THE CHILDREN'S HOUR

"Does a boy get a chance to whitewash a fence every day?"

Old Time Favorites

A BOOK TO GROW ON

CONSULTANT EDITORS FOR THE CHILDREN'S HOUR

MARJORIE BARROWS, *Editor*

Old Time Favorites

MATHILDA SCHIRMER
Associate Editor

DOROTHY SHORT
Art Editor

THE CHILDREN'S HOUR

PRINTED IN THE UNITED STATES OF AMERICA

Acknowledgments

The editor and publishers wish to thank the following publishers and artists for permission to use and reprint stories and illustrations included in this book:

GINN AND COMPANY and Marguerite Davis for illustrations by Marguerite Davis from *Heidi* by Johanna Spyri, copyright, 1927.

HOUGHTON MIFFLIN COMPANY for "Rebecca at the Brick House" from *Rebecca of Sunnybrook Farm* by Kate Douglas Wiggin.

LITTLE, BROWN & COMPANY for an illustration by Jessie Wilcox Smith from the Orchard House edition of Louisa May Alcott's *Little Women, or Meg, Jo, Beth, and Amy,* originally published by Little, Brown & Company.

THE MACMILLAN COMPANY for illustrations by E. A. Verpilleux from *The Picture Book of Robinson Crusoe.* Copyright, 1931, by The Macmillan Company and E. A. Verpilleux.

THE WORLD PUBLISHING COMPANY for illustrations by Fritz Kredel from The Rainbow Classics edition of John Ruskin's "The King of the Golden River."

Contents

Samuel Clemens

THE GLORIOUS WHITEWASHER
AND HIS FRIENDS

ILLUSTRATED BY *James Murray Haddow*

SATURDAY morning was come, and all the summer world was bright and fresh, and brimming with life. There was a song in every heart; and if the heart was young the music issued at the lips. There was cheer in every face and a spring in every step. The locust trees were in bloom and the fragrance of the blossoms filled the air. Cardiff Hill, beyond the village and above it, was green with vegetation, and it lay just far enough away to seem a Delectable Land, dreamy, reposeful, and inviting.

Tom appeared on the sidewalk with a bucket of whitewash and a long-handled brush. He surveyed the fence, and all gladness left him and a deep melancholy settled down upon his spirit. Thirty yards of board fence nine feet high. Life to him seemed hollow, and existence but a burden. Sighing he dipped his brush and passed it along the topmost plank; repeated the operation; did it again; compared the insignificant whitewashed streak with the far-reaching continent of unwhitewashed fence, and sat down on a tree-box discouraged. Jim came skipping out at the gate with a tin pail, and singing "Buffalo Gals." Bringing water from the town pump had always been hateful work in Tom's eyes, before, but now it did not strike him so. He remembered that there was company at the pump. White, mulatto, and negro boys and girls were always there waiting their turns, resting, trading playthings, quarreling, fighting, skylarking. And he remembered that although the pump was only a hundred and fifty yards off, Jim never got back with a bucket of water under an hour—and even then some-

1

body generally had to go after him. Tom said,—

"Say, Jim, I'll fetch the water if you'll whitewash some."

Jim shook his head and said,—

"Can't, Mars Tom. Ole missis, she tole me I got to go an' git dis water an' not stop foolin' roun' wid anybody. She say she spec' Mars Tom gwine to ax me to whitewash, an' so she tole me go 'long an' 'tend to my own business—she 'lowed she'd 'tend to de whitewashin'."

"Oh, never you mind what she said, Jim. That's the way she always talks. Gimme the bucket—I won't be gone only a minute. *She* won't ever know."

"Oh, I dasn't, Mars Tom. Ole missis she'd take an' tar de head off'n me. 'Deed she would."

"*She!* She never licks anybody—whacks 'em over the head with her thimble—and who cares for that, I'd like to know. She talks awful, but talk don't hurt—anyways it don't if she don't cry. Jim, I'll give you a marvel. I'll give you a white alley!"

Jim began to waver.

"White alley, Jim! And it's a bully taw."

"My! Dat's a mighty gay marvel, *I* tell you! But, Mars Tom I's powerful 'fraid ole missis—"

"And besides, if you will I'll show you my sore toe."

Jim was only human—this attraction was too much for him. He put down his pail, took the white alley, and bent over the toe with absorbing interest while the bandage was being unwound. In another moment he was flying down the street with his pail and a tingling rear, Tom was whitewashing with vigor, and Aunt Polly was retiring from the field with a slipper in her hand and triumph in her eye.

But Tom's energy did not last. He began to think of the fun he had planned for this day, and his sorrows multiplied. Soon the free boys would come tripping along on all sorts of delicious expeditions, and they would make a world of fun of him for having to work—the very thought of it burnt him like fire. He got out his worldly wealth and examined it—bits of toys, marbles, and trash; enough to buy an exchange of *work*, maybe, but not half enough to buy so much as half an hour of pure

2

freedom. So he returned his straitened means to his pocket, and gave up the idea of trying to buy the boys. At this dark and hopeless moment an inspiration burst upon him! Nothing less than a great, magnificent inspiration.

He took up his brush and went tranquilly to work. Ben Rogers hove in sight presently—the very boy, of all boys, whose ridicule he had been dreading. Ben's gait was the hop-skip-and-jump—proof enough that his heart was light and his anticipations high. He was eating an apple and giving a long, melodious whoop, at intervals, followed by a deep-toned ding-dong-dong, ding-dong-dong, for he was personating a steamboat. As he drew near, he slackened speed, took the middle of the street, leaned far over to starboard and rounded to ponderously and with laborious pomp and circumstance—for he was personating the *Big Missouri*, and considered himself to be drawing nine feet of water. He was boat and captain and engine-bells combined, so he had to imagine himself standing on his own hurricane-deck giving the orders and executing them:

"Stop her, sir! Ting-a-ling-ling!" The headway ran almost out and he drew up slowly toward the sidewalk.

"Ship up to back! Ting-a-ling-ling!" His arms straightened and stiffened down his sides.

"Set her back on the stabboard! Ting-a-ling-ling! Chow! ch-chow-wow! Chow!" His right hand, meantime, describing stately circles—for it was representing a forty-foot wheel.

"Let her go back on the labboard! Ting-a-ling-ling! Chow-ch-chow-chow!" The left hand began to describe circles.

"Stop the stabboard! Ting-a-ling-ling! Stop the labboard! Come ahead on the stabboard! Stop her! Let your outside turn over slow! Ting-a-ling-ling! Chow-ow-ow! Get out that head-line! *Lively* now! Come—out with your spring-line—what're you about there! Take a turn round that stump with the bight of it! Stand by that stage, now—let her go! Done with the engines, sir! Ting-a-ling-ling! *Sh't! s'h't! sh't!*" (trying the gauge-cocks).

Tom went on whitewashing—paid no attention to the steamboat. Ben stared a moment and then said,—

"Hi-*yi! You're* up a stump, ain't you!"

3

No answer. Tom surveyed his last touch with the eye of an artist, then he gave his brush another gentle sweep and surveyed the result, as before. Ben ranged up alongside of him. Tom's mouth watered for the apple, but he stuck to his work. Ben said,—

"Hello, old chap, you got to work, hey?"

Tom wheeled suddenly and said,—

"Why, it's you, Ben! I warn't noticing."

"Say—*I'm* going in a-swimming, *I* am. Don't you wish you could? But of course you'd druther *work*—wouldn't you? Course you would!"

Tom contemplated the boy a bit, and said,—

"What do you call work?"

"Why, ain't *that* work?"

Tom resumed his whitewashing, and answered carelessly,—

"Well, maybe it is, and maybe it ain't. All I know, is, it suits Tom Sawyer."

"Oh come, now, you don't mean to let on that you *like* it?"

The brush continued to move.

"Like it? Well, I don't see why I oughtn't to like it. Does a boy get a chance to whitewash a fence every day?"

That put the thing in a new light. Ben stopped nibbling his apple. Tom swept his brush daintily back and forth—stepped back to note the effect—added a touch here and there—criticized the effect again—Ben watching every move and getting more and more interested, more and more absorbed. Presently he said,—

"Say, Tom, let *me* whitewash a little."

Tom considered, was about to consent; but he altered his mind,—

"No—no—I reckon it wouldn't hardly do, Ben. You see, Aunt Polly's awful particular about this fence—right here on the street, you know—but if it was the back fence I wouldn't mind and *she* wouldn't. Yes, she's awful particular about this fence; it's got to be done very careful; I reckon there ain't one boy in a thousand, maybe two thousand, that can do it the way it's got to be done."

4

"No—is that so? Oh come, now—lemme just try. Only just a little—I'd let *you*, if you was me, Tom."

"Ben, I'd like to, honest injun; but Aunt Polly—well, Jim wanted to do it, but she wouldn't let him; Sid wanted to do it, and she wouldn't let Sid. Now don't you see how I'm fixed? If you was to tackle this fence and anything was to happen to it—"

"Oh, shucks, I'll be just as careful. Now lemme try. Say—I'll give you the core of my apple."

"Well, here— No, Ben, now don't. I'm afeard—"

"I'll give you *all* of it!"

Tom gave up the brush with reluctance in his face, but alacrity in his heart. And while the late steamer *Big Missouri* worked and sweated in the sun, the retired artist sat on a barrel in the shade close by, dangled his legs, munched his apple, and planned the slaughter of more innocents. There was no lack of material; boys happened along every little while; they came to jeer, but remained to whitewash. By the time Ben was fagged out, Tom had traded the next chance to Billy Fisher for a kite, in good repair; and when *he* played out, Johnny Miller bought in for a dead rat and a string to swing it with—and so on, and

so on, hour after hour. And when the middle of the afternoon came, from being a poor poverty-stricken boy in the morning, Tom was literally rolling in wealth. He had beside the things before mentioned, twelve marbles, part of a jews'-harp, a piece of blue bottle-glass to look through, a spool cannon, a key that wouldn't unlock anything, a fragment of chalk, a glass stopper of a decanter, a tin soldier, a couple of tadpoles, six firecrackers, a kitten with only one eye, a brass door-knob, a dog-collar—but no dog—the handle of a knife, four pieces of orange-peel, and a dilapidated old window-sash.

He had had a nice, good, idle time all the while—plenty of company—and the fence had three coats of whitewash on it! If he hadn't run out of whitewash, he would have bankrupted every boy in the village.

Tom said to himself that it was not such a hollow world, after all. He had discovered a great law of human action, without knowing it—namely, that in order to make a man or a boy covet a thing, it is only necessary to make the thing difficult to attain. If he had been a great and wise philosopher, like the writer of this book, he would now have comprehended that Work consists of whatever a body is *obliged* to do, and that Play consists of whatever a body is not obliged to do. And this would help him to understand why constructing artificial flowers or performing on a treadmill is work, while rolling tenpins or climbing Mont Blanc is only amusement. There are wealthy gentlemen in England who drive four-horse passenger-coaches twenty or thirty miles on a daily line, in the summer, because the privilege costs them considerable money; but if they were offered wages for the service, that would turn it into work and then they would resign.

The boy mused awhile over the substantial change which had taken place in his worldly circumstances, and then wended toward headquarters to report.

Tom presented himself before Aunt Polly, who was sitting by an open window in a pleasant rearward apartment, which was bedroom, breakfast room, dining room, and library, combined. The balmy summer air, the restful quiet, the odor of the flowers, and the drowsing murmur of the bees had had their effect, and she was nodding over her knitting—for she had no company but the cat, and it was asleep in her lap. Her spectacles were propped up on her gray head for safety. She had thought that of course Tom had deserted long ago, and she wondered at seeing him place himself in her power again in this intrepid way. He said,—

"Mayn't I go and play now, aunt?"

"What, a'ready? How much have you done?"

"It's all done, aunt."

"Tom, don't lie to me—I can't bear it."

"I ain't, aunt; it *is* all done."

Aunt Polly placed small trust in such evidence. She went out to see for herself; and she would have been content to find twenty per cent of Tom's statement true. When she found the entire fence whitewashed, and not only whitewashed but elaborately coated and recoated, and even a streak added to the ground, her astonishment was almost unspeakable. She said,—

"Well, I never! There's no getting round it, you *can* work when you're a mind to, Tom." And then she diluted the compliment by adding, "But it's powerful seldom you're a mind to, I'm bound to say. Well, go 'long and play; but mind you get back some time in a week, or I'll tan you."

She was so overcome by the splendor of his achievement that she took him into the closet and selected a choice apple and delivered it to him, along with an improving lecture upon the added value and flavor a treat took to itself when it came without sin through virtuous effort. And while she closed with a happy Scriptural flourish, he "hooked" a doughnut.

Then he skipped out, and saw Sid just starting up the outside stairway that led to the back rooms on the second floor. Clods were handy and the air was full of them in a twinkling. They raged around Sid like a hailstorm; and before Aunt Polly could collect her surprised faculties and sally to the rescue, six or seven clods had taken personal effect, and Tom was over the fence and gone. There was a gate, but as a general thing he was too crowded for time to make use of it.

7

Tom skirted the block, and came round into a muddy alley that led by the back of his aunt's cow-stable. He presently got safely beyond the reach of capture and punishment, and hastened toward the public square of the village, where two "military" companies of boys had met for conflict, according to previous appointment. Tom was General of one of these armies, Joe Harper (a bosom friend) General of the other. These two great commanders did not condescend to fight in person—that being better suited to the still smaller fry—but sat together on an eminence and conducted the field operations by orders delivered through aides-de-camp. Tom's army won a great victory, after a long and hard-fought battle. Then the dead were counted, prisoners exchanged, the terms of the next disagreement agreed upon, and the day for the necessary battle appointed; after which the armies fell into line and marched away, and Tom turned homeward alone.

As he was passing by the house where Jeff Thatcher lived, he saw a new girl in the garden—a lovely little blue-eyed creature with yellow hair plaited into two long tails, white summer frock and embroidered pantalettes. The fresh-crowned hero fell without firing a shot. A certain Amy Lawrence vanished out of his heart and left not even a memory of herself behind. He had thought he loved her to distraction, he had regarded his passion as adoration; and behold it was only a poor little evanescent partiality. He had been months winning her; she had confessed hardly a week ago; he had been the happiest and the proudest boy in the world only seven short days, and here in one instant of time she had gone out of his heart like a casual stranger whose visit is done.

He worshiped this new angel with furtive eye, till he saw that she had discovered him; then he pretended he did not know she was present and began to "show off" in all sorts of absurd boyish ways, in order to win her admiration. He kept up this grotesque foolishness for some time; but by and by, while he was in the midst of some dangerous gymnastic performances, he glanced aside and saw that the little girl was wending her way toward the house. Tom came up to the fence and leaned

8

on it, grieving, and hoping she would tarry yet awhile longer. She halted a moment on the steps and then moved toward the door. Tom heaved a great sigh as she put her foot on the threshold. But his face lit up, right away, for she tossed a pansy over the fence a moment before she disappeared.

The boy ran around and stopped within a foot or two of the flower, and then shaded his eyes with his hand and began to look down street as if he had discovered something of interest going on in that direction. Presently he picked up a straw and began trying to balance it on his nose, with his head tilted far back; and as he moved from side to side, in his efforts, he edged nearer and nearer toward the pansy; finally his bare foot rested upon it, his pliant toes closed upon it, and he hopped away with the treasure and disappeared round the corner. But only for a minute—only while he could button the flower inside his jacket, next his heart—or next his stomach, possibly, for he was not much posted in anatomy, and not hypercritical, anyway.

He returned, now, and hung about the fence till nightfall, "showing off," as before; but the girl never exhibited herself

9

again, though Tom comforted himself a little with the hope that she had been near some window, meantime, and been aware of his attentions. Finally he rode home reluctantly, with his poor head full of visions.

All through supper his spirits were so high that his aunt wondered "what had got into the child." He took a good scolding about clodding Sid and did not seem to mind it in the least. He tried to steal sugar under his aunt's very nose and got his knuckles rapped for it. He said,—

"Aunt, you don't whack Sid when he takes it."

"Well, Sid don't torment a body the way you do. You'd be always into that sugar if I warn't watching you."

Presently she stepped into the kitchen, and Sid, happy in his immunity, reached for the sugar-bowl—a sort of glorying over Tom which was well-nigh unbearable. But Sid's fingers slipped, and the bowl dropped and broke. Tom was in ecstasies. In such ecstasies that he even controlled his tongue and was silent. He said to himself that he would not speak a word, even when his aunt came in, but would sit perfectly still till she asked who did the mischief; and then he would tell, and there would be nothing so good in the world as to see that pet model "catch it." He was so brim full of exultation that he could hardly hold himself when the old lady came back and stood above the wreck, discharging lightnings of wrath from over her spectacles. He said to himself, "Now it's coming!" And the next instant he was sprawling on the floor! The potent palm was uplifted to strike again when Tom cried out,—

"Hold on, now, what 'er you belting *me* for?—Sid broke it!"

Aunt Polly paused, perplexed, and Tom looked for healing pity. But when she got her tongue again, she only said,—

"Umf! Well, you didn't get a lick amiss, I reckon. You been into some other audacious mischief when I wasn't around, like enough."

Then her conscience reproached her, and she yearned to say something kind and loving; but she judged that this would be construed into a confession that she had been in the wrong, and discipline forbade that. So she kept silence and went about her

10

affairs with a troubled heart. Tom sulked in a corner and exalted his woes. He knew that in her heart his aunt was on her knees to him, and he was morosely gratified by the consciousness of it. He would hang out no signals, he would take notice of none. He knew that a yearning glance fell upon him, now and then, through a film of tears, but he refused recognition of it. He pictured himself lying sick unto death and his aunt bending over him beseeching one little forgiving word, but he would turn his face to the wall and die with that word unsaid. Ah, how would she feel then? And he pictured himself brought home from the river, dead, with his curls all wet, and his sore heart at rest. How she would throw herself upon him, and how her tears would fall like rain, and her lips pray God to give her back her boy and she would never, never abuse him any more! But he would lie there cold and white and make no sign—a poor little sufferer, whose griefs were at an end. He so worked upon his feelings with the pathos of these dreams, that he had to keep swallowing, he was so like to choke; and his eyes swam in a blur of water, which overflowed when he winked, and ran down and trickled from the end of his nose. And such a luxury to him was this petting of his sorrows, that he could not bear to have any worldly cheeriness or any grating delight intrude upon it; it was too sacred for such contact; and so, presently, when his cousin Mary danced in, all alive with the joy of seeing home again after an age-long visit of one week to the country, he got up and moved in clouds and darkness out at one door as she brought song and sunshine in at the other.

He wandered far from the accustomed haunts of boys and sought desolate places that were in harmony with his spirit. A log raft in the river invited him, and he seated himself on its outer edge and contemplated the dreary vastness of the stream, wishing, the while, that he could only be drowned all at once and unconsciously, without undergoing the uncomfortable routine devised by nature. Then he thought of his flower. He got it out, rumpled and wilted, and it mightily increased his dismal felicity. He wondered if *she* would pity him if she knew? Would she cry and wish that she had a right to put her arms around his

11

neck and comfort him? Or would she turn coldly away like all
the hollow world? This picture brought such an agony of pleasurable suffering that he worked it over and over again in his
mind and set it up in new and varied lights, till he wore it
threadbare. At last he rose up sighing and departed in the
darkness.

About half past nine or ten o'clock he came along the deserted
street to where the Adored Unknown lived; he paused a moment; no sound fell upon his listening ear; a candle was casting
a dull glow upon the curtain of a second-story window. Was
the sacred presence there? He climbed the fence, threaded his
stealthy way through the plants, till he stood under that window; he looked up at it long, and with emotion; then he laid
him down on the ground under it, disposing himself upon his
back, with his hands clasped upon his breast and holding his
poor wilted flower. And thus he would die—out in the cold
world, with no shelter over his homeless head, no friendly hand
to wipe the death-damps from his brow, no loving face to bend
pityingly over him when the great agony came. And thus *she*
would see him when she looked out upon the glad morning, and
oh! would she drop one little tear upon his poor, lifeless form,
would she heave one little sigh to see a bright young life so
rudely blighted, so untimely cut down?

12

The window went up, a maid-servant's discordant voice profaned the holy calm, and a deluge of water drenched the prone martyr's remains!

The strangling hero sprang up with a relieving snort. There was a whiz as of a missile in the air, mingled with the murmur of a curse, a sound as of shivering glass followed, and a small, vague form went over the fence and shot away in the gloom.

Not long after, as Tom, all undressed for bed, was surveying his drenched garments by the light of a tallow dip, Sid woke up; but if he had any dim idea of making any "references to allusions," he thought better of it and held his peace, for there was danger in Tom's eye.

Tom turned in without the added vexation of prayers, and Sid made mental note of the omission.

Monday morning found Tom Sawyer miserable. Monday morning always found him so—because it began another week's slow suffering in school. He generally began that day with wishing he had had no intervening holiday, it made the going into captivity and fetters again so much more odious.

Tom lay thinking. Presently it occurred to him that he wished he was sick; then he could stay home from school. Here was a vague possibility. He canvassed his system. No ailment was found, and he investigated again. This time he thought he could detect colicky symptoms, and he began to encourage them with considerable hope. But they soon grew feeble, and presently died wholly away. He reflected further. Suddenly he discovered something. One of his upper front teeth was loose. This was lucky; he was about to begin to groan, as a "starter," as he called it, when it occurred to him that if he came into court with that argument, his aunt would pull it out, and that would hurt. So he thought he would hold the tooth in reserve for the present, and seek further. Nothing offered for some little time, and then he remembered hearing the doctor tell about a certain thing that laid up a patient for two or three weeks and threatened to make him lose a finger. So the boy eagerly drew his sore toe from under the sheet and held it up for inspection. But now he did not know the necessary symptoms. However, it seemed

13

well worth while to chance it, so he fell to groaning with considerable spirit.

But Sid slept on unconscious.

Tom groaned louder and fancied that he began to feel pain in the toe.

No result from Sid.

Tom was panting with his exertions by this time. He took a rest and then swelled himself up and fetched a succession of admirable groans.

Sid snored on.

Tom was aggravated. He said, "Sid, Sid!" and shook him. This course worked well, and Tom began to groan again. Sid yawned, stretched, then brought himself up on his elbow with a snort, and began to stare at Tom. Tom went on groaning. Sid said,—

"Tom! Say, Tom!" (No response.) "Here, Tom! *Tom!* What is the matter, Tom?" And he shook him and looked in his face anxiously.

Tom moaned out,—

"Oh, don't, Sid. Don't joggle me."

"Why, what's the matter, Tom? I must call auntie."

"No—never mind. It'll be over by and by, maybe. Don't call anybody."

"But I must! *Don't* groan so, Tom, it's awful. How long you been this way?"

"Hours. Ouch! Oh, don't stir so, Sid, you'll kill me."

"Tom, why didn't you wake me sooner? Oh, Tom, *don't!* It makes my flesh crawl to hear you! Tom, what *is* the matter?"

"I forgive you everything, Sid. (Groan.) Everything you've ever done to me. When I'm gone—"

"Oh, Tom, you ain't dying, are you? Don't, Tom—oh, don't. Maybe—"

"I forgive everybody, Sid. (Groan.) Tell 'em so, Sid. And, Sid, you give my window-sash and my cat with one eye to that new girl that's come to town, and tell her—"

But Sid had snatched his clothes and gone. Tom was suffering in reality, now, so handsomely was his imagination working, and so his groans had gathered quite a genuine tone.

Sid flew downstairs and said,—

"Oh, Aunt Polly, come! Tom's dying!"

"Dying!"

"Yes'm. Don't wait—come quick!"

"Rubbage! I don't believe it!"

But she fled upstairs, nevertheless, with Sid and Mary at her heels. And her face grew white, too, and her lip trembled. When she reached the bedside she gasped out,—

"You, Tom! Tom, what's the matter with you?"

"Oh, auntie, I'm—"

"What's the matter with you—what *is* the matter with you, child?"

"Oh, auntie, my sore toe's mortified!"

The old lady sank down into a chair and laughed a little, then cried a little, then did both together. This restored her and she said,—

"Tom, what a turn you did give me. Now you shut up that nonsense and climb out of this."

The groans ceased and the pain vanished from the toe. The boy felt a little foolish, and he said,—

"Aunt Polly, it *seemed* mortified, and it hurt so I never minded my tooth at all."

"Your tooth, indeed! What's the matter with your tooth?"

"One of them's loose, and it aches perfectly awful."

"There, there, now, don't begin that groaning again. Open your mouth. Well—your tooth *is* loose, but you're not going to die about that. Mary, get me a silk thread, and a chunk of fire out of the kitchen."

Tom said,—

"Oh, please auntie, don't pull it out. It don't hurt any more. I wish I may never stir if it does. Please don't, auntie. *I* don't want to stay home from school."

"Oh, you don't, don't you? So all this row was because you thought you'd get to stay home from school and go a-fishing? Tom, Tom, I love you so, and you seem to try every way you can to break my old heart with your outrageousness." By this time the dental instruments were ready. The old lady made one

end of the silk thread fast to Tom's tooth with a loop and tied the other to the bedpost. Then she seized the chunk of fire and suddenly thrust it almost into the boy's face. The tooth hung dangling by the bedpost, now.

But all trials bring their compensations. As Tom wended to school after breakfast, he was the envy of every boy he met because the gap in his upper row of teeth enabled him to expectorate in a new and admirable way. He gathered quite a following of lads interested in the exhibition; and one that had cut his finger and had been a center of fascination and homage up to this time, now found himself suddenly without an adherent, and shorn of his glory. His heart was heavy, and he said with a disdain which he did not feel, that it wasn't anything to spit like Tom Sawyer; but another boy said, "Sour grapes!" and he wandered away a dismantled hero.

Shortly Tom came upon the juvenile pariah of the village, Huckleberry Finn, son of the town drunkard. Huckleberry was cordially hated and dreaded by all the mothers of the town, because he was idle and lawless and vulgar and bad—and be-

16

cause all their children admired him so, and delighted in his forbidden society, and wished they dared to be like him. Tom was like the rest of the respectable boys, in that he envied Huckleberry his gaudy outcast condition, and was under strict orders not to play with him. So he played with him every time he got a chance. Huckleberry was always dressed in the cast-off clothes of full-grown men, and they were in perennial bloom and fluttering with rags. His hat was a vast ruin with a wide crescent lopped out of its brim; his coat, when he wore one, hung nearly to his heels and had the rearward buttons far down the back; but one suspender supported his trousers; the seat of the trousers bagged low and contained nothing; the fringed legs dragged in the dirt when not rolled up.

Huckleberry came and went, at his own free will. He slept on doorsteps in fine weather and in empty hogsheads in wet; he did not have to go to school or to church, or call any being master or obey anybody; he could go fishing or swimming when and where he chose, and stay as long as it suited him; nobody forbade him to fight; he could sit up as late as he pleased; he was always the first boy that went barefoot in the spring and the last to resume leather in the fall; he never had to wash, nor put on clean clothes; he could swear wonderfully. In a word, everything that goes to make life precious, that boy had. So thought every harassed, hampered, respectable boy in St. Petersburg.

Tom hailed the romantic outcast,—

"Hello, Huckleberry!"

"Hello yourself, and see how you like it."

"What's that you got?"

"Dead cat."

"Lemme see him, Huck. My, he's pretty stiff. Where'd you get him?"

"Bought him off'n a boy."

"What did you give?"

"I give a blue ticket and a bladder that I got at the slaughter-house."

"Where'd you get the blue ticket?"

"Bought it off'n Ben Rogers two weeks ago for a hoopstick."

"Say—what is dead cats good for, Huck?"

"Good for? Cure warts with."

"No! Is that so? I know something that's better."

"I bet you don't. What is it?"

"Why, spunk-water."

"Spunk-water! I wouldn't give a dern for spunk-water."

"You wouldn't, wouldn't you? D'you ever try it?"

"No, I hain't. But Bob Tanner did."

"Who told you so?"

"Why, he told Jeff Thatcher, and Jeff told Johnny Baker, and Johnny told Jim Hollis, and Jim told Ben Rogers, and Ben told me. There now!"

"Well, what of it? They'll all lie. Now you tell me how Bob Tanner done it, Huck."

"Why, he took and dipped his hand in a rotten stump where the rain-water was."

"In the daytime?"

"Certainly."

"With his face to the stump?"

"Yes. Least I reckon so."

"Did he *say* anything?"

"I don't reckon he did. I don't know."

"Aha! Talk about trying to cure warts with spunk-water such a blame-fool way as that! Why, that ain't a-going to do any good. You got to go all by yourself, to the middle of the woods, where you know there's a spunk-water stump, and just as it's midnight you back up against the stump and jam your hand in and say,—

> 'Barley-corn, Barley-corn, injun-meal shorts,
> Spunk-water, spunk-water, swaller these warts,'

and then walk away quick, eleven steps, with your eyes shut, and then turn around three times and walk home without speaking to anybody. Because if you speak the charm's busted."

"Well, that sounds like a good way; but that ain't the way Bob Tanner done."

"No, sir, you can bet he didn't, becuz he's the wartiest boy in this town; and he wouldn't have a wart on him if he'd knowed how to work spunk-water. I've took off thousands of warts off of my hands that way, Huck. I play with frogs so much that I've always got considerable many warts. Sometimes I take 'em off with a bean."

"Yes, bean's good. I've done that."

"Have you? What's your way?"

"You take and split the bean, and cut the wart so as to get some blood, and then you put the blood on one piece of the bean and take and dig a hole and bury it 'bout midnight at the crossroads in the dark of the moon, and then you burn up the rest of the bean. You see that piece that's got the blood on it will keep drawing and drawing, trying to fetch the other piece to it, and so that helps the blood to draw the wart, and pretty soon off she comes."

"Yes, that's it, Huck—that's it; though when you're burying it if you say 'Down bean; off wart; come no more to bother me!' it's better. That's the way Joe Harper does, and he's been nearly to Coonville and most everywheres. But say—how do you cure 'em with dead cats?"

"Why, you take your cat and go and get in the graveyard 'long about midnight when somebody that was wicked has been buried; and when it's midnight a devil will come, or maybe two or three, but you can't see 'em, you can only hear something

19

like the wind, or maybe hear 'em talk; and when they're taking that feller away, you heave your cat after 'em and say, 'Devil follow corpse, cat follow devil, warts follow cat, *I'm* done with ye!' That'll fetch *any* wart."

"Sounds right. D'you ever try it, Huck?"

"No, but old Mother Hopkins told me."

"Well, I reckon it's so, then. Becuz they say she's a witch."

"Say! Why, Tom, I *know* she is. She witched Pap. Pap says so his own self. He come along one day, and he see she was a-witching him, so he took up a rock, and if she hadn't dodged, he'd 'a' got her. Well, that very night he rolled off'n a shed, wher' he was a-layin' drunk, and broke his arm."

"Why, that's awful. How did he know she was a-witching him?"

"Lord, Pap can tell, easy. Pap says when they keep looking at you right stiddy, they're a-witching you. Specially if they mumble. Becuz when they mumble they're saying the Lord's Prayer backards."

"Say, Hucky, when you going to try the cat?"

"Tonight. I reckon they'll come after old Hoss Williams tonight."

"But they buried him Saturday. Didn't they get him Saturday night?"

"Why, how you talk! How could their charms work till midnight?—and *then* it's Sunday. Devils don't slosh around much of a Sunday, I don't reckon."

"I never thought of that. That's so. Lemme go with you?"

"Of course—if you ain't afeard."

"Afeard! 'Tain't likely. Will you meow?"

"Yes—and you meow back, if you get a chance. Last time, you kep' me a-meowing around till old Hays went to throwing rocks at me and says, 'Dern that cat!' and so I hove a brick through his window—but don't you tell."

"I won't. I couldn't meow that night, becuz auntie was watching me, but I'll meow this time. Say—what's that?"

"Nothing but a tick."

"Where'd you get him?"

20

"Out in the woods."

"What'll you take for him?"

"I don't know. I don't want to sell him."

"All right. It's a mighty small tick, anyway."

"Oh, anybody can run a tick down that don't belong to them.
I'm satisfied with it. It's a good enough tick for me."

"Sho, there's ticks a-plenty. I could have a thousand of 'em
if I wanted to."

"Well, why don't you? Becuz you know mighty well you
can't. This is a pretty early tick, I reckon. It's the first one I've
seen this year."

"Say, Huck—I'll give you my tooth for him."

"Less see it."

Tom got out a bit of paper and carefully unrolled it. Huckleberry viewed it wistfully. The temptation was very strong. At
last he said,—

"Is it genuwyne?"

Tom lifted his lip and showed the vacancy.

"Well, all right," said Huckleberry, "it's a trade."

Tom inclosed the tick in the percussion-cap box that had

lately been the pinchbug's prison, and the boys separated, each feeling wealthier than before.

When Tom reached the little isolated frame schoolhouse, he strode in briskly, with the manner of one who had come with all honest speed. He hung his hat on a peg and flung himself into his seat with business-like alacrity. The master, throned on high in his great splint-bottom armchair, was dozing, lulled by the drowsy hum of study. The interruption roused him.

"Thomas Sawyer!"

Tom knew that when his name was pronounced in full, it meant trouble.

"Sir!"

"Come up here. Now, sir, why are you late again, as usual?"

Tom was about to take refuge in a lie, when he saw two long tails of yellow hair hanging down a back that he recognized by the electric sympathy of love; and by that form was *the only vacant place* on the girls' side of the schoolhouse. He instantly said,—

"I stopped to talk with Huckleberry Finn!"

The master's pulse stood still, and he stared helplessly. The buzz of study ceased. The pupils wondered if this foolhardy boy had lost his mind. The master said,—

"You—you did what?"

"Stopped to talk with Huckleberry Finn."

There was no mistaking the words.

"Thomas Sawyer, this is the most astounding confession I have ever listened to. No mere ferule will answer for this offense. Take off your jacket."

The master's arm performed until it was tired and the stock of switches notably diminished. Then the order followed:

"Now, sir, go and sit with the *girls!* And let this be a warning to you."

The titter that rippled around the room appeared to abash the boy, but in reality that result was caused rather more by his worshipful awe of his unknown idol and the dread pleasure that lay in his high good fortune. He sat down upon the end of the pine bench, and the girl hitched herself away from him

22

with a toss of her head. Nudges and winks and whispers traversed the room, but Tom sat still, with his arms upon the long, low desk before him, and seemed to study his book.

By and by attention ceased from him, and the accustomed school murmur rose upon the dull air once more. Presently the boy began to steal furtive glances at the girl. She observed it, "made a mouth" at him and gave him the back of her head for the space of a minute. When she cautiously faced around again, a peach lay before her. She thrust it away. Tom gently put it back. She thrust it away again, but with less animosity. Tom patiently returned it to its place. Then she let it remain. Tom scrawled on his slate, "Please take it—I got more." The girl glanced at the words, but made no sign. Now the boy began to draw something on the slate, hiding his work with his left hand. For a time the girl refused to notice; but her human curiosity presently began to manifest itself by hardly perceptible signs. The boy worked on, apparently unconscious. The girl made a sort of non-committal attempt to see it, but the boy did not betray that he was aware of it. At last she gave in and hesitatingly whispered,—

"Let me see it."

Tom partly uncovered a dismal caricature of a house with two gable ends to it and a corkscrew of smoke issuing from the chimney. Then the girl's interest began to fasten itself upon the work, and she forgot everything else. When it was finished, she gazed a moment, then whispered,—

"It's nice—make a man."

The artist erected a man in the frontyard, that resembled a derrick. He could have stepped over the house; but the girl was not hypercritical; she was satisfied with the monster, and whispered,—

"It's a beautiful man—now make me coming along."

Tom drew an hourglass with a full moon and straw limbs to it and armed the spreading fingers with a portentous fan. The girl said,—

"It's ever so nice—I wish I could draw."

"It's easy," whispered Tom, "I'll learn you."

23

"Oh, will you? When?"

"At noon. Do you go home to dinner?"

"I'll stay if you will."

"Good—that's a whack. What's your name?"

"Becky Thatcher. What's yours? Oh, I know. It's Thomas Sawyer."

"That's the name they lick me by. I'm Tom when I'm good. You call me Tom, will you?"

"Yes."

Now Tom began to scrawl something on the slate, hiding the words from the girl. But she was not backward this time. She begged to see. Tom said,—

"Oh, it ain't anything."

"Yes it is."

"No it ain't. You don't want to see."

"Yes I do, indeed I do. Please let me."

"You'll tell."

"No I won't—deed and deed and double deed I won't."

"You won't tell anybody at all? Ever, as long as you live?"

"No, I won't ever tell *any*body. Now let me."

"Oh, *you* don't want to see!"

"Now that you treat me so, I *will* see." And she put her small hand upon his and a little scuffle ensued, Tom pretending to resist in earnest but letting his hand slip by degrees till these words were revealed: *"I love you."*

"Oh, you bad thing!" And she hit his hand a smart rap, but reddened and looked pleased, nevertheless.

Just at this juncture the boy felt a slow, fateful grip closing on his ear, and a steady lifting impulse. In that vise he was borne across the house and deposited in his own seat, under a peppering fire of giggles from the whole school. Then the master stood over him during a few awful moments, and finally moved away to his throne without saying a word. But although Tom's ear tingled, his heart was jubilant.

As the school quieted down Tom made an honest effort to study, but the turmoil within him was too great. In turn he took his place in the reading class and made a botch of it; then in the geography class and turned lakes into mountains, mountains into rivers, and rivers into continents, till chaos was come again; then in the spelling class, and got "turned down," by a succession of mere baby words, till he brought up at the foot and yielded up the pewter medal which he had worn with ostentation for months.

Johanna Spyri

HEIDI'S
ADVENTURES
ON THE MOUNTAIN

ILLUSTRATED BY *Marguerite Davis*
AND *Barbara Fitzgerald*

HEIDI, still a favorite classic, is the story of a little orphan who went to live high up in the Swiss mountains near eleven-year-old Peter and the pet goats. She went to live with her gruff old grandfather in his lonely mountain hut. Grandfather had lived alone before that, and the rumors about his fiery temper frightened his nearest neighbors down in the valley so that the mere sight of him with his bushy gray eyebrows, his immense beard, and his big stick made them tremble.

Then Heidi, brought there by cross Aunt Dete, came to live with him.

AS SOON as Aunt Dete had disappeared Heidi's grandfather went back to his bench and sat there without saying a word while thick clouds of smoke floated upward from his pipe. As for Heidi, she was enjoying herself in her new surroundings. She looked about till she found the goat shed, built against the hut. She peeped in and saw it was empty. She continued her search and soon came to the pine trees behind the hut. The wind was blowing through them, and there was a roaring in their topmost branches. Heidi stood still and listened. The sound grew fainter, and she went on again, to the farther corner of the hut, and around to where her grandfather was sitting. Since he was in exactly the same place where she left him, she went and stood in front of the old man. She put her

26

hands behind her back and gazed at him. Her grandfather looked up, and as she continued standing there without moving, he spoke to her.

"What is it you want?" he asked.

"I want to see what you have inside the house," said Heidi.

"Come along then!" said her grandfather who rose and led the way towards the hut.

"Bring your bundle of clothes in with you," he said as she was following him.

"I shan't want them any more," replied Heidi promptly.

The old man turned and looked searchingly at the child, whose dark eyes were sparkling in expectation of what she was going to see inside.

"She is certainly not wanting in intelligence," he murmured to himself. "And why shall you not want them any more?" he asked aloud.

"Because I want to go about like the goats with their swift little legs," said Heidi.

"Well, you can do so if you like," said her grandfather, "but bring the clothes in. We must put them in the cupboard."

Heidi did as she was told. The old man now opened the door, and she stepped inside after him.

She found herself in a good-sized room, which covered the whole ground floor of the hut. A table and a chair were the only furniture; in one corner stood her grandfather's bed, in another was the hearth with a large kettle hanging above it; and on the further side was a large door in the wall—this was the cupboard. Her grandfather opened it; inside were his clothes, some hanging up, others, a couple of shirts and some socks and handkerchiefs, lying on a shelf. On a second shelf were some plates and cups and glasses, and on a higher one still, a round loaf, smoked meat, and cheese, for everything that the old man needed for his food and clothing was kept in this cupboard.

Heidi, as soon as it was opened, ran quickly forward and thrust in her bundle of clothes, as far back behind her grandfather's things as possible, so that they might not easily be found again. She then looked carefully round the room and asked,

27

"Where am I to sleep, Grandfather?"

"Wherever you like," he answered.

Heidi was delighted and began at once to examine all the nooks and corners to see where would be the best place to sleep. In the corner near her grandfather's bed she saw a short ladder against the wall; up she climbed and found herself in the hay-loft. There lay a large heap of fresh sweet-smelling hay, while through a round window in the wall she could see right down the valley.

"I shall sleep up here, Grandfather," she called down to him. "It's lovely! Come up and see how lovely it is!"

"Oh, I know all about it," he said.

"I am getting the bed ready now," she called down again, as she went busily to and fro at her work, "but I shall want you to bring me up a sheet; I really need a sheet to sleep upon."

"All right," said her grandfather, and he went to the cupboard, and after rummaging about inside for a few minutes he drew out a long, coarse piece of cloth which was all he had to do duty for a sheet. He carried it up to the loft, where he found Heidi had already made quite a nice bed. She had put an extra

28

heap of hay at one end for a pillow, and had so arranged it that, when in bed, she would be able to see comfortably out through the round window.

"That is fine," said her grandfather. "Now we must put on the sheet, but wait a moment first," and he went and brought another large bundle of hay to make the bed thicker, so that the child should not feel the hard floor under her, "there, now bring it here."

Heidi had got hold of the sheet, but it was almost too heavy for her to carry. This was a good thing, however, as the close thick cloth would prevent the sharp stalks of the hay from pricking her. The two together now spread the sheet over the bed, and where it was too long or too wide, Heidi quickly tucked it in under the hay. It looked now as tidy and comfortable a bed as you could wish for, and Heidi stood gazing thoughtfully at it.

"We have forgotten something now, Grandfather," she said after a short silence.

"What's that?" he asked.

"A quilt; when you get into bed, you have to creep in between the sheet and the quilt."

"But suppose I have not got a quilt?"

"Well, never mind, Grandfather," said Heidi in a consoling tone of voice. "I can take some more hay to put over me," and she was turning quickly to fetch another armful from the heap, when her grandfather stopped her.

"Wait a moment," he said, and he climbed down the ladder again and went towards his bed. He returned to the loft with a large, thick sack, made of flax, which he threw down exclaiming, "There, that is better than hay, isn't it?"

Heidi began tugging away at the sack with all her might, in her efforts to get it smooth and straight, but her small hands were not fitted for so heavy a job. Her grandfather came to her assistance, and when they had got it tidily spread over the bed, it all looked so nice and warm and comfortable that Heidi stood gazing at it in delight. "That is a splendid quilt," she said, "and the bed looks very comfortable! How I wish it were night, so that I might get right in it."

"I think we might have something to eat first," said her grand-father. "What do you think?"

Heidi, in the excitement of bed-making, had forgotten every-thing else. But now she felt terribly hungry, so she answered quickly, "Yes, I think so too."

"Let us go down then, as we both think alike," said the old man, and he followed the child down the ladder. Then he went up to the hearth, pushed the big kettle aside, and pulled for-ward the little one that was hanging on the chain. Then seating himself on the round-topped, three-legged stool before the fire, he blew it up into a clear bright flame. The kettle soon began to boil, and meanwhile the old man held a large piece of cheese on a long iron fork over the fire, turning it round and round till it was toasted a nice golden yellow on each side.

Heidi watched all that was going on with eager attention. Suddenly a new idea came to her, for she turned and ran to the cupboard, and then began going busily backwards and for-wards. Presently her grandfather got up and came to the table with a jug and the cheese, and there he saw it already tidily laid with the round loaf and two plates and two knives each in its right place; for Heidi had noticed that morning all that there was in the cupboard, and she knew which things would be wanted for their meal.

"Ah, that's right," said her grandfather. "I am glad to see that you have some ideas of your own," and as he spoke he laid the toasted cheese on a layer of bread. "But there is still something missing."

Heidi looked at the jug that was steaming away invitingly and ran quickly back to the cupboard. At first she could only see a small bowl left on the shelf, but a moment later she caught sight of two glasses further back, and she quickly returned with these and the bowl and put them down on the table.

"Good, I see you know how to set about things; but where are you going to sit?" Her grandfather himself was sitting on the only chair in the room. Heidi flew to the hearth, and dragging the three-legged stool up to the table, sat down.

"Well, you have managed to find a seat for yourself, I see;

only it is rather low, I am afraid," said her grandfather, "but you would not be tall enough to reach the table even if you sat in my chair. Now it is time to have something to eat, so come along."

With that he stood up, filled the bowl with milk, and placing it on the chair, pushed it in front of Heidi on her little three-legged stool, so that now she had a table to herself. Then he brought her a large slice of bread and a piece of the golden cheese, and told her to eat. After that he went and sat down on the corner of the table and began his own meal. Heidi lifted the bowl with both hands and drank without stopping till it was empty, for she was very thirsty after her long, hot journey.

"Was the milk nice?" asked her grandfather.

"I never drank any so good before," answered Heidi.

"Then you must have some more," said the old man, and he filled her bowl again to the brim and set it before her. Heidi was now hungrily beginning her bread, having first spread it with the cheese. This, after being toasted, was soft as butter. The bread and cheese tasted delicious, and the child looked very contented as she sat eating. The meal being over, her grandfather went outside to put the goatshed in order, and Heidi watched with interest while he first swept it out, and then put fresh straw for the goats to sleep upon. Then he went to his little shop, and there he cut some long round sticks, and a small round board. In this he made some holes and stuck the sticks into them, and there, as if made by magic, was a three-legged stool just like her grandfather's, only higher. Heidi stood and looked at it, speechless with astonishment.

"What do you think that is?" asked her grandfather.

"It's my stool, I know, because it is such a high one; and it was made all of a minute," said the child.

"She understands what she sees; her eyes are in the right place," remarked her grandfather to himself. Then he went round the hut, knocking in a nail here and there. Heidi followed him step by step, her eyes attentively taking in all that he did, and everything that he did interested her.

And so the time passed happily on till evening. Then the wind began to roar louder than ever through the old fir trees. Heidi listened with delight to the sound, and skipped and danced around the old trees joyously. Her grandfather stood and watched her from the shed.

Suddenly a shrill whistle was heard. Heidi paused in her dancing, and her grandfather came out. Down from the heights above the goats came springing one after another, with Peter the goatherd in their midst. Heidi sprang forward with a cry of joy and rushed among the flock, greeting first one and then another of her old friends, for she had met them earlier that day. As they neared the hut the goats stood still, and then two of their number, two beautiful slender animals, one white and one brown, ran forward to where Heidi's grandfather was standing and began licking his hands, for he was holding a little salt which he always had ready for his goats on their return home. Peter disappeared with the remainder of his flock.

Heidi tenderly stroked the two goats in turn, running first to one side of them and then the other, and jumping about in her glee at their antics.

"Are they ours, Grandfather? Are they both ours? Are you going to put them in the shed? Will they always stay with us?"

Heidi's questions came tumbling out one after the other, so that her grandfather had only time to answer each of them with "Yes, yes."

When the goats had finished licking up the salt, her grandfather told her to go and fetch her bowl and the bread.

Heidi obeyed and was soon back again. Her grandfather milked the white goat and filled her bowl, and then he broke off a piece of bread.

"Now eat your supper," he said, "and then go up to bed. Aunt Dete left another little bundle for you with a nightgown and other small things in it, which you will find at the bottom of the cupboard if you want them. I must go and shut up the goats, so be off and sleep well."

"Good night, Grandfather! good night. What are their names, Grandfather, what are their names?" she called out as she ran after the old man and the goats.

"The white one is named Little Swan, and the brown one Little Bear," he answered.

"Good night, Little Swan, good night, Little Bear!" she called again at the top of her voice, for they were already inside the shed. Then she sat down on the seat and began to eat and drink, but the wind was so strong that it almost blew her away; so she hurried and finished her supper and then went indoors and climbed up to her bed, where she was soon lying as soundly asleep as any young princess on her couch of silk.

Not long after, and while it was still twilight, her grandfather also went to bed, for he was up every morning at sunrise, and the sun came climbing up over the mountains at a very early hour during these summer months.

The wind blew with such force during the night, and in such gusts against the walls, that the hut trembled and the old beams groaned and creaked. It came howling and wailing down the chimney like voices of those in pain, and it raged with such fury among the old fir trees that here and there a branch was snapped and fell. In the middle of the night the old man got up.

"The child will be frightened," he murmured half aloud. He mounted the ladder and went and stood by the child's bed.

Outside the moon was struggling with the dark, fast-driving clouds, which at one moment left it clear and shining, and the next swept over it, and all again was dark. Just now the moonlight was falling through the round window straight on Heidi's bed. She lay under the heavy quilt, her cheeks rosy with sleep, her head peacefully resting on her little round arm, and with a happy expression on her face as if dreaming of something pleasant. The old man stood looking down on the sleeping child until the moon again disappeared behind the clouds, and he could see no more; then he went back to bed.

Heidi was awakened early the next morning by a loud whistle; the sun was shining through the round window and falling on her bed and on the large heap of hay, and as she opened her eyes everything in the loft seemed gleaming with gold. She looked around her in astonishment and could not imagine for a while where she was. But her grandfather's deep voice was

33

now heard outside, and then Heidi began to recall all that had happened: how she had come away from her former home and was now on the mountain with her grandfather. She felt very happy this morning as she woke up in her new home and remembered all the many new things that she had seen the day before and which she would see again that day, and above all she thought with delight of the two goats. Heidi jumped quickly out of bed and dressed rapidly. Then she climbed down the ladder and ran outside the hut.

There stood Peter already with his flock of goats, and her grandfather was just bringing his two out of the shed to join the others. Heidi ran forward to wish good morning to him and the goats.

"Do you want to go with them on to the mountain?" asked her grandfather. Heidi jumped for joy.

"But you must first wash and make yourself tidy. The sun that shines so brightly overhead will laugh at you for being dirty; see, I have everything ready for you," and her grandfather pointed to a large tub full of water, which stood in the sun before the door.

Heidi ran to it and began splashing and rubbing, till she quite glistened with cleanliness. Grandfather meanwhile went inside the hut, calling to Peter to follow him and bring in his wallet. Peter obeyed with astonishment and laid down the little bag which held his meager dinner.

"Open it," said the old man, and inside it he put a large piece of bread and an equally large piece of cheese, which made Peter open his eyes, for each was twice the size of the two portions which he had for his own dinner.

"There, now there is only a little bowl to add," continued Heidi's grandfather, "for the child cannot drink her milk as you do from the goat; she is not accustomed to do that. You must milk two bowlfuls for her when she has her dinner, for she is going with you and will remain with you till you return this evening. Take care she does not fall over any of the rocks!"

Heidi now came running in. "Will the sun laugh at me now, Grandfather?" she asked anxiously. Her grandfather had left a coarse towel hanging up for her near the tub, and with this she had so thoroughly scrubbed herself, for fear of the sun, that as she stood there she was as red as a lobster. He gave a little laugh.

"No, there is nothing for him to laugh at now," he assured her. "But I tell you what—when you come home this evening, you will have to get right into the tub, like a fish, for if you run about like the goats you will get your feet dirty. Now you can be off."

They started joyfully for the mountain. During the night the wind had blown away all the clouds; the dark blue sky was spreading overhead, and in its midst was the bright sun shining down on the green slopes of the mountain where the flowers opened their little blue and yellow cups.

Heidi went running hither and thither, shouting with delight, for here were whole patches of delicate red primroses, and there the blue gleam of the lovely gentian, while above them all laughed and nodded the golden cistus. Enchanted with all this waving field of brightly-colored flowers, Heidi forgot even Peter and the goats. She ran on in front and then off to the side, tempted first one way and then the other, as she caught sight of some bright spot of glowing red or yellow. And all the while she was picking whole handfuls of flowers which she put into her apron, for she wanted to take them all home and stick them in the hay.

Peter had to be very alert, and his round eyes, which did not move very quickly, had more work than they could well manage, for the goats were as lively as Heidi. They ran in all directions, and Peter had to follow whistling and calling and swinging his stick to get all the runaways together again.

"Where have you got to now, Heidi?" he called out somewhat crossly.

"Here," she called. Peter could see no one, for Heidi was seated on the ground at the foot of a small hill thickly overgrown with sweet-smelling prunella. The air was filled with its fragrance, and Heidi thought she had never smelt anything so delicious. She sat surrounded by the flowers.

"Come along here!" called Peter again. "You are not to fall over the rocks. Your grandfather gave orders that you were not to do so."

"Where are the rocks?" asked Heidi. But she did not move from her seat, for the scent of the flowers seemed sweeter to her with every breath of wind.

"Up above, right up above. We have a long way to go yet, so come along! And on the topmost peak of all the old bird of prey sits and croaks."

That did it. Heidi immediately sprang to her feet and ran up to Peter with her apron full of flowers.

"You have got enough now," said the boy as they began climbing together. "You will stay here forever if you go on picking, and if you gather all the flowers now there will be none for tomorrow."

This last argument seemed to convince Heidi; besides, her apron was already so full that there was hardly room for another flower, and it would never do to leave nothing to pick for another day. So she now kept with Peter, and the goats also became more orderly, for they were beginning to smell the plants they loved that grew on the higher slopes and clambered up now without stopping. The spot where Peter generally pastured his goats lay at the foot of the high rocks, which were covered for some distance up by bushes and fir trees, beyond which rose their bare and rugged summits. On one side of the mountain the rock was split into deep clefts, and Grandfather had reason to warn Peter of danger. Having climbed as far as the halting-place, Peter unslung his wallet and put it carefully in a little hollow of the ground, for he knew what the wind was like up there and did not want to see his precious belongings sent rolling down the mountain by a sudden gust. Then he threw himself at full length on the warm ground, for he was tired after all his climbing.

Heidi meanwhile had unfastened her apron and rolling it carefully round the flowers laid it beside Peter's wallet inside the hollow. She then sat down beside him and looked about her. The valley lay far below in the sunlight. In front of her rose a wide snowfield, high against the dark blue sky, while to the left was a huge pile of rocks on each of which a bare lofty peak, that seemed to pierce the blue, looked frowningly down upon her. The child sat without moving, her eyes taking in the whole scene, and all around was a great stillness, only broken by soft, light puffs of wind that swayed the light bells of the blue flowers, and the shining gold heads of the cistus, and set them nodding merrily on their slender stems. Peter had fallen asleep and the goats were climbing about among the bushes overhead. Heidi had never felt so happy in her life before. She loved the golden sunlight, the fresh air, the sweet smell of the flowers, and wished for nothing better than to stay there always. So the time went on, while to Heidi, who had so often looked up from the valley at the mountains above, these seemed now to have faces, and to be looking down at her like old friends. Suddenly she heard a loud harsh cry overhead and lifting up her eyes she saw a bird, larger than any she had ever seen before, with great, spreading wings, wheeling round and round in a wide circle, and uttering a piercing, croaking kind of sound above her.

"Peter, Peter, wake up!" called out Heidi. "See, the great bird is there—look, look!"

Peter got up on hearing her call, and together they sat and watched the bird, which rose higher and higher in the blue air till it disappeared behind the gray mountain tops.

"Where has it gone?" asked Heidi, who had followed the bird's movements with intense interest.

"Home to its nest," said Peter.

"Is his home right up there? Oh, how nice to be up so high! Why does he make that noise?"

"Because he can't help it," explained Peter.

"Let us climb up there and see where his nest is," said Heidi.

"Oh! oh! oh!" exclaimed Peter, in disapproval. "Why, even the goats cannot climb as high as that; besides, didn't your grandfather say that you were not to fall over the rocks?"

Peter now began whistling and calling so loudly that Heidi could not think what was happening; but the goats evidently understood his voice, for one after another they came springing down the rocks until they were all assembled on the green plateau, some continuing to nibble at the juicy stems, others skipping about here and there or pushing at each other with their horns for pastime.

Heidi jumped up and ran in and out among them. She made friends with them all in turn. Meanwhile Peter had taken the wallet out of the hollow and placed the pieces of bread and cheese on the ground in the shape of a square.

Now he called Heidi to come, but she was so excited and amused at the capers and lively games of her new playfellows that she saw and heard nothing else. But Peter knew how to make himself heard, for he shouted till the very rocks above echoed his voice, and at last Heidi appeared, and when she saw the inviting meal spread out upon the ground she went skipping round it for joy.

"Leave off jumping about, it is time for dinner," said Peter. "Sit down now and begin."

Heidi sat down. "Is the milk for me?" she asked, giving another look of delight at the beautifully arranged square with the bowl as a chief ornament in the center.

"Yes," replied Peter, "and the two large pieces of bread and cheese are yours also, and when you have drunk up that milk, you are to have another bowlful from the white goat, and then it will be my turn."

"And which do you get your milk from?" inquired Heidi.

"From my own goat, the piebald one. But go on now with your dinner," said Peter, again reminding her it was time to eat. Heidi now took up the bowl and drank her milk, and as soon as she had put it down empty Peter rose and filled it again for her. Then she broke off a piece of her bread and held out the remainder, which was still larger than Peter's own piece, together with the whole big slice of cheese to her companion, saying, "You can have that, I have plenty."

Peter looked at Heidi, unable to speak for astonishment, for he never would have done anything like that. He hesitated a moment, for he could not believe that Heidi was in earnest; but she kept on holding out the bread and cheese, and as Peter still did not take it, she laid it on his knees. He saw then that she really meant it. He seized the food, nodded his thanks and ate the best dinner of his goatherd life. Heidi still continued to watch the goats. "Tell me all their names," she said.

Peter knew these by heart. So he began, telling Heidi the name of each goat in turn as he pointed it out to her. Heidi listened with great attention, and it was not long before she could herself distinguish the goats from one another and could call each by name. Every goat had its own peculiarities which anyone might remember. One had only to watch them closely, and this Heidi did. There was the great Turk with his big horns, who was always wanting to butt the others, so that most of them ran away when they saw him coming and would have nothing to do with their rough companion. Only Greenfinch, the slender, nimble little goat was brave enough to face him, and would make a rush at him, three or four times in succession, so swiftly and skillfully that the great Turk often stood still quite astounded, not venturing to attack her again, for Green-

39

finch was fronting him, prepared for more warlike action, and her horns were sharp. Then there was little White Snowflake, who bleated in such a plaintive and beseeching manner that Heidi already had several times run to it and taken its head in her hands to comfort it.

Just at this moment the pleading young cry was heard again, and Heidi jumped up running and, putting her arms around the little creature's neck, asked in a sympathetic voice, "What is it, little Snowflake? Why do you cry so?" The goat pressed close to Heidi in a confiding way and left off bleating.

Peter called out from where he was sitting—for he had not yet got to the end of his bread and cheese, "She cries like that because the old goat is not with her; she was sold at Mayenfeld the day before yesterday, and so will not come up the mountain any more."

"Who is the old goat?" asked Heidi.

"Why, her mother, of course," was the answer.

"Where is her grandmother?" called Heidi again.

"She had none."

"Oh, you poor little Snowflake!" exclaimed Heidi, clasping the animal gently to her. "Do not cry like that any more. See now, I shall come up here with you every day, so that you will not be alone any more, and if you want anything you have only to come to me."

The young animal rubbed its head contentedly against Heidi's shoulder, and no longer gave such plaintive bleats. Peter now having finished his meal joined Heidi and the goats, Heidi having by this time found out a great many things about them. She decided that by far the handsomest and best behaved of the goats were Little Swan and Little Bear, the two belonging to her grandfather. They carried themselves with a certain air of distinction and generally went their own way, and as to the great Turk they treated him with scorn.

The goats were now beginning to climb the rocks again. Each was seeking for the plants it liked in its own fashion. Some jumped over everything they met till they found what they wanted. Others went more carefully and cropped all the best

leaves by the way. The Turk now and then still gave the others a poke with his horns. Little Swan and Little Bear clambered lightly up and never failed to find leaves. Heidi stood with her hands behind her back, carefully noting all they did.

"Peter," she said to the boy who had again thrown himself down on the ground, "the prettiest of all the goats are Little Swan and Little Bear."

"Yes, I know they are," was the answer. "Your grandfather brushes them down and washes them and gives them salt, and he has the nicest shed for them."

All of a sudden Peter leaped to his feet and ran hastily after the goats. Heidi followed him as fast as she could, for she was too eager to know what had happened to stay behind. Peter dashed through the middle of the flock towards the side of the mountain where the rocks were very steep and bare, and where any thoughtless goat, if it went too near, might fall over and break all its legs. He had caught sight of the venturesome Greenfinch taking leaps in that direction, and he was only just in time, for the animal had already sprung to the edge of the cliff. All Peter could do was to throw himself down and seize one of her hind legs. Greenfinch, thus taken by surprise, began bleating furiously, angry at being held so fast and prevented from continuing her voyage of discovery. She struggled to get loose, and tried so hard to leap forward that Peter shouted to Heidi to come and help him, for he could not get up and was afraid of pulling out the goat's leg altogether.

Heidi had already run up, and she saw at once the danger both Peter and the animal were in. She quickly gathered a bunch of sweet-smelling leaves, and then holding them under Greenfinch's nose, said coaxingly, "Come, come, Greenfinch, you must not be naughty! Look, you might fall down there and break your leg, and that would give you dreadful pain!"

The young animal turned quickly and began contentedly eating the leaves out of Heidi's hand. Meanwhile Peter got to his feet again and took hold of Greenfinch by the band round her neck from which her bell was hung. Heidi, taking hold of her in the same way on the other side, helped lead the wanderer back to the rest of the flock that had remained peacefully feeding. Peter, now he had his goat in safety, lifted his stick in order to give her a good beating, and Greenfinch, seeing what was coming, shrank back in fear. But Heidi cried out, "No, no, Peter, you must not strike her; see how frightened she is!"

"She deserves it," growled Peter, and again lifted his stick. Then Heidi flung herself against him and cried indignantly. "You have no right to touch her; it will hurt her; let her alone!"

Peter looked with surprise at the commanding little figure, whose dark eyes were flashing, and reluctantly he let his stick drop. "Well, I will let her off if you will give me some of your cheese tomorrow," he said, for he was determined to have something to make up to him for his fright.

"You shall have it all, tomorrow and every day. I do not want it," replied Heidi, giving ready consent to his demand. "And I will give you bread as well, a large piece like you had today. But then you must promise never to beat Greenfinch, or Snowflake, or any of the goats."

"All right," said Peter, "I don't care," which meant that he would agree to the bargain. He now let go of Greenfinch, who joyfully sprang to join her companions.

The day had crept on to its close, and now the sun was on the point of sinking out of sight behind the high mountains. Heidi was again sitting on the ground, silently gazing at the blue bell-shaped flowers, as they glistened in the evening sun, for a golden light lay on the grass and flowers, and the rocks above were beginning to shine and glow.

All at once she sprang to her feet. "Peter! Peter! everything is on fire! All the rocks are burning, and the great snow mountains and the sky! Oh, the beautiful, fiery snow! Stand up, Peter! See, the fire has reached the great bird's nest. Look at the rocks! Look at the fir trees! Everything, everything is on fire!"

"It is always like that," said Peter calmly continuing to peel his stick; "but it is not really fire."

"What is it then?" cried Heidi, as she ran backwards and forwards to look first on one side and then the other, for she felt she could not have enough of such a beautiful sight. "What

43

is it, Peter, what is it?" she repeated.

"It gets like that of itself," exclaimed Peter.

"Look, look!" cried Heidi in fresh excitement, "now they have turned all rose color! Look at that one covered with snow, and that with the high pointed rocks! What do you call them?"

"Mountains have no names," he answered.

"Oh, how beautiful, look at the crimson snow! And up there on the rocks there are ever so many roses. Oh! now they are turning gray! Oh! oh! now all the color has died away! It is all gone, Peter!" And Heidi sat down on the ground looking disappointed.

"It will come again tomorrow," said Peter. "Get up, we must go home now." He whistled to his goats and together they all started on their homeward way.

"Is it like that every day? Shall we see it every day when we bring the goats up here?" asked Heidi, as she clambered down the mountain at Peter's side. She waited eagerly for his answer, hoping that he would tell her it was so.

"It is like that most days," he replied.

"But will it be like that tomorrow for certain?" Heidi persisted.

"Yes, yes, tomorrow for certain," Peter assured her.

Heidi now felt quite happy again, and her little brain was so full of new impressions and new thoughts that she did not speak any more until they had reached the hut. Her grandfather was sitting under the fir trees, where he had also put up a seat, waiting as usual for his goats which returned down the mountain on this side.

Heidi ran up to him followed by the white and brown goats, for they knew their own master and stall. Peter called out after her, "Come with me again tomorrow! Good night!" For he was anxious for more than one reason that Heidi should go with him the next day.

Heidi ran back quickly and gave Peter her hand, promising to go with him, and then making her way through the goats she once more clasped Snowflake, "And remember that I shall be with you again tomorrow, so you must not bleat so sadly any

44

more." Snowflake gave her a friendly and grateful look, and then went leaping joyfully after the other goats.

Heidi returned to the fir trees. "Oh, Grandfather," she cried, even before she had come up to him. "It was so beautiful. The fire, and the roses on the rocks, and the blue and yellow flowers, and look what I have brought you!" And opening the apron that held her flowers she shook them all out at her grandfather's feet. But the poor flowers, how changed they were! Heidi hardly knew them again. They looked like dried bits of hay, not a single little flower cup stood open. "Oh, Grandfather, what is the matter with them?" exclaimed Heidi in shocked surprise, "They were not like that this morning, why do they look so now?"

"They like to stand out there in the sun and not be shut up in an apron," said her grandfather.

"Then I will never gather any more. But, Grandfather, why did the great bird go on croaking so?" she continued eagerly.

"Go along now and get into your bath while I go and get some milk. When we are together at supper I will tell you all about it."

Heidi obeyed, and when later she was sitting on her high stool before her milk bowl with her grandfather beside her, she repeated her question, "Why does the great bird go on croaking and screaming down at us, Grandfather?"

"He is mocking the people who live down below in the villages, because they all go huddling and gossiping together. He calls out, 'If you would separate and each go your own way and come up here and live on a height as I do, it would be better for you!' There was a wild tone in the old man's voice as he spoke, so that Heidi seemed to hear the croaking of the bird again even more distinctly.

"Why haven't the mountains any names?" Heidi went on.

"They have names," answered her grandfather, "and if you can describe one of them to me that I know I will tell you what it is called."

Heidi then described to him the rocky mountain with the two high peaks so exactly that her grandfather was delighted. "Just so, I know it," and he told her its name. "Did you see any other?"

45

Then Heidi told him of the mountain with the great snow field, and how it had been on fire, and had turned rosy red and then all of a sudden had grown quite pale again, and all the color had disappeared.

"I know that one, too," he said, giving her its name. "So you enjoyed being out with the goats?"

Then Heidi went on to give him an account of the whole day, and of how delightful it had all been, and particularly described the fire that had burst out everywhere in the evening. And then nothing would do but that her grandfather must tell how it came, for Peter knew nothing about it.

Her grandfather explained to her that it was the sun that did it. "When he says good night to the mountains he throws his most beautiful colors over them, so that they may not forget him before he comes again the next day."

Heidi was delighted with this explanation and could hardly bear to wait for another day to come that she might once more climb up with the goats and see how the sun bids good night to the mountains. But she had to go to bed first, and all night she slept soundly on her bed of hay, dreaming of nothing but shining mountains with red roses all over them, among which happy little Snowflake went leaping in and out.

As HEIDI grows older she is taken to be a companion to Clara Sesemann, a little cripple down in Frankfurt. Heidi has many sad and glad adventures in this wealthy household, but, finally, homesickness for her grandfather and for Peter's blind grandmother brings her back to her mountain home.

Soon Clara and her grandmother come to visit Heidi. They embrace each other lovingly.

After the first words of greeting had been exchanged Clara's grandmamma cried admiringly, "What a fine place you have, Sir! I could hardly have believed it was so beautiful! A king might well envy you! And how my little Heidi looks—like a wild rose!" She drew the child towards her and patted her fresh pink cheeks. "I don't know which way to look first, it is all so lovely! What do you say to it, Clara, what do you say?"

Clara was gazing around entranced; she had never imagined anything so beautiful. She cried with delight, "Oh, Grandmamma, I should like to remain here forever!"

Heidi's grandfather had meanwhile drawn up Clara's wheel chair and spread some of the wraps over it; he now went up to Clara.

"Supposing we carry the little daughter now to her accustomed chair. I think she will be more comfortable; the traveling sedan is rather hard," he said, and without waiting for anyone to help him, he lifted the child in his strong arms and let her gently down on her wheel chair. He then covered her over carefully and arranged her feet on the soft cushion, as if he had never done anything all his life but wait on cripples. Clara's grandmamma looked on with surprise.

"My dear Sir," she exclaimed, "how do you know how to care so well for the sick?"

Grandfather smiled. "I know more from experience than training," he answered, for he had once cared for a sick friend in Sicily.

The sky spread blue and cloudless over the hut and fir trees and high lofty cliffs which towered up so gray and sparkling.

Clara could not stop looking at all the beauty around her.

She was charmed. "Oh, Heidi, if only I could walk about with you," she said longingly, "if I could only go and look at the fir trees and at all the things you've told me about."

Then Heidi made a great effort and managed to wheel Clara's chair round the hut to the fir trees. There they paused.

Clara had never seen such trees before, with their tall, straight trunks, and long thick branches, growing thicker and thicker till they touched the ground. Even her grandmamma, who had followed the children, was astonished at the sight of them. She hardly knew what to admire most in these ancient trees: the lofty tops rising in their full green splendor towards the sky, or the pillar-like trunks with their straight and gigantic boughs, that could tell of the many long years during which they had looked down upon the valley below, where men came and went, on all things continually changing, while they stood undisturbed and changeless.

Heidi had now wheeled Clara in front of the goat shed, and had flung open the door, so that Clara might have a full view of all that was inside. There was not much to see just now, as the goats were gone. Clara cried out regretfully that they would have to leave early before the goats came home. "I should so like to have seen Peter and his whole flock," she said.

"Dear child, let us enjoy all the beautiful things that we can see, and not think about those that we cannot," Grandmamma replied as she followed the chair which Heidi was pushing further on.

"Oh, the flowers!" exclaimed Clara. "Look at the bushes of red flowers, and all the nodding bluebells! Oh, if I could only pick some."

Heidi ran off at once and picked her a large bunch of them.

"But these are nothing, Clara," she said, laying the flowers on her lap. "If you could come up higher to where the goats are feeding, then you would indeed see something! Bushes on bushes of the red centaury, and ever so many more of the bluebells and then the bright yellow rock roses, that gleam like pure gold, and all crowding together in the one spot. And then there are others with the large leaves that Grandfather calls Bright

48

Eyes, and the brown ones with little round heads that smell so good. Oh, it is beautiful up there, and if you sit down among them you never want to get up again, everything is so fragrant and beautiful."

Heidi's eyes sparkled; she was longing herself to see it all again, and Clara caught her enthusiasm and looked back at her with equal longing in her soft blue eyes.

"Grandmamma, do you think I could get up there? Is it possible for me to go?" she asked eagerly. "If only I could walk and climb about everywhere with you, Heidi!"

"I am sure I could push you up; the chair goes easily," said Heidi, and in proof of her words, she sent the chair at such a pace around the corner that it nearly went flying down the mountainside. Grandmamma being at hand, however, stopped it in time.

Heidi's grandfather, meantime, had not been idle. He had by this time put the table and extra chairs in front of the hut, so that they might all sit out here and eat their dinner. The milk and cheese were soon ready, and then the company sat down in high spirits to their mid-day meal.

49

Grandmamma was enchanted with their dining room. From there one could see far along the valley, and far over the mountains to the farthest stretch of blue sky. A light wind blew over them as they sat at the table, and the rustling of the fir trees seemed like music ordered for the feast.

"I never enjoyed anything as much as this. It is really superb!" cried Grandmamma two or three times. "Do I really see you taking a second piece of toasted cheese, Clara?"

There, sure enough, was a second golden-colored slice of cheese on Clara's plate.

"Oh, it does taste so good, Grandmamma—better than all the dishes we have at Ragatz," replied Clara, as she continued eating with great relish.

"That's right, eat what you can!" exclaimed Heidi's grandfather. "It's the mountain air which makes you so hungry!"

And so the meal went on. Grandmamma and the old man became more and more lively. They so agreed in their opinions of men and things and the world in general that they might have been friends for years.

Suddenly Grandmamma looked towards the west and said, "We must soon get ready to go, Clara; the sun is a good way down; the men will soon be here with the horse and sedan."

Clara's face fell, and she said beseechingly, "Oh, just another hour, Grandmamma, or two hours. We haven't seen the inside of the hut yet, or Heidi's bed, or any of the other things. If only the day was ten hours longer!"

"Well, that is impossible," said Grandmamma, but she herself was anxious to see the inside of the hut, so they all rose from the table and Heidi's grandfather wheeled Clara's chair to the door. But there they came to a standstill, for the chair was much too broad to pass through the door. Grandfather, however, soon settled the difficulty by lifting Clara in his strong arms and carrying her inside.

Grandmamma went all round and examined the household arrangements, and was very much amused and pleased at their orderliness and the cozy appearance of everything.

"And this is your bedroom up here, Heidi, is it not?" she asked, as she fearlessly climbed the ladder to the hayloft. "Oh, it does smell sweet! What a healthy place to sleep in."

She went up to the round window and looked out, and Grandfather followed up with Clara in his arms, Heidi springing up after them. Then they all stood and examined Heidi's wonderful hay-bed, and Grandmamma looked thoughtfully at it and drew in from time to time deep breaths of the new hay's spicy fragrance.

"It is delightful for you up here, Heidi! You can look from your bed straight into the sky, and then such a delicious smell all round you! And outside the fir trees waving and rustling. I have never seen such a pleasant, cheerful bedroom before."

Heidi's grandfather looked over at Clara's grandmamma. "I have been thinking," he said to her, "that if you were willing to agree to it, your little granddaughter might remain up here, and I am sure she would grow stronger. You have brought up all kinds of shawls and covers with you, and we could make a soft bed out of them, and as to looking after the child, you need not fear, for I will see to that."

Clara and Heidi were as overjoyed at these words as if they were two birds let out of their separate cages, and Grandmamma's face beamed with satisfaction.

"You are very kind, indeed, my dear Sir," she exclaimed. "You say what was in my own mind. I was only asking myself whether a stay up here might not be the very thing she needed. But then the trouble and inconvenience to yourself! And you speak of nursing and looking after her as if it was a mere nothing! I thank you sincerely, I thank you from my whole heart, Sir." And she shook his hand again and again.

The old man immediately set to work to get things ready. He carried Clara back to her chair outside, Heidi following, not knowing how to jump high enough into the air to express her delight. Then he gathered up a whole pile of shawls and furs and said, smiling, "It is a good thing that Grandmamma came up well provided for a winter's campaign; we shall be able to make good use of these."

"Foresight is a virtue," responded the lady, amused, "and

prevents many misfortunes. If we have made the journey over your mountains without meeting with storms, winds, and cloud-bursts, we are thankful and my provision against these disasters now comes in usefully, as you say."

The two had meanwhile ascended to the hayloft and had begun to prepare a bed. There were so many covers one over the other that the bed looked like a little fortress. Grandmamma passed her hand carefully over it to make sure that there were no bits of hay sticking out. "If there's a bit that can come through, it will," she said. The soft mattress, however, was so smooth and thick that nothing could penetrate it.

Then they went down again well satisfied, and found the children laughing and talking together, and arranging all they were going to do from morning to night as long as Clara stayed. The older people had decided that Clara should try the mountain air for at least a month. The children clapped their hands, for they had not expected to be together for so long a time.

The porters and the horse and guide were now seen approaching; the former were sent back at once, and Grandmamma prepared to mount for her return journey.

"It is not saying good-bye, Grandmamma," Clara called out, "for you will come up now and then and see how we are getting on. And we shall so look forward to your visits, shan't we, Heidi?"

Heidi nodded and jumped high with delight.

Grandmamma being now seated on her sturdy animal, Heidi's grandfather took the bridle to lead her down the steep mountain path. She begged him not to come far with her, but he insisted on seeing her safely as far as Dörfli, for the mountain was steep and dangerous. Grandmamma did not care to stay alone in Dörfli, and therefore decided to return to Ragatz, and journey up the mountain from time to time.

Peter came down with his goats before Grandfather had returned. As soon as the animals caught sight of Heidi they all came flocking towards her, and she, as well as Clara in her chair, was soon surrounded by the goats, pushing and poking their heads one over the other, while Heidi introduced each in turn by its name to Clara.

It was not long before Clara had met little Snowflake, the lively Greenfinch, and the well-behaved goats belonging to Grandfather, as well as many of the others, including the Great Turk. Peter meanwhile stood apart looking on and casting somewhat unfriendly glances towards Clara.

When the two children called out, "Good evening, Peter," he made no answer, but swung up his stick angrily, as if wanting to cut the air in two, and then ran off with his goats after him.

The climax to all the beautiful things that Clara had already seen upon the mountain came at the close of the day.

As she lay on the large soft bed in the hayloft with Heidi near her, she looked out through the round open window right into the middle of the shining clusters of stars, and she exclaimed in delight, "Heidi, it's just as if we were in a high carriage and were riding in the sky."

"Yes, and do you know why the stars are so happy and look down and nod to us like that?" asked Heidi.

"No, why is it?" asked Clara.

"Because they live up in heaven and know how well God arranges everything for us, so that we need have no more fear or trouble and may be quite sure that all things will come right in the end. That's why they are so happy, and they nod to us because they want us to be happy, too. But then we must never forget to pray, and to ask God to remember us when He is

53

arranging things. Then we may feel safe and happy, and not be afraid."

The two children now sat up and said their prayers, and then Heidi put her head down on her little round arm and fell off to sleep at once. Clara, however, lay awake some time, for she could not get over the wonder of this new experience, of being in bed up here among the stars. She had, indeed, seldom seen a star, for she never went outside the house at night, and the curtains at home were always drawn before the stars came out. Each time she closed her eyes she felt she must open them again to see if the two very large stars were still looking in, and nodding to her as Heidi said they did. There they were, always in the same place, and Clara felt she could not look long enough into their bright sparkling faces. Then at last her eyes closed, and it was only in her dreams that she still saw the two large friendly stars shining down upon her.

The sun had just risen above the mountains and was casting its first golden beams over the hut and the valley below. Grandfather, as was his custom, had been standing in a quiet and devout attitude for some little while, watching the light mists gradually lifting, and the heights and valley emerging from their twilight shadows and awakening to another day.

The light morning clouds overhead grew brighter and brighter, till at last the sun shone out in all its glory, and rock and wood and hill were bathed in golden light.

Grandfather now stepped back into the hut and went softly up the ladder. Clara had just opened her eyes and was looking with wonder at the bright sunlight that shone through the round window and danced and sparkled about her bed. She could not at first think what she was looking at or where she was. Then she caught sight of Heidi sleeping beside her, and now she heard Grandfather's cheery voice asking her if she had slept well and was feeling rested. She assured him she was not tired, and that when she had once fallen asleep she had not opened her eyes again all night. Grandfather was pleased and immediately began to care for her with so much gentleness that it seemed as if his chief calling had been to look after sick children.

Heidi now awoke and was surprised to see Clara dressed and already in Grandfather's arms ready to be carried down. She must get up, too, and she dressed as quickly as lightning. Then she ran down the ladder and out of the hut, and rubbed her eyes in surprise, for Grandfather had been busy the night before after they were in bed. Seeing that it was impossible to get Clara's chair through the hut door, he had taken down two of the boards at the side of the shed and made an opening large enough to admit the chair; these he left loose so that they might be taken away and put up at pleasure. He was at this moment wheeling Clara out into the sun; he left her in front of the hut while he went to look after the goats, and Heidi ran up to her friend.

The fresh morning breeze blew round the children's faces, and every fresh puff brought to them the spicy fragrance of the fir trees. Clara drew in deep breaths with delight and lay back in her chair with a feeling of health she had never had before. It was the first time in her life that she had been out in the open country at this early hour and felt the fresh morning breeze, and the pure mountain air was so cool and refreshing that every breath was a pleasure. And the bright sun, which was not hot and sultry up here, lay soft and warm on her hands and on the grass at her feet. Clara had not imagined that it would be like this on the mountain.

"Oh, Heidi, if only I could stay up here forever with you," she exclaimed happily, turning in her chair from side to side.

"Now you see that it is just what I told you," replied Heidi, delighted. "It is the most beautiful thing in the world to be up here with Grandfather!"

The old man at that moment came out from the goat shed and brought two small bowls of foaming snow-white milk—one for Clara and one for Heidi.

"That will do the little girl good," he said, nodding to Clara. "It is from Little Swan and will make her strong. To your health, child! Drink it up!"

Clara had never tasted goat's milk before. She hesitated before putting it to her lips, but seeing how Heidi drank hers

55

without hesitating, and how much she seemed to like it, Clara did the same, and drank till there was not a drop left, for she too found it delicious, tasting just as if sugar and cinnamon had been mixed with it.

"Tomorrow we will drink two," said Grandfather, who had looked on with satisfaction at seeing her follow Heidi's example.

Peter now arrived with the goats, and while Heidi was receiving her usual crowded morning's greetings, Grandfather drew Peter aside to speak to him, for the goats bleated so loudly and continuously that no one could be heard near them.

"Listen to what I have to say," he said. "From now on be sure to let Little Swan go where she likes. She knows where to find the best food for herself, and so if she wants to climb higher, you follow her, and it will do the others no harm if they go, too. On no account bring her back. A little more climbing won't hurt you, and in this matter she probably knows better than you what is good for her. I want her to give as fine milk as possible. Why are you looking over there as if you wanted to eat somebody? Nobody will interfere with you. So now be off and remember what I say."

Peter was accustomed to obeying Grandfather at once, and he marched off with his goats, but with a turn of the head and roll of the eye that showed something was disturbing him. The goats carried Heidi along with them a little way, which was what Peter wanted. "You will have to come with them," he called to her, "for I shall be obliged to follow Little Swan."

"I cannot," Heidi called back from the midst of her friends, "and I shall not be able to come for a long, long time—not as long as Clara is with me. Grandfather, however, has promised to go up the mountain with both of us one day."

Heidi had now torn herself away from the goats and she ran back to Clara. Peter doubled his fists and made threatening gestures towards the invalid in her chair, and then climbed up some distance without pause until he was out of sight, for he was afraid Grandfather might have seen him, and he did not care to know what he might have thought of the fists.

Clara and Heidi had made so many plans for themselves that

they hardly knew where to begin. Heidi suggested that they should first write to Grandmamma, to whom they had promised to send word every day, for Grandmamma had not felt sure that Clara would like it up there or that her health would improve. With daily news of her granddaughter she could stay on without anxiety at Ragatz, and be ready to go to Clara at a moment's notice.

"Must we go indoors to write?" asked Clara, who agreed to write a letter, but did not want to move from where she was, as it was so much nicer outside.

Heidi was ready to arrange everything. She ran in and brought out her school materials and her own little stool. She put her reading book and copybook on Clara's knees, to make a desk for her to write upon, and she herself took her seat on the stool and sat by the bench, and then they both began writing to Grandmamma. Clara, however, paused after every sentence to look about her. It was too beautiful for much letter writing. The breeze had died down a little, and now only gently fanned her face and whispered lightly through the fir trees. Little winged insects hummed and danced around her in the clear air, and a great stillness lay over the far, wide, sunny pastures. Lofty and silent rose the high mountain peaks above her, and below lay the whole broad valley full of quiet peace. Now and then only the call of some shepherd boy rang out through the air, and an echo answered softly from the rocks.

The morning passed, the children hardly knew how, and now Grandfather came with the mid-day bowls of steaming milk, for Clara, he said, was to remain out as long as there was a gleam of sun in the sky. The mid-day meal was again eaten in the open air. Then Heidi pushed Clara's chair under the fir trees, so that they could spend the afternoon there and tell each other all that had happened since Heidi left Frankfurt. Heidi wanted to hear about the various people in the Sesemann household who were all so well known to her.

So they sat and chatted under the trees, and the more lively grew their conversation, the more loudly sang the birds overhead, as if wishing to take part in the children's chatter, which

57

evidently pleased them. Then, all of a sudden, the evening came with the returning of Peter, who still scowled and looked gray.

"Good night, Peter," called out Clara in a friendly voice. Peter took no notice and went sullenly on with his goats.

As Clara saw Grandfather leading away Little Swan to milk her, she suddenly longed for another bowlful of the fragrant milk, and waited impatiently for it.

"Isn't it curious, Heidi," she said, astonished at herself. "As long as I can remember I have only eaten because I was obliged to. Everything used to taste queer, and I was always wishing there was no need to eat or drink. But now I am longing for Grandfather to bring me the milk!"

"Yes, I know what it feels like," replied Heidi, who remembered the many homesick days in Frankfurt when all her food seemed to stick in her throat.

Clara, however, could not understand it. The fact was that she had never before spent a whole day in the open air, much less in such high, life-giving mountain air. When Grandfather at last brought her the evening milk, she drank it up so quickly that she had emptied her bowl before Heidi, and then she asked for a little more. Grandfather went inside with both the children's bowls, and when he brought them out again full he had something else to add to their supper. He had walked over that afternoon to a herdsman's house where the sweet-tasting butter was made, and had brought home a large pat, some of which he had now spread thickly on two good slices of bread. He stood and watched with pleasure while Clara and Heidi ate their appetizing meal with such enjoyment.

That night, when Clara lay down in her bed and prepared to watch the stars, her eyes would not keep open, and she fell asleep as soon as Heidi and slept soundly all night—a thing she never remembered having done before.

The following day and the day after passed in the same pleasant fashion, and the third day there came a surprise for the children.

Two stout porters came up the mountain, each carrying a bed on his shoulders with bedding of all kinds and two beautiful new white quilts. The men also had a letter with them from Grand-mamma. These beds were for Clara and Heidi, she wrote, and Heidi in the future was always to sleep in a proper bed. When she went down to Dörfli in the winter she was to take one with her and leave the other at the hut, so that Clara might always know there was a bed ready for her when she paid a visit to the mountain. She went on to thank the children for their long letters and hoped they would continue writing daily, so that she might be able to picture all they were doing.

So Grandfather went up and threw back the hay from Heidi's bed on to the great heap, and then with his help the beds were transported to the loft. He put them close to one another so that the children might still be able to see out of the window, for he knew what pleasure they had in the light from the sun and stars.

Meanwhile Grandmamma down at Ragatz was rejoicing at the excellent news of the sick child which reached her daily from the mountain. Clara found the life more delightful each day and could not say enough of the kindness and care which Grandfather lavished upon her, nor of Heidi's lively and amusing companionship. Heidi, indeed, was more entertaining than she was in Frankfurt, and Clara's first thought when she woke each morning was, "Oh, how glad I am to be here!"

Having such assurances each day that all was going well with Clara, Grandmamma thought she might put off her visit to the children a little longer. The steep ride up and down was some-what tiring to her.

Grandfather tried to think of something fresh every day to help forward Clara's recovery. He climbed up the mountain every afternoon, higher and higher each day, and came home in the evening with a large bunch of leaves. These perfumed the air with a mingled fragrance as of carnations and thyme, even from afar. He hung it up in the goat shed, and the goats on their return were wild to get at it, for they recognized the smell. But Grandfather did not go climbing after rare plants to give the goats the pleasure of eating them. What he gathered was for Little Swan alone, that she might give extra fine milk. The effect of the extra feeding was soon shown in the way she flung her head in the air more and more gaily. It also showed in the bright glow of her eye.

Clara had now been on the mountain for three weeks. For some days past Grandfather, after carrying her down each morning, had said, "Won't you try to stand for a minute or two?" Clara had made the effort in order to please him. But she had clung to him as soon as her feet touched the ground, it hurt her so. He let her try a little longer, however, each day.

It was many years since they had had such a splendid sum-mer among the mountains. Day after day there was the same cloudless sky and the same brilliant sun. The flowers opened wide their fragrant blossoms, and everywhere the eye was greeted with a glow of color. And when the evening came the crimson light fell on mountain peaks and on the great snow-field, till at last the sun sank in a sea of golden flame.

And Heidi never tired of telling Clara of all this, for only higher up could the full glory of the colors be rightly seen. Most of all she pictured the beauty of the spot on the higher slope of the mountain. There the bright golden rock-roses grew in masses, and the blue flowers were in such numbers that the very grass seemed to have turned blue. While near these, were whole bushes of the brown blossoms, with their delicious scent, so that you never wanted to move again when you once sat down among them.

She had just been talking about the flowers as she sat with Clara under the fir trees one evening, and had been telling her again of the wonderful light from the evening sun, when such a longing came over her to see it all once more that she jumped up and ran to her grandfather, who was in the shed.

"Grandfather," she called, "will you take us out with the goats tomorrow? Oh, it is so lovely up there now!"

"Very well," he answered, "but if I do, little Clara must do something to please me. She must try her best again this evening to stand on her feet."

Heidi ran back with the good news to Clara, and Clara promised to try her very best as Grandfather wished. She looked forward eagerly to the next day's excursion. Heidi was so pleased and excited that she called out to Peter as soon as she caught sight of him that evening, "Peter, Peter, we are all coming out with you tomorrow and are going to stay up there the whole day!"

Peter, cross as a bear, grumbled some reply. He lifted his stick to give Greenfinch a blow for no reason in particular. But Greenfinch saw the movement, and with a leap over Snowflake's back, got out of the way, and the stick only hit the air.

Clara and Heidi got into their two fine beds that night looking forward to tomorrow's excursion. They were so full of their plans that they agreed to keep awake all night and talk over them until it was time to get up. But their heads had no sooner touched their soft pillows than the conversation suddenly ceased. Clara fell into a dream of an immense field, which looked the color of the sky, so thickly inlaid was it with blue bell-shaped flowers. And Heidi heard the great bird of prey calling to her from the heights above, "Come! Come! Come!"

Grandfather went out early the next morning to see what kind of a day it was going to be. There was a reddish gold light over the higher peaks. A light breeze was springing up. And the branches of the fir trees moved gently to and fro. The sun was on its way.

The old man stood and watched the green slopes under the higher peaks gradually growing brighter with the coming day.

He watched the dark shadows lifting from the valley, until a rosy light filled its hollows. Then he saw the morning gold flooding every height and depth—the sun had risen.

Grandfather wheeled the chair out of the shed ready for the coming journey and then went in to call the children and tell them what a lovely sunrise it was.

Peter came up at this moment. The goats did not gather round him so trustfully as usual. They seemed to avoid him, for Peter was angry and bitter and was using his stick unnecessarily. And where it fell the blow was no light one. For weeks now he had not had Heidi all to himself. When he came up in the morning the invalid child was always already in her chair and Heidi was talking to her. And it was the same thing again when he came down in the evening. She had not come out with the goats once this summer. And now today she was only coming with her friend and the chair, and would stick by the chair's side the whole time. It was the thought of this which was making him particularly cross this morning.

There stood the chair on its high wheels. Peter seemed to see something proud and disdainful about it. He glared at it, his enemy that had done him harm, and was likely to do him more

harm still today. He glanced round—there was no sound anywhere, no one to see him. He sprang forward like a wild creature, caught hold of it, and gave it a violent and angry push in
the direction of the slope.

The chair rolled swiftly forward and in another minute had
disappeared.

Peter now sped up the mountain, not pausing till he was well
in the shelter of a large blackberry bush. He had no wish to be
seen by Grandfather. But he was anxious to see what had become of the chair, and his bush was well placed for that. If
hidden, he could watch what happened below and see what
Grandfather did without being discovered himself. So he
looked, and there he saw his enemy running faster and faster
downhill. Then it turned head over heels several times. Finally, after one great bound, it rolled over and over to its complete destruction. The pieces flew in every direction—feet, arms,
and torn fragments of the padded seat and bolster—and Peter
experienced a feeling of such unbounded delight at the sight
that he leapt in the air, laughing aloud and stamping for joy.
Then he took a run round, jumping over bushes on the way,
only to return to the same spot and fall into fresh fits of laughter.
He was beside himself with delight, for he could see only good
results for himself in this disaster to his enemy. Now Heidi's
friend would be obliged to go away. She would have no means
of going about. Then, when Heidi was alone again, she would
come out with him as in the old days, and everything would
go on as before.

Peter did not realize that when we do a wrong thing trouble
is sure to follow.

Heidi now came running out of the hut and round to the shed.
Grandfather was behind with Clara in his arms. The shed stood
wide open, the two loose planks having been taken down, and
it was quite light inside. Heidi looked in every corner and ran
from one end to the other, and then stood still, wondering what
could have happened to the chair. Grandfather now came up.

"How is this, have you wheeled the chair away, Heidi?"

"I have been looking everywhere for it, Grandfather," she

answered. "You said it was standing ready outside." And again she searched every corner of the shed.

At that moment the wind, which had risen suddenly, blew open the shed door and sent it banging back against the wall.

"It must have been the wind, Grandfather," exclaimed Heidi, and her eyes grew anxious at this sudden discovery. "Oh! if it has blown the chair all the way down to Dörfli we shall not get it back in time, and shall not be able to go."

"If it has rolled as far as that it will never come back, for it is in a hundred pieces by now," said Grandfather, going round the corner and looking down. "But it's a curious thing to have happened!" he added, for, as he thought over the matter, the chair would have had to turn a corner before starting downhill!

"Oh, I am sorry," lamented Clara, "for we shall not be able to go today, or perhaps any other day. I shall have to go home, I suppose, if I have no chair. Oh, I am so sorry, I am so sorry!"

But Heidi looked towards her grandfather with her usual expression of confidence.

"Grandfather, you will be able to do something, won't you, so that Clara need not go home?"

"Well, for the present we will go up the mountain as we had arranged, and then later on we will see what can be done," he answered, much to the children's delight.

He went indoors, fetched out a pile of shawls, and laying them on the sunniest spot he could find, set Clara down upon them. Then he fetched the children's morning milk and brought out his two goats.

"Why is Peter not here yet," thought Grandfather to himself, for Peter's whistle had not been sounded that morning. Grandfather now took Clara up on one arm, and the shawls on the other.

"Now then we will start," he said. "The goats can come with us."

Heidi was pleased at this and walked on after her grandfather with an arm over each of the goats' necks. The animals were so overjoyed to have her again that they nearly squeezed her flat between them out of sheer affection. When they reached

the spot where the goats usually pastured they were surprised to find them already feeding there, climbing about the rocks, and Peter with them, lying his full length on the ground.

"I'll teach you another time to go by like that, you lazy rascal! What do you mean by it?" Grandfather called to him.

Peter, recognizing the voice, jumped up like a shot. "No one was up," he answered.

"Have you seen anything of the chair?" asked Grandfather.

"Of what chair?" asked Peter crossly.

Grandfather said no more. He spread the shawls on the sunny slope, and setting Clara upon them asked if she was comfortable.

"As comfortable as in my chair," she said, thanking him, "and this seems the most beautiful spot. Oh, Heidi, it is lovely! It is lovely!" she cried, looking round her with delight.

Grandfather prepared to leave them. They would now be safe and happy together he said, and when it was time for dinner Heidi was to go and fetch the bag from the shady hollow where he had put it; Peter was to bring them as much milk as they wanted, but Heidi was to see that it was Little Swan's milk. He would come and fetch them towards evening. He must now be off to go after the chair and see what had become of it.

The sky was dark blue, and not a single cloud was to be seen from one horizon to the other. The great snowfield overhead sparkled as if set with thousands and thousands of gold and silver stars. The two gray mountain peaks lifted their lofty heads against the sky and looked solemnly down upon the valley as of old. The great bird was poised aloft in the clear blue air. And the mountain wind came over the heights and blew refreshingly around the children as they sat on the sunlit slope. It was all beauty to Clara and Heidi. Now and again a young goat came and lay down beside them; Snowflake came oftenest, putting her little head down near Heidi, and only moving because another goat came and drove her away. Clara had learned to know them all so well that she never mistook one for the other now, for each one had a quite different face and manner. And the goats had also grown friendly with Clara and would rub their heads against her shoulder, which was always a sign of goodwill.

Some hours went by, and Heidi began to think that she might just go over to the spot where all the flowers grew to see if they were fully blown and looking as lovely as they had the year before. Clara could not go until Grandfather came back that evening, when the flowers probably would be already closed. The longing to go became stronger and stronger.

"Would you think me unkind, Clara," she said rather hesitatingly, "if I left you for a few minutes? I should run there and back very quickly. I want so to see how the flowers are looking—but wait—" for an idea had come into Heidi's head. She ran and picked a bunch or two of green leaves, and then took hold of Snowflake and led her up to Clara.

"There, now you will not be alone," said Heidi, giving the goat a little push to show her she was to lie down near Clara, which the animal quite understood. Heidi threw the leaves into Clara's lap. And her friend told her to go at once to look at the flowers as she was quite happy to be left with the goat. It was something she had never done before.

Heidi ran off, and Clara began to hold out the leaves one by one to Snowflake, who snoozled up to her new friend in a confiding manner and slowly ate the leaves from her hand. It was easy to see that Snowflake enjoyed this peaceful and sheltered way of feeding. And Clara found a strange new pleasure in sitting all alone like this on the mountainside, her only companion a little goat that looked to her for protection. She suddenly wanted to get well and be independent. She longed to go on living in the sunshine, and to be doing something that would bring happiness to another, as now she was helping to make the goat happy. Suddenly she felt full of joy and happiness and threw her arms round the little goat's neck, and exclaimed, "Oh, Snowflake, how delightful it is up here! If only I could stay on forever with you beside me!"

Heidi had meanwhile reached her field of flowers, and as she caught sight of it she uttered a cry of joy. The whole ground in front of her was a mass of shimmering gold, where the cistus flowers spread their yellow blossoms. Above them waved whole bushes of the deep blue bellflowers, while a rare fragrance arose from the whole sunlit expanse. The scent, however, came from the small brown flowers, the little round heads of which rose modestly here and there among the yellow blossoms. Heidi stood and gazed and breathed in the delicious air. Suddenly she turned round and reached Clara's side out of breath with running and excitement.

"Oh, you must come," she called out as soon as she came in sight. "It is more beautiful than you can imagine, and perhaps this evening it may not be so lovely. I believe I could carry you, don't you think I could?"

Clara looked at her and shook her head. "Why, Heidi, what can you be thinking of! You are smaller than I am. Oh, if only I could walk!"

Heidi looked round as if in search of something, some new idea had evidently come into her head. Peter was sitting up above looking down on the two children. He had been sitting and staring before him in the same way for hours, as if he could not make out what he saw. He had destroyed the chair so that the friend might not be able to move anywhere and so that her visit might come to an end. Then, a little while after, she had appeared right up here under his very nose with Heidi beside her. There she was and no mistake about it.

Heidi now looked up to where he was sitting and called out in a decided voice, "Peter, come down here!"

"I don't wish to come," he called in reply.

"But you must! I cannot do it alone, and you must come here and help me. Hurry and come down," called Heidi.

"I shall do nothing of the kind," said Peter.

Heidi ran some way up the slope towards him, and then pausing called again, her eyes ablaze with anger, "If you don't come at once, Peter, I will do something to you that you won't like! I mean what I say."

These words stabbed Peter, and he was seized with great fear. He had done something wicked which he wanted no one to know about, and so far he had thought himself safe. But now Heidi spoke exactly as if she knew everything. And whatever she did know she would tell her grandfather. And Peter was more afraid of him than of anyone else. Supposing he were to suspect what had happened about the chair. Peter grew very frightened. He stood up and went down to where Heidi was waiting for him.

"I am coming, but then you mustn't do it," he said meekly.

Peter seemed so frightened that Heidi felt quite sorry for him and answered reassuringly, "No, no, of course not; come along with me. There is nothing to be afraid of in what I want you to do."

As soon as they got to Clara, Heidi gave her orders. Peter was to take hold of her under the arms on one side and she on the other, and together they were to lift her up. This first movement was successfully carried through, but then came the difficulty. As Clara could not even stand, how were they to support her and get her along? Heidi was too small for Clara to lean upon.

"You must put one arm well round my neck—so, and put the other through Peter's arm and lean firmly upon it; then we shall be able to carry you," she said.

Peter, however, had never given his arm to anyone in his life. Clara put hers in his, but he kept his own hanging down straight beside him like a stick.

"That's not the way, Peter," said Heidi in an authoritative voice. "You must put your arm out in the shape of a ring, and Clara must put hers through it and lean her weight upon you, and whatever you do, don't let your arm give way. That way I am sure we shall be able to manage."

Peter did as he was told, but still they did not get on very well. Clara was not so light, and the team did not match very well in size; it was up one side and down the other, so that the supports were rather wobbly.

Clara tried to use her own feet a little, but each time drew them quickly back.

"Put your foot down firmly once," suggested Heidi, "I am sure it will hurt you less after that."

"Do you think so?" said Clara hesitatingly, but she followed Heidi's advice and ventured one firm step on the ground and

then another; she called out a little as she did it; then she lifted her foot again and went on, "Oh, that was less painful already," she exclaimed joyfully.

"Try again," said Heidi encouragingly.

And Clara went on putting one foot out after another until all at once she called out, "I can do it, Heidi! Look! Look! I can make proper steps!"

And Heidi cried out with even greater delight, "Can you really make steps, can you really walk? Really walk by yourself? Oh, if only Grandfather were here!" and she continued to exclaim, "You can walk now, Clara. You can walk!"

Clara still held on firmly to Heidi and Peter. But with every step she felt safer on her feet. All three saw this, and Heidi was beside herself with joy.

"Now we shall be able to come up here together every day, and just go where we like," she said, "and you will be able all your life to walk about as I do, and not have to be pushed in a chair, and will get quite strong and well. Isn't it wonderful!"

And Clara agreed, for she could think of no greater joy in the world than to be strong and able to go about like other people. No longer to have to lie from day to day in her invalid chair!

They had not far to go to reach the field of flowers, and could already catch sight of the cistus flowers glowing gold in the sun. As they came to the bushes of the blue bellflowers, with sunny, inviting patches of warm ground between them, Clara said, "Mightn't we sit down here for a while?"

This was just what Heidi enjoyed, and so the children sat down in the midst of the flowers, Clara for the first time on the dry, warm mountain grass. This pleased her more than she could tell. Around her were the blue flowers softly waving to and fro, and beyond the gleaming patches of the cistus flowers and the red centaury, while the sweet scent of the brown blossoms and of the fragrant prunella came to her. Everything was so lovely! So beautiful! Heidi, too, who was beside her, thought she had never seen it so beautiful up here before, and she did not know herself why she felt so joyful that she longed to shout aloud. Then she suddenly remembered that Clara was cured. That was

70

the greatest joy of all. Clara sat silent, looking over the beauty around her and thinking of all the happiness that was now before her.

Peter also lay among the flowers without moving or speaking, for he was fast asleep. The breeze came blowing softly from behind the sheltering rocks, and passed through the bushes overhead. Heidi got up now and then to run about, for the flowers waving in the warm wind seemed to smell sweeter and to grow more thickly whichever way she went, and she felt she must sit down everywhere. So the hours went by.

It was long past noon when a small troop of goats advanced solemnly towards the field of flowers. It was not a feeding-place of theirs, for they did not care to graze on flowers. They looked like an embassy arriving, with Greenfinch as their leader. They had evidently come in search of their companions who had left them in the lurch, and who had, contrary to all custom, remained away so long, for the goats could tell the time without mistake. As soon as Greenfinch caught sight of the three missing friends amid the flowers she set up an extra loud bleat, whereupon all the others joined in a chorus of bleats, and the whole company came trotting towards the children. Peter woke up, rubbing his eyes, for he had been dreaming that he saw the chair again with its beautiful red padding standing whole and uninjured before Grandfather's door. Indeed, just as he awoke, he thought he was looking at the brass-headed nails that studded it all round, but it was only the bright yellow flowers beside him. He was frightened again. Even though Heidi had promised not to do anything, there still remained the lively dread that his deed might be found out in some other way. He was very meek and willing to be the guide and do everything exactly as Heidi wished.

When all three had got back to their old pasture, Heidi ran and brought forward the dinner bag. She had seen her grandfather putting in all sorts of good things, and had been pleased to think of Peter having a large share of them. Indeed, she had meant Peter to understand when he refused at first to help her that he would get nothing for his dinner. But Peter's conscience

71

had put another meaning to her words. Heidi took the food out of the bag and divided it into three portions, and each was of such a big helping that she thought to herself, "There will be plenty of ours left for him to have more still."

She gave the other two their dinners and sat down with her own beside Clara, and they all three enjoyed their dinner.

It ended as Heidi had expected, and Peter got as much food again as his own share with what Clara and Heidi had over from theirs after they had both eaten as much as they wanted. Peter ate up every bit of food to the last crumb, but there was something lacking to his usual enjoyment of a good dinner, for every mouthful he swallowed seemed to choke him.

They were so late at their dinner that they had not long to wait after they had finished before Grandfather came to take them home. Heidi rushed forward to meet him as soon as he appeared, as she wanted to be the first to tell him the good news. She was so excited that she could hardly get her words out when she did get up to him, but he soon understood, and his face lighted up with joy. He hurried up to where Clara was sitting and said with a cheerful smile, "So, we've made the effort, have we, and won the day!"

Then he lifted her up, and putting his left arm behind her and giving her his right to lean upon, made her walk a little way, which she did with less trembling and hesitation than before, for now she had such a strong arm round her.

Heidi skipped along beside her in glee, and Grandfather looked too as if some happiness had befallen him. But now he took Clara up in his arms. "We must not overdo it," he said, "and it is high time we went home." Then he started off down the mountain path, for he was anxious to get her indoors that she might rest after her great exertion.

When Peter got to Dörfli that evening he found a large group of people collected round a certain spot, pushing one another and looking over each other's shoulders in their eagerness to catch sight of something lying on the ground. Peter thought he should like to see too, and poked and elbowed till he made his way through.

72

There it lay, the thing he had wanted to see. Scattered about the grass were the remains of Clara's chair; part of the back and the middle bit, and enough of the red padding and the bright nails to show how magnificent the chair had been when it was whole.

"I was here when the men passed carrying it up," said the baker, who was standing near Peter. "I'll bet anyone that it was worth at least a hundred dollars. I cannot think how such an accident could have happened."

"Heidi's grandfather said the wind might perhaps have done it," remarked one of the women, who was admiring the red upholstery.

"It's a good job that no one but the wind did it," said the baker again, "or he might smart for it! No doubt the gentleman in Frankfurt when he hears what has happened will make all inquiries about it. I am glad for myself that I have not been seen up the mountain for a good two years, as suspicion is likely to fall on anyone who was about up there at the time."

Many more opinions were passed on the matter, but Peter had heard enough. He crept quietly away out of the crowd and then took to his heels and ran up home as fast as he could, as if he thought someone was after him. The baker's words had filled him with fear and trembling. He was sure now that any day a constable might come over from Frankfurt and inquire about the destruction of the chair. Then everything would come out. He would be seized and carried off to Frankfurt and there put in prison. The whole picture of what was coming was clear before him, and he was terrified.

He reached home much distressed. He would not open his mouth in reply to anything that was said to him. He would not eat his potatoes. All he did was to creep off to bed as quickly as possible and hide under the bedclothes and groan.

"Peter has been eating sorrel again, and is evidently in pain by the way he is groaning," said Brigitta, his mother.

"You must give him a little more bread to take with him. Give him a bit of mine tomorrow," said Peter's grandmother sympathetically.

As the children lay that night in bed looking out at the stars Heidi said, "I have been thinking all day what a happy thing it is that God does not give us what we ask for, even when we pray and pray and pray, if he knows there is something better for us. Have you felt like that?"

"Why do you ask me that tonight all of a sudden?" asked Clara.

"Because I prayed so hard when I was in Frankfurt that I might go home at once, and because I was not allowed to I thought God had forgotten me. And now you see, if I had come away at first when I wanted to, you would never have come here, and would never have got well."

Clara had in her turn become thoughtful. "But, Heidi," she began again, "in that case we ought never to pray for anything, as God always intends something better for us than we know or wish for."

"You must not think it is like that, Clara," replied Heidi eagerly. "We must go on praying for everything, for everything, so that God may know we do not forget that it all comes from Him. If we forget God, then He lets us go our own way and we get into trouble. Grandmamma told me so. And if He does not give us what we ask for we must not think that He has not heard us and leave off praying. We must still pray and say, 'I am sure, dear God, that You are keeping something better for me, and I will not be unhappy, for I know that You will make everything right in the end.'"

"How did you learn all that?" asked Clara.

"Grandmamma explained it to me first of all, and then when it all happened just as she said, I knew it myself," said Heidi, "and I think, Clara, we ought certainly to thank God tonight that you can walk now, and that He has made us so happy."

"Yes, Heidi," said Clara, "I am sure you are right and I am glad you reminded me; I was so excited I almost forgot my prayers."

Both children said their prayers, and each thanked God in her own way for the blessing he had bestowed on Clara, who had for so long lain weak and ill.

The next morning Grandfather suggested that they should now write to Clara's grandmamma and ask her if she would not come and pay them a visit, as they had something new to show her. But the children had another plan in their heads, for they wanted to prepare a great surprise for Grandmamma. Clara was first to have more practice in walking so that she might be able to go a little way by herself. Above all things Grandmamma was not to have the least suspicion. They asked Grandfather how long he thought this would take, and when he told them about a week or less, they immediately sat down and wrote a pressing invitation to Grandmamma, asking her to come soon, but no word was said about there being anything new to see.

The following days were some of the most beautiful that Clara had spent on the mountain. She awoke each morning with these delightful words in her mind. "I am well now! I am well now! I shan't have to go about in a chair. I can walk by myself like other people!"

Then came the walking, and every day she found it easier and was able to go a longer distance. The exercise gave her such an appetite that Grandfather cut his bread and butter a little thicker each day, and was well pleased to see it disappear. He now brought out with it a large jugful of the foaming milk, and filled her little bowl over and over again.

And so another week went by, and the day came which was to bring Grandmamma up the mountain for her second visit.

Grandmamma wrote the day before her arrival to let the children know that they might expect her without fail. Peter brought up the letter early the following morning. Grandfather and the children were already outside the hut and the goats were awaiting him, shaking their heads gaily in the cool morning air, while the children stroked them and wished them a pleasant journey up the mountain. Grandfather stood near, looking now at the young faces of the children, now at his clean, well-kept goats. Both pleased him, for he smiled.

As Peter came along, he slowed down, and the instant he had handed the letter to the old man he turned quickly away as if frightened. And as he went he gave a hasty glance behind him

75

as if the thing he feared was pursuing him. Then he gave a leap
and ran off up the mountain.

"Grandfather," said Heidi, who had been watching him with
astonished eyes, "why does Peter always behave now like the
Great Turk when he thinks somebody is after him with a stick?
He turns and shakes his head and goes off with a bound just
like that."

"Perhaps Peter fancies he sees the stick which he so well
deserves coming after him," answered Grandfather.

Peter ran up the slope without stopping. When he was well
out of sight, however, he stood still and looked suspiciously
about him. Suddenly he gave a jump and looked behind him
with a terrified expression, as if someone had caught hold of
him by the nape of the neck. Peter thought every minute that
the policeman from Frankfurt would leap out upon him from

behind some bush or hedge. The longer his suspense lasted, the more frightened and miserable he became. He did not have a moment's peace.

Heidi now set about tidying the hut, as Grandmamma must find everything clean and tidy when she came.

Clara looked on with interest. She was glad to watch Heidi at work.

So the morning soon went by, and Grandmamma was expected to arrive at any minute. The children came and sat together outside on the bench ready to receive her.

Grandfather joined them. He had gathered a fine bunch of blue gentians up in the mountains, and the children exclaimed with delight when they saw them shine in the morning sun. Grandfather carried them indoors. Heidi jumped up from time to time to see if there was any sign of Grandmamma's approach.

At last she saw the procession winding up the mountain. First there was the guide. Then came the white horse with Grandmamma mounted upon it. And last of all, the porter with a heavy basket on his back, for Grandmamma would not think of going up the mountain without plenty of wraps.

Nearer and nearer they came. At last they reached the top and Grandmamma was there looking down on the children from her horse.

"What is this?" she cried, dismounting from her horse. "Why are you not lying in your chair, Clara? What are you all thinking about?" But even before she had reached them she threw up her hands and exclaimed, "Is it really you, dear child? Why, your cheeks have grown quite round and rosy! I should hardly have known you again!"

Then she was rushing forward, when Heidi slipped down from the bench and Clara leaned on her shoulder. The two children started away quite calmly to take a little walk.

Grandmamma stood still, alarmed. She thought at first that Heidi was trying to do something rash.

But no—Clara was actually walking uprightly and safely beside Heidi. Then the two children turned and came towards her with beaming faces and rosy cheeks.

77

Grandmamma rushed towards them. Laughing and crying she embraced first Clara and then Heidi and then Clara again. In her delight she could find no words.

All at once she caught sight of Heidi's grandfather standing by the bench, smiling as he watched the three of them. She took Clara's arm in hers, and with continual cries of delight she went up to the old man. Then letting go Clara's arm, she seized his hands.

"My dear Sir! my dear Sir! How much we have to thank you for. It is all your doing! It is your care and nursing—"

"And God's good sun and mountain air," he interrupted, smiling.

"Yes, and don't forget Little Swan's good milk, too," added Clara. "Grandmamma, you can't think how much goat's milk I drink, and how good it is!"

"I can see that by your cheeks, child," answered Grandmamma. "I really should scarcely have known you. You have grown quite strong and plump, and taller too! I never dreamed you could look like that. I cannot take my eyes off you. I can hardly yet believe it! But now I must telegraph at once to my son in Paris and tell him he must come here. I shall not say why; it will be the greatest joy he has ever known. My dear Sir, how can I send a telegram? Have you sent the men away already?"

"They have gone," he answered, "but if you are in a hurry I will send for Peter, and he can take it for you."

Grandmamma thanked him, for she was anxious that the good news should not be kept from her son a single day.

So the old man went aside a little way and blew such a re-sounding whistle through his fingers that he awoke an echo among the rocks far overhead. It was not long before Peter came running down, for he knew the sound of the whistle. Peter arrived, looking as white as a ghost, for he was sure Grandfather was sending for him to give him up to the police. But only a written paper was given him with instructions to take it down at once to the post office at Dörfli. Grandfather would pay for it later, as it was not safe to give Peter too much to look after.

Peter went off with the paper in his hand, feeling much relieved for this time as no policeman had yet arrived.

At last they could all sit down quietly to their dinner round the table in front of the hut, and Grandmamma was told of all that had taken place. How Grandfather had made Clara try first to stand and then to move her feet a little every day, and how they had taken the day's excursion up the mountain and the chair had been blown away. How Clara's desire to see the flowers had induced her to take the first walk, and so one thing had led to another. The story took some time, for Grandmamma continually interrupted it with fresh exclamations of surprise and thankfulness. "It hardly seems possible! I can scarcely believe it is not all a dream! Are we really awake, and are we all sitting here by the mountain hut, and is that round-faced, healthy-looking child my poor little, white, sickly Clara?"

And Clara and Heidi were still pleased with the surprise they had so carefully arranged for Grandmamma and that had succeeded so well.

Meanwhile, Herr Sesemann, who had finished his business in Paris, had also been preparing a surprise. Without saying a word to his mother he took the train one sunny morning and traveled that day to Basle. The next morning he continued his journey, for he greatly longed to see his little daughter from whom he had been separated all summer. He arrived at Ragatz a few hours after his mother had left.

When he heard that she had that very day started for the mountain, he immediately hired a carriage and drove off to Mayenfeld. Here he found that he could if he liked drive on as far as Dörfli. This he did, for he thought that would be far enough to have to walk up the mountain.

Herr Sesemann found he was right. The climb up the mountain, as it was, proved long and tiring to him. He went on and on, but still no hut came in sight. Yet he knew that Peter lived halfway up, for the path had been described to him over and over again.

There were footpaths of climbers to be seen on all sides. The narrow footpaths seemed to run in every direction, and Herr

Sesemann began to wonder whether the hut might not, perhaps, lie on the other side of the mountain. He looked round to
see if there was anyone in sight of whom he could ask the way.
But far and wide there was not a soul to be seen or a sound to
be heard. Now and then the mountain wind whistled through
the air, and the insects hummed in the sunshine, or a happy bird
sang out from the branches of a solitary larch tree. Herr Sesemann stood still for a while to let the cool Alpine wind blow on
his hot face. But now someone came running down the mountainside—it was Peter with the telegram in his hand. He ran
straight down the steep slope, not following the path on which
Herr Sesemann was standing. As soon as he caught sight of
Peter he beckoned to him. Peter advanced towards him slowly
and timidly, with a sort of sidelong movement, as if he could
only move one leg properly and had to drag the other after him.

"Hurry up, lad," called Herr Sesemann, and when Peter was near enough he added, "Is this the way to the hut where the old man and the child Heidi live, and where the visitors from Frankfurt are staying?"

Peter gave a gasp of terror and turned to run away in such haste that he fell head over heels several times and went rolling and bumping down the slope just in the same way as the chair. Peter, however, did not fall to pieces. Only the telegram came to grief, and that was torn into fragments and flew away.

"How extraordinarily timid these mountain dwellers are!" thought Herr Sesemann to himself, for he quite believed that it was the sight of a stranger that had made such an impression on this child of the mountains.

After watching Peter's violent descent towards the valley for a few minutes he continued his journey.

Peter, meanwhile, could not stop himself, but went rolling on, still tumbling head over heels, in a most remarkable fashion.

But far worse than his fall was his fear that the policeman had really come for him. He had no doubt at all that the stranger who had asked him the way was the policeman himself. Just as he had rolled to the edge of the last high slope above Dörfli he was caught in a bush, and at last able to keep himself from falling any farther. He lay still for a moment or two to think over matters.

"Well done! Another of you come bumping along like this!" said a voice close to Peter, "and which of you tomorrow is the wind going to send rolling down like a badly-sewn sack of potatoes?" It was the baker, who stood there laughing. He had been strolling out to refresh himself after his hot day's work and had watched with amusement as he saw Peter come rolling over and over in much the same way as the wheel chair had done.

Peter was on his feet in a moment. He had received a fresh shock. Without once looking behind him he began hurrying up the slope again. He would have liked best to go home and creep into bed, so as to hide himself, for he felt safest when there. But he had left the goats up above, and Grandfather had given

81

him strict instructions to hurry back so that they might not be alone too long. And he stood more in awe of Grandfather than anyone and would not have dared to disobey him. There was no help for it, he had to go back, and Peter went on, groaning and limping. And so he slowly made his way up the mountain.

Soon after meeting Peter, Herr Sesemann passed the first hut, and so felt sure that he was on the right path. He continued his climb and at last, after a long and exhausting walk, he came in sight of his goal. There, only a little distance farther up, stood Grandfather's home, with the dark tops of the fir trees waving above its roof.

Herr Sesemann was delighted to have come to the last steep bit of his journey. In another minute or two he would be with his little daughter, and he was happy with thinking of her surprise. But Grandfather and the others had seen his approach. They recognized him and they were preparing a surprise of their own.

When he had taken the last step up the mountain two young people came towards him. One was a tall fair girl with pink cheeks, leaning on little Heidi, whose dark eyes were dancing with joy. Herr Sesemann suddenly stopped, staring at the two children, and all at once the tears started to his eyes. What memories arose! Just so had Clara's mother looked, the fair-haired girl with the delicate pink-and-white complexion. Herr Sesemann did not know whether he was awake or dreaming.

"Don't you know me, Papa?" called Clara to him, her face beaming with happiness. "Am I so changed since you saw me?"

Then Herr Sesemann ran to his child and clasped her in his arms.

"Yes, you are indeed changed! Is it possible? Is it really so?" And the delighted father stepped back again to see whether the picture would not vanish before his eyes.

"Are you my little Clara, really my little Clara?" he kept on saying. Then he clasped her in his arms again.

And now Grandmamma came up, anxious for a sight of her son's happy face.

"Well, what do you say now, dear son?" she exclaimed. "You

have given us a pleasant surprise, but it is nothing to the surprise we have prepared for you, is it?" And she gave her son an affectionate kiss. "But now," she went on, "you must come and pay your respects to Grandfather, our chief benefactor."

"Yes, indeed, and to our little Heidi, too," said Herr Sesemann, as he shook Heidi's hand. "Well? Are you still well and happy in your mountain home? But I need not ask. No Alpine rose could look more blooming. I am glad, child. It is a great pleasure to see you so."

Heidi looked up at Herr Sesemann's kind face and smiled. How good he had always been to her! How happy she was in his new happiness!

Grandmamma now introduced him to Heidi's grandfather, and while the two men were shaking hands and Herr Sesemann was thanking the old man, Grandmamma wandered round to the back to see the old fir trees again.

Here, where the long branches had left a clear space on the

ground, stood a great bunch of the most wonderful blue gentians, as fresh and shining as if they were growing on the spot. She clasped her hands with delight.

"What a lovely sight!" she exclaimed. "Heidi, dearest child, come here! Is it you who have prepared this pleasure for me? It is perfectly wonderful!"

The children ran up.

"No, no, I did not put them there," said Heidi, "but I know who did."

"They grow just like that on the mountain, Grandmamma, only they look still more beautiful," Clara said. "But guess who brought those down today!" As she spoke she gave such a pleased smile that Grandmother thought for a moment the child herself must have gathered them. But that was hardly possible.

At this moment a slight rustling was heard behind the fir trees. It was Peter, who had just arrived. He had made a long way round, having seen from the distance who it was standing beside Grandfather in front of the hut, and he was trying to slip by unobserved. But Grandmamma had seen and recognized him, and thought it might be Peter who had brought the flowers.

"Come along, boy. Come here. Do not be afraid," she called to him.

Peter stood still, speechless with fear. After all he had gone through that day he felt he had no longer any power of resistance left. All he could think was, "It's all up with me now." He stepped forth from behind the fir trees, his face pale and frightened.

"Come here, boy," said Grandmamma. "Tell me, now, was it you who did it?"

Peter did not lift his eyes and therefore did not see that Grandmamma was pointing to the flowers. But he knew that Heidi's grandfather was standing at the corner of the hut, staring at him, while beside him stood the policeman from Frankfurt.

Quaking in every limb, and with trembling lips he muttered a low "Yes."

"Well, and what is there dreadful about that?" said Grand-mamma.

"Because—because—it is all broken to pieces and no one can put it together again." Peter brought out his words with difficulty, and his knees knocked together so that he could hardly stand.

Grandmamma went up to Heidi's grandfather. "Is that poor boy really out of his mind?" she asked sympathetically.

"Not in the least," Grandfather assured her. "It is only that he was the wind that sent the chair rolling down the slope, and he is expecting his well-deserved punishment."

Grandmamma found this hard to believe, for in her opinion Peter did not look like a bad boy, who would do a thing like that.

But his confession confirmed Grandfather's suspicion about the broken chair. He explained Peter's bitter feelings towards Clara to Grandmamma.

She burst out excitedly, "Dear Sir, we will not punish the poor boy any further. One must be fair. Here are all these strangers from Frankfurt who come and carry away Heidi, his one friend, and a friend well worth having, too. He is left then to sit alone day after day for weeks with nothing to do but brood. No, no, let us be fair to him; his anger got the upper hand and drove him to an act of revenge—a foolish one, indeed, but then we all behave foolishly when we are angry."

After saying this she went back to Peter, who still stood frightened and trembling. She sat down on the seat under the fir trees and said, "Come here, boy, to me, for I have something to say to you. Stop shaking and trembling, for I want you to listen to me. You sent the chair rolling down the mountain so that it was broken to pieces. That was a very wrong thing to do, as you yourself knew very well at the time. You also knew that you deserved to be punished for it. In order to escape this you have been doing all you can to hide the truth from everybody. But be sure of this, Peter, that those who do wrong make a mistake when they think no one knows anything about it. For God sees and hears everything. And so your conscience pricks you, and you never know a moment's happiness or peace. Is that not so, Peter?"

Peter nodded, quite crushed, and as one who knew all about it. For lately, indeed, he had had no happiness or peace.

"But," continued Grandmamma, "see how the harm you intended has turned out for the best for those you wished to hurt. As Clara had no chair to go in and yet wanted so much to see the flowers, she made the effort to walk. And every day since she has been walking better and better. And if she remains up here she will in time be able to go up the mountain every day, much oftener than she would have done in her chair. So you see, Peter, God is able to bring good out of evil for those whom you meant to injure, and you who did the evil were left to suffer the unhappy consequences of it. Do you understand all I have said to you, Peter? If so, do not forget my words, and whenever you want to do anything wrong, think of your unhappiness now. Will you remember all this?"

"Yes, I will," answered Peter, still very subdued, for he did not yet know how the matter was going to end. For wasn't the policeman still standing with Heidi's grandfather?

"That's right, and now the thing is over and done for," said Grandmamma. "But I should like you to have something for a pleasant reminder of the visitors from Frankfurt. Can you tell me anything that you have wished very much to have? What would you like best as a present?"

Peter lifted his head at this, and stared open-eyed at Grandmamma. Up to the last minute he had been expecting something dreadful to happen, and now he might have anything that he wanted. He felt confused.

"I mean what I say," went on Grandmamma. "You shall choose what you would like to have as a remembrance from the Frankfurt visitors, and as a token that they will not think any more of the wrong thing you did. Now do you understand me, boy?"

It began to dawn upon Peter that he had no further punishment to fear, and that the kind lady sitting in front of him had saved him from the policeman. He suddenly felt as if the weight of a mountain had fallen off him. He was also convinced now that it was better to confess one's faults, and so he said, "And I lost the paper, too."

Grandmamma had to consider a moment what he meant, but soon recalled his connection with her telegram, and answered kindly, "You are a good boy to tell me! Never conceal anything you have done wrong, and then all will come right again. And now what would you like me to give you?"

Peter grew almost giddy with the thought that he could have anything in the world that he wished for. He had a vision of the yearly fair at Mayenfeld with the glittering stalls and all the lovely things that he had stood gazing at for hours, without a hope of ever possessing one of them. Peter's purse, indeed, never held more than a halfpenny, and all these fascinating objects cost double that amount. There were the pretty little red whistles that he could use to call his goats, and the splendid knives with rounded handles, with which one could do such fine work among the hazel bushes.

Peter remained pondering. He was trying to think which of these two desirable objects he should like best. It was hard to decide. Then a bright thought occurred to him; he would then be able to think over the matter between now and next year's fair.

"A penny," answered Peter, who was no longer in doubt.

Grandmamma could not help laughing. "That is not an extravagant request. Come here then!" and she pulled out her purse and put four bright round shillings in his hand and then laid some pennies on the top of it. "We will settle our accounts at once," she continued, "and I will explain them to you. I have given you as many pennies as there are weeks in the year, and so every Sunday throughout the year you can take out a penny to spend."

"As long as I live?" asked Peter innocently.

Grandmamma laughed still more at this, and the men hearing her, paused in their talk to listen to what was going on.

"Yes, boy, you shall have it all your life—I will put it down in my will. Do you hear, my son? And you are to put it down in

87

yours as well: a penny a week to Peter as long as he lives!"

Herr Sesemann nodded his assent and joined in the laughter.

Peter looked again at the present in his hand to make sure he was not dreaming, and then said, "God bless you!"

And he went off running and leaping, and this time managed to keep his feet, for it was not fear, but joy such as he had never known before in his life, that now sent him flying up the mountain. All trouble and trembling had disappeared, and he was to have a penny every week for life.

Later, after dinner, the company were sitting together chatting. Clara drew her father a little aside and said with an eagerness that had been unknown to the little tired invalid, "Oh, Papa, if you only knew all that Grandfather has done for me from day to day! I cannot count his kindnesses, but I shall never forget them as long as I live. And I keep on thinking what I could do for him, or what present I could make him that would give him half as much pleasure as he has given me."

"That is just what I wish most myself, Clara," replied her father, whose face grew happier each time he looked at his little daughter. "I have been also thinking how we can best show our gratitude to our kind friend."

Herr Sesemann now went over to where the old man and Grandmamma were engaged in lively conversation. Herr Sesemann, taking him by the hand said, "Dear friend, let us have a word together. Believe me I have known no real happiness for years past. What was money when it was unable to make my poor child well and happy? With the help of God you have made her whole and strong, and you have given new life not only to her but to me. Tell me now, in what way can I show my gratitude to you? I can never repay all you have done, but whatever is in my power to do is at your service. Speak, friend, and tell me what I can do."

Grandfather had listened to him quietly, with a smile of pleasure on his face.

"Herr Sesemann," he replied with dignity, "I, too, have my share in the joy of your daughter's recovery, and my trouble is well repaid by it. I thank you for all you have said, but I have

88

need of nothing. I have enough for myself and the child as long as I live. One wish alone I have, and if that could be satisfied I should have no further care in life."

"Speak, dear friend, and tell me what it is," said Herr Sesemann.

"I am growing old," Grandfather went on, "and shall not be here much longer. I have nothing to leave the child when I die, and she has no relations, except one person who will always like to make what profit out of her she can. If you could promise me that Heidi shall never have to go and earn her living among strangers, then you would richly reward me for all I have done for your child."

"There could never be any question of such a thing as that, my dear friend," said Herr Sesemann, quickly. "I look upon the child as our own. Ask my mother, my daughter. You may be sure that they will never allow the child to be left in anyone else's care! But if it will make you happier I give you here my hand upon it. I promise you; Heidi shall never have to go and earn her living among strangers. But now I have something else to say. The child is totally unfitted to live a life away from home; we found out that when she was with us. But she has made friends, and among them I know one who is at this moment in Frankfurt. He is winding up his affairs there, that he may be free to retire. I am speaking of my friend, the doctor, who came over here in the autumn. He has taken your advice and intends to settle in this neighbourhood, for he has never felt so well and happy anywhere. So you see the child will henceforth have two protectors near her—and may they both live long to share the task!"

"God grant indeed it may be so!" added Grandmamma, shaking Grandfather's hand warmly as she spoke. Then putting her arm around Heidi, who was standing near, she drew the child to her.

"And I have a question to ask you too, dear Heidi. Tell me if there is anything you particularly wish for?"

"Yes, there is," answered Heidi promptly, looking up delightedly at Grandmamma.

89

"Then tell me at once, dear, what it is."

"I want to have the bed I slept in at Frankfurt with the high pillows and the thick coverlid, and then Peter's blind grandmother will not have to lie with her head downhill and hardly able to breathe. She will be warm enough under the coverlid not to have to wear her shawl in bed."

Heidi said this eagerly, all in one breath.

"Dearest child," answered Grandmamma, moved by Heidi's speech, "what is this you tell me of Peter's grandmother! You are right to remind me. In the midst of our own happiness we forget too often what we ought to think of most. When God has shown us some special mercy we should think at once of those who are denied so many things. I will telegraph to Frankfurt at once. Fraulein Rottenmeier shall pack up the bed this very day, and it will be here in two days' time. God willing, Peter's grandmother shall soon be sleeping comfortably upon it."

Heidi skipped round Grandmamma in her glee, and then stopping all of a sudden, said quickly, "I must make haste down and tell Peter's grandmother. She will be worried at my not having been to see her for such a long time." She felt she could not wait another moment before carrying the good news down to the old blind woman.

"No, no, Heidi, what can you be thinking of," said her grandfather reprovingly. "You can't be running backwards and forwards like that when you have visitors."

But Grandmamma took Heidi's part. "The child is right, Sir," she said. "Peter's poor grandmother has too long been deprived of Heidi for our sakes. Let us all go down to see her. I believe my horse is waiting for me and I can ride down from there, and as soon as I get to Dörfli the message shall be sent off. What do you think of my plan, Son?"

Herr Sesemann had not yet had time to speak of his traveling plans, so he begged his mother to wait a few moments that he might tell her what he wanted to do.

Herr Sesemann, it seems, planned to make a little tour in Switzerland. First, though, he had wanted to see if Clara was well enough to go part of the way with them. But now he saw

Clara could take the journey, too, and he was anxious to start at once.

Clara was rather upset at first at the thought of saying good-bye like this to the mountain. She could not help being pleased, however, at the thought of the trip.

Grandmamma had already taken Heidi by the hand, when she suddenly turned. "But what is to become of Clara?" she asked, remembering all at once that the child could not yet take so long a walk. She gave a nod of satisfaction as she saw that Grandfather had already taken Clara up in his arms and was following her with sturdy strides. Herr Sesemann brought up the rear, and so they all started down the mountain.

Heidi kept jumping for joy as she and Grandmamma walked along side by side, and Grandmamma asked all about Peter's grandmother, how she lived, and what she did, especially in the winter when it was so cold. And Heidi told her about everything, for she knew all that went on at Peter's grandmother's. She was able also to give her exact particulars of what they had to eat. Grandmamma listened with interest and sympathy until they came to the hut. Brigitta was just hanging out Peter's second shirt in the sun. As soon as she saw the company approaching she rushed indoors.

"The whole party of them are just going past, Mother, evidently all returning home again," she informed the old woman. "Heidi's grandfather is with them, carrying the sick child."

"Alas, is it really to be so then?" sighed the Grandmother. "And you saw Heidi with them? Then they are taking her away. If only she could come and put her hand in mine again! If I could but hear her voice once more!"

At this moment the door flew open and Heidi sprang across to the corner and threw her arms round Peter's grandmother.

"Grandmother! Grandmother! My bed is to be sent from Frankfurt with all the three pillows and the thick coverlid. Grandmamma says it will be here in two days." Heidi could not get out her words quickly enough, for she could hardly wait to see the old lady's great joy at the news. Peter's grandmother smiled, but said a little sadly,—

"She must indeed be a good kind lady, and I ought to be glad to think she is taking you with her."

"What is this I hear? Who has been telling this good woman such tales?" exclaimed a kindly voice, and Peter's grandmother felt her hand taken and warmly pressed, for Grandmamma had followed Heidi in and heard all that was said. "No, no, there is no thought of such a thing! Heidi is going to stay with you and make you happy. We want to see her again, but we shall come to her. We hope to pay a visit to the Alm every year, for we have good cause to offer up especial thanks to God upon this spot where so great a miracle has been wrought upon our child."

And now the true light of joy came into the old lady's face and she pressed Frau Sesemann's hand over and over again, unable to speak her thanks. And large tears of joy rolled down her aged cheeks. Heidi now saw the old lady's happiness and was happy, too.

"Truly, Grandmother," she said hugging her, "hasn't everything come out beautifully?"

"Yes, Heidi," said Peter's grandmother, deeply moved. "And many, many other good things, too, God has sent me."

Toby Tyler, a favorite with three generations of boys and girls, is the story of a small boy who ran away from Uncle Dan'l's farm and its chores and joined the circus because he thought it would be fun. The circus showed him strange people and strange animals, but it wasn't fun. Helping cross Mr. Lord with his candy counter wasn't fun either. But with Mr. Stubbs, the monkey, his exciting adventures begin.

James Otis

TOBY TYLER

AND MR. STUBBS

ILLUSTRATED BY *Kay Lovelace*

NOW, then, lazybones," was Mr. Lord's warning cry as Toby came out of the tent, "if you've fooled away enough of your time, you can come here an' tend shop for me while I go to supper. You crammed yourself this noon, an' it'll teach you a good lesson to make you go without anything to eat tonight; it'll make you move round more lively in the future."

Instead of becoming accustomed to such treatment as he was receiving from his employers, Toby's heart grew more tender with each brutal word, and this last punishment—that of losing his supper—caused the poor boy more sorrow than blows would. Mr. Lord started for the hotel as he concluded his cruel speech, and poor little Toby, going behind the counter, leaned his head upon the boards and cried as if his heart would break.

All the fancied brightness and pleasure of a circus life had vanished, and in its place was the bitterness of remorse that he had repaid Uncle Daniel's kindness by the ingratitude of running away. Toby thought that if he could only nestle his little red head on the pillows of his little bed in that rough room at Uncle Daniel's, he would be the happiest and best boy in the future, in all the great, wide world.

While he was still sobbing away at a most furious rate, he heard a voice close at his elbow and, looking up, saw the thinnest man he had ever seen in all his life. The man had flesh-colored tights on, and a spangled red velvet garment that was neither pants, because there were no legs to it, nor a coat, because it did not come above his waist, made up the remainder of his costume. Because he was so wonderfully thin, because of the costume which he wore, and because of a highly colored painting which was hanging in front of one of the small tents, Toby knew that the Living Skeleton was before him, and his big, brown eyes opened all the wider as he gazed at him.

"What is the matter, little fellow?" asked the man in a kindly tone. "What makes you cry so? Has Job been up to his old tricks again?"

"I don't know what his old tricks are," and Toby sobbed, the tears coming again because of the sympathy which this man's voice expressed for him, "but I know that he's a mean, ugly thing—that's what I know. An' if I could only get back to Uncle Dan'l, there hain't elephants enough in all the circuses in the world to pull me away again."

"Oh, you run away from home, did you?"

"Yes, I did," sobbed Toby, "an' there hain't any boy in any Sunday-school book that ever I read that was half so sorry he'd been bad as I am. It's awful, an' now I can't have any supper, 'cause I stopped to talk with Mr. Stubbs."

"Is Mr. Stubbs one of your friends?" asked the skeleton as he seated himself in Mr. Lord's own private chair.

"Yes, he is, an' he's the only one in this whole circus who 'pears to be sorry for me. You'd better not let Mr. Lord see you sittin' in that chair or he'll raise a row."

"Job won't raise any row with me," said the skeleton. "But who is this Mr. Stubbs? I don't seem to know anybody by that name."

"I don't think that is his name. I only call him so, 'cause he looks so much like a feller I know who is named Stubbs."

This satisfied the skeleton that this Mr. Stubbs must be someone attached to the show, and he asked,—

"Has Job been whipping you?"

"No; Ben, the driver on the wagon where I ride, told him not to do that again; but he hain't going to let me have any supper, 'cause I was so slow about my work—though I wasn't slow. I only talked to Mr. Stubbs when there wasn't anybody round his cage."

"Sam! Sam! Sam-u-el!"

This name, which was shouted twice in a quick, loud voice and the third time in a slow manner, ending almost in a screech, did not come from either Toby or the skeleton, but from an enormously large woman, dressed in a gaudy red-and-black dress, cut very short and with low neck and an apology for sleeves, who had just come out from the tent whereon the picture of the Living Skeleton hung.

"Samuel," she screamed again, "come inside this minute, or you'll catch your death o' cold, an' I shall have you wheezin' around with the phthisic all night. Come in, Sam-u-el."

"That's her," said the skeleton to Toby, as he pointed his thumb in the direction of the fat woman, but paying no attention to the outcry she was making, "that's my wife, Lilly, an' she's the Fat Woman of the show. She's always yellin' after me that way the minute I get out for a little fresh air, an' she's always sayin' just the same thing. Bless you, I never have the phthisic, but she does awful. An' I s'pose 'cause she's so large she can't feel all over her, an' thinks it's me that has it."

"Is—is all that—is that your wife?" stammered Toby, in astonishment, as he looked at the enormously fat woman who stood in the tent door and then at the wonderfully thin man who sat beside him.

"Yes, that's her," said the skeleton. "She weighs pretty nigh

95

four hundred, though of course the show cards says it's over six hundred, an' she earns almost as much money as I do. Of course she can't get so much, for skeletons is much scarcer than fat folks; but we make a pretty good thing travelin' together."

"Sam-u-el!" again came the cry from the fat woman, "are you never coming in?"

"Not yet, my angel," said the skeleton, placidly, as he crossed one thin leg over the other and looked calmly at her. "Come here an' see Job's new boy."

"Your imprudence is wearin' me away so that I sha'n't be worth five dollars a week to any circus," she said, impatiently, at the same time coming toward the candy stand quite as rapidly as her very great size would admit.

"This is my wife Lilly—Mrs. Treat," said the skeleton, with a proud wave of his hand, as he rose from his seat and gazed admiringly at her. "This is my flower—my queen, Mr.—Mr.—"

"Tyler," said Toby, supplying the name which the skeleton—or Mr. Treat, as Toby now learned his name was—did not know, "Tyler is my name—Toby Tyler."

"Why, what a little chap you are!" said Mrs. Treat, paying no attention to the awkward little bend of the head which Toby intended for a bow. "How small he is, Samuel!"

"Yes," said the skeleton, reflectively, as he looked Toby over from head to foot, as if he were mentally trying to calculate exactly how many inches high he was, "he is small; but he's got all the world before him to grow in, an' if he only eats enough— There, that reminds me. Job isn't going to give him any supper, because he didn't work hard enough."

"He won't, won't he?" exclaimed the large lady, savagely. "Oh, he's a precious one, he is. An' some day I shall just give him a good shakin'-up, that's what I'll do. I get all out of patience with that man's ugliness."

"An' she'll do just what she says," said the skeleton to Toby, with an admiring shake of the head. "That woman hain't afraid of anybody, an' I wouldn't be a bit surprised if she did give Job a pretty rough time."

Toby thought, as he looked at her, that she was large enough

to give 'most anyone a pretty rough time, but he did not venture to say so. While he was looking first at her and then at her very thin husband, the skeleton told his wife the little that he had learned regarding the boy's history; and when he had concluded, she waddled away toward her tent.

"Great woman that," said the skeleton, as he saw her disappear within the tent.

"Yes," said Toby, "she's the greatest I ever saw."

"I mean that she's got a great head. Now you'll see about how much she cares for what Job says."

"If I was as big as her," said Toby, with just a shade of envy in his voice, "I wouldn't be afraid of anybody."

"It hain't so much the size," said the skeleton, sagely, "it hain't so much the size, my boy; for I can scare that woman almost to death when I feel like it."

Toby looked for a moment at Mr. Treat's thin legs and arms and then he said, warningly, "I wouldn't feel like it very often if I was you, Mr. Treat, 'cause she might break some of your bones if you didn't happen to scare her enough."

"Don't fear for me, my boy—don't fear for me. You'll see how I manage her if you stay with the circus long enough. Now, I often—"

If Mr. Treat was about to confide a family secret to Toby, it was fated that he should not hear it then, for Mrs. Treat had just come out of her tent, carrying in her hands a large tin plate piled high with a miscellaneous assortment of pie, cake, bread, and meat.

She placed this in front of Toby, and as she did so, she handed him two pictures.

"There, little Toby Tyler," she said, "there's something for you to eat, if Mr. Job Lord and his precious partner Jacobs did say you shouldn't have any supper; an' I've brought you a picture of Samuel an' me. We sell 'em for ten cents apiece, but I'm going to give them to you, because I like the looks of you."

Toby was quite overcome with the presents and seemed at a loss how to thank her for them. He attempted to speak but could not get the words out at first. Then he said, as he put the two photographs in the same pocket with his money, "You're awful good to me, an' when I get to be a man, I'll give you lots of things. I wasn't so very hungry, if I am such a big eater, but I did want something."

"Bless your dear little heart, and you *shall* have something to eat," said the Fat Woman, as she seized Toby, squeezed him close up to her, and kissed his freckled face as kindly as if it had been as fair and white as possible. "You shall eat all you want to; an' if you get the stomach-ache, as Samuel does sometimes when he's been eatin' too much, I'll give you some catnip tea out of the same dipper that I give him his. He's a great eater, Samuel is," she added, in a burst of confidence, "an' it's a wonder to me what he does with it all sometimes."

"Is he?" exclaimed Toby, quickly. "How funny that is, for I'm an awful eater. Why, Uncle Dan'l used to say that I ate twice as much as I ought to, an' it never made me any bigger. I wonder what's the reason?"

"I declare I don't know," said the Fat Woman, thoughtfully,

"an' I've wondered at it time an' time again. Some folks is made that way, an' some folks is made different. Now, I don't eat enough to keep a chicken alive, an' yet I grow fatter an' fatter every day. Don't I, Samuel?"

"Indeed you do, my love," said the skeleton, with a world of pride in his voice, "but you mustn't feel bad about it, for every pound you gain, makes you worth just so much more to the show."

"Oh, I wasn't worryin', I was only wonderin'. But we must go, Samuel, for the poor child won't eat a bit while we are here. After you've eaten what there is there, bring the plate in to me," she said to Toby, as she took her lean husband by the arm and walked him off toward their own tent.

Toby gazed after them a moment, and then he commenced a vigorous attack upon the eatables which had been so kindly given him. Of the food which he had taken from the dinner table he had eaten some while he was in the tent, and after that he had entirely forgotten that he had any in his pocket; therefore, at the time that Mrs. Treat had brought him such a liberal supply he was really very hungry.

He succeeded in eating nearly all the food which had been brought to him, and the very small quantity which remained he readily found room for in his pockets. Then he washed the plate nicely, and seeing no one in sight, he thought he could leave the booth long enough to return the plate.

He ran with it quickly into the tent occupied by the thin man and fat woman and handed it to her, with a profusion of thanks for her kindness.

"Did you eat it all?" she asked.

"Well," hesitated Toby, "there was three doughnuts an' a piece of pie left over, an' I put them in my pocket. If you don't care, I'll eat them some time tonight."

"You shall eat it whenever you want to, an' any time that you get hungry again, you come right to me."

"Thank you, ma'am. I must go now, for I left the store all alone."

"Run, then; an' if Job Lord abuses you, just let me know it, an'

99

I'll keep him from cuttin' up any monkeyshines."

Toby hardly heard the end of her sentence, so great was his haste to get back to the booth. And just as he emerged from the tent on a quick run, he received a blow on the ear which sent him sprawling in the dust, and he heard Mr. Job Lord's angry voice as it said, "So, just the moment my back is turned, you leave the stand to take care of itself, do you, an' run around tryin' to plot some mischief against me, eh?" And the brute kicked the prostrate boy twice with his heavy boot.

"Please don't kick me again!" pleaded Toby. "I wasn't gone but a minute, an' I wasn't doing anything bad."

"You're lying now, an' you know it, you young cub!" exclaimed the angry man as he advanced to kick the boy again. "I'll let you know who you've got to deal with when you get hold of me!"

"And I'll let you know who you've got to deal with when you get hold of me!" said a woman's voice, and, just as Mr. Lord raised his foot to kick the boy again, the Fat Woman seized him by the collar, jerked him back over one of the tent ropes, and left him quite as prostrate as he had left Toby. "Now, Job Lord," said the angry woman, as she towered above the thoroughly enraged but thoroughly frightened man, "I want you to understand that you can't knock and beat this boy while I'm around. I've seen enough of your capers, an' I'm going to put a stop to them. That boy wasn't in this tent more than two minutes, an' he attends to his work better than anyone you have ever had, so see that you treat him decent. Get up," she said to Toby, who had not dared to rise from the ground, "and if he offers to strike you again, come to me."

Toby scrambled to his feet and ran to the booth in time to attend to one or two customers who had just come up. He could see from out the corner of his eye that Mr. Lord had arisen to his feet also and was engaged in an angry conversation with Mrs. Treat, the result of which he very much feared would be another and a worse whipping for him.

But in this he was mistaken, for Mr. Lord, after the conversation was ended, came toward the booth and began to attend to his business without speaking one word to Toby. When Mr. Jacobs returned from his supper, Mr. Lord took him by the arm and walked him out toward the rear of the tents; and Toby was very positive that he was to be the subject of their conversation, which made him not a little uneasy.

It was not until nearly time for the performance to begin that Mr. Lord returned, and he had nothing to say to Toby, save to tell him to go into the tent and begin his work there. The boy was only too glad to escape so easily, and he went to his work with as much alacrity as if he were about entering upon some pleasure.

When he met Mr. Jacobs, that gentleman spoke to him very sharply about being late and seemed to think it no excuse at all that he had just been relieved from the outside work by Mr. Lord.

Mr. Jacobs scolded and swore alternately, and the boy really surprised him by his way of selling goods, though he was very careful not to say anything about it, but made Toby believe that he was doing only about half as much work as he ought

101

to do. Toby's private hoard of money was increased that evening, by presents, ninety cents, and he began to look upon himself as almost a rich man.

When the performance was nearly over, Mr. Jacobs called to him to help in packing up; and by the time the last spectator had left the tent, the worldly possessions of Messrs. Lord and Jacobs were ready for removal, and Toby allowed to do as he had a mind to, as long as he was careful to be on hand when Old Ben was ready to start.

Toby thought that he would have time to pay a visit to his friends, the skeleton and the Fat Woman, and to that end started toward the place where their tent had been standing. But to his sorrow he found that it was already being taken down, and he had only time to thank Mrs. Treat and to press the fleshless hand of her shadowy husband as they entered their wagon to drive away.

He was disappointed, for he had hoped to be able to speak with his new-made friends a few moments before the weary night's ride commenced; but, failing in that, he went hastily back to the monkey's cage. Old Ben was there, getting things ready for a start, but the wooden sides of the cage had not been put up, and Toby had no difficulty in calling the aged monkey up to the bars. He held one of the Fat Woman's doughnuts in his hand and said, as he passed it through to the animal,—

"I thought perhaps you might be hungry, Mr. Stubbs, and this is some of what the skeleton's wife give me. I hain't got very much time to talk with you now, but the first chance I can get away tomorrow, an' when there hain't anybody 'round, I want to tell you something."

The monkey had taken the doughnut in his handlike paws and was tearing it to pieces, eating small portions of it very rapidly.

"Don't hurry yourself," said Toby, warningly, "for Uncle Dan'l always told me the worst thing a feller could do was to eat fast. If you want any more before we start, just put your hand through the little hole up there near the seat, an' I'll give you all you want."

From the look on his face Toby confidently believed the monkey was about to make some reply, but just then Ben shut up the sides, separating Toby and Mr. Stubbs, and the order was given to start.

Toby clambered up on to the high seat, Ben followed him, and in another instant the team was moving along slowly down the dusty road, preceded and followed by the many wagons, with their tiny, swinging lights.

"Well," said Ben, when he had got his team well under way and felt that he could indulge in a little conversation, "how did you get along today?"

Toby related all of his movements and gave the driver a faithful account of all that had happened to him, concluding his story by saying, "That was one of Mrs. Treat's doughnuts that I just gave to Mr. Stubbs."

"To whom?" asked Ben, in surprise.

"To Mr. Stubbs—the old fellow here in the cart, you know, that's been so good to me."

Toby heard a sort of gurgling sound, saw the driver's body sway back and forth in a trembling way, and was just becoming thoroughly alarmed, when he thought of the previous night and understood that Ben was only laughing in his own peculiar way.

"How did you know his name was Stubbs?" asked Ben, after he had recovered his breath.

"Oh, I don't know that that is his real name," was the quick reply, "I only call him that because he looks so much like a feller with that name that I knew at home. He don't seem to mind because I call him Stubbs."

Ben looked at Toby earnestly for a moment, acting all the time as if he wanted to laugh again, but didn't dare to, for fear he might burst a blood vessel; and then he said, as he patted him on the shoulder, "Well, you are the queerest little fish that I ever saw in all my travels. You seem to think that that monkey knows all you say to him."

"I'm sure he does," said Toby, positively. "He don't say anything right out to me, but he knows everything I tell him. Do you suppose he could talk if he tried to?"

103

"Look here, Mr. Toby Tyler," and Ben turned half around in his seat and looked Toby full in the face, so as to give more emphasis to his words, "are you heathen enough to think that that monkey could talk if he wanted to?"

"I know I hain't a heathen," said Toby, thoughtfully, "for if I had been some of the missionaries would have found me out a good while ago; but I never saw anybody like this old Mr. Stubbs before, an' I thought he could talk if he wanted to, just as the Living Skeleton does, or his wife. Anyhow, Mr. Stubbs winks at me; an' how could he do that if he didn't know what I've been sayin' to him?"

"Look here, my son," said Ben, in a most fatherly fashion, "monkeys hain't anything but beasts, an' they don't know how to talk any more than they know what you say to 'em."

"Didn't you ever hear any of them speak a word?"

"Never. I've been in a circus, man an' boy, nigh on to forty years, an' I never seen nothin' in a monkey more'n any other beast, except their awful mischiefness."

"Well," said Toby, still unconvinced, "I believe Mr. Stubbs knows what I say to him, anyway."

"Now don't be foolish, Toby," pleaded Ben. "You can't show me one thing that a monkey ever did because you told him to."

Just at that moment, Toby felt someone pulling at the back of his coat and, looking round, he saw that it was a little brown hand reaching through the bars of the air hole of the cage, that was tugging away at his coat.

"There!" he said, triumphantly, to Ben. "Look there! I told Mr. Stubbs if he wanted anything more to eat, to tell me, an' I would give it to him. Now you can see for yourself that he's come for it." And Toby took a doughnut from his pocket and put it into the tiny hand, which was immediately withdrawn. "Now what do you think of Mr. Stubbs knowing what I say to him?"

"They often stick their paws up through there," said Ben, in a matter-of-fact tone. "I've had 'em pull my coat in the night till they made me as nervous as ever any old woman was. You see, Toby, my boy, monkeys is monkeys; an' you mustn't go to

104

gettin' the idea that they're anything else, for it's a mistake. You think this old monkey in here knows what you say? Why, that's just the cuteness of the old fellow. He watches you to see if he can't do just as you do, an' that's all there is about it."

Toby was more than half convinced that Ben was putting the matter in its proper light, and he would have believed all that had been said if, just at that moment, he had not seen that brown hand reaching through the hole to clutch him again by the coat.

The action seemed so natural, so like a hungry boy who gropes in the dark pantry for something to eat, that it would have taken more arguments than Ben had at his disposal to persuade Toby that his Mr. Stubbs could not understand all that was said to him. Toby put another doughnut in the outstretched hand and then sat silently, as if in a brown study over some difficult problem.

For some time the ride was continued in silence. Ben was going through all the motions of whistling without uttering a sound a favorite amusement of his—and Toby's thoughts were far away in the humble home he had scorned, with Uncle Daniel, whose virtues had increased in his esteem with every mile of distance which had been put between them, and whose faults had decreased in a corresponding ratio.

Toby's thoughtfulness had made him sleepy, and his eyes were almost closed in slumber, when he was startled by a crashing sound, was conscious of a feeling of being hurled from his seat by some great force, and then he lay senseless by the side of the road, while the wagon became a perfect wreck, from out of which a small army of monkeys was escaping. Ben's experienced ear had told him at the first crash that his wagon was breaking down, and, without having time to warn Toby of his peril, he had leaped clear of the wreck, keeping his horses under perfect control, and thus averting more trouble. It was the breaking of one of the axles which Toby had heard just before he was thrown from his seat, and when the body of the wagon came down upon the hard road.

The monkeys, thus suddenly released from confinement, had

105

scampered off in every direction, and by a singular chance, Toby's aged friend started for the woods in such a direction as to bring him directly before the boy's insensible form. The monkey, on coming up to Toby, stopped, urged by the well-known curiosity of its race, and began to examine the boy's person carefully, prying into pockets and trying to open the boy's half-closed eyelids. Fortunately for Toby, he had fallen upon a mud bank and was only stunned for the moment, having received no serious bruises. The attentions bestowed upon him by the monkey served the purpose of bringing him to his senses; and, after he had looked around him in the gray light of the coming morning, it would have taken far more of a philosopher than Old Ben was to persuade the boy that monkeys did not possess reasoning faculties.

The monkey was busy at Toby's ears, nose, and mouth, as monkeys will do when they get an opportunity, and the expression of its face was as grave as possible. Toby firmly believed that the monkey's face showed sorrow at his fall, and he imagined that the attentions which were bestowed upon him were for the purpose of learning whether he had been injured or not.

"Don't worry, Mr. Stubbs," said Toby, anxious to reassure his friend, as he sat upright and looked about him. "I didn't get hurt any; but I would like to know how I got 'way over here."

It really seemed as if the monkey was pleased to know that his little friend was not hurt, for he seated himself on his haunches, and his face expressed the liveliest pleasure that Toby was well again—or at least that was how the boy interpreted the look.

By this time the news of the accident had been shouted ahead from one team to the other, and all hands were hurrying to the scene for the purpose of rendering aid. As Toby saw them coming, he also saw a number of small forms, looking something like diminutive men, hurrying past him, and for the first time he understood how it was that the aged monkey was at liberty, and knew that those little dusky forms were the other occupants of the cage escaping to the woods.

106

"See there, Mr. Stubbs! See there!" he exclaimed, pointing toward the fugitives, "they're all going off into the woods! What shall we do?"

The sight of the runaways seemed to excite the old monkey quite as much as it did the boy. He sprang to his feet, chattering in the most excited way, screamed two or three times, as if he were calling them back, and then started off in vigorous pursuit.

"Now he's gone, too!" said Toby, disconsolately, believing that the old fellow had run away from him. "I didn't think Mr. Stubbs would treat me this way!"

The boy tried to rise to his feet, but his head whirled so, and he felt so dizzy and sick from the effects of his fall, that he was obliged to sit down again until he should feel able to stand. Meanwhile the crowd around the wagon paid no attention to him, and he lay there quietly enough, until he heard the hateful voice of Mr. Lord, asking if his boy were hurt.

The sound of his voice affected Toby very much as the chills and fever affect a sufferer, and he shook so with fear and his heart beat so loudly, that he thought Mr. Lord must know where he was by the sound. Seeing, however, that his employer did not come directly toward him, the thought flashed upon his mind that now would be a good chance to run away, and he acted upon it at once. He rolled himself over in the mud until he reached a low growth of fir trees that skirted the road, and when beneath their friendly shade, he arose to his feet and walked swiftly toward the woods, following the direction the monkeys had taken.

He no longer felt dizzy and sick: the fear of Mr. Lord had dispelled all that, and he felt strong and active again.

He had walked rapidly for some distance and was nearly beyond the sound of the voices in the road, when he was startled by seeing quite a procession of figures emerge from the trees and come directly toward him.

He could not understand the meaning of this strange company, and it so frightened him that he attempted to hide behind a tree, in the hope that they might pass without seeing

108

him. But no sooner had he secreted himself than a strange, shrill chattering came from the foremost of the group, and in an instant Toby emerged from his place of concealment.

He had recognized the peculiar sound as that of the old monkey who had left him a few moments before, and he knew now what he did not know then, owing to the darkness. The newcomers were the monkeys that had escaped from the cage and had been overtaken and compelled to come back by the old monkey, who seemed to have the most perfect control over them.

The old fellow was leading the band, and all were linked "hand in hand" with each other, which gave the whole crowd a most comical appearance as they came up to Toby, half hopping, half walking upright, and all chattering and screaming like a crowd of children out for a holiday.

Toby stepped toward the noisy crowd, held out his hand gravely to the old monkey, and said, in tones of heartfelt sorrow,—

"I felt awful bad because I thought you had gone off an' left

109

me, when you only went off to find the other fellows. You're awful good, Mr. Stubbs, an' now, instead of runnin' away, as I was goin' to do, we'll all go back together."

The old monkey grasped Toby's extended hand with his disengaged paw and, clinging firmly to it, the whole crowd followed in unbroken line, chattering and scolding at the most furious rate, while every now and then Mr. Stubbs would look back and scream out something, which would cause the confusion to cease for an instant.

It was really a comical sight, but Toby seemed to think it the most natural thing in the world that they should follow him in this manner, and he chattered to the old monkey quite as fast as any of the others were doing. He told him very gravely all that he knew about the accident, explained why it was that he conceived the idea of running away, and really believed that Mr. Stubbs understood every word he was saying.

Very shortly after Toby had started to run away, the proprietor of the circus drove up to the scene of disaster; and, after seeing that the wagon was being rapidly fixed up so that it could be hauled to the next town, he ordered that search should be made for the monkeys. It was very important that they should be captured at once, and he appeared to think more of the loss of the animals than of the damage done to the wagon.

While the men were forming a plan for a search for the truants, so that in case of a capture they could let each other know, the noise made by Toby and his party was heard, and the men stood still to learn what it meant.

The entire party burst into shouts of laughter as Toby and his companions walked into the circle of light formed by the glare of the lanterns, and the merriment was by no means abated at Toby's serious demeanor. The wagon was now standing upright, with the door open, and Toby therefore led his companions directly to it, gravely motioning them to enter.

The old monkey, instead of obeying, stepped back to Toby's side and screamed to the others in such a manner that they all entered the cage, leaving him on the outside with the boy.

Toby motioned him to get in, too, but he clung to his hand

110

and scolded so furiously that it was apparent he had no idea of leaving his boy companion. One of the men stepped up and was about to force him into the wagon, when the proprietor ordered him to stop.

"What boy is that?" he asked.

"Job Lord's new boy," said someone in the crowd.

The man asked Toby how it was that he had succeeded in capturing all the runaways, and he answered, gravely,—

"Mr. Stubbs an' I are good friends, an' when he saw the others runnin' away, he just stopped 'em an' brought 'em back to me. I wish you'd let Mr. Stubbs ride with me; we like each other a good deal."

"You can do just what you please with Mr. Stubbs, as you call him. I expected to lose half the monkeys in that cage, and you have brought back every one. That monkey shall be yours, and you may put him in the cage whenever you want to or take him with you, just as you choose, for he belongs entirely to you."

Toby's joy knew no bounds; he put his arm around the monkey's neck, and the monkey clung firmly to him, until even Job Lord was touched at the evidence of affection between the two.

While the wagon was being repaired, Toby and the monkey stood hand in hand watching the work go on, while those in the cage scolded and raved because they had been induced to return to captivity. After a while the old monkey seated himself on Toby's arm and cuddled close up to him, uttering now and then a contented sort of little squeak as the boy talked to him.

That night Mr. Stubbs slept in Toby's arms, in the band wagon, and both boy and monkey appeared very well contented with their lot, which a short time previous had seemed so hard.

When Toby awakened to his second day's work with the circus, his monkey friend was seated by his side, gravely exploring his pockets, and all the boy's treasures were being spread out on the floor of the wagon by his side. Toby remonstrated with him on this breach of confidence, but Mr. Stubbs was more in the mood for sport than for grave conversation, and the more Toby talked, the more mischievous did he become, until at length the boy gathered up his little store of

111

treasures, took the monkey by the paw, and walked him toward the cage from which he had escaped on the previous night.

"Now, Mr. Stubbs," said Toby, speaking in an injured tone, "you must go in here and stay till I have got more time to fool with you."

He opened the door of the cage, but the monkey struggled as well as he was able, and Toby was obliged to exert all his strength to put him in.

When once the door was fastened upon him, Toby tried to impress upon his monkey friend's mind the importance of being more sedate, and he was convinced that the words had sunk deep into Mr. Stubbs's heart, for, by the time he had concluded, the old monkey was seated in the corner of the cage, looking up from under his shaggy eyebrows in the most reproachful manner possible.

Toby felt sorry that he had spoken so harshly and was about to make amends for his severity, when Mr. Lord's gruff voice recalled him to the fact that his time was not his own, and he therefore commenced his day's work, but with a lighter heart than he had had since he stole away from Uncle Daniel and Guilford. . . .

As far as his relations with members of the company were concerned, Toby now stood in a much better position than before. Those who had witnessed the scene told the others how Toby had led in the monkeys on the night previous, and nearly every member of the company had a kind word for the little fellow whose head could hardly be seen above the counter of Messrs. Lord and Jacobs's booth.

Louisa May Alcott

UNEXPECTED CHRISTMAS

ILLUSTRATED BY *James Ponter*

CHRISTMAS won't be Christmas without any presents," grumbled Jo, lying on the rug.

"It's so dreadful to be poor!" sighed Meg, looking down at her old dress.

"I don't think it's fair for some girls to have plenty of pretty things, and other girls nothing at all," added little Amy, with an injured sniff.

"We've got Father and Mother and each other," said Beth contentedly, from her corner.

The four young faces on which the firelight shone brightened at the cheerful words, but darkened again as Jo said sadly,—

"We haven't got Father, and shall not have him for a long time." She didn't say "perhaps never," but each silently added it, thinking of Father far away, where the fighting was.

Nobody spoke for a minute; then Meg said in an altered tone,—

"You know the reason Mother proposed not having any presents this Christmas was because it is going to be a hard winter for everyone; and she thinks we ought not to spend money for pleasure, when our men are suffering so in the army. We can't do much, but we can make our little sacrifices, and ought to do it gladly. But I am afraid I don't"; and Meg shook her head, as she thought regretfully of all the pretty things she wanted.

"But I don't think the little we should spend would do any good. We've each got a dollar, and the army wouldn't be much helped by our giving that. I agree not to expect anything from Mother or you, but I do want to buy Undine and Sintram for

113

myself; I've wanted it *so* long," said Jo, who was a bookworm.

"I planned to spend mine in new music," said Beth, with a little sigh, which no one heard but the hearth-brush and kettle-holder.

"I shall get a nice box of Faber's drawing-pencils; I really need them," said Amy decidedly.

"Mother didn't say anything about our money, and she won't wish us to give up everything. Let's each buy what we want and have a little fun; I'm sure we work hard enough to earn it," cried Jo, examining the heels of her shoes in a gentlemanly manner.

"I know *I* do,—teaching those tiresome children nearly all day, when I'm longing to enjoy myself at home," began Meg, in the complaining tone again.

"You don't have half such a hard time as I do," said Jo. "How would you like to be shut up for hours with a nervous, fussy old lady, who keeps you trotting, is never satisfied, and worries you till you're ready to fly out of the window or cry?"

"It's naughty to fret; but I do think washing dishes and keeping things tidy is the worst work in the world. It makes me cross; and my hands get so stiff, I can't practice well at all"; and Beth looked at her rough hands with a sigh that anyone could hear that time.

"I don't believe any of you suffer as I do," cried Amy; "for you don't have to go to school with impertinent girls, who plague you if you don't know your lessons, and laugh at your dresses, and label your father if he isn't rich, and insult you when your nose isn't nice."

"If you mean *libel*, I'd say so, and not talk about *labels*, as if papa was a pickle-bottle," advised Jo, laughing.

"I know what I mean, and you needn't be *statirical* about it. It's proper to use good words, and improve your *vocabilary*," returned Amy, with dignity.

"Don't peck at one another, children. Don't you wish we had the money Papa lost when we were little, Jo? Dear me! how happy and good we'd be, if we had no worries!" said Meg, who could remember better times.

"You said the other day, you thought we were a deal happier than the King children, for they were fighting and fretting all the time, in spite of their money."

"So I did, Beth. Well, I think we are; for, though we do have to work, we make fun for ourselves, and are a pretty jolly set, as Jo would say."

"Jo does use such slang words!" observed Amy, with a reproving look at the long figure stretched on the rug. Jo immediately sat up, put her hands in her pockets, and began to whistle.

"Don't, Jo; it's so boyish!"

"That's why I do it."

"I detest rude, unlady-like girls!"

"I hate affected, niminy-piminy chits!"

" 'Birds in their little nests agree,' " sang Beth, the peace-maker, with such a funny face that both sharp voices softened to a laugh, and the "pecking" ended for that time.

"Really, girls, you are both to be blamed," said Meg, begin-ning to lecture in her elder-sisterly fashion. "You are old enough to leave off boyish tricks and to behave better, Josephine. It didn't matter so much when you were a little girl; but now you are so tall and turn up your hair, you should remember that you are a young lady."

"I'm not! and if turning up my hair makes me one, I'll wear it in two tails till I'm twenty," cried Jo, pulling off her net, and shaking down a chestnut mane. "I hate to think I've got to grow up, and be Miss March, and wear long gowns, and look as prim as a China-aster! It's bad enough to be a girl, anyway, when I like boys' games and work and manners! I can't get over my disappointment in not being a boy; and it's worse than ever now, for I'm dying to go and fight with Papa, and I can only stay at home and knit, like a poky old woman!" And Jo shook the blue army-sock till the needles rattled like castanets, and her ball bounded across the room.

"Poor Jo! It's too bad, but it can't be helped; so you must try to be contented with making your name boyish, and playing brother to us girls," said Beth, stroking the rough head at her knee with a hand that all the dish-washing and dusting in the world could not make ungentle in its touch.

"As for you, Amy," continued Meg, "you are altogether too particular and prim. Your airs are funny now; but you'll grow up an affected little goose, if you don't take care. I like your nice manners and refined ways of speaking, when you don't try to be elegant; but your absurd words are as bad as Jo's slang."

"If Jo is a tomboy and Amy a goose, what am I, please?" asked Beth, ready to share the lecture.

"You're a dear, and nothing else," answered Meg warmly; and no one contradicted her, for the "Mouse" was the pet of the family.

As young readers like to know "how people look," we will take this moment to give them a little sketch of the four sisters, who sat knitting away in the twilight, while the December snow fell quietly without, and the fire crackled cheerfully within. It was a comfortable old room, though the carpet was faded and the furniture very plain; for a good picture or two hung on the walls, books filled the recesses, chrysanthemums and Christmas roses bloomed in the windows, and a pleasant atmosphere of home-peace pervaded it.

Margaret, the eldest of the four, was sixteen, and very pretty, being plump and fair, with large eyes, plenty of soft, brown hair, a sweet mouth, and white hands, of which she was rather vain. Fifteen-year-old Jo was very tall, thin, and brown, and reminded one of a colt; for she never seemed to know what to do with her long limbs, which were very much in her way. She had a decided mouth, a comical nose, and sharp, gray eyes, which appeared to see everything, and were by turns fierce, funny, or thoughtful. Her long, thick hair was her one beauty; but it was usually bundled into a net, to be out of her way. Round shoulders had Jo, big hands and feet, a fly-away look to her clothes, and the uncomfortable appearance of a girl who was rapidly shooting up into a woman, and didn't like it. Elizabeth—or Beth, as every one called her—was a rosy, smooth-haired, bright-eyed girl of thirteen, with a shy manner, a timid voice, and a peaceful expression, which was seldom disturbed. Her father called her "Little Tranquillity," and the name suited her excellently; for she

116

seemed to live in a happy world of her own, only venturing out to meet the few whom she trusted and loved. Amy, though the youngest, was a most important person,—in her own opinion at least. A regular snow-maiden, with blue eyes, and yellow hair, curling on her shoulders, pale and slender, and always carrying herself like a young lady mindful of her manners. What the characters of the four sisters were we will leave to be found out.

The clock struck six; and, having swept up the hearth, Beth put a pair of slippers down to warm. Somehow the sight of the old shoes had a good effect upon the girls; for Mother was coming, and everyone brightened to welcome her. Meg stopped lecturing and lighted the lamp. Amy got out of the easy-chair without being asked, and Jo forgot how tired she was as she sat up to hold the slippers nearer to the blaze.

"They are quite worn out; Marmee must have a new pair."

"I thought I'd get her some with my dollar," said Beth.

"No, I shall!" cried Amy.

"I'm the oldest," began Meg, but Jo cut in with a decided,—

"I'm the man of the family now Papa is away, and *I* shall provide the slippers, for he told me to take special care of Mother while he was gone."

"I'll tell you what we'll do," said Beth; "let's each get her something for Christmas, and not get anything for ourselves."

"That's like you, dear! What will we get?" exclaimed Jo.

Everyone thought soberly for a minute; then Meg announced, as if the idea was suggested by the sight of her own pretty hands, "I shall give her a nice pair of gloves."

"Army shoes, best to be had," cried Jo.

"Some handkerchiefs, all hemmed," said Beth.

"I'll get a little bottle of cologne; she likes it, and it won't cost much, so I'll have some left to buy my pencils," added Amy.

"How will we give the things?" asked Meg.

"Put them on the table, and bring her in and see her open the bundles. Don't you remember how we used to do on our birthdays?" answered Jo.

"I used to be *so* frightened when it was my turn to sit in the big chair with the crown on, and see you all come marching round to give the presents, with a kiss. I liked the things and the kisses, but it was dreadful to have you sit looking at me while I opened the bundles," said Beth, who was toasting her face and the bread for tea, at the same time.

"Let Marmee think we are getting things for ourselves, and then surprise her. We must go shopping tomorrow afternoon,

Meg; there is so much to do about the play for Christmas night," said Jo, marching up and down, with her hands behind her back and her nose in the air.

"I don't mean to act any more after this time; I'm getting too old for such things," observed Meg, who was as much a child as ever about "dressing-up" frolics.

"You won't stop, I know, as long as you can trail round in a white gown with your hair down, and wear gold-paper jewelry. You are the best actress we've got, and there'll be an end of everything if you quit the boards," said Jo. "We ought to rehearse tonight. Come here, Amy, and do the fainting scene, for you are as stiff as a poker in that."

"I can't help it; I never saw anyone faint, and I don't choose to make myself all black and blue, tumbling flat as you do. If I can go down easily, I'll drop; if I can't, I shall fall into a chair and be graceful; I don't care if Hugo does come at me with a pistol," returned Amy, who was not gifted with dramatic power, but was chosen because she was small enough to be borne out shrieking by the villain of the piece.

"Do it this way; clasp your hands so, and stagger across the room, crying frantically, 'Roderigo! save me! save me!'" and away went Jo, with a melodramatic scream which was truly thrilling.

Amy followed, but she poked her hands out stiffly before her, and jerked herself along as if she went by machinery; and her "Ow!" was more suggestive of pins being run into her than of fear and anguish. Jo gave a despairing groan, and Meg laughed outright, while Beth let her bread burn as she watched the fun, with interest.

"It's no use! Do the best you can when the time comes, and if the audience laughs don't blame me. Come on, Meg."

Then things went smoothly, for Don Pedro defied the world in a speech of two pages without a single break; Hagar, the witch, chanted an awful incantation over her kettleful of simmering toads, with weird effect; Roderigo rent his chains asunder manfully, and Hugo died in agonies of remorse and arsenic, with a wild "Ha! ha!"

"It's the best we've had yet," said Meg, as the dead villain sat up and rubbed his elbows.

"I don't see how you can write and act such splendid things, Jo. You're a regular Shakespeare!" exclaimed Beth, who firmly believed that her sisters were gifted with wonderful genius.

"Not quite," replied Jo modestly. "I do think 'The Witch's Curse, an Operatic Tragedy,' is rather a nice thing; but I'd like to try Macbeth, if we only had a trap door for Banquo. I always wanted to do the killing part. 'Is that a dagger that I see before me?'" muttered Jo, rolling her eyes and clutching at the air, as she had seen a famous tragedian do.

"No, it's the toasting fork, with Mother's shoe on it instead of the bread. Beth's stage-struck!" cried Meg, and the rehearsal ended in a general burst of laughter.

"Glad to find you so merry, my girls," said a cheery voice at the door, and actors and audience turned to welcome a tall, motherly lady, with a "can-I-help-you" look about her which was truly delightful. She was not elegantly dressed, but a noble-looking woman, and the girls thought the gray cloak and un-fashionable bonnet covered the most splendid mother in the world.

"Well, dearies, how have you got on today? There was so much to do, getting the boxes ready to go tomorrow, that I didn't come home to dinner. Has anyone called, Beth? How is your cold, Meg? Jo, you look tired to death. Come and kiss me, baby."

While making these maternal inquiries Mrs. March got her wet things off, her warm slippers on, and sitting down in the easy-chair, drew Amy to her lap, preparing to enjoy the happiest hour of her busy day. The girls flew about, trying to make things comfortable, each in her own way. Meg arranged the teatable; Jo brought wood and set chairs, dropping, overturning, and clattering everything she touched; Beth trotted to and fro between parlor and kitchen, quiet and busy; while Amy gave directions to everyone, as she sat with her hands folded.

As they gathered about the table, Mrs. March said, with a particularly happy face, "I've got a treat for you after supper."

A quick, bright smile went round like a streak of sunshine.

120

Beth clapped her hands, regardless of the biscuit she held, and Jo tossed up her napkin, crying, "A letter! a letter! Three cheers for Father!"

"Yes, a nice long letter. He is well, and thinks he shall get through the cold season better than we feared. He sends all sorts of loving wishes for Christmas, and an especial message to you girls," said Mrs. March, patting her pocket as if she had got a treasure there.

"Hurry and get done! Don't stop to quirk your little finger and simper over your plate, Amy," cried Jo, choking in her tea, and dropping her bread, butter side down, on the carpet, in her haste to get at the treat.

Beth ate no more, but crept away, to sit in her shadowy corner and brood over the delight to come, till the others were ready.

"I think it was so splendid in Father to go as a chaplain when he was too old to be drafted, and not strong enough for a soldier," said Meg warmly.

"Don't I wish I could go as a drummer, a *vivan*—what's its name? or a nurse, so I could be near him and help him," exclaimed Jo, with a groan.

"It must be very disagreeable to sleep in a tent, and eat all sorts of bad-tasting things, and drink out of a tin mug," sighed Amy.

"When will he come home, Marmee?" asked Beth, with a little quiver in her voice.

"Not for many months, dear, unless he is sick. He will stay and do his work faithfully as long as he can, and we won't ask for him back a minute sooner than he can be spared. Now come and hear the letter."

They all drew to the fire, Mother in the big chair with Beth at her feet, Meg and Amy perched on either arm of the chair, and Jo leaning on the back, where no one would see any sign of emotion if the letter should happen to be touching.

Very few letters were written in those hard times that were not touching, especially those which fathers sent home. In this one little was said of the hardships endured, the dangers faced, or the homesickness conquered; it was a cheerful, hopeful letter,

121

full of lively descriptions of camp life, marches, and military news; and only at the end did the writer's heart overflow with fatherly love and longing for the little girls at home.

"Give them all my dear love and a kiss. Tell them I think of them by day, pray for them by night, and find my best comfort in their affection at all times. A year seems very long to wait before I see them, but remind them that while we wait we may all work, so that these hard days need not be wasted. I know they will remember all I said to them, that they will be loving children to you, will do their duty faithfully, fight their bosom enemies bravely, and conquer themselves so beautifully, that when I come back to them I may be fonder and prouder than ever of my little women."

Everybody sniffed when they came to that part; Jo wasn't ashamed of the great tear that dropped off the end of her nose, and Amy never minded the rumpling of her curls as she hid her face on her mother's shoulder and sobbed out, "I *am* a selfish girl! but I'll truly try to be better, so he mayn't be disappointed in me by and by."

"We all will!" cried Meg. "I think too much of my looks, and hate to work, but won't any more, if I can help it."

"I'll try and be what he loves to call me, 'a little woman,' and not be rough and wild; but do my duty here instead of wanting to be somewhere else," said Jo, thinking that keeping her temper at home was a much harder task than facing a rebel or two down South.

Beth said nothing, but wiped away her tears with the blue army-sock, and began to knit with all her might, losing no time in doing the duty that lay nearest her, while she resolved in her quiet little soul to be all that Father hoped to find her when the year brought round the happy coming home.

Mrs. March broke the silence that followed Jo's words, by saying in her cheery voice, "Do you remember how you used to play Pilgrim's Progress when you were little things? Nothing delighted you more than to have me tie my piece-bags on your backs for burdens, give you hats and sticks and rolls of paper, and let you travel through the house from the cellar, which was

122

the City of Destruction, up, up, to the housetop, where you had all the lovely things you could collect to make a Celestial City."

"What fun it was, especially going by the lions, fighting Apollyon, and passing through the Valley where the hobgoblins were!" said Jo.

"I liked the place where the bundles fell off and tumbled downstairs," said Meg.

"My favorite part was when we came out on the flat roof where our flowers and arbors and pretty things were, and all stood and sung for joy up there in the sunshine," said Beth, smiling, as if that pleasant moment had come back to her.

"I don't remember much about it, except that I was afraid of the cellar and the dark entry, and always liked the cake and milk we had up at the top. If I wasn't too old for such things, I'd rather like to play it over again," said Amy, who began to talk of renouncing childish things at the mature age of twelve.

"We never are too old for this, my dear, because it is a play we are playing all the time in one way or another. Our burdens are here, our road is before us, and the longing for goodness and happiness is the guide that leads us through many troubles and mistakes to the peace which is a true Celestial City. Now, my little pilgrims, suppose you begin again, not in play, but in earnest, and see how far on you can get before Father comes home."

"Really, Mother? Where are our bundles?" asked Amy, who was a very literal young lady.

"Each of you told what your burden was just now, except Beth; I rather think she hasn't got any," said her mother.

"Yes, I have; mine is dishes and dusters, and envying girls with nice pianos, and being afraid of people."

Beth's bundle was such a funny one that everybody wanted to laugh; but nobody did, for it would have hurt her feelings very much.

"Let us do it," said Meg thoughtfully. "It is only another name for trying to be good, and the story may help us; for though we do want to be good, it's hard work, and we forget, and don't do our best."

"We were in the Slough of Despond tonight, and Mother

123

came and pulled us out as Help did in the book. We ought to have our roll of directions, like Christian. What shall we do about that?" asked Jo, delighted with the fancy which lent a little romance to the very dull task of doing her duty.

"Look under your pillows, Christmas morning, and you will find your guidebook," replied Mrs. March.

They talked over the new plan while old Hannah cleared the table; then out came the four little work-baskets, and the needles flew as the girls made sheets for Aunt March. It was uninteresting sewing, but tonight no one grumbled. They adopted Jo's plan of dividing the long seams into four parts, and calling the quarters Europe, Asia, Africa, and America, and in that way got on capitally, especially when they talked about the different countries as they stitched their way through them.

At nine they stopped work, and sung, as usual, before they went to bed. No one but Beth could get much music out of the old piano; but she had a way of softly touching the yellow keys, and making a pleasant accompaniment to the simple songs they sung. Meg had a voice like a flute, and she and her mother led the little choir. Amy chirped like a cricket, and Jo wandered through the airs at her own sweet will, always coming out at the wrong place with a croak or a quaver that spoilt the most pensive tune. They had always done this from the time they could lisp

"Crinkle, crinkle, 'ittle 'tar,"

and it had become a household custom, for the mother was a born singer. The first sound in the morning was her voice, as she went about the house singing like a lark; and the last sound at night was the same cheery sound, for the girls never grew too old for that familiar lullaby.

Jo was the first to wake in the gray dawn of Christmas morning. No stockings hung at the fireplace, and for a moment she felt as much disappointed as she did long ago, when her little sock fell down because it was so crammed with goodies. Then she remembered her mother's promise, and, slipping her hand under her pillow, drew out a little crimson-covered book. She knew it very well, for it was that beautiful old story of the best life ever lived, and Jo felt that it was a true guidebook for any pilgrim going the long journey. She woke Meg with a "Merry Christmas," and bade her see what was under her pillow. A green-covered book appeared, with the same picture inside, and a few words written by their mother, which made their one present very precious in their eyes. Presently Beth and Amy woke, to rummage and find their little books also,—one dove-colored, the other blue; and all sat looking at and talking about them, while the east grew rosy with the coming day.

In spite of her small vanities, Margaret had a sweet and pious nature, which unconsciously influenced her sisters, especially Jo, who loved her very tenderly and obeyed her because her advice was so gently given.

"Girls," said Meg seriously, looking from the tumbled head beside her to the two little night-capped ones in the room beyond, "Mother wants us to read and love and mind these books, and we must begin at once. We used to be faithful about it; but since father went away, and all this war trouble unsettled us, we have neglected many things. You can do as you please; but I shall keep my book on the table here and read a little every morning as soon as I wake, for I know it will do me good and help me through the day."

Then she opened her new book and began to read. Jo put her arm round her, and, leaning cheek to cheek, read also, with the quiet expression so seldom seen on her restless face.

"How good Meg is! Come, Amy, let's do as they do. I'll help you with the hard words, and they'll explain things if we don't understand," whispered Beth, very much impressed by the pretty books and her sisters' example.

"I'm glad mine is blue," said Amy; and then the rooms were very still while the pages were softly turned, and the winter sunshine crept in to touch the bright heads and serious faces with a Christmas greeting.

"Where is Mother?" asked Meg, as she and Jo ran down to thank her for their gifts, half an hour later.

"Goodness only knows. Some poor creeter come a-beggin', and your ma went straight off to see what was needed. There

125

never *was* such a woman for givin' away vittles and drink, clothes and firin'," replied Hannah, who had lived with the family since Meg was born, and was considered by them all more as a friend than a servant.

"She will be back soon, I think; so fry your cakes and have everything ready," said Meg, looking over the presents which were collected in a basket and kept under the sofa, ready to be produced at the proper time. "Why, where is Amy's bottle of cologne?" she added, as the little flask did not appear.

"She took it out a minute ago and went off with it to put a ribbon on it, or some such notion," replied Jo, dancing about the room to take the first stiffness off the new army-slippers.

"How nice my handkerchiefs look, don't they? Hannah washed and ironed them for me, and I marked them all myself," said Beth, looking proudly at the somewhat uneven letters which had cost her such labor.

"Bless the child! she's gone and put 'Mother' on them instead of 'M. March.' How funny!" cried Jo, taking up one.

"Isn't it right? I thought it was better to do it so, because Meg's initials are 'M. M.,' and I don't want anyone to use these but Marmee," said Beth, looking troubled.

"It's all right, dear, and a very pretty idea,—quite sensible, too, for no one can ever mistake now. It will please her very much, I know," said Meg, with a frown for Jo and a smile for Beth.

"There's Mother. Hide the basket, quick!" cried Jo, as a door slammed, and steps sounded in the hall.

Amy came in hastily and looked rather abashed when she saw her sisters all waiting for her.

"Where have you been, and what are you hiding behind you?" asked Meg, surprised to see, by her hood and cloak, that lazy Amy had been out so early.

"Don't laugh at me, Jo! I didn't mean anyone should know till the time came. I only meant to change the little bottle for a big one, and I gave *all* my money to get it, and I'm truly trying not to be selfish any more."

As she spoke, Amy showed the handsome flask which replaced the cheap one; and looked so earnest and humble in her little

126

effort to forget herself that Meg hugged her on the spot, and Jo pronounced her "a trump," while Beth ran to the window and picked her finest rose to ornament the stately bottle.

"You see I felt ashamed of my present, after reading and talking about being good this morning, so I ran round the corner and changed it the minute I was up: and I'm *so* glad, for mine is the handsomest now."

Another bang of the street-door sent the basket under the sofa, and the girls to the table, eager for breakfast.

"Merry Christmas, Marmee! Many of them! Thank you for our books; we read some, and mean to every day," they cried, in chorus.

"Merry Christmas, little daughters! I'm glad you began at once and hope you will keep on. But I want to say one word before we sit down. Not far away from here lies a poor woman with a little new-born baby. Six children are huddled into one bed to keep from freezing, for they have no fire. There is nothing to eat over there; and the oldest boy came to tell me they were suffering hunger and cold. My girls, will you give them your breakfast as a Christmas present?"

They were all unusually hungry, having waited nearly an hour, and for a minute no one spoke; only a minute, for Jo exclaimed impetuously,—

"I'm so glad you came before we began!"

"May I go and help carry the things to the poor little children?" asked Beth, eagerly.

"*I* shall take the cream and the muffins," added Amy, heroically giving up the articles she most liked.

Meg was already covering the buckwheats, and piling the bread into one big plate.

"I thought you'd do it," said Mrs. March, smiling as if satisfied. "You shall all go and help me, and when we come back we will have bread and milk for breakfast, and make it up at dinnertime."

They were soon ready, and the procession set out. Fortunately it was early, and they went through back streets, so few people saw them, and no one laughed at the queer party.

A poor, bare, miserable room it was, with broken windows, no fire, ragged bedclothes, a sick mother, wailing baby, and a group of pale, hungry children cuddled under one old quilt, trying to keep warm.

How the big eyes stared and the blue lips smiled as the girls went in!

"Ach, mein Gott! it is good angels come to us!" said the poor woman, crying for joy.

"Funny angels in hoods and mittens," said Jo, and set them laughing.

In a few minutes it really did seem as if kind spirits had been at work there. Hannah, who had carried wood, made a fire, and stopped up the broken panes with old hats and her own cloak. Mrs. March gave the mother tea and gruel, and comforted her with promises of help, while she dressed the little baby as tenderly as if it had been her own. The girls, meantime, spread the table, set the children round the fire, and fed them like so many hungry birds,—laughing, talking, and trying to understand the funny broken English.

"Das ist gut!" "Die Engel-kinder!" cried the poor things, as they ate and warmed their purple hands at the comfortable blaze.

The girls had never been called angel children before, and

128

thought it very agreeable, especially Jo, who had been considered a "Sancho" ever since she was born. That was a very
happy breakfast, though they didn't get any of it; and when
they went away, leaving comfort behind, I think there were
not in all the city four merrier people than the hungry little
girls who gave away their breakfasts and contented themselves
with bread and milk on Christmas morning.

"That's loving our neighbor better than ourselves, and I like
it," said Meg, as they set out their presents, while their mother
was upstairs collecting clothes for the poor Hummels.

Not a very splendid show, but there was a great deal of love
done up in the few little bundles; and the tall vase of red roses,
white chrysanthemums, and trailing vines, which stood in the
middle, gave quite an elegant air to the table.

"She's coming! Strike up, Beth! Open the door, Amy! Three
cheers for Marmee!" cried Jo, prancing about, while Meg went
to conduct mother to the seat of honor.

Beth played her gayest march, Amy threw open the door, and
Meg enacted escort with great dignity. Mrs. March was both
surprised and touched, and smiled with her eyes full as she
examined her presents and read the little notes which accompanied them. The slippers went on at once, a new handkerchief
was slipped into her pocket, well scented with Amy's cologne,

the rose was fastened in her bosom, and the nice gloves were pronounced a "perfect fit."

There was a good deal of laughing and kissing and explaining, in the simple, loving fashion which makes these home-festivals so pleasant at the time, so sweet to remember long afterward, and then all fell to work.

The morning charities and ceremonies took so much time that the rest of the day was devoted to preparations for the evening festivities. Being still too young to go often to the theatre, and not rich enough to afford any great outlay for private perform-ances, the girls put their wits to work, and—necessity being the mother of invention—made whatever they needed. Very clever were some of their productions—pasteboard guitars, antique lamps made of old-fashioned butter-boats covered with silver paper, gorgeous robes of old cotton, glittering with tin spangles from a pickle factory, and armor covered with the same useful diamond-shaped bits, left in sheets when the lids of tin preserve-pots were cut out. The furniture was used to being turned topsy-turvy, and the big chamber was the scene of many inno-cent revels.

No gentlemen were admitted; so Jo played male parts to her heart's content and took immense satisfaction in a pair of russet-leather boots given her by a friend, who knew a lady who knew an actor. These boots, an old foil, and a slashed doublet once used by an artist for some picture, were Jo's chief treasures, and appeared on all occasions. The smallness of the company made it necessary for the two principal actors to take several parts apiece; and they certainly deserved some credit for the hard work they did in learning three or four different parts, whisking in and out of various costumes, and managing the stage besides. It was excellent drill for their memories, a harmless amusement, and employed many hours which otherwise would have been idle, lonely, or spent in less profitable society.

On Christmas night, a dozen girls piled on to the bed which was the dress-circle, and sat before the blue and yellow chintz curtains in a most flattering state of expectancy. There was a good deal of rustling and whispering behind the curtain, a trifle of lamp-smoke, and an occasional giggle from Amy, who was apt to get hysterical. Presently a bell sounded, the curtains flew apart, and the Operatic Tragedy began.

"A gloomy wood," according to the one playbill, was represented by a few shrubs in pots, green baize on the floor, and a cave in the distance. This cave was made with a clotheshorse for a roof, bureaus for walls; and in it was a small furnace in full blast, with a black pot on it, and an old witch bending over it. The stage was dark, and the glow of the furnace had a fine effect, especially as real steam issued from the kettle when the witch took off the cover. A moment was allowed for the first thrill to subside; then Hugo, the villain, stalked in with a clanking sword at his side, a slouched hat, black beard, mysterious cloak, and the boots. After pacing to and fro in much agitation, he struck his forehead, and burst out in a wild strain, singing of his hatred to Roderigo, his love for Zara, and his pleasing resolution to kill the one and win the other. The gruff tones of Hugo's voice, with an occasional shout when his feelings overcame him, were very impressive, and the audience applauded the moment he paused for breath. Bowing with the air of one accustomed to public praise, he stole to the cavern and ordered Hagar to come forth with a commanding "What ho, minion! I need thee!"

Out came Meg, with gray horsehair hanging about her face, a red and black robe, a staff, and cabalistic signs upon her cloak. Hugo demanded a potion to make Zara adore him, and one to destroy Roderigo. Hagar, in a fine dramatic melody, promised both, and proceeded to call up the spirit who would bring the love philter,—

> "Hither, hither, from thy home,
> Airy sprite, I bid thee come!
> Born of roses, fed on dew,
> Charms and potions canst thou brew?
> Bring me here, with elfin speed,
> The fragrant philter which I need;
> Make it sweet and swift and strong,
> Spirit, answer now my song!"

A soft strain of music sounded, and then at the back of the cave appeared a little figure in cloudy white, with glittering wings, golden hair, and a garland of roses on its head. Waving a wand, it sang,—

"Hither I come,
From my airy home,
Afar in the silver moon.
Take the magic spell,
And use it well,
Or its power will vanish soon!"

And, dropping a small, gilded bottle at the witch's feet, the spirit vanished. Another chant from Hagar produced another apparition,—not a lovely one; for, with a bang, an ugly black imp appeared, and, having croaked a reply, tossed a dark bottle at Hugo, and disappeared with a mocking laugh. Having warbled his thanks and put the potions in his boots, Hugo departed; and Hagar informed the audience that, as he had killed a few of her friends in times past, she has cursed him, and intends to thwart his plans, and be revenged on him. Then the curtain fell, and the audience reposed and ate candy while discussing the merits of the play.

A good deal of hammering went on before the curtain rose again; but when it became evident what a masterpiece of stage-carpentering had been got up, no one murmured at the delay. It was truly superb! A tower rose to the ceiling; halfway up appeared a window, with a lamp burning at it, and behind the white curtain appeared Zara in a lovely blue and silver dress, waiting for Roderigo. He came in gorgeous array, with plumed cap, red cloak, chestnut lovelocks, a guitar, and the boots, of course. Kneeling at the foot of the tower, he sang a serenade in melting tones. Zara replied, and, after a musical dialogue, consented to fly. Then came the grand effect of the play. Roderigo produced a rope ladder, with five steps to it, threw up one end, and invited Zara to descend. Timidly she crept from her lattice, put her hand on Roderigo's shoulder, and was about to leap gracefully down, when, "Alas! alas for Zara!" she forgot her

train,—it caught in the window; the tower tottered, leaned forward, fell with a crash, and buried the unhappy lovers in the ruins!

A universal shriek arose as the russet boots waved wildly from the wreck, and a golden head emerged, exclaiming, "I told you so! I told you so!" With wonderful presence of mind, Don Pedro, the cruel sire, rushed in, dragged out his daughter, with a hasty aside,—

"Don't laugh! Act as if it was all right!"—and, ordering Roderigo up, banished him from the kingdom with wrath and scorn. Though decidedly shaken by the fall of the tower upon him, Roderigo defied the old gentleman and refused to stir. This dauntless example fired Zara: she also defied her sire, and he ordered them both to the deepest dungeons of the castle. A stout little retainer came in with chains, and led them away, looking very much frightened, and evidently forgetting the speech he ought to have made.

Act third was the castle hall; and here Hagar appeared, having come to free the lovers and finish Hugo. She hears him coming and hides; sees him put the potions into two cups of wine and bid the timid little servant "Bear them to the captives in their cells and tell them I shall come anon." The servant takes Hugo aside to tell him something, and Hagar changes the cups for two others which are harmless. Ferdinando, the "minion," carries them away, and Hagar puts back the cup which holds the poison meant for Roderigo. Hugo, getting thirsty after a long warble, drinks it, loses his wits, and, after a good deal of clutching and stamping, falls flat and dies; while Hagar informs him what she has done in a song of exquisite power and melody.

This was a truly thrilling scene, though some persons might have thought that the sudden tumbling down of a quantity of long hair rather marred the effect of the villain's death. He was called before the curtain, and with great propriety appeared, leading Hagar, whose singing was considered more wonderful than all the rest of the performance put together.

Act fourth displayed the despairing Roderigo on the point of

134

stabbing himself, because he has been told that Zara has deserted him. Just as the dagger is at his heart, a lovely song is sung under his window, informing him that Zara is true, but in danger, and he can save her, if he will. A key is thrown in, which unlocks the door, and in a spasm of rapture he tears off his chains and rushes away to find and rescue his ladylove.

Act fifth opened with a stormy scene between Zara and Don Pedro. He wishes her to go into a convent, but she won't hear of it; and, after a touching appeal, is about to faint, when Roderigo dashes in and demands her hand. Don Pedro refuses, because he is not rich. They shout and gesticulate tremendously, but cannot agree, and Roderigo is about to bear away the exhausted Zara, when the timid servant enters with a letter and a bag from Hagar, who has mysteriously disappeared. The latter informs the party that she bequeaths untold wealth to the young pair, and an awful doom to Don Pedro, if he doesn't make them happy. The bag is opened, and several quarts of tin money shower down upon the stage, till it is quite glorified with the glitter. This entirely softens the "stern sire": he consents without a murmur, all join in a joyful chorus, and the curtain falls upon the lovers kneeling to receive Don Pedro's blessing in attitudes of the most romantic grace.

Tumultuous applause followed, but received an unexpected check; for the cot-bed, on which the "dress-circle" was built, suddenly shut up and extinguished the enthusiastic audience. Roderigo and Don Pedro flew to the rescue, and all were taken out unhurt, though many were speechless with laughter. The excitement had hardly subsided, when Hannah appeared, with "Mrs. March's compliments, and would the ladies walk down to supper."

This was a surprise, even to the actors; and, when they saw the table, they looked at one another in rapturous amazement. It was like Marmee to get up a little treat for them; but anything so fine as this was unheard-of since the departed days of plenty. There was ice cream,—actually two dishes of it, pink and white, —and cake and fruit and distracting French bonbons, and, in the middle of the table, four great bouquets of hothouse flowers!

It quite took their breath away; and they stared first at the table and then at their mother, who looked as if she enjoyed it immensely.

"Is it fairies?" asked Amy.

"It's Santa Claus," said Beth.

"Mother did it"; and Meg smiled her sweetest, in spite of her gray beard and white eyebrows.

"Aunt March had a good fit and sent the supper," cried Jo, with a sudden inspiration.

"All wrong. Old Mr. Laurence sent it," replied Mrs. March.

"The Laurence boy's grandfather! What in the world put such a thing into his head? We don't know him!" exclaimed Meg.

"Hannah told one of his servants about your breakfast party. He is an odd old gentleman, but that pleased him. He knew my father, years ago; and he sent me a polite note this afternoon, saying he hoped I would allow him to express his friendly feeling toward my children by sending them a few trifles in honor of the day. I could not refuse; and so you have a little feast at night to make up for the bread-and-milk breakfast."

"That boy put it into his head, I know he did! He's a capital fellow, and I wish we could get acquainted. He looks as if he'd like to know us; but he's bashful, and Meg is so prim she won't let me speak to him when we pass," said Jo, as the plates went round, and the ice began to melt out of sight, with "Ohs!" and "Ahs!" of satisfaction.

"You mean the people who live in the big house next door, don't you?" asked one of the girls. "My mother knows old Mr. Laurence; but says he's very proud and doesn't like to mix with his neighbors. He keeps his grandson shut up, when he isn't riding or walking with his tutor, and makes him study very hard. We invited him to our party, but he didn't come. Mother says he's very nice, though he never speaks to us girls."

"Our cat ran away once, and he brought her back, and we talked over the fence and were getting on capitally,—all about cricket, and so on,—when he saw Meg coming and walked off. I mean to know him some day; for he needs fun, I'm sure he does," said Jo decidedly.

"I like his manners, and he looks like a little gentleman; so I've no objection to your knowing him, if a proper opportunity comes. He brought the flowers himself; and I should have asked him in, if I had been sure what was going on upstairs. He looked so wistful as he went away, hearing the frolic and evidently having none of his own."

"It's a mercy you didn't, Mother!" laughed Jo, looking at her boots. "But we'll have another play, some time, that he *can* see. Perhaps he'll help act; wouldn't that be jolly?"

"I never had such a fine bouquet before! How pretty it is!" And Meg examined her flowers with great interest.

"They *are* lovely! But Beth's roses are sweeter to me," said Mrs. March, smelling the half-dead posy in her belt.

Beth nestled up to her, and whispered softly, "I wish I could send my bunch to father. I'm afraid he isn't having such a merry Christmas as we are."

Louisa May Alcott

JO MEETS LAURIE

ILLUSTRATED BY *James Ponter*
COLOR PAGE BY *Jessie Wilcox Smith*

WHAT in the world are you going to do now, Jo?" asked Meg, one snowy afternoon, as her sister came tramping through the hall, in rubber boots, old sack and hood, with a broom in one hand and a shovel in the other.

"Going out for exercise," answered Jo, with a mischievous twinkle in her eyes.

"I should think two long walks this morning would have been enough! It's cold and dull out; and I advise you to stay, warm and dry, by the fire, as I do," said Meg, with a shiver.

"Never take advice! Can't keep still all day, and, not being a pussycat, I don't like to doze by the fire. I like adventures, and I'm going to find some."

Meg went back to toast her feet and read "Ivanhoe"; and Jo began to dig paths with great energy. The snow was light, and with her broom she soon swept a path all round the garden, for Beth to walk in when the sun came out; and the invalid dolls needed air. Now, the garden separated the Marches' house from that of Mr. Laurence. Both stood in a suburb of the city, which was still countrylike, with groves and lawns, large gardens, and quiet streets. A low hedge parted the two estates. On one side was an old, brown house, looking rather bare and shabby, robbed of the vines that in summer covered its walls, and the flowers which then surrounded it. On the other side was a stately stone mansion, plainly betokening every sort of comfort and luxury, from the big coachhouse and well-kept grounds to the conservatory and the glimpses of lovely things one caught between the rich curtains. Yet it seemed a lonely, lifeless sort of house; for no children frolicked on the lawn, no motherly face ever smiled at the windows, and few people went in and out, except the old gentleman and his grandson.

To Jo's lively fancy, this fine house seemed a kind of enchanted palace, full of splendors and delights, which no one enjoyed. She had long wanted to behold these hidden glories, and to know the "Laurence boy," who looked as if he would like to be known, if he only knew how to begin. Since the party, she had been more eager than ever, and had planned many ways of making friends with him; but he had not been seen lately, and Jo began to think he had gone away, when she one day spied a brown face at an upper window, looking wistfully down into their garden, where Beth and Amy were snowballing one another.

"That boy is suffering for society and fun," she said to herself. "His grandpa does not know what's good for him and keeps him shut up all alone. He needs a party of jolly boys to play with, or somebody young and lively. I've a great mind to go over and tell the old gentleman so!"

The idea amused Jo, who liked to do daring things, and was always scandalizing Meg by her queer performances. The plan of "going over" was not forgotten; and when the snowy afternoon came, Jo resolved to try what could be done. She saw Mr. Laurence drive off, and then sallied out to dig her way down to the hedge, where she paused, and took a survey. All quiet,—curtains down at the lower windows; servants out of sight, and nothing human visible but a curly black head leaning on a thin hand at the upper window.

"There he is," thought Jo, "poor boy! all alone and sick this dismal day. It's a shame! I'll toss up a snowball, and make him look out, and then say a kind word to him."

Up went a handful of soft snow, and the head turned at once, showing a face which lost its listless look in a minute, as the big eyes brightened and the mouth began to smile. Jo nodded and laughed, and flourished her broom as she called out,—

"How do you do? Are you sick?"

Laurie opened the window, and croaked out as hoarsely as a raven,—

"Better, thank you. I've had a bad cold, and been shut up a week."

"I'm sorry. What do you amuse yourself with?"

"Nothing; it's as dull as tombs up here."

"Don't you read?"

"Not much; they won't let me."

"Can't somebody read to you?"

"Grandpa does, sometimes; but my books don't interest him, and I hate to ask Brooke all the time."

"Have someone come and see you, then."

"There isn't anyone I'd like to see. Boys make such a row, and my head is weak."

"Isn't there some nice girl who'd read and amuse you? Girls are quiet and like to play nurse."

"Don't know any."

"You know us," began Jo, then laughed, and stopped.

"So I do! Will you come, please?" cried Laurie.

"I'm not quiet and nice; but I'll come, if mother will let me. I'll go ask her. Shut that window, like a good boy, and wait till I come."

With that, Jo shouldered her broom and marched into the house, wondering what they would all say to her. Laurie was in a flutter of excitement at the idea of having company and flew about to get ready; for, as Mrs. March said, he was "a little gentleman," and did honor to the coming guest by brushing his curly pate, putting on a fresh collar, and trying to tidy up the room, which, in spite of half a dozen servants, was anything but neat. Presently there came a loud ring, then a decided voice, asking for "Mr. Laurie," and a surprised-looking servant came running up to announce a young lady.

"All right, show her up, it's Miss Jo," said Laurie, going to the door of his little parlor to meet Jo, who appeared, looking rosy and kind and quite at her ease, with a covered dish in one hand and Beth's three kittens in the other.

"Here I am, bag and baggage," she said briskly. "Mother sent her love and was glad if I could do anything for you. Meg wanted me to bring some of her blancmange; she makes it very nicely, and Beth thought her cats would be comforting. I knew you'd laugh at them, but I couldn't refuse, she was so anxious to do something."

It so happened that Beth's funny loan was just the thing; for, in laughing over the kits, Laurie forgot his bashfulness, and grew sociable at once.

"That looks too pretty to eat," he said, smiling with pleasure, as Jo uncovered the dish, and showed the blancmange, surrounded by a garland of green leaves, and the scarlet flowers of Amy's pet geranium.

141

"It isn't anything, only they all felt kindly and wanted to show it. Tell the girl to put it away for your tea: it's so simple, you can eat it; and, being soft, it will slip down without hurting your sore throat. What a cosy room this is!"

"It might be if it was kept nice; but the maids are lazy, and I don't know how to make them mind. It worries me, though."

"I'll right it up in two minutes; for it only needs to have the hearth brushed, so,—and the things made straight on the mantel-piece so,—and the books put here, and the bottles there, and your sofa turned from the light, and the pillows plumped up a bit. Now, then, you're fixed."

And so he was; for, as she laughed and talked, Jo had whisked things into place and given quite a different air to the room. Laurie watched her in respectful silence; and when she beck-oned him to his sofa, he sat down with a sigh of satisfaction, saying gratefully,—

"How kind you are! Yes, that's what it wanted. Now please take the big chair, and let me do something to amuse my company."

"No; I came to amuse you. Shall I read aloud?" and Jo looked affectionately toward some inviting books near by.

"Thank you; I've read all those, and if you don't mind, I'd rather talk," answered Laurie.

"Not a bit; I'll talk all day if you'll only set me going. Beth says I never know when to stop."

"Is Beth the rosy one, who stays at home a good deal, and sometimes goes out with a little basket?" asked Laurie, with interest.

"Yes, that's Beth; she's my girl, and a regular good one she is, too."

"The pretty one is Meg, and the curly-haired one is Amy, I believe?"

"How did you find that out?"

Laurie colored up, but answered frankly, "Why, you see, I often hear you calling to one another, and when I'm alone up here, I can't help looking over at your house, you always seem to be having such good times. I beg your pardon for being so

142

rude, but sometimes you forget to put down the curtain at the window where the flowers are; and when the lamps are lighted, it's like looking at a picture to see the fire, and you all round the table with your mother; her face is right opposite, and it looks so sweet behind the flowers, I can't help watching it. I haven't got any mother, you know"; and Laurie poked the fire to hide a little twitching of the lips that he could not control.

The solitary, hungry look in his eyes went straight to Jo's warm heart. She had been so simply taught that there was no nonsense in her head, and at fifteen she was as innocent and frank as any child. Laurie was sick and lonely; and, feeling how rich she was in homelove and happiness, she gladly tried to share it with him. Her face was very friendly and her sharp voice unusually gentle as she said,—

"We'll never draw that curtain any more, and I give you leave to look as much as you like. I just wish, though, instead of peeping, you'd come over and see us. Mother is so splendid, she'd do you heaps of good, and Beth would sing to you if *I* begged her to, and Amy would dance; Meg and I would make you laugh over our funny stage properties, and we'd have jolly times. Wouldn't your grandpa let you?"

"I think he would, if your mother asked him. He's very kind, though he does not look so; and he lets me do what I like, pretty much, only he's afraid I might be a bother to strangers," began Laurie, brightening more and more.

"We are not strangers, we are neighbors, and you needn't think you'd be a bother. We *want* to know you, and I've been trying to do it this ever so long. We haven't been here a great while, you know, but we have got acquainted with all our neighbors but you."

"You see Grandpa lives among his books, and doesn't mind much what happens outside. Mr. Brooke, my tutor, doesn't stay here, you know, and I have no one to go about with me, so I just stop at home and get on as I can."

"That's bad. You ought to make an effort and go visiting everywhere you are asked; then you'll have plenty of friends, and pleasant places to go to. Never mind being bashful; it won't last long if you keep going."

Laurie turned red again, but wasn't offended at being accused of bashfulness; for there was so much good will in Jo, it was impossible not to take her blunt speeches as kindly as they were meant.

"Do you like your school?" asked the boy, changing the subject, after a little pause, during which he stared at the fire, and Jo looked about her, well pleased.

"Don't go to school; I'm a business man—girl, I mean. I go to wait on my great-aunt, and a dear, cross old soul she is, too," answered Jo.

Laurie opened his mouth to ask another question; but remembering just in time that it wasn't manners to make too many inquiries into people's affairs, he shut it again, and looked uncomfortable. Jo liked his good breeding and didn't mind having a laugh at Aunt March, so she gave him a lively description of the fidgety old lady, her fat poodle, the parrot that talked Spanish, and the library where she revelled. Laurie enjoyed that immensely; and when she told about the prim old gentleman who came once to woo Aunt March, and, in the middle of a fine speech, how Poll had tweaked his wig off to his great dismay, the boy lay back and laughed till the tears ran down his cheeks, and a maid popped her head in to see what was the matter.

"Oh! that does me no end of good. Tell on, please," he said, taking his face out of the sofa cushion, red and shining with merriment.

Much elated with her success, Jo did "tell on," all about their plays and plans, their hopes and fears for father, and the most interesting events of the little world in which the sisters lived. Then they got to talking about books; and to Jo's delight, she found that Laurie loved them as well as she did, and had read even more than herself.

"If you like them so much, come down and see ours. Grandpa is out, so you needn't be afraid," said Laurie, getting up.

"I'm not afraid of anything," returned Jo, tossing her head.

"I don't believe you are!" exclaimed the boy, looking at her with much admiration, though he privately thought she would have good reason to be a trifle afraid of the old gentleman, if she met him in some of his moods.

The atmosphere of the whole house being summer-like, Laurie led the way from room to room, letting Jo stop to examine whatever struck her fancy; and so at last they came to the library, where she clapped her hands, and pranced, as she always did when especially delighted. It was lined with books, and there were pictures and statues, and distracting little cabinets full of coins and curiosities, and sleepy-hollow chairs, and queer tables, and bronzes; and, best of all, a great open fireplace, with quaint tiles all round it.

"What richness!" sighed Jo, sinking into the depth of a velvet chair, and gazing about her with an air of intense satisfaction. "Theodore Laurence, you ought to be the happiest boy in the world," she added impressively.

"A fellow can't live on books," said Laurie, shaking his head, as he perched on a table opposite.

Before he could say more, a bell rang, and Jo flew up, exclaiming with alarm, "Mercy me! it's your grandpa!"

145

"Well, what if it is? You are not afraid of anything, you know," returned the boy, looking wicked.

"I think I am a little bit afraid of him, but I don't know why I should be. Marmee said I might come, and I don't think you're any the worse for it," said Jo, composing herself, though she kept her eyes on the door.

"I'm a great deal better for it, and ever so much obliged. I'm only afraid you are very tired talking to me; it was *so* pleasant, I couldn't bear to stop," said Laurie gratefully.

"The doctor to see you, sir," and the maid beckoned as she spoke.

"Would you mind if I left you for a minute? I suppose I must see him," said Laurie.

"Don't mind me. I'm as happy as a cricket here," answered Jo.

Laurie went away, and his guest amused herself in her own way. She was standing before a fine portrait of the old gentleman, when the door opened again, and, without turning, she said decidedly, "I'm sure now that I shouldn't be afraid of him, for he's got kind eyes, though his mouth is grim, and he looks as if he had a tremendous will of his own. He isn't as handsome as *my* grandfather, but I like him."

"Thank you, ma'am," said a gruff voice behind her; and there, to her great dismay, stood old Mr. Laurence.

Poor Jo blushed till she couldn't blush any redder, and her heart began to beat uncomfortably fast as she thought what she had said. For a minute a wild desire to run away possessed her; but that was cowardly, and the girls would laugh at her: so she resolved to stay, and get out of the scrape as she could. A second look showed her that the living eyes, under the bushy gray eyebrows, were kinder even than the painted ones; and there was a sly twinkle in them, which lessened her fear a good deal. The gruff voice was gruffer than ever, as the old gentleman said abruptly, after that dreadful pause, "So you're not afraid of me, hey?"

"Not much, sir."

"And you don't think me as handsome as your grandfather?"

"Not quite, sir."

"And I've got a tremendous will, have I?"

"I only said I thought so."

"But you like me, in spite of it?"

"Yes, I do, sir."

That answer pleased the old gentleman; he gave a short laugh, shook hands with her, and, putting his finger under her chin, turned up her face, examined it gravely, and let it go, saying, with a nod, "You've got your grandfather's spirit, if you haven't his face. He *was* a fine man, my dear; but, what is better, he was a brave and an honest one, and I was proud to be his friend."

"Thank you, sir"; and Jo was quite comfortable after that, for it suited her exactly.

"What have you been doing to this boy of mine, hey?" was the next question, sharply put.

"Only trying to be neighborly, sir"; and Jo told how her visit came about.

"You think he needs cheering up a bit, do you?"

"Yes, sir; he seems a little lonely, and young folks would do him good perhaps. We are only girls, but we should be glad to help if we could, for we don't forget the splendid Christmas present you sent us," said Jo eagerly.

"Tut, tut, tut! that was the boy's affair. How is the poor woman?"

"Doing nicely, sir"; and off went Jo, talking very fast, as she told all about the Hummels, in whom her mother had interested richer friends than they were.

"Just her father's way of doing good. I shall come and see your mother some fine day. Tell her so. There's the tea-bell; we have it early, on the boy's account. Come down, and go on being neighborly."

"If you'd like to have me, sir."

"Shouldn't ask you, if I didn't"; and Mr. Laurence offered her his arm with old-fashioned courtesy.

"What *would* Meg say to this?" thought Jo, as she was marched away, while her eyes danced with fun as she imagined herself telling the story at home.

"Hey! Why, what the dickens has come to the fellow?" said the old gentleman, as Laurie came running downstairs, and brought up with a start of surprise at the astonishing sight of Jo arm-in-arm with his redoubtable grandfather.

"I didn't know you'd come, sir," he began, as Jo gave him a triumphant little glance.

"That's evident, by the way you racket downstairs. Come to your tea, sir, and behave like a gentleman"; and having pulled the boy's hair by way of a caress, Mr. Laurence walked on, while Laurie went through a series of comic evolutions behind their backs, which nearly produced an exposion of laughter from Jo.

The old gentleman did not say much as he drank his four cups of tea, but he watched the young people, who soon chatted away like old friends, and the change in his grandson did not escape him. There was color, light, and life in the boy's face now, vivacity in his manner, and genuine merriment in his laugh.

"She's right; the lad is lonely. I'll see what these little girls can do for him," thought Mr. Laurence, as he looked and listened. He liked Jo, for her odd, blunt ways suited him; and she seemed to understand the boy almost as well as if she had been one herself.

If the Laurences had been what Jo called "prim and poky," she would not have got on at all, for such people always made her shy and awkward; but finding them free and easy, she was so herself, and made a good impression. When they rose she proposed to go, but Laurie said he had something more to show her, and took her away to the conservatory, which had been lighted for her benefit. It seemed quite fairylike to Jo, as she went up and down the walks, enjoying the blooming walls on either side, the soft light, the damp sweet air, and the wonderful vines and trees that hung above her,—while her new friend cut the finest flowers till his hands were full; then he tied them up, saying, with the happy look Jo liked to see, "Please give these to your mother and tell her I like the medicine she sent me very much."

They found Mr. Laurence standing before the fire in the

great drawing-room, but Jo's attention was entirely absorbed by a grand piano, which stood open.

"Do you play?" she asked, turning to Laurie with a respectful expression.

"Sometimes," he answered modestly.

"Please do now. I want to hear it, so I can tell Beth."

"Won't you first?"

"Don't know how; too stupid to learn, but I love music dearly."

So Laurie played, and Jo listened, with her nose luxuriously buried in heliotrope and tea roses. Her respect and regard for the "Laurence boy" increased very much, for he played remarkably well and didn't put on any airs. She wished Beth could hear him, but she did not say so; only praised him till he was quite abashed, and his grandfather came to the rescue. "That will do, that will do, young lady. Too many sugarplums are not good for him. His music isn't bad, but I hope he will do as well in more important things. Going? Well, I'm much obliged to you, and I hope you'll come again. My respects to your mother. Good night, Doctor Jo."

He shook hands kindly, but looked as if something did not please him. When they got into the hall, Jo asked Laurie if she had said anything amiss. He shook his head.

"No, it was me; he doesn't like to hear me play."

"Why not?"

"I'll tell you some day. John is going home with you, as I can't."

"No need of that; I am not a young lady, and it's only a step. Take care of yourself, won't you?"

"Yes; but you will come again, I hope?"

"If you promise to come and see us after you are well."

"I will."

"Good night, Laurie!"

"Good night, Jo, good night!"

When all the afternoon's adventures had been told, the family felt inclined to go visiting in a body, for each found something very attractive in the big house on the other side of the hedge. Mrs. March wanted to talk of her father with the old man who

had not forgotten him; Meg longed to walk in the conservatory; Beth sighed for the grand piano; and Amy was eager to see the fine pictures and statues.

"Mother, why didn't Mr. Laurence like to have Laurie play?" asked Jo, who was of an inquiring disposition.

"I am not sure, but I think it was because his son, Laurie's father, married an Italian lady, a musician, which displeased the old man, who is very proud. The lady was good and lovely and accomplished, but he did not like her and never saw his son after he married. They both died when Laurie was a little child, and then his grandfather took him home. I fancy the boy, who was born in Italy, is not very strong, and the old man is afraid of losing him, which makes him so careful. Laurie comes naturally by his love of music, for he is like his mother, and I dare say his grandfather fears that he may want to be a musician; at any rate, his skill reminds him of the woman he did not like, and so he 'glowered,' as Jo said."

"Dear me, how romantic!" exclaimed Meg.

"How silly!" said Jo. "Let him be a musician, if he wants to, and not plague his life out sending him to college."

"That's why he has such handsome black eyes and pretty manners, I suppose. Italians are always nice," said Meg, who was a little sentimental.

"What do you know about his eyes and his manners? You never spoke to him, hardly," cried Jo, who was *not* sentimental.

"I saw him at the party, and what you tell shows that he knows how to behave. That was a nice little speech about the medicine mother sent him."

"He meant the blancmange, I suppose."

"How stupid you are, child! He meant you, of course."

"Did he?" and Jo opened her eyes as if it had never occurred to her before.

"I never saw such a girl! You don't know a compliment when you get it," said Meg, with the air of a young lady who knew all about the matter.

"I think they are great nonsense, and I'll thank you not to be silly and spoil my fun. Laurie's a nice boy, and I like him, and I won't have any sentimental stuff about compliments and such rubbish. We'll all be good to him, because he hasn't got any mother, and he *may* come over, mayn't he, Marmee?"

"Yes, Jo, your friend is welcome, and I hope Meg will remember that children should be children as long as they can."

"I don't call myself a child, and I'm not in my teens yet," observed Amy. "What do you say, Beth?"

"I was thinking about our 'Pilgrim's Progress,'" answered Beth, who had not heard a word. "How we got out of the Slough and through the Wicket Gate by resolving to be good, and up the steep hill by trying; and that maybe the house over there, full of splendid things, is going to be our Palace Beautiful."

"We have got to get by the lions, first," said Jo, as if she rather liked the prospect.

Daniel Defoe

ROBINSON CRUSOE
IS SHIPWRECKED

ILLUSTRATED BY *E. A. Verpilleux*

OUR ship was about a hundred and twenty tons' burthen, carried six guns and fourteen men, besides the master, his boy, and myself. We had on board no large cargo of goods, except of such toys as were fit for our trade with the natives—such as beads, bits of glass, shells, and odd trifles, especially little looking glasses, knives, scissors, hatchets, and the like.

The same day I went on board we set sail, standing away to the northward upon our own coast, with design to stretch over for the African coast, when they came about ten or twelve degrees of northern latitude, which, it seems, was the manner of their course in those days. We had very good weather, only excessive hot, all the way upon our own coast, till we came the height of Cape St. Augustino, from whence, keeping farther off at sea, we lost sight of land, and steered as if we were bound for the Isle Fernando de Noronha, holding our course N. E. by N., and leaving those isles on the east. In this course we passed the line in about twelve days' time, and were, by our last observation, in 7° 22′ northern latitude, when a violent tornado, or hurricane, took us quite out of our knowledge. It began from the southeast, came about to the northwest, and then settled into the northeast, from whence it blew in such a terrible manner that for twelve days together we could do nothing but drive,

153

and, scudding away before it, let it carry us wherever fate and the fury of the winds directed. And during these twelve days, I need not say that I expected every day to be swallowed up, nor, indeed, did any in the ship expect to save their lives.

In this distress we had, besides the terror of the storm, one of our men died of fever, and one man and the boy washed overboard. About the twelfth day, the weather abating a little, the master made an observation, as well as he could, and found that he was in about eleven degrees north latitude, but that he was twenty-two degrees of longitude difference west from Cape St. Augustino. Thus he found he had gotten upon the coast of Guiana, or the north part of Brazil, beyond the river Amazon, toward that of the river Orinoco, commonly called the Great River, and began to consult with me what course he should take, for the ship was leaky and very much disabled, and he was going directly back to the coast of Brazil.

I was positively against that; and looking over the charts of the seacoast of America with him, we concluded there was no inhabited country for us to have recourse to till we came within the circle of the Caribbee Islands. Therefore we resolved to stand away for Barbados, which by keeping off at sea, to avoid the indraft of the Bay or Gulf of Mexico, we might easily perform, as we hoped, in about fifteen days' sail; whereas we could not possibly make our voyage to the coast of Africa without some assistance, both to our ship and to ourselves.

With this design we changed our course and steered away N. W. by W. in order to reach some of our English islands, where I hoped for relief. But our voyage was otherwise determined; for being in the latitude of 12° 18', a second storm came upon us, which carried us away with the same impetuosity westward, and drove us so out of the very way of all human commerce that had all our lives been saved as to the sea, we were rather in danger of being devoured by savages than ever returning to our own country.

In this distress, the wind still blowing very hard, one of our men early in the morning cried out, "Land!" and we had no sooner run out of the cabin to look out, in hopes of seeing whereabouts in the world we were, but the ship struck upon a sand, and in a moment, her motion being so stopped, the sea broke over her in such a manner that we expected we should all have perished immediately; and we were immediately driven into our close quarters, to shelter us from the very foam and spray of the sea.

It is not easy for anyone who has not been in the like condition to describe or conceive the consternation of men in such circumstances. We knew nothing where we were, or upon what land it was we were driven, whether an island or the main, whether inhabited or not inhabited; and as the rage of the wind was still great, though rather less than at first, we could not so much as hope to have the ship hold many minutes without breaking in pieces, unless the winds, by a kind of miracle, should turn immediately about. In a word, we sat looking one upon another, and expecting death every moment, and every man acting accordingly, as preparing for another world; for there was little or nothing more for us to do in this. That which was our present comfort, and all the comfort we had, was that, contrary to our expectation, the ship did not break yet, and that the master said the wind began to abate.

Now, though we thought that the wind did a little abate, yet the ship having thus struck upon the sand, and sticking too fast for us to expect her getting off, we were in a dreadful condition indeed, and had nothing to do but to think of saving our lives as well as we could. We had a boat at our stern just before the storm, but she was first staved by dashing against the ship's rudder, and in the next place she broke away, and either sunk or was driven off to sea. There was no hope from her. We had another boat on board, but how to get her off into the sea was a doubtful thing. However, there was no room to debate, for we fancied the ship would break in pieces every minute, and some told us she was actually broken already.

In this distress, the mate of our vessel laid hold of the boat, and with the help of the rest of the men they got her slung over the ship's side; and getting all into her, let go, and committed ourselves, being eleven in number, to God's mercy and the wild

155

sea. Though the storm was abated considerably, the sea went dreadful high upon the shore, and might well be called *den wild Zee*, as the Dutch call the sea in a storm.

And now our case was very dismal indeed, for we all saw plainly that the sea went so high that the boat could not live, and that we should be inevitably drowned. As to making sail, we had none; nor if we had, could we have done anything with it. So we worked at the oar towards the land, though with heavy hearts, like men going to execution, for we all knew that when the boat came nearer the shore, she would be dashed in a thousand pieces by the breach of the sea. However, we committed our souls to God in the most earnest manner; and the wind driving us towards the shore, we hastened our destruction with our own hands, pulling as well as we could towards land.

What the shore was, whether rock or sand, whether steep or shoal, we knew not. The only hope that could rationally give us the least shadow of expectation was, if we might happen into some bay or gulf, or the mouth of some river, where by great chance we might have run our boat in, or got under the lee of the land, and perhaps made smooth water. But there was nothing of this appeared; but as we made nearer and nearer the shore, the land looked more frightful than the sea.

After we had rowed, or rather driven, about a league and a half, as we reckoned it, a raging wave, mountain-like, came rolling astern of us, and plainly bade us expect the *coup de grâce*. In a word, it took us with such a fury that it overset the boat at once; and separating us, as well from the boat as from one another, gave us not time hardly to say, "O God!" for we were all swallowed up in a moment.

Nothing can describe the confusion of thought which I felt when I sunk into the water. Though I swam very well, yet I could not deliver myself from the waves so as to draw breath, till that wave having driven me, or rather carried me, a vast way on towards the shore, and having spent itself, went back, and left me upon the land almost dry, but half dead with the water I took in. I had so much presence of mind, as well as breath left, that seeing myself nearer the mainland than I ex-

pected, I got upon my feet and endeavored to make on towards the land as fast as I could, before another wave should return and take me up again. But I soon found it was impossible to avoid it; for I saw the sea come after me as high as a great hill, and as furious as an enemy, which I had no means or strength to contend with. My business was to hold my breath and raise myself upon the water, if I could; and so, by swimming, to preserve my breathing, and pilot myself towards the shore, if possible; my greatest concern now being that the sea, as it would carry me a great way towards the shore when it came on, might not carry me back again with it when it gave back towards the sea.

The wave that came upon me again buried me at once twenty or thirty feet deep in its own body, and I could feel myself carried with a mighty force and swiftness towards the shore a very great way; but I held my breath and assisted myself to swim still forward with all my might. I was ready to burst with holding my breath when, as I felt myself rising up, so, to my immediate relief, I found my head and hands shoot out above the surface of the water; and though it was not two seconds of time that I could keep myself so, yet it relieved me greatly, gave me breath and new courage. I was covered again with water a good while, but not so long but I held it out; and finding the water had spent itself, and began to return, I struck forward against the return of the waves, and felt ground again with my feet. I stood still a few moments to recover breath, and till the water went from me, and then took to my heels and ran with what strength I had farther towards the shore. But neither would this deliver me from the fury of the sea, which came pouring in after me again, and twice more I was lifted up by the waves and carried forwards as before, the shore being very flat.

The last time of these two had well near been fatal to me; for the sea, having hurried me along as before, landed me, or rather dashed me, against a piece of a rock, and that with such force as it left me senseless, and indeed helpless as to my own deliverance; for the blow taking my side and breast, beat the breath as it were quite out of my body; and had it returned again immediately, I must have been strangled in the water. But I recovered a little before the return of the waves, and seeing I should be covered again with the water, I resolved to hold fast by a piece of the rock, and so to hold my breath, if possible, till the wave went back. Now as the waves were not so high as at first, being near land, I held my hold till the wave abated and then fetched another run, which brought me so near the shore that the next wave, though it went over me, yet did not so swallow me up as to carry me away, and the next run I took I got to the mainland, where, to my great comfort, I clambered up the cliffs of the shore and sat me down upon the grass, free from danger and quite out of the reach of the water.

I was now landed, and safe on shore, and began to look up and thank God that my life was saved in a case wherein there was some minutes before scarce any room to hope. I believe it is impossible to express to the life what the ecstasies and transports of the soul are when it is so saved, as I may say, out of the very grave; and I do not wonder now at that custom, viz., that when a malefactor who has the halter about his neck, is tied up, and just going to be turned off, and has a reprieve brought to him—I say, I do not wonder that they bring a surgeon with it, to let him blood that very moment they tell him of it, that the surprise may not drive the animal spirits from the heart, and overwhelm him:—

"For sudden joys, like griefs, confound at first."

I walked about on the shore, lifting up my hands, and my whole being, as I may say, wrapt up in the contemplation of my deliverance, making a thousand gestures and motions which I cannot describe, reflecting upon all my comrades that were drowned, and that there should not be one soul saved but my-self; for, as for them, I never saw them afterwards, or any sign of them, except three of their hats, one cap, and two shoes that were not fellows

I cast my eyes to the stranded vessel, where the breach and froth of the sea being so big I could hardly see it, it lay so far off, and considered, Lord, how was it possible I could get on shore?

After I had solaced my mind with the comfortable part of my condition, I began to look round me to see what kind of place I was in, and what was next to be done, and I soon found my comforts abate, and that, in a word, I had a dreadful deliver-ance; for I was wet, had no clothes to shift me, nor anything either to eat or drink to comfort me, neither did I see any pros-pect before me but that of perishing with hunger or being de-voured by wild beasts; and that which was particularly afflicting to me was, that I had no weapon either to hunt and kill any creature for my sustenance or to defend myself against any other creatures that might desire to kill me for theirs. In a word, I had nothing about me but a knife, a tobacco-pipe, and a little tobacco in a box. This was all my provision; and this threw me into terrible agonies of mind, that for a while I ran about like a madman. Night coming upon me, I began, with a heavy heart, to consider what would be my lot if there were any ravenous beasts in that country, seeing at night they always come abroad for their prey.

All the remedy that offered to my thoughts at that time was, to get up into a thick bushy tree like a fir, but thorny, which grew near me, and where I resolved to sit all night, and consider the next day what death I should die, for as yet I saw no prospect of life. I walked about a furlong from the shore, to see if I could find any fresh water to drink, which I did, to my great joy; and having drunk, and put a little tobacco in my mouth to prevent hunger, I went to the tree, and getting up into it, endeavored to place myself so, as that if I should sleep I might not fall; and having cut me a short stick, like a truncheon for my defense, I took up my lodging, and having been excessively fatigued, I fell fast asleep, and slept as comfortably as, I believe, few could have done in my condition, and found myself the most refreshed with it that I think I ever was on such an occasion. . . .

When I waked it was broad day, the weather clear, and the storm abated, so that the sea did not rage and swell as before;

but that which surprised me most was, that the ship was lifted off in the night from the sand where she lay by the swelling of the tide, and was driven up almost as far as the rock which I first mentioned, where I had been so bruised by the dashing me against it. This being within about a mile from the shore where I was, and the ship seeming to stand upright still, I wished myself on board, that, at least, I might save some necessary things for my use.

When I came down from my apartment in the tree, I looked about me again, and the first thing I found was the boat, which lay as the wind and the sea had tossed her, up upon the land, about two miles on my right hand. I walked as far as I could upon the shore to have got to her, but found a neck or inlet of water between me and the boat, which was about half a mile broad; so I came back for the present, being more intent upon getting at the ship, where I hoped to find something for my present subsistence.

A little after noon I found the sea very calm, and the tide ebbed so far out that I could come within a quarter of a mile of the ship, and here I found a fresh renewing of my grief; for I saw evidently, that if we had kept on board, we had been all safe, that is to say, we had all got safe on shore, and I had not been so miserable as to be left entirely destitute of all comfort and company, as I now was. This forced tears from my eyes again, but as there was little relief in that, I resolved, if possible, to get to the ship, so I pulled off my clothes, for the weather was hot to extremity, and took the water; but when I came to the ship, my difficulty was still greater to know how to get on board, for as she lay aground, and high out of the water, there was nothing within my reach to lay hold of. I swam round her twice, and the second time I spied a small piece of rope, which I wondered I did not see at first, hang down by the fore-chains so low as that with great difficulty I got hold of it, and by the help of that rope got up into the forecastle of the ship. Here I found that the ship was bulged, and had a great deal of water in her hold, but that she lay so on the side of a bank of hard sand, or rather earth, that her stern lay lifted up upon the bank,

161

and her head low almost to the water. By this means all her quarter was free, and all that was in that part was dry; for you may be sure my first work was to search and to see what was spoiled and what was free; and first I found that all the ship's provisions were dry and untouched by the water; and being very well disposed to eat, I went to the breadroom and filled my pockets with biscuit, and eat it as I went about other things, for I had no time to lose. I also found some rum in the great cabin, of which I took a large dram, and which I had indeed need enough of to spirit me for what was before me. Now I wanted nothing but a boat to furnish myself with many things which I foresaw would be very necessary to me.

It was in vain to sit still and wish for what was not to be had, and this extremity roused my application. We had several spare yards, and two or three large spars of wood, and a spare topmast or two in the ship. I resolved to fall to work with these, and flung as many of them overboard as I could manage for their weight, tying every one with a rope that they might not drive away; when this was done I went down the ship's side, and pulling them to me, I tied four of them fast together at both ends, as well as I could, in the form of a raft, and laying two or three short pieces of plank upon them crossways, I found I could walk upon it very well, but that it was not able to bear any great weight, the pieces being too light; so I went to work, and with the carpenter's saw I cut a spare topmast into three lengths, and added them to my raft, with a great deal of labor and pains: but hope of furnishing myself with necessaries encouraged me to go beyond what I should have been able to have done upon another occasion.

My raft was now strong enough to bear any reasonable weight; my next care was what to load it with, and how to preserve what I laid upon it from the surf of the sea; but I was not long considering this. I first laid all the planks or boards upon it that I could get, and having considered well what I most wanted, I first got three of the seamen's chests, which I had broken open and emptied, and lowered them down upon my raft. The first of these I filled with provisions, namely, bread,

162

rice, three Dutch cheeses, five pieces of dried goat's flesh, which we lived much upon, and a little remainder of European corn which had been laid by for some fowls which we brought to sea with us, but the fowls were killed. There had been some barley and wheat together; but, to my great disappointment, I found afterwards that the rats had eaten or spoiled it all. As for liquors, I found several cases of bottles belonging to our skipper, in which were some cordial waters, and in all about five or six gallons of rack; these I stowed by themselves, there being no need to put them into the chest, nor no room for them. While I was doing this, I found the tide began to flow, though very calm; and I had the mortification to see my coat, shirt, and waistcoat which I had left on shore, upon the sand, swim away; as for my breeches, which were only linen and open-kneed, I swam on board in them and my stockings. However, this put me upon rummaging for clothes, of which I found enough, but took no more than I wanted for present use; for I had other things which my eye was more upon—as, first, tools to work with on shore; and it was after long searching that I found out the carpenter's chest, which was indeed a very useful prize to me, and much more valuable than a ship-loading of gold would have been at that time. I got it down to my raft, even whole as it was, without losing time to look into it, for I knew in general what it contained.

My next care was for some ammunition and arms. There were two very good fowling pieces in the great cabin, and two pistols; these I secured first, with some powder horns, and a small bag of shot, and two old rusty swords. I knew there were three barrels of powder in the ship, but knew not where our gunner had stowed them; but with much search I found them, two of them dry and good, the third had taken water. Those two I got to my raft, with the arms; and now I thought myself pretty well freighted, and began to think how I should get to shore with them, having neither sail, oar, nor rudder, and the least capful of wind would have overset all my navigation.

I had three encouragements: a smooth, calm sea, the tide rising and setting into the shore, and what little wind there was blew me towards the land; and thus, having found two or three broken oars belonging to the boat, and besides the tools which were in the chest, I found two saws, an axe and a hammer, and with this cargo I put to sea. For a mile, or thereabouts, my raft went very well, only that I found it drive a little distant from the place where I had landed before, by which I perceived that there was some indraft of the water, and consequently I earnestly hoped to find some creek or river there, which I might make use of as a port to get to land with my cargo.

As I imagined, so it was. There appeared before me a little opening of the land, and I found a strong current of the tide set into it, so I guided my raft as well as I could to keep in the middle of the stream; but here I had like to have suffered a second shipwreck, which, if I had, I think verily would have broke my heart; for knowing nothing of the coast, my raft ran aground at one end of it upon a shoal, and not being aground at the other end, it wanted but a little that all my cargo had slipped off towards that end that was afloat, and so fallen into the water. I did my utmost, by setting my back against the chests, to keep them in their places, but could not thrust off the raft with all my strength; neither durst I stir from the posture I was in; but holding up the chests with all my might, stood in that manner near half an hour, in which time the rising of the water brought me a little more upon a level; and a little after, the water still rising, my raft floated again, and I thrust her off with the oar I had into the channel; and then driving up higher, I at length found myself in the mouth of a little river, with land on both sides, and a strong current or tide running up. I looked on both sides for a proper place to get to shore, for I was not willing to be driven too high up the river, hoping in time to see some ship at sea, and therefore resolved to place myself as near the coast as I could.

At length I spied a little cove on the right shore of the creek, to which, with great pain and difficulty, I guided my raft, and at last got so near, as that, reaching ground with my oar, I could thrust her directly in. But here I had liked to have dipped all my cargo into the sea again: for that shore lying pretty steep,

that is to say sloping, there was no place to land, but where one end of the float, if it ran on shore, would lie so high, and the other sink lower as before, that it would endanger my cargo again. All that I could do, was to wait till the tide was at the highest, keeping the raft with my oar like an anchor to hold the side of it fast to the shore, near a flat piece of ground, which I expected the water would flow over; and so it did. As soon as I found water enough (for my raft drew about a foot of water), I thrust her on upon that flat piece of ground, and there fastened or moored her by sticking my two broken oars into the ground; one on one side near one end, and one on the other side near the other end; and thus I lay till the water ebbed away and left my raft and all my cargo safe on shore.

My next work was to view the country, and seek a proper place for my habitation, and where to stow my goods to secure them from whatever might happen. Where I was I yet knew not; whether on the continent or on an island, whether inhabited or not inhabited, whether in danger of wild beasts or not. There was a hill not above a mile from me, which rose up very steep and high, and which seemed to overtop some other hills which lay as in a ridge from it northward. I took out one of the fowling pieces, and one of the pistols, and an horn of powder, and thus armed, I traveled for discovery up to the top of that hill; where, after I had with great labor and difficulty got to the top, I saw my fate to my great affliction, namely, that I was in an island environed every way with the sea, no land to be seen, except some rocks which lay a great way off, and two small islands less than this, which lay about three leagues to the west.

I found also that the island I was in was barren, and, as I saw good reason to believe, uninhabited, except by wild beasts, of whom however I saw none; yet I saw abundance of fowls, but knew not their kinds, neither when I killed them could I tell what was fit for food, and what not. At my coming back, I shot at a great bird, which I saw sitting upon a tree on the side of a great wood—I believe it was the first gun that had been fired there since the creation of the world. I had no sooner fired, when from all parts of the wood there arose an innumerable number of fowls of many sorts, making a confused screaming, and crying every one according to his usual note; but not one of them of any kind that I knew. As for the creature I killed, I took it to be a kind of hawk, its color and beak resembling it, but had no talons or claws more than common; its flesh was carrion and fit for nothing.

Contented with this discovery, I came back to my raft, and fell to work to bring my cargo on shore, which took me up the rest of that day; and what to do with myself at night, I knew not, nor indeed where to rest; for I was afraid to lie down on the ground, not knowing but some wild beast might devour me, though, as I afterwards found, there was really no need for those fears.

However, as well as I could, I barricaded myself round with the chests and boards that I had brought on shore, and made a kind of a hut for that night's lodging. As for food, I yet saw not which way to supply myself, except that I had seen two or three creatures, like hares, run out of the wood where I shot the bird.

I now began to consider that I might yet get a great many things out of the ship which would be useful to me, and particularly some of the rigging and sails, and such other things as might come to land; and I resolved to make another voyage on board the vessel, if possible. And as I knew that the first storm that blew must necessarily break her all in pieces, I resolved to set all other things apart till I got everything out of the ship that I could get. Then I called a council, that is to say, in my thoughts, whether I should take back the raft, but this appeared impracticable; so I resolved to go as before, when the tide was down; and I did so, only that I stripped before I went from my hut, having nothing on but a chequered shirt and a pair of linen drawers, and a pair of pumps on my feet.

I got on board the ship as before and prepared a second raft, and having had experience of the first, I neither made this so unwieldy, nor loaded it so hard; but yet I brought away several things very useful to me; as, first, in the carpenter's stores I found two or three bags full of nails and spikes, a great screw jack, a dozen or two of hatchets, and, above all, that most useful thing called a grindstone. All these I secured, together with several things belonging to the gunner, particularly two or three iron crows, and two barrels of musket bullets, seven muskets, and another fowling piece, with some small quantity of powder more; a large bag full of smallshot, and a great roll of sheet lead; but this last was so heavy I could not hoist it up to get it over the ship's side. Besides these things, I took all the men's clothes that I could find, and a spare foretop sail, a hammock, and some bedding; and with this I loaded my second raft, and brought them all safe on shore, to my very great comfort.

I was under some apprehensions during my absence from the land that at least my provisions might be devoured on shore; but when I came back, I found no sign of any visitor, only there sat a creature like a wildcat upon one of the chests, which, when I came towards it, ran away a little distance, and then stood still. She sat very composed and unconcerned, and looked full in my face, as if she had a mind to be acquainted with me. I presented my gun at her; but as she did not understand it, she was per-

167

fectly unconcerned at it, nor did she offer to stir away; upon which I tossed her a bit of biscuit, though, by the way, I was not very free of it, for my store was not great. However, I spared her a bit, I say, and she went to it, smelled of it, and ate it, and looked (as pleased) for more; but I thanked her, and could spare no more, so she marched off.

Having got my second cargo on shore, though I was fain to open the barrels of powder and bring them by parcels, for they were too heavy, being large casks, I went to work to make me a little tent with the sail and some poles which I cut for that purpose; and into this tent I brought everything that I knew would spoil either with rain or sun; and I piled all the empty chests and casks up in a circle round the tent, to fortify it from any sudden attempt, either from man or beast.

When I had done this I blocked up the door of the tent with some boards within, and an empty chest set up on end without; and spreading one of the beds upon the ground, laying my two pistols just at my head, and my gun at length by me, I went to bed for the first time, and slept very quietly all night, for I was very weary and heavy; for the night before I had slept little, and had labored very hard all day, as well to fetch all those things from the ship, as to get them on shore.

I had the biggest magazine of all kinds now that ever was laid up, I believe, for one man; but I was not satisfied still, for while the ship sat upright in that posture, I thought I ought to get everything out of her that I could. So every day at low water I went on board and brought away something or other; but, particularly, the third time I went I brought away as much of the rigging as I could, as also all the small ropes and rope-twine I could get, with a piece of spare canvas, which was to mend the sails upon occasion, and the barrel of wet gunpowder; in a word, I brought away all the sails first and last, only that I was fain to cut them in pieces, and bring as much at a time as I could; for they were no more useful to be sails, but as mere canvas only.

But that which comforted me more still was that, at last of all, after I had made five or six such voyages as these, and thought

168

I had nothing more to expect from the ship that was worth my meddling with,—I say, after all this, I found a great hogshead of bread, and three large runlets of rum or spirits, and a box of sugar, and a barrel of fine flour; this was surprising to me, because I had given over expecting any more provisions, except what was spoilt by the water. I soon emptied the hogshead of that bread, and wrapped it up parcel by parcel in pieces of the sails, which I cut out; and, in a word, I got all this safe on shore also.

The next day I made another voyage. And now, having plundered the ship of what was portable and fit to hand out, I began with the cables; and cutting the great cable into pieces, such as I could move, I got two cables and a hawser on shore, with all the iron-work I could get; and having cut down the sprit-sail yard, and the mizzon yard, and everything I could to make a large raft, I loaded it with all those heavy goods, and came away. But my good luck began now to leave me; for this raft was so unwieldy, and so overladen, that after I was entered the little cove where I had landed the rest of my goods, not being able to guide it so handily as I did the other, it overset, and threw me and all my cargo into the water. As for myself, it was no great harm, for I was near the shore; but as to my cargo, a great part of it was lost, especially the iron, which I expected would have been of great use to me. However, when the tide was out I got most of the pieces of cable ashore, and some of the iron, though with infinite labor; for I was fain to dip for it into the water, a work which fatigued me very much. After this I went every day on board and brought away what I could get.

I had been now thirteen days on shore and had been eleven times on board the ship; in which time I had brought away all that one pair of hands could well be supposed capable to bring, though I believe verily, had the calm weather held, I should have brought away the whole ship piece by piece. But preparing the twelfth time to go on board, I found the wind begin to rise. However, at low water I went on board, and though I thought I had rummaged the cabin so effectually so that nothing more could be found, yet I discovered a locker with drawers

169

in it, in one of which I found two or three razors, and one pair of large scissors, with some ten or a dozen of good knives and forks; in another, I found about thirty-six pounds value in money, some European coin, some Brazil, some pieces of eight, some gold, some silver.

I smiled to myself at the sight of this money. "O drug!" said I aloud, "what art thou good for? Thou art not worth to me, no, not the taking off of the ground; one of those knives is worth all this heap. I have no manner of use for thee; even remain where thou art, and go to the bottom as a creature whose life is not worth saving." However, upon second thought I took it away; and wrapping all this in a piece of canvas, I began to think of making another raft; but while I was preparing this, I found the sky overcast, and the wind began to rise, and in a quarter of an hour it blew a fresh gale from the shore. It presently occurred to me that it was in vain to pretend to make a raft with the wind off shore, and that it was my business to be gone before the tide of flood began, otherwise I might not be able to reach the shore at all. Accordingly I let myself down into the water, and swam across the channel, which lay between the ship and the sands, and even that with difficulty enough, partly with the weight of the things I had about me, and partly the roughness of the water; for the wind rose very hastily, and before it was quite high water it blew a storm.

But I was gotten home to my little tent, where I lay with all my wealth about me very secure. It blew very hard all that night, and in the morning when I looked out, behold, no more ship was to be seen. I was a little surprised, but recovered myself with this satisfactory reflection, that I had lost no time, nor abated no diligence, to get everything out of her that could be useful to me, and that indeed there was little left in her that I was able to bring away if I had had more time.

I now gave over any more thoughts of the ship, or of anything out of her, except what might drive on shore from her wreck, as indeed divers pieces of her afterwards did; but those things were of small use to me.

My thoughts were now wholly employed about securing myself against either savages, if any should appear, or wild beasts, if any were in the island; and I had many thoughts of the method how to do this, and what kind of dwelling to make, whether I should make me a cave in the earth, or a tent upon the earth; and, in short, I resolved upon both, the manner and description of which it may not be improper to give an account of.

I soon found the place I was in was not for my settlement, particularly because it was upon a low moorish ground near the sea, and I believed would not be wholesome; and more particularly because there was no fresh water near it. So I resolved to find a more healthy and more convenient spot of ground.

I consulted several things in my situation, which I found would be proper for me. First, health and fresh water, I just now mentioned. Secondly, shelter from the heat of the sun. Thirdly, security from ravenous creatures, whether men or beasts. Fourthly, a view to the sea, that if God sent any ship in sight I might not lose any advantage for my deliverance, of which I was not to banish all my expectation yet.

In search of a place proper for this, I found a little plain on the side of a rising hill, whose front towards this little plain was steep as a houseside, so that nothing could come down upon me from the top. On the side of this rock there was a hollow place, worn a little way in, like the entrance or door of a cave; but there was not really any cave, or way into the rock at all.

On the flat of the green, just before this hollow place, I resolved to pitch my tent. This plain was not above a hundred yards broad, and about twice as long, and lay like a green before my door, and at the end of it descended irregularly every way down into the low grounds by the seaside. It was on the N. N. W. side of the hill, so that I was sheltered from the heat every day, till it came to a W. and by S. sun, or thereabouts, which in those countries is near the setting.

Before I set up my tent, I drew a half-circle before the hollow place, which took in about ten yards in its semi-diameter from the rock, and twenty yards in its diameter from its beginning and ending. In this half-circle I pitched two rows of strong

171

stakes, driving them into the ground till they stood very firm like piles, the biggest end being out of the ground about five feet and a half and sharpened on the top. The two rows did not stand above six inches from one another.

Then I took the pieces of cable which I had cut in the ship, and laid them in rows one upon another, within the circle, between these two rows of stakes, up to the top, placing other stakes in the inside leaning against them, about two feet and a half high, like a spur to a post; and this fence was so strong that neither man nor beast could get into it, or over it. This cost me a great deal of time and labor, especially to cut the piles in the woods, bring them to the place, and drive them into the earth.

The entrance into this place I made to be not by a door, but by a short ladder to go over the top; which ladder, when I was in, I lifted over after me, and so I was completely fenced in, and fortified, as I thought, from all the world, and consequently slept secure in the night, which otherwise I could not have done;

172

though, as it appeared afterward, there was no need of all this caution from the enemies that I apprehended danger from.

Into this fence or fortress, with infinite labor, I carried all my riches, all my provisions, ammunition, and stores, of which you have the account above; and I made me a large tent, which, to preserve me from the rains that in one part of the year are very violent there, I made double, one smaller tent within, and one larger tent above it, and covered the uppermost with a large tarpaulin, which I had saved among the sails. And now I lay no more for a while in the bed which I had brought on shore, but in a hammock, which was indeed a very good one, and belonged to the mate of the ship.

Into this tent I brought all my provisions, and everything that would spoil by the wet; and having thus enclosed all my goods, I made up the entrance, which, till now, I had left open, and so passed and repassed, as I said, by a short ladder.

When I had done this, I began to work my way into the rock; and bringing all the earth and stones that I dug down out through my tent, I laid them up within my fence in the nature of a terrace, so that it raised the ground within about a foot and a half; and thus I made me a cave just behind my tent which served me like a cellar to my house.

It cost me much labor and many days before all these things were brought to perfection, and therefore I must go back to some other things which took up some of my thoughts. At the same time it happened, after I had laid my scheme for the setting up my tent and making the cave, that a storm of rain falling from a thick dark cloud, a sudden flash of lightning happened, and after that a great clap of thunder, as is naturally the effect of it. I was not so much surprised with the lightning as I was with a thought which darted into my mind as swift as the lightning itself. Oh, my powder! My very heart sunk within me when I thought, that at one blast all my powder might be destroyed, on which, not my defense only, but the providing me food, as I thought, entirely depended. I was nothing near so anxious about my own danger; though had the powder taken fire, I had never known who had hurt me.

173

Such impression did this make upon me that after the storm was over I laid aside all my works, my building and fortifying, and applied myself to make bags and boxes to separate the powder, and keep it a little and a little in a parcel, in hope that whatever might come it might not all take fire at once, and to keep it so apart that it should not be possible to make one part fire another. I finished this work in about a fortnight; and I think my powder, which in all was about 240 pounds' weight, was divided in not less than a hundred parcels. As to the barrel that had been wet, I did not apprehend any danger from that, so I placed it in my new cave, which in my fancy I called my kitchen, and the rest I hid up and down in holes among the rocks, so that no wet might come to it, marking very carefully where I laid it.

In the interval of time while this was doing, I went out once, at least, every day with my gun, as well to divert myself as to see if I could kill anything fit for food, and as near as I could to acquaint myself with what the island produced. The first time I went out, I presently discovered that there were goats in the island, which was a great satisfaction to me; but then it was attended with this misfortune to me, that they were so shy, so subtle, and so swift of foot that it was the difficultest thing in the world to come at them. But I was not discouraged at this, not doubting but I might now and then shoot one, as it soon happened; for after I had found their haunts a little, I laid wait in this manner for them. I observed if they saw me in the valleys, though they were upon the rocks, they would run away as in a terrible fright; but if they were feeding in the valleys, and I was upon the rocks, they took no notice of me, from whence I concluded that, by the position of their optics, their sight was so directed downward that they did not readily see objects that were above them. So afterward I took this method: I always climbed the rocks first to get above them, and then had frequently a fair mark. The first shot I made among these creatures I killed a she-goat, which had a little kid by her, which she gave suck to, which grieved me heartily; but when the old one fell, the kid stood stock still by her till I came and took her up; and

174

not only so, but when I carried the old one with me upon my shoulders, the kid followed me quite to my enclosure; upon which I laid down the dam, and took the kid in my arms, and carried it over my pale, in hopes to have bred it up tame; but it would not eat, so I was forced to kill it, and eat it myself. These two supplied me with flesh a great while, for I eat sparingly, and saved my provisions, my bread especially, as much as possibly I could.

Having now fixed my habitation, I found it absolutely necessary to provide a place to make a fire in and fuel to burn; and what I did for that, as also how I enlarged my cave, and what conveniences I made, I shall give a full account of in its place. But I must first give some little account of myself, and of my thoughts about living, which it may well be supposed were not a few.

I had a dismal prospect of my condition; for as I was not cast away upon that island without being driven, as is said, by a violent storm, quite out of the course of our intended voyage, and a great way, some hundreds of leagues, out of the ordinary course of the trade of mankind, I had great reason to consider it as a determination of Heaven that in this desolate place, and in this desolate manner, I should end my life. The tears would run plentifully down my face when I made these reflections, and sometimes I would expostulate with myself, why Providence should thus completely ruin its creatures, and render them so absolutely miserable, so without help, abandoned, so entirely depressed, that it could hardly be rational to be thankful for such a life.

But something always returned swift upon me to check these thoughts and to reprove me; and particularly one day, walking with my gun in my hand by the seaside, I was very pensive upon the subject of my present condition, when Reason, as it were, expostulated with me t' other way, thus: "Well, you are in a desolate condition, it is true, but pray remember, where are the rest of you? Did not you come eleven of you into the boat? Where are the ten? Why were not they saved, and you lost? Why were you singled out? Is it better to be here, or there?"

And then I pointed to the sea. All evils are to be considered with the good that is in them, and with what worse attends them.

Then it occurred to me again, how well I was furnished for my subsistence, and what would have been my case if it had not happened, which was an hundred thousand to one, that the ship floated from the place where she first struck and was driven so near to the shore that I had time to get all these things out of her; what would have been my case, if I had been to have lived in the condition in which I at first came on shore, without necessaries of life, or necessaries to supply and procure them? "Particularly," said I aloud (though to myself), "what should I have done without a gun, without ammunition, without any tools to make anything or to work with, without clothes, bedding, a tent, or any manner of covering?" and that now I had all these to a sufficient quantity, and was in a fair way to provide myself in such a manner, as to live without my gun when my ammunition was spent; so that I had a tolerable view of subsisting without any want as long as I lived. For I considered from the beginning how I would provide for the accidents that might happen, and for the time that was to come, even not only after my ammunition should be spent, but even after my health or strength should decay.

I confess I had not entertained any notion of my ammunition being destroyed at one blast—I mean, my powder being blown up by lightning; and this made the thoughts of it so surprising to me when it lightened and thundered, as I observed just now.

You may be sure my thoughts ran many times upon the prospect of land which I had seen from the other side of the island, and I was not without secret wishes that I were on shore there, fancying that seeing the mainland, and in an inhabited country, I might find some way or other to convey myself farther, and perhaps at last find some means of escape.

But all this while I made no allowance for the dangers of such a condition, and how I might fall into the hands of savages, and perhaps such as I might have reason to think far worse than the lions and tigers of Africa; that if I once came into their power, I should run a hazard more than a thousand to one of being killed, and perhaps of being eaten; for I had heard that the people of the Caribbean coasts were cannibals, or man-eaters, and I knew by the latitude that I could not be far off from that shore. That suppose they were not cannibals, yet that they might kill me, as many Europeans who had fallen into their hands had been served, even when they had been ten or twenty together, much more I, that was but one, and could make little or no defense,—all these things, I say, which I ought to have considered well of, and did cast up in my thoughts afterwards, yet took up none of my apprehensions at first, but my head ran mightily upon the thought of getting over to the shore.

Now I wished for my boy Xury, and the longboat with the shoulder-of-mutton sail, with which I sailed above a thousand miles on the coast of Africa; but this was in vain. Then I thought I would go and look at our ship's boat, which, as I have said, was blown up upon the shore a great way, in the storm, when we were first cast away. She lay almost where she did at first, but not quite; and was turned, by the force of the waves and the winds, almost bottom upwards, against a high ridge of beachy rough sand, but no water about her, as before.

If I had had hands to have refitted her, and to have launched her into the water, the boat would have done well enough, and I might have gone back into the Brazils with her easily enough; but I might have foreseen that I could no more turn her, and set her upright upon her bottom, than I could remove the island. However, I went to the woods, and cut levers and rollers, and brought them to the boat, resolved to try what I could do; suggesting to myself that if I could but turn her down, I might easily repair the damage she had received, and she would be a very good boat, and I might go to sea in her very easily.

I spared no pains, indeed, in this piece of fruitless toil, and spent, I think, three or four weeks about it. At last, finding it impossible to heave it up with my little strength, I fell to digging away the sand, to undermine it, and so to make it fall down, setting pieces of wood to thrust and guide it right in the fall. But when I had done this, I was unable to stir it up again, or to get under it, much less to move it forward towards the

177

water; so I was forced to give it over. And yet, though I gave over the hopes of the boat, my desire to venture over for the main increased, rather than decreased, as the means for it seemed impossible.

This at length put me upon thinking whether it was not possible to make myself a canoe, or *periagua*, such as the natives of those climates make, even without tools, or, as I might say, without hands, of the trunk of a great tree. This I not only thought possible, but easy, and pleased myself extremely with the thoughts of making it, and with my having much more convenience for it than any of the natives; but not at all considering the particular inconveniences which I lay under more than the Indians did, want of hands to move it, when it was made, into the water, a difficulty much harder for me to surmount than all the consequences of want of tools could be to them. For what was it to me, that when I had chosen a vast tree in the woods, I might with much trouble cut it down, if, after I might be able with my tools to hew and dub the outside into the proper shape of a boat, and burn or cut out the inside to make it hollow, so to make a boat of it; if, after all this, I must leave it just there where I found it, and was not able to launch it into the water?

One would have thought I could not have had the least reflection upon my mind of my circumstance while I was making this boat, but I should have immediately thought how I should get it into the sea; but my thoughts were so intent upon my voyage over the sea in it that I never once considered how I should get it off of the land; and it was really, in its own nature, more easy for me to guide it over forty-five miles of sea than about forty-five fathoms of land, where it lay, to set it afloat in the water.

I went to work upon this boat the most like a fool that ever man did who had any of his senses awake. I pleased myself with the design, without determining whether I was ever able to undertake it. Not but that the difficulty of launching my boat came often into my head; but I put a stop to my own inquiries into it by this foolish answer which I gave myself: "Let's

first make it; I 'll warrant I 'll find some way or other to get it along when 't is done."

This was a most preposterous method; but the eagerness of my fancy prevailed, and to work I went. I felled a cedar tree: I question much whether Solomon ever had such a one for the building of the Temple at Jerusalem. It was five feet ten inches diameter at the lower part next the stump, and four feet eleven inches diameter at the end of twenty-two feet, after which it lessened for a while, and then parted into branches. It was not without infinite labor that I felled this tree. I was twenty days hacking and hewing at it at the bottom; I was fourteen more getting the branches and limbs, and the vast spreading head of it cut off, which I hacked and hewed through with axe and hatchet, and inexpressible labor. After this, it cost me a month to shape it and dub it to a proportion, and to something like

179

the bottom of a boat, that it might swim upright as it ought to do. It cost me near three months more to clear the inside, and work it so as to make an exact boat of it. This I did, indeed, without fire, by mere mallet and chisel, and by the dint of hard labor, till I had brought it to be a very handsome *periagua*, and big enough to have carried six and twenty men, and consequently big enough to have carried me and all my cargo.

When I had gone through this work, I was extremely delighted with it. The boat was really much bigger than I ever saw a canoe or *periagua* that was made of one tree, in my life. Many a weary stroke it had cost, you may be sure; and there remained nothing but to get it into the water; and had I gotten it into the water, I make no question but I should have begun the maddest voyage, and the most unlikely to be performed, that ever was undertaken.

But all my devices to get it into the water failed me, though they cost me infinite labor too. It lay about one hundred yards from the water, and not more; but the first inconvenience was, it was uphill towards the creek. Well, to take away this discouragement, I resolved to dig into the surface of the earth, and so make a declivity. This I began, and it cost me a prodigious deal of pains; but who grudges pains that have their deliverance in view? But when this was worked through, and this difficulty managed, it was still much at one, for I could no more stir the canoe than I could the other boat.

Then I measured the distance of ground and resolved to cut a dock or canal, to bring the water up to the canoe, seeing I could not bring the canoe down to the water. Well, I began this work; and when I began to enter into it, and calculate how deep it was to be dug, how broad, how the stuff to be thrown out, I found that by the number of hands I had, being none but my own, it must have been ten or twelve years before I should have gone through with it; for the shore lay high, so that at the upper end it must have been at least twenty feet deep; so at length, though with great reluctancy, I gave this attempt over also.

This grieved me heartily; and now I saw, though too late, the folly of beginning a work before we count the cost and before we judge rightly of our own strength to go through with it.

I was somewhat impatient to have the use of my boat; and therefore sometimes I sat contriving ways to get her about the island, and at other times I sat myself down contented enough without her. But I had a strange uneasiness in my mind to go down to the point of the island where I went up the hill to see how the shore lay, and how the current set, that I might see what I had to do. This inclination increased upon me every day, and, at length, I resolved to travel thither by land, following the edge of the shore. I did so; but had anyone in England been to meet such a man as I was, it must either have frighted him or raised a great deal of laughter; and as I frequently stood still to look at myself, I could not but smile at the notion of my traveling through Yorkshire, with such an equipage, and in such a dress.

I had a great high shapeless cap, made of a goatskin, with a flap hanging down behind, as well to keep the sun from me, as to shoot the rain off from running into my neck, nothing being so hurtful in these climates as the rain upon the flesh, under the clothes.

I had a short jacket of goatskin, the skirts coming down to about the middle of my thighs; and a pair of open-kneed breeches of the same. The breeches were made of the skin of an old he-goat, whose hair hung down such a length on either side, that, like pantaloons, it reached to the middle of my legs. Stockings and shoes I had none, but had made me a pair of some-things, I scarce know what to call them, like buskins, to flap over my legs, and lace on either side like spatterdashes; but of a most barbarous shape, as indeed were all the rest of my clothes.

I had on a broad belt of goatskin dried, which I drew together with two thongs of the same, instead of buckles; and in a kind of frog on either side of this, instead of a sword and a dagger, hung a little saw and a hatchet, one on one side, one on the other. I had another belt, not so broad, and fastened in the same manner, which hung over my shoulder; and at the end of

181

it, under my left arm, hung two pouches, both made of goat-skin, too; in one of which hung my powder, in the other my shot. At my back I carried my basket, on my shoulder my gun, and over my head a great clumsy, ugly goatskin umbrella, but which, after all, was the most necessary thing I had about me, next to my gun. As for my face, the color of it was really not so mulatto-like as one might expect from a man not at all careful of it, and living within nineteen degrees of the equinox. My beard I had once suffered to grow till it was about a quarter of a yard long; but as I had both scissors and razors sufficient, I had cut it pretty short, except what grew on my upper lip, which I had trimmed into a large pair of Mahometan whiskers such as I had seen worn by some Turks whom I saw at Sallee; for the Moors did not wear such, though the Turks did. Of these mustachios or whiskers, I will not say they were long enough to hang my hat upon them, but they were of a length and shape monstrous enough, and such as, in England, would have passed for frightful.

But all this is by the bye; for as to my figure I had so few to observe me that it was of no manner of consequence; so I say no more to that part. In this kind of figure I went my journey, and was out five or six days. I was surprised to see the sea all smooth and quiet, no rippling, no motion, no current, any more there than in other places.

I was at a strange loss to understand this, and resolved to spend some time in the observing of it, to see if nothing from the sets of the tide had occasioned it. But I was presently convinced how it was, that the tide of ebb setting from the west, and join-ing with the current of waters from some great river on the shore, must be the occasion of this current; and that according as the wind blew more forcibly from the west, or from the north, this current came near, or went farther from the shore; for waiting thereabouts till evening, I went up to the rock again, and then the tide of ebb being made, I plainly saw the current again as before, only that it ran farther off, being near half a league from the shore.

I took up a resolution, and this was, that I would build, or

182

rather make me another *periagua*, or canoe, and so have one for one side of the island, and one for the other.

You are to understand that now I had, as I may call it, two plantations in the island; one, my little fortification or tent, with the wall about it, under the rock, with the cave behind me, which, by this time, I had enlarged into several apartments or caves, one within another. One of these, which was the driest and largest, and had a door out beyond my wall or fortification, that is to say, beyond where my wall joined to the rock, was all filled up with the large earthen pots, and with fourteen or fifteen great baskets, which would hold five or six bushels each, where I laid up my stores of provision, especially my corn, some in the ear, cut off short from the straw, and the other rubbed out with my hand.

As for my wall, made, as before, with long stakes or piles, those piles grew all like trees, and were by this time grown so big, and spread so very much, that there was not the least appearance, to anyone's view, of any habitation behind them.

Near this dwelling of mine, but a little farther within the land, and upon lower ground, lay my two pieces of corn ground, which I kept duly cultivated and sowed, and which duly yielded me their harvest in its season; and whenever I had occasion for more corn, I had more land adjoining as fit as that.

Besides this, I had my country seat, and I had now a tolerable plantation there also; for, first, I had my little bower, as I called it, which I kept in repair; that is to say, I kept the hedge which circled it in constantly fitted up to its usual height, the ladder standing always in the inside. I kept the trees, which at first were no more than my stakes, but were now grown very firm and tall,—I kept them always so cut that they might spread and grow thick and wild, and make the more agreeable shade, which they did effectually to my mind. In the middle of this, I had my tent always standing, being a piece of a sail spread over poles, set up for that purpose, and which never wanted any repair or renewing; and under this I had made me a squab or couch, with the skins of the creatures I had killed, and with other soft things, and a blanket laid on them, such as belonged

183

to our sea-bedding, which I had saved, and a great watchcoat to cover me; and here, whenever I had occasion to be absent from my chief seat, I took up my country habitation.

Adjoining to this I had my enclosures for my cattle, that is to say, my goats. And as I had taken an inconceivable deal of pains to fence and enclose this ground, I was so uneasy to see it kept entire, lest the goats should break through, that I never left off till, with infinite labor, I had stuck the outside of the hedge so full of small stakes, and so near to one another, that it was rather a pale than a hedge, and there was scarce room to put a hand through between them; which afterwards, when those stakes grew, as they all did in the next rainy season, made the enclosure strong like a wall,—indeed, stronger than any wall.

This will testify for me that I was not idle, and that I spared no pains to bring to pass whatever appeared necessary for my comfortable support; for I considered the keeping up a breed of tame creatures thus at my hand would be a living magazine of flesh, milk, butter, and cheese for me as long as I lived in the place, if it were to be forty years; and that keeping them in my reach depended entirely upon my perfecting my enclosures to

such a degree that I might be sure of keeping them together; which, by this method, indeed, I so effectually secured that when these little stakes began to grow, I had planted them so very thick I was forced to pull some of them up again.

In this place also I had my grapes growing, which I principally depended on for my winter store of raisins, and which I never failed to preserve very carefully, as the best and most agreeable dainty of my whole diet. And indeed they were not only agreeable, but physical, wholesome, nourishing, and refreshing to the last degree.

As this was also about halfway between my other habitation and the place where I had laid up my boat, I generally stayed and lay here in my way thither; for I used frequently to visit my boat, and I kept all things about or belonging to her in very good order.

It happened one day, about noon, going towards my boat, I was exceedingly surprised with the print of a man's naked foot on the shore, which was very plain to be seen in the sand. I stood like one thunderstruck, or as if I had seen an apparition. I listened, I looked round me, I could hear nothing, nor see anything. I went up to a rising ground, to look farther. I went up the shore and down the shore, but it was all one; I could see no other impression but that one. I went to it again to see if there were any more, and to observe if it might not be my fancy; but there was no room for that, for there was exactly the very print of a foot—toes, heel, and every part of a foot. IIow it came thither I knew not, nor could in the least imagine. But after innumerable fluttering thoughts, like a man perfectly confused and out of myself, I came home to my fortification, not feeling, as we say, the ground I went on, but terrified to the last degree, looking behind me at every two or three steps, mistaking every bush and tree, and fancying every stump at a distance to be a man; nor is it possible to describe how many various shapes affrighted imagination represented things to me, how many wild ideas were found every moment in my fancy, and what strange, unaccountable whimsies came into my thoughts by the way.

When I came to my castle, for so I think I called it ever after this, I fled into it like one pursued. Whether I went over by the ladder, as first contrived, or went in at the hole in the rock, which I called a door, I cannot remember; no, nor could I remember the next morning, for never frighted hare fled to cover, or fox to earth, with more terror of mind than I to this retreat.

I slept none that night. The farther I was from the occasion of my fright, the greater my apprehensions were; which is something contrary to the nature of such things, and especially to the usual practice of all creatures in fear. But I was so embarrassed with my own frightful ideas of the thing that I formed nothing but dismal imaginations to myself, even though I was now a great way from it.

I presently concluded that it must be some dangerous creature, that it must be some of the savages of the mainland, who had wandered out to sea in their canoes, and, either driven by the currents or by contrary winds, had made the island, and had been on shore, but were gone away again to sea, being as loath, perhaps, to stay in this desolate island as I should have been to have them.

While these reflections were rolling upon my mind, I was very thankful in my thoughts that I was so happy as not to be thereabouts at that time, or that they did not see my boat, by which they would have concluded that some inhabitants had been in the place, and perhaps have searched farther for me. Then terrible thoughts racked my imagination about their having found my boat, and that there were people here; and that if so, I should certainly have them come again in greater numbers, and devour me; that if it should happen so that they should not find me, yet they would find my enclosure, destroy all my corn, carry away all my flock of tame goats, and I should perish at last for mere want.

These thoughts took me up many hours, days, nay, I may say, weeks and months; and one particular effect of my reflections on this occasion I cannot omit. One morning early, lying in my bed and filled with thought about my danger from the appearance of savages, I found it discomposed me very much; upon which those words of the Scripture came into my thoughts,

"Call upon Me in the day of trouble, and I will deliver thee, and thou shalt glorify Me."

Upon this, rising cheerfully out of my bed, my heart was not only comforted, but I was guided and encouraged to pray earnestly to God for deliverance. When I had done praying, I took up my Bible, and opening it to read, the first words that presented to me were, "Wait on the Lord, and be of good cheer, and He shall strengthen thy heart; wait, I say, on the Lord." It is impossible to express the comfort this gave me. In answer, I thankfully laid down the book, and was no more sad, at least, not on that occasion.

In the middle of these cogitations, apprehensions, and reflections, it came into my thought one day that all this might be a mere chimera of my own; and that this foot might be the print of my own foot, when I came on shore from my boat. This cheered me up a little, too, and I began to persuade myself it was all a delusion, that it was nothing else but my own foot; and why might not I come that way from the boat, as well as I was going that way to the boat? Again, I considered also that I could by no means tell, for certain, where I had trod, and where I had not; and that if, at last, this was only the print of my own foot, I had played the part of those fools who strive to make stories of specters and apparitions, and then are frighted at them more than anybody.

Now I began to take courage and to peep abroad again, for I had not stirred out of my castle for three days and nights, so that I began to starve for provision; for I had little or nothing within doors but some barley cakes and water. Then I knew that my goats wanted to be milked, too, which usually was my evening diversion.

Heartening myself, therefore, with the belief that this was nothing but the print of one of my own feet, and so I might be truly said to start at my own shadow, I began to go abroad again, and went to my country house to milk my flock. But to see with what fear I went forward, how often I looked behind me, how I was ready, every now and then, to lay down my basket, and run for my life, it would have made anyone have thought I was haunted with an evil conscience, or that I had been lately most terribly frighted; and so, indeed, I had.

However, as I went down thus two or three days, and having seen nothing, I began to be a little bolder, and to think there was really nothing in it but my own imagination. But I could not persuade myself fully of this till I should go down to the shore again, and see this print of a foot, and measure it by my own, and see if there was any similitude or fitness, that I might be assured it was my own foot. But when I came to the place, first, it appeared evident to me that when I laid up my boat, I could not possibly be on shore anywhere thereabout; secondly, when I came to measure the mark with my own foot, I found my foot not so large by a great deal. Both these things filled my head with new imaginations and gave me the vapors again to the highest degree; so that I shook with cold, like one in an ague; and I went home again, filled with the belief that some man or men had been on shore there; or, in short, that the island was inhabited, and I might be surprised before I was aware. And what course to take for my security, I knew not.

This confusion of my thoughts kept me waking all night, but in the morning I fell asleep; and having, by the amusement of my mind, been, as it were, tired, and my spirits exhausted, I slept very soundly, and waked much better composed than I had ever been before. And now I began to think sedately; and upon the utmost debate with myself, I concluded that this island, which was so exceeding pleasant, fruitful, and no farther from the mainland than as I had seen, was not so entirely abandoned as I might imagine; that although there were no stated inhabitants who lived on the spot, yet that there might sometimes come boats off from the shore, who, either with design, or perhaps never but when they were driven by cross winds, might come to this place; that I had lived here fifteen years now, and had not met with the least shadow or figure of any people yet; and that if at any time they should be driven here, it was probable they went away again as soon as ever they could, seeing they had never thought fit to stay there; that the most I could suggest any danger from, was from any such casual accidental

landing of straggling people from the main, who, as it was likely, if they were driven hither, were here against their wills; so they made no stay here, but went off again with all possible speed, seldom staying one night on shore, lest they should not have the help of the tides and daylight back again; and that, therefore, I had nothing to do but to consider of some safe retreat, in case I should see any savages land upon the spot.

I was surprised, one morning early, with seeing no less than five canoes all on shore together on my side of the island, and the people who belonged to them all landed, and out of my sight. The number of canoes broke all my measures; for seeing so many, and knowing that they always came four, or six, or sometimes more, in a boat, I could not tell what to think of it, or how to take my measures to attack twenty or thirty men single-handed; so I lay still in my castle, perplexed and discomforted. However, I put myself into all the same postures for an attack that I had formerly provided and was ready for action. Having waited a good while, listening to hear if they made any noise, at length, being very impatient, I set my guns at the foot of my ladder and clambered up to the top of the hill, by my two stages, as usual; standing so, however, that my head did not appear above the hill, so that they could not perceive me by any means. Here I observed, by the help of my perspective glass, that they were no less than thirty in number, that they had a fire kindled, that they had had meat dressed. How they had cooked it, that I knew not, or what it was; but they were all dancing, in I know not how many barbarous gestures and figures, their own way, round the fire.

While I was thus looking on them, I perceived by my perspective two miserable wretches dragged from the boats, where, it seems, they were laid by, and were now brought out for the slaughter. I perceived one of them immediately fell, being knocked down, I suppose, with a club or wooden sword, for that was their way, and two or three others were at work immediately, cutting him open for their cookery, while the other victim was left standing by himself, till they should be ready for him. In that very moment, this poor wretch seeing himself a little at liberty, Nature inspired him with hopes of life, and he started away from them, and ran with incredible swiftness along the sands directly towards me,—I mean towards that part of the coast where my habitation was.

I was dreadfully frighted (that I must acknowledge) when I perceived him to run my way, and especially when, as I thought, I saw him pursued by the whole body; and now I expected that part of my dream was coming to pass, and that he would certainly take shelter in my grove; but I could not depend, by any means, upon my dream for the rest of it, that the other savages would not pursue him thither, and find him there. However, I kept my station, and my spirits began to recover when I found that there were not above three men that followed him; and still more was I encouraged when I found that he outstripped them exceedingly in running, and gained ground of them; so that if he could but hold it for half an hour, I saw easily he would fairly get away from them all.

There was between them and my castle the creek, and this I

saw plainly he must necessarily swim over, or the poor wretch
would be taken there. But when the savage escaping came
thither he made nothing of it, though the tide was then up; but
plunging in, swam through it in about thirty strokes or thereabouts, landed, and ran on with exceeding strength and swiftness. When the three pursuers came to the creek, I found that
two of them could swim, but the third could not, and that,
standing on the other side, he looked at the other, but went no
further, and soon after went softly back, which, as it happened,
was very well for him in the main.

I observed that the two who swam were twice as long swimming over the creek as was the fellow that fled from them. It
came now very warmly upon my thoughts, and indeed irresist-
ibly, that now was my time to get me a servant, and perhaps a
companion or assistant, and that I was called plainly by Providence to save this poor creature's life. I immediately ran down
the ladders with all possible expedition, fetched my two guns,
for they were both at the foot of the ladders, and getting up
again, with the same haste, to the top of the hill, I crossed
toward the sea, and having a very short cut, and all downhill,

put myself between the pursuers and the pursued, hallooing aloud to him that fled, who, looking back, was at first perhaps as much frighted at me as at them; but I beckoned with my hand to him to come back; and, in the meantime, I slowly advanced towards the two that followed; then rushing at once upon the foremost, I knocked him down with the stock of my piece. I was loath to fire, because I would not have the rest hear; though, at that distance, it would not have been easily heard, and being out of sight of the smoke, too, they would not have known what to make of it. Having knocked this fellow down, the other who pursued with him stopped, as if he had been frighted, and I advanced towards him; but as I came nearer, I perceived presently he had a bow and arrow, and was fitting it to shoot at me; so I was necessitated to shoot at him first, which I did, and killed him at the first shot.

The poor savage who fled, but had stopped, though he saw both his enemies fallen and killed, as he thought, yet was so frighted with the fire and noise of my piece that he stood stock still, and neither came forward or went backward, though he seemed rather inclined to fly still than to come on. I hallooed again to him, and made signs to come forward, which he easily understood, and came a little way, then stopped again, and then a little further, and stopped again; and I could then perceive that he stood trembling, as if he had been taken prisoner, and would be killed, as his two enemies were. I beckoned him again to come to me, and gave him all the signs of encouragement that I could think of; and he came nearer and nearer, kneeling down every ten or twelve steps, in token of acknowledgment for my saving his life. I smiled at him, and looked pleasantly, and beckoned to him to come still nearer. At length he came close to me, and then he kneeled down again, kissed the ground, and laid his head upon the ground, and taking me by the foot, set my foot upon his head. This, it seems, was in token of swearing to be my slave forever. I took him up, and made much of him, and encouraged him all I could. But there was more work to do yet; for I perceived the savage whom I knocked down was not killed, but stunned with the blow, and began to come to himself;

so I pointed to him, and showing him the savage, that he was not dead, upon this he spoke some words to me; and though I could not understand them, yet I thought they were pleasant to hear; for they were the first sound of a man's voice that I had heard, my own excepted, for above twenty-five years. But there was no time for such reflections now. The savage who was knocked down recovered himself so far as to sit up upon the ground, and I perceived that my savage began to be afraid; but when I saw that, I presented my other piece at the man, as if I would shoot him. Upon this my savage, for so I call him now, made a motion to me to lend him my sword, which hung naked in a belt by my side; so I did. He no sooner had it but he ran to his enemy, and, at one blow, cut off his head, which I thought very strange for one who, I had reason to believe, never saw a sword in his life before, except their own wooden swords. However, it seems, as I learned afterwards, they make their wooden swords so sharp, so heavy, and the wood is so hard, that they will cut off heads and arms, and that at one blow, too. When he had done this, he comes laughing to me in sign of triumph, and brought me the sword again, and with abundance of gestures, which I did not understand, laid it down, with the head of the savage that he had killed, just before me.

But that which astonished him most was to know how I had killed the other Indian so far off; so pointing to him, he made signs to me to let him go to him; so I bade him go, as well as I could. When he came to him, he stood like one amazed, looking at him, turned him first on one side, then on t'other, looked at the wound the bullet had made, which, it seems, was just in his breast, where it had made a hole, and no great quantity of blood had flowed; but he had bled inwardly, for he was quite dead. He took up his bow and arrows and came back; so I turned to go away and beckoned to him to follow me, making signs to him that more might come after them.

Upon this he signed to me that he should bury them with sand, that they might not be seen by the rest if they followed; and so I made signs again to him to do so. He fell to work, and in an instant he had scraped a hole in the sand with his hands big enough to bury the first in, and then dragged him into it, and covered him, and did so also by the other. I believe he had buried them both in a quarter of an hour. Then calling him away, I carried him, not to my castle, but to my cave, on the farther part of the island; so I did not let my dream come to pass in that part, that he came into my grove for shelter.

Here I gave him bread and a bunch of raisins to eat, and a draught of water, which I found he was indeed in great distress for, by his running; and having refreshed him, I made signs for him to go lie down and sleep, pointing to a place where I had laid a great parcel of rice-straw, and a blanket upon it, which I used to sleep upon myself sometimes; so the poor creature laid down and went to sleep.

He was a comely, handsome fellow, perfectly well made, with straight strong limbs, not too large, tall and well-shaped, and, as I reckon, about twenty-six years of age. He had a very good countenance, not a fierce and surly aspect, but seemed to have something very manly in his face; and yet he had all the sweetness and softness of a European in his countenance too, especially when he smiled. His hair was long and black; his forehead very high and large; and a great vivacity and sparkling sharpness in his eyes. The color of his skin was not quite black, but very tawny, of a bright kind of a dun olive color, that had in it something very agreeable, though not very easy to describe. His face was round and plump; his nose small; a very good mouth, thin lips, and his fine teeth well set, and white as ivory.

After he had slumbered about half an hour, he waked, and came out of the cave to me, for I had been milking my goats, which I had in the enclosure just by. When he espied me, he came running to me, laying himself down again upon the ground, with all the possible signs of a humble, thankful disposition, making many antic gestures to show it. At last he lay his head flat upon the ground, close to my foot, and set my other foot upon his head, as he had done before, and after this made all the signs to me of subjection, servitude, and submission imaginable, to let me know how he would serve me as long as he lived. I understood him in many things, and let him know I was very well pleased with him. In a little time I began to speak to him, and teach him to speak to me; and first I made him know his name should be Friday, which was the day I saved his life. I likewise taught him to say master, and then let him know that was to be my name. I likewise taught him to say yes and no, and to know the meaning of them. I gave him some milk in an earthen pot, and let him see me drink it before him, and sop my bread in it; and I gave him a cake of bread to do the like, which he quickly complied with, and made signs that it was very good.

I stayed with him all that night; but as soon as it was day, I beckoned to him to come with me. As we went by the place where he had buried the two men, he pointed exactly to the spot, and showed me the marks that he had made to find them again, making signs to me that we should dig them up, and eat them. At this I appeared very angry and beckoned with my hand to him to come away; which he did immediately, with great submission. I then led him up to the top of the hill, to see if his enemies were gone; and pulling out my glass, I looked,

195

and saw plainly the place where they had been, but no appearance of them or of their canoes.

I was not content with this discovery, but having now more courage, and consequently more curiosity, I took my man Friday with me, giving him the sword in his hand, with the bow and arrows at his back, which I found he could use very dexterously, making him carry one gun for me, and I two for myself, and away we marched to the place where these creatures had been. When I came to the place, my very blood ran chill in my veins, and my heart sank within me, at the horror of the spectacle. Indeed, it was a dreadful sight, at least it was so to me, though Friday made nothing of it. The place was covered with human bones, the ground dyed with their blood, great pieces of flesh left here and there, half-eaten, mangled, and scorched; and, in short, all the tokens of the triumphant feast they had been making there, after a victory over their enemies. I saw three skulls, five hands, and the bones of three or four legs and feet, and abundance of other parts of the bodies; and Friday, by his signs, made me understand that they brought over four prisoners to feast upon; that three of them were eaten, and that he, pointing to himself, was the fourth; that there had been a great battle between them and their next king, whose subjects it seems he had been one of, and that they had taken a great number of prisoners; all which were carried to several places by those that had taken them in the fight, in order to feast upon them, as was done here by these wretches upon those they brought hither.

I caused Friday to gather all the skulls, bones, flesh, and whatever remained, and lay them together on a heap, and make a great fire upon it, and burn them all to ashes. I found Friday had still a hankering stomach after some of the flesh, and was still a cannibal in his nature; but I showed so much abhorrence at the very thoughts of it, and at the least appearance of it, that he durst not touch it.

When we had done this we came back to our castle, and there I fell to work for my man Friday; and, first of all, I gave him a pair of linen drawers, which I had found in the wreck; and which, with a little alteration, fitted him very well. Then I made him a jerkin of goatskin; and I gave him a cap, which I had made of a hareskin, very convenient and fashionable enough; and thus he was clothed for the present tolerably well, and was mighty well pleased to see himself almost as well clothed as his master. It is true he went awkwardly in these things at first; wearing the drawers was very awkward to him, and the sleeves of the waistcoat galled his shoulders, and the inside of his arms; but at length he took to them very well.

The next day after I came home to my hutch with him, I began to consider where I should lodge him. And that I might do well for him, and yet be perfectly easy myself, I made a little tent for him in the vacant place between my two fortifications, in the inside of the last and in the outside of the first; and as there was a door or entrance there into my cave, I made a formal framed doorcase, and a door to it of boards, and set it up in the passage, a little within the entrance; and causing the door to open on the inside, I barred it up in the night, taking in my ladders too; so that Friday could no way come at me in the inside of my innermost wall without making so much noise in getting over that it must needs waken me; for my first wall had now a complete roof over it of long poles, covering all my tent, and leaning up to the side of the hill, which was again laid cross with smaller sticks instead of laths, and then thatched over a great thickness with the rice straw, which was strong, like reeds; and at the hole or place which was left to go in or out by the ladder, I had placed a kind of trap door, which, if it had been attempted on the outside, would not have opened at all, but would have fallen down, and made a great noise; and as to weapons, I took them all into my side every night.

But I needed none of this precaution; for never was a more faithful, loving, sincere servant than Friday was to me; without passions, sullenness, or designs, his very affections were tied to me, like those of a child to a father; and I dare say he would have sacrificed his life to save mine, upon any occasion whatsoever.

AFTER Crusoe has spent some years on the island, an English vessel appears and a number of men come ashore. They prove to be mutineers who have brought their captain and two other men to be left on the island. By the aid of Crusoe and Friday, the captain regains possession of his vessel.

I laid me down; and it having been a day of great fatigue to me, I slept very sound, till I was surprised with the noise of a gun; and presently starting up, I heard a man call me by the name of "Governor," "Governor," and presently I knew the captain's voice; when climbing up to the top of the hill, there he stood, and pointing to the ship, he embraced me in his arms.

"My dear friend and deliverer," he said, "there's your ship, for she is all yours, and so are we, and all that belongs to her."

I cast my eyes to the ship, and there she rode within little more than half a mile of the shore; for they had weighed her anchor as soon as they were masters of her, and, the weather being fair, had brought her to anchor just against the mouth of the little creek, and the tide being up, the captain had brought the pinnace in near the place where I at first landed my rafts and so landed just at my door.

I was at first ready to sink down with surprise; for I saw my deliverance, indeed, visibly put into my hands, all things easy, and a large ship just ready to carry me away whither I pleased to go. At first, for some time, I was not able to answer him one word; but as he had taken me in his arms, I held fast by him, or I should have fallen to the ground.

He perceived the surprise, and immediately pulled a bottle out of his pocket, and gave me a dram of cordial, which he had brought on purpose for me. After I drank it, I sat down upon the ground; and though it brought me to myself, yet it was a good while before I could speak a word to him.

Then I took my turn, and embraced him as my deliverer, and we rejoiced together. I told him I looked upon him as a man sent from heaven to deliver me, and that the whole transaction seemed to be a chain of wonders; that such things as these were the testimonies we had of a secret hand of Providence governing the world, and an evidence that the eyes of an infinite Power

could search into the remotest corner of the world, and send help to the miserable whenever He pleased. I forgot not to lift up my heart in thankfulness to heaven.

When we had talked a while, the captain told me he had brought me some little refreshment, such as the ship afforded, and such as the wretches that had been so long his masters had not plundered him of. Upon this he called aloud, and bade his men bring the things ashore that were for the governor; and, indeed, it was a present as if I had been one, not that was to be carried away along with them, but as if I had been to dwell upon the island still, and they were to go without me.

First, he had brought me a case of bottles full of excellent cordial waters, six large bottles of Madeira wine (the bottles held two quarts apiece), two pounds of excellent good tobacco, twelve good pieces of the ship's beef, and six pieces of pork, with a bag of peas, and about a hundredweight of biscuit.

He had brought me also a box of sugar, a box of flour, a bag full of lemons, and two bottles of lime juice, and abundance of other things; but besides these, and what was a thousand times more useful to me, he brought me six clean new shirts, six very good neckcloths, two pair of gloves, one pair of shoes, a hat, one pair of stockings, and a very good suit of clothes of his own, which had been worn but very little; in a word, he clothed me from head to foot.

It was a very kind and agreeable present, as anyone may imagine, to one in my circumstances; but never was anything in the world of that kind so unpleasant, awkward, and uneasy as it was to me to wear such clothes at their first putting on.

After these ceremonies passed, and after all his good things were brought into my little apartment, we began to consult what was to be done with the prisoners we had; for it was worth considering whether we might venture to take them away with us or no, especially two of them, whom we knew to be incorrigible and refractory to the last degree; and the captain said he knew they were such rogues that there was no obliging them; and if he did carry them away, it must be in irons, as malefactors, to be delivered over to justice at the first English colony he could come at; and I found that the captain himself was very anxious about it.

Upon this I told him that, if he desired it, I durst undertake to bring the two men he spoke of to make it their own request that he should leave them upon the island. "I should be very glad of that," said the captain, "with all my heart."

"Well," I said, "I will send for them and talk with them for you."

I caused the men to be brought before me, and I told them I had had a full account of their villainous behavior to the captain, and how they had run away with the ship, and were preparing to commit further robberies, but that Providence had ensnared them in their own ways, and that they were fallen into the pit which they had digged for others.

I let them know that by my direction the ship had been seized, that she lay now in the road, and they might see, by and by, that their new captain had received the reward of his villainy, for that they might see him hanging at the yardarm; that as to them, I wanted to know what they had to say why I should not execute them as pirates, taken in the fact, as by my commission they could not doubt I had authority to do.

One of them answered in the name of the rest that they had nothing to say but this, that when they were taken the captain promised them their lives, and they humbly implored my mercy. But I told them I knew not what mercy to show them; for as for myself, I had resolved to quit the island with all my men, and had taken passage with the captain to go for England. And as for the captain, he could not carry them to England other than as prisoners in irons, to be tried for mutiny, and running away with the ship; the consequence of which, they must needs know, would be the gallows; so that I could not tell which was best for them, unless they had a mind to take their fate in the island. If they desired that, I did not care, as I had liberty to leave it. I had some inclination to give them their lives, if they thought they could shift on shore.

They seemed very thankful for it, said they would much rather venture to stay there than to be carried to England to be hanged; so I left it on that issue.

When they had all declared their willingness to stay, I then told them I would let them into the story of my living there, and put them into the way of making it easy to them. Accordingly I gave them the whole history of the place, and of my coming to it, showed them my fortifications, the way I made my bread, planted my corn, cured my grapes; and in a word, all that was necessary to make them easy.

I left them my firearms, five muskets, three fowling pieces, and three swords. I had above a barrel and a half of powder left; for after the first year or two I used but little, and wasted none. I gave them a description of the way I managed the goats, and directions to milk and fatten them, and to make both butter and cheese.

In a word, I gave them every part of my own story, and I told them I would prevail with the captain to leave them two barrels of gunpowder more, and some garden seeds, which I told them I would have been very glad of. Also I gave them the bag of peas which the captain had brought me to eat, and bade them be sure to sow and increase them.

Having done all this, I left them the next day and went on board the ship. We prepared to sail, but did not weigh anchor that night. The next morning early two of the five men came swimming to the ship's side, and, making a most lamentable complaint of the other three, begged to be taken into the ship for God's sake, for they should be murdered, and begged the captain to take them on board, though he hanged them immediately.

Upon this the captain pretended to have no power without me; but after some difficulty, and after their solemn promises of amendment, they were taken on board, and were some time after soundly whipped, after which they proved very honest and quiet fellows.

Some time after this the boat was ordered on shore, the tide being up, with the things promised to the men, to which the captain, at my intercession, caused their chests and clothes to be added, which they took, and were very thankful for. I also encouraged them by telling them that if it lay in my way to send any vessel to take them in, I would not forget them.

When I took leave of this island, I carried on board, for relics, the great goatskin cap I had made, my umbrella, and my parrot; also I forgot not to take the money I formerly mentioned, which had lain by me so long useless that it was grown rusty or tarnished, and could hardly pass for silver till it had been a little rubbed and handled.

Kate Douglas Wiggin

REBECCA AT THE BRICK HOUSE

ILLUSTRATED BY *Lillian B. Wuerfel*

THE old stagecoach was rumbling along the dusty road that runs from Maplewood to Riverboro. The day was as warm as midsummer, though it was only the middle of May, and Mr. Jeremiah Cobb was favoring the horses as much as possible, yet never losing sight of the fact that he carried the mail. The hills were many, and the reins lay loosely in his hands as he lolled back in his seat and extended one foot and leg luxuriously over the dashboard. His brimmed hat of worn felt was well pulled over his eyes, and he revolved a quid of tobacco in his left cheek.

There was one passenger in the coach,—a small dark-haired person in a glossy buff calico dress. She was so slender and so stiffly starched that she slid from space to space on the leather cushions, though she braced herself against the middle seat with her feet and extended her cotton-gloved hands on each side, in order to maintain some sort of balance. Whenever the wheels sank farther than usual into a rut, or jolted suddenly over a stone, she bounded involuntarily into the air, came down again, pushed back her funny little straw hat, and picked up or settled more firmly a small pink sunshade, which seemed to be her chief responsibility,—unless we except a bead purse, into which she looked whenever the condition of the roads would permit, finding great apparent satisfaction in that its precious contents neither disappeared nor grew less. Mr. Cobb guessed nothing of these harassing details of travel, his business being to carry people to their destinations, not, necessarily, to make them comfortable on the way. Indeed he had forgotten the very existence of this one unnoteworthy little passenger.

When he was about to leave the post office in Maplewood that morning, a woman had alighted from a wagon, and coming up to him, inquired whether this were the Riverboro stage, and if he were Mr. Cobb. Being answered in the affirmative, she nodded to a child who was eagerly waiting for the answer, and who ran towards her as if she feared to be a moment too late. The child might have been ten or eleven years old perhaps, but whatever the number of her summers, she had an air of being small for her age. Her mother helped her into the stage-coach, deposited a bundle and a bouquet of lilacs beside her, superintended the "roping on" behind of an old hair trunk, and finally paid the fare, counting out the silver with great care.

"I want you should take her to my sisters' in Riverboro," she said. "Do you know Mirandy and Jane Sawyer? They live in the brick house."

Lord bless your soul, he knew 'em as well as if he'd made 'em!

"Well, she's going there, and they're expecting her. Will you keep an eye on her, please? If she can get out anywhere and get with folks, or get anybody in to keep her company, she'll do it. Good-bye, Rebecca; try not to get into any mischief, and sit quiet, so you'll look neat an' nice when you get there. Don't be any trouble to Mr. Cobb.—You see, she's kind of excited.—We came on the cars from Temperance yesterday, slept all night

at my cousin's, and drove from her house—eight miles it is—
this morning."

"Good-bye, Mother, don't worry; you know it isn't as if I
hadn't traveled before."

The woman gave a short sardonic laugh and said in an ex-
planatory way to Mr. Cobb, "She's been to Wareham and stayed
overnight; that isn't much to be journey-proud on!"

"It *was traveling*, Mother," said the child eagerly and will-
fully. "It was leaving the farm, and putting up lunch in a basket,
and a little riding and a little steamcars, and we carried our
nightgowns."

"Don't tell the whole village about it, if we did," said the
mother, interrupting the reminiscences of this experienced
voyager. "Haven't I told you before," she whispered, in a last
attempt at discipline, "that you shouldn't talk about nightgowns and stockings and—things like that, in a loud tone of
voice, and especially when there's men-folks round?"

"I know, Mother, I know, and I won't. All I want to say is"—
here Mr. Cobb gave a cluck, slapped the reins, and the horses
started sedately on their daily task—"all I want to say is that it

205

is a journey when"—the stage was really under way now and Rebecca had to put her head out of the window over the door in order to finish her sentence—"it *is* a journey when you carry a nightgown!"

The objectionable word, uttered in a high treble, floated back to the offended ears of Mrs. Randall, who watched the stage out of sight, gathered up her packages from the bench at the store door, and stepped into the wagon that had been standing at the hitching-post. As she turned the horse's head towards home she rose to her feet for a moment, and shading her eyes with her hand, looked at a cloud of dust in the dim distance.

"Mirandy'll have her hands full, I guess," she said to herself; "but I shouldn't wonder if it would be the making of Rebecca."

All this had been half an hour ago, and the sun, the heat, the dust, the contemplation of errands to be done in the great metropolis of Milltown, had lulled Mr. Cobb's never active mind into complete oblivion as to his promise of keeping an eye on Rebecca.

Suddenly he heard a small voice above the rattle and rumble of the wheels and the creaking of the harness. At first he thought it was a cricket, a tree toad, or a bird, but having determined the direction from which it came, he turned his head over his shoulder and saw a small shape hanging as far out of the window as safety would allow. A long black braid of hair swung with the motion of the coach; the child held her hat in one hand and with the other made ineffectual attempts to stab the driver with her microscopic sunshade.

"Please let me speak!" she called.

Mr. Cobb drew up the horses obediently.

"Does it cost any more to ride up there with you?" she asked. "It's so slippery and shiny down here, and the stage is so much too big for me, that I rattle round in it till I'm 'most black and blue. And the windows are so small I can only see pieces of things, and I've 'most broken my neck stretching round to find out whether my trunk has fallen off the back. It's my mother's trunk, and she's very choice of it."

Mr. Cobb waited until this flow of conversation, or more

206

properly speaking this flood of criticism, had ceased, and then said jocularly,—

"You can come up if you want to; there ain't no extry charge to sit side o' me." Whereupon he helped her out, "boosted" her up to the front seat, and resumed his own place.

Rebecca sat down carefully, smoothing her dress under her with painstaking precision, and putting her sunshade under its extended folds between the driver and herself. This done she pushed back her hat, pulled up her darned white cotton gloves, and said delightedly,—

"Oh! this is better! This is like traveling! I am a real passenger now, and down there I felt like our setting hen when we shut her up in a coop. I hope we have a long, long ways to go?"

"Oh! we've only just started on it," Mr. Cobb responded genially; "it's more'n two hours."

"Only two hours," she sighed. "That will be half-past one; mother will be at Cousin Ann's, the children at home will have had their dinner, and Hannah cleared all away. I have some lunch, because mother said it would be a bad beginning to get to the brick house hungry and have Aunt Mirandy have to get me something to eat the first thing.—It's a good growing day, isn't it?"

"It is, certain; too hot, most. Why don't you put up your parasol?"

She extended her dress still farther over the article in question as she said, "Oh, dear, no! I never put it up when the sun shines; pink fades awfully, you know, and I only carry it to meetin' cloudy Sundays; sometimes the sun comes out all of a sudden, and I have a dreadful time covering it up; it's the dearest thing in life to me, but it's an awful care."

At this moment the thought gradually permeated Mr. Jeremiah Cobb's slow-moving mind that the bird perched by his side was a bird of very different feather from those to which he was accustomed in his daily drives. He put the whip back in its socket, took his foot from the dashboard, pushed his hat back, blew his quid of tobacco into the road, and having thus cleared his mental decks for action, he took his first good look at the passenger, a look which she met with a grave, childlike stare of friendly curiosity.

The buff calico was faded, but scrupulously clean, and starched within an inch of its life. From the little standing ruffle at the neck the child's slender throat rose very brown and thin, and the head looked small to bear the weight of dark hair that hung in a thick braid to her waist. She wore an odd little vizored cap of white leghorn, which may either have been the latest thing in children's hats, or some bit of ancient finery furbished up for the occasion. It was trimmed with a twist of buff ribbon and a cluster of black and orange porcupine quills, which hung or bristled stiffly over one ear, giving her the quaintest and most unusual appearance. Her face was without color and sharp in outline. As to features, she must have had the usual number, though Mr. Cobb's attention never proceeded so far as nose, forehead, or chin, being caught on the way and held fast by the eyes. Rebecca's eyes were like faith,—"the substance of things hoped for, the evidence of things not seen." Under her delicately etched brows they glowed like two stars, their dancing lights half hidden in lustrous darkness. Their glance was eager and full of interest, yet never satisfied; their steadfast gaze was brilliant and mysterious, and had the effect of looking directly through the obvious to something beyond, in the object, in the landscape, in you. They had never been accounted for, Rebecca's eyes. The schoolteacher and the minister at Temperance had tried and failed; the young artist who came for the summer to sketch the red barn, the ruined mill, and the bridge ended by giving up all these local beauties and devoting herself to the face of a child,—a small, plain face illuminated by a pair of eyes carrying such messages, such suggestions, such hints of sleeping power and insight, that one never tired of looking into their shining depths, nor of fancying that what one saw there was the reflection of one's own thought.

Mr. Cobb made none of these generalizations; his remark to his wife that night was simply to the effect that whenever the child looked at him she knocked him galley-west.

"Miss Ross, a lady that paints, gave me the sunshade," said

Rebecca, when she had exchanged looks with Mr. Cobb and learned his face by heart. "Did you notice the pinked double ruffle and the white tip and handle? They're ivory. The handle is scarred, you see. That's because Fanny sucked and chewed it in meeting when I wasn't looking. I've never felt the same to Fanny since."

"Is Fanny your sister?"

"She's one of them."

"How many are there of you?"

"Seven. There's verses written about seven children:—

> "Quick was the little Maid's reply,
>   'O master! we are seven!'"

I learned it to speak in school, but the scholars were hateful and laughed. Hannah is the oldest, I come next, then John, then Jenny, then Mark, then Fanny, then Mira."

"Well, that *is* a big family!"

"Far too big, everybody says," replied Rebecca with an unexpected and thoroughly grown-up candor that induced Mr. Cobb to murmur, "I swan!" and insert more tobacco in his left cheek.

"They're dear, but such a bother, and cost so much to feed, you see," she rippled on. "Hannah and I haven't done anything but put babies to bed at night and take them up in the morning for years and years. But it's finished, that's one comfort, and we'll have a lovely time when we're all grown up and the mortgage is paid off."

"All finished? Oh, you mean you've come away?"

"No, I mean they're all over and done with; our family's finished. Mother says so, and she always keeps her promises. There hasn't been any since Mira, and she's three. She was born the day father died. Aunt Miranda wanted Hannah to come to Riverboro instead of me, but mother couldn't spare her; she takes hold of housework better than I do, Hannah does. I told mother last night if there was likely to be any more children while I was away I'd have to be sent for, for when there's a baby it always takes Hannah and me both, for mother has the cooking and the farm."

"Oh, you live on a farm, do ye? Where is it?—near to where you got on?"

"Near? Why, it must be thousands of miles! We came from Temperance in the cars. Then we drove a long ways to Cousin Ann's and went to bed. Then we got up and drove ever so far to Maplewood, where the stage was. Our farm is away off from everywheres, but our school and meetinghouse is at Temperance, and that's only two miles. Sitting up here with you is most as good as climbing the meetinghouse steeple. I know a boy who's been up on our steeple. He said the people and cows looked like flies. We haven't met any people yet, but I'm *kind* of disappointed in the cows;—they don't look so little as I hoped they would; still (brightening) they don't look quite as big as if we were down side of them, do they? Boys always do the nice splendid things, and girls can only do the nasty dull ones that get left over. They can't climb so high, or go so far, or stay out so late, or run so fast, or anything."

Mr. Cobb wiped his mouth on the back of his hand and gasped. He had a feeling that he was being hurried from peak to peak of a mountain range without time to take a good breath in between.

"I can't seem to locate your farm," he said, "though I've been to Temperance and used to live up that way. What's your folks' name?"

"Randall. My mother's name is Aurelia Randall; our names are Hannah Lucy Randall, Rebecca Rowena Randall, John Halifax Randall, Jenny Lind Randall, Marquis Randall, Fanny Ellsler Randall, and Miranda Randall. Mother named half of us and father the other half, but we didn't come out even, so they both thought it would be nice to name Mira after Aunt Miranda in Riverboro; they hoped it might do some good, but it didn't, and now we call her Mira. We are all named after somebody in particular. Hannah is 'Hannah at the Window Binding Shoes,' and I am taken out of 'Ivanhoe'; John Halifax was a gentleman in a book; Mark is after his uncle, Marquis de

211

Lafayette, that died a twin. (Twins very often don't live to grow up, and triplets almost never—did you know that, Mr. Cobb?) We don't call him Marquis, only Mark. Jenny is named for a singer and Fanny for a beautiful dancer, but mother says they're both misfits, for Jenny can't carry a tune and Fanny's kind of stiff-legged. Mother would like to call them Jane and Frances and give up their middle names, but she says it wouldn't be fair to father. She says we must always stand up for father, because everything was against him, and he wouldn't have died if he hadn't had such bad luck. I think that's all there is to tell about us," she finished seriously.

"Land o' Liberty! I should think it was enough," ejaculated Mr. Cobb. "There wa'n't many names left when your mother got through choosin'! You've got a powerful good memory! I guess it ain't no trouble for you to learn your lessons, is it?"

"Not much; the trouble is to get the shoes to go and learn 'em. These are spandy new I've got on, and they have to last six months. Mother always says to save my shoes. There don't seem to be any way of saving shoes but taking 'em off and going barefoot; but I can't do that in Riverboro without shaming Aunt Mirandy. I'm going to school right along now when I'm living with Aunt Mirandy, and in two years I'm going to the seminary at Wareham; mother says it ought to be the making of me! I'm going to be a painter like Miss Ross when I get through school. At any rate, that's what *I* think I'm going to be. Mother thinks I'd better teach."

"Your farm ain't the old Hobbs place, is it?"

"No, it's just Randall's Farm. At least that's what mother calls it. I call it Sunnybrook Farm."

"I guess it don't make no difference what you call it so long as you know where it is," remarked Mr. Cobb sententiously.

Rebecca turned the full light of her eyes upon him reproachfully, almost severely, as she answered,—

"Oh! don't say that, and be like all the rest! It does make a difference what you call things. When I say Randall's Farm, do you see how it looks?"

"No, I can't say I do," responded Mr. Cobb uneasily.

"Now when I say Sunnybrook Farm, what does it make you think of?"

Mr. Cobb felt like a fish removed from his native element and left panting on the sand; there was no evading the awful responsibility of a reply, for Rebecca's eyes were searchlights that pierced the fiction of his brain and perceived the bald spot on the back of his head.

"I s'pose there's a brook somewheres near it," he said timorously.

Rebecca looked disappointed but not quite disheartened. "That's pretty good," she said encouragingly. "You're warm but not hot; there's a brook, but not a common brook. It has young trees and baby bushes on each side of it, and it's a shallow chattering little brook with a white sandy bottom and lots of little shiny pebbles. Whenever there's a bit of sunshine the brook catches it, and it's always full of sparkles the livelong day. Don't your stomach feel hollow? Mine does! I was so 'fraid I'd miss the stage I couldn't eat any breakfast."

"You'd better have your lunch, then. I don't eat nothin' till I get to Milltown; then I get a piece o' pie and cup o' coffee."

"I wish I could see Milltown. I suppose it's bigger and grander even than Wareham; more like Paris? Miss Ross told me about Paris; she bought my pink sunshade there and my bead purse. You see how it opens with a snap? I've twenty cents in it, and it's got to last three months, for stamps and paper and ink. Mother says Aunt Mirandy won't want to buy things like those when she's feeding and clothing me and paying for my school-books."

"Paris ain't no great," said Mr. Cobb disparagingly. "It's the dullest place in the State o' Maine. I've druv there many a time."

Again Rebecca was obliged to reprove Mr. Cobb, tacitly and quietly, but none the less surely, though the reproof was dealt with one glance, quickly sent and as quickly withdrawn.

"Paris is the capital of France, and you have to go to it on a boat," she said instructively. "It's in my geography, and it says: 'The French are a gay and polite people, fond of dancing and light wines.' I asked the teacher what light wines were, and he

213

thought it was something like new cider, or maybe ginger pop. I can see Paris as plain as day by just shutting my eyes. The beautiful ladies are always gayly dancing around with pink sunshades and bead purses, and the grand gentlemen are politely dancing and drinking ginger pop. But you can see Milltown most every day with your eyes wide open," Rebecca said wistfully.

"Milltown ain't no great, neither," replied Mr. Cobb, with the air of having visited all the cities of the earth and found them as naught. "Now you watch me heave this newspaper right onto Mis' Brown's doorstep."

Piff! and the packet landed exactly as it was intended, on the cornhusk mat in front of the screen door.

"Oh, how splendid that was!" cried Rebecca with enthusiasm. "Just like the knife-thrower Mark saw at the circus. I wish there was a long, long row of houses each with a cornhusk mat and a screen door in the middle, and a newspaper to throw on everyone!"

"I might fail on some of 'em, you know," said Mr. Cobb, beaming with modest pride. "If your Aunt Mirandy 'll let you, I'll take you down to Milltown some day this summer when the stage ain't full."

A thrill of delicious excitement ran through Rebecca's frame, from her new shoes up, up to the leghorn cap and down the black braid. She pressed Mr. Cobb's knee ardently and said in a voice choking with tears of joy and astonishment, "Oh, it can't be true, it can't; to think I should see Milltown. It's like having a fairy godmother who asks you your wish and then gives it to you! Did you ever read 'Cinderella,' or 'The Yellow Dwarf,' or 'The Enchanted Frog,' or 'The Fair One with Golden Locks'?"

"No," said Mr. Cobb cautiously, after a moment's reflection. "I don't seem to think I ever did read jest those partic'lar ones. Where'd you get a chance at so much readin'?"

"Oh, I've read lots of books," answered Rebecca casually. "Father's and Miss Ross's and all the dif'rent school teachers', and all in the Sunday-School library. I've read 'The Lamplighter,' and 'Scottish Chiefs,' and 'Ivanhoe,' and 'The Heir of

Redclyffe,' and 'Cora, the Doctor's Wife,' and 'David Copperfield,' and 'The Gold of Chickaree,' and 'Plutarch's Lives,' and 'Thaddeus of Warsaw,' and 'Pilgrim's Progress,' and lots more.—What have you read?"

"I've never happened to read those partic'lar books; but land! I've read a sight in my time! Nowadays I'm so drove I get along with the Almanac, the 'Weekly Argus,' and the 'Maine State Agriculturist.'—There's the river again; this is the last long hill, and when we get to the top of it we'll see the chimbleys of Riverboro in the distance. 'T ain't fur. I live 'bout half a mile beyond the brick house myself."

Rebecca's hand stirred nervously in her lap and she moved in her seat. "I didn't think I was going to be afraid," she said almost under her breath; "but I guess I am, just a little mite—when you say it's coming so near."

"Would you go back?" asked Mr. Cobb curiously.

She flashed him an intrepid look and then said proudly, "I'd never go back—I might be frightened, but I'd be ashamed to run. Going to Aunt Mirandy's is like going down cellar in the dark. There might be ogres and giants under the stairs,—but, as I tell Hannah, there *might* be elves and fairies and enchanted frogs!—Is there a main street in the village, like that in Wareham?"

"I s'pose you might call it a main street, an' your Aunt Sawyer lives on it, but there ain't no stores nor mills, an' it's an awful one-horse village! You have to go 'cross the river an' get to our side if you want to see anything goin' on."

"I'm almost sorry," she sighed, "because it would be so grand to drive down a real main street, sitting high up like this behind two splendid horses, with my pink sunshade up, and everybody in town wondering who the bunch of lilacs and the hair trunk belongs to. It would be just like the beautiful lady in the parade. Last summer the circus came to Temperance, and they had a procession in the morning. Mother let us all walk in and wheel Mira in the baby carriage, because we couldn't afford to go to the circus in the afternoon. And there were lovely horses and animals in cages, and clowns on horseback; and at the very end

215

came a little red and gold chariot drawn by two ponies, and in it, sitting on a velvet cushion, was the snake charmer, all dressed in satin and spangles. She was so beautiful beyond compare, Mr. Cobb, that you had to swallow lumps in your throat when you looked at her, and little cold feelings crept up and down your back. Don't you know how I mean? Didn't you ever see anybody that made you feel like that?"

Mr. Cobb was more distinctly uncomfortable at this moment than he had been at any one time during the eventful morning, but he evaded the point dexterously by saying, "There ain't no harm, as I can see, in our makin' the grand entry in the biggest style we can. I'll take the whip out, set up straight, an' drive fast; you hold your bo'quet in your lap, an' open your little red parasol, an' we'll jest make the natives stare!"

The child's face was radiant for a moment, but the glow faded just as quickly as she said, "I forgot—mother put me inside, and maybe she'd want me to be there when I got to Aunt Mirandy's. Maybe I'd be more genteel inside, and then I wouldn't have to be jumped down and my clothes fly up, but could open the door and step down like a lady passenger. Would you please stop a minute, Mr. Cobb, and let me change?"

The stage-driver good-naturedly pulled up his horses, lifted the excited little creature down, opened the door, and helped her in, putting the lilacs and the pink sunshade beside her.

"We've had a great trip," he said, "and we've got real well acquainted, haven't we?—You won't forget about Milltown?"

"Never!" she exclaimed fervently; "and you're sure you won't either?"

"Never! Cross my heart!" vowed Mr. Cobb solemnly, as he remounted his perch.

And as the stage rumbled down the village street between the green maples, those who looked from their windows saw a little brown elf in buff calico sitting primly on the back seat holding a great bouquet tightly in one hand and a pink parasol in the other. Had they been far-sighted enough they might have seen, when the stage turned into the side dooryard of the old brick house, a calico yoke rising and falling tempestuously over the

216

beating heart beneath, the red color coming and going in two pale cheeks, and a mist of tears swimming in two brilliant dark eyes.

Rebecca's journey had ended.

"There's the stage turnin' into the Sawyer girls' dooryard," said Mrs. Perkins to her husband. "That must be the niece from up Temperance way. It seems they wrote to Aurelia and invited Hannah, the oldest, but Aurelia said she could spare Rebecca better, if 't was all the same to Mirandy an' Jane; so it's Rebecca that's come. She'll be good comp'ny for our Emma Jane, but I don't believe they'll keep her three months! She looks black as an Injun what I can see of her; black and kind of up-an'-comin'. They used to say that one o' the Randalls married a Spanish woman, somebody that was teachin' music and languages at a boardin' school. Lorenzo was dark complected, you remember, and this child is, too. Well, I don't know as Spanish blood is any real disgrace, not if it's a good ways back and the woman was respectable." . . .

SOME DAY you will want to read Rebecca's various adventures at the brick house, and how she finally makes her Aunt Miranda approve of her.

Here is one experience she has playing hostess to some missionaries.

The Aid Society had called its meeting for a certain Wednesday in March of the year in which Rebecca ended her Riverboro school days and began her studies in Wareham. It was a raw, blustering day, snow on the ground, and a look in the sky of more to follow. Both Miranda and Jane had taken cold and decided that they could not leave the house in such weather, and this deflection from the path of duty worried Miranda, since she was an officer of the society. After making the breakfast table sufficiently uncomfortable and wishing plaintively that Jane wouldn't always insist on being sick at the same time she was, she decided that Rebecca must go to the meeting in their stead. "You'll be better than nobody, Rebecca," she said

flatteringly; "your Aunt Jane shall write an excuse from afternoon school for you; you can wear your rubber boots and come
home by the way of the meetin' house. This Mr. Burch, if I
remember right, used to know your Grandfather Sawyer and
stayed here once when he was candidatin'. He'll mebbe look
for us there, and you must just go and represent the family, an'
give him our respects. Be careful how you behave. Bow your
head in prayer; sing all the hymns, but not too loud and bold;
ask after Mis' Strout's boy; tell everybody what awful colds
we've got; if you see a good chance, take your pocket handkerchief and wipe the dust off the melodeon before the meetin'
begins, and get twenty-five cents out of the sittin'-room match-
box in case there should be a collection."

Rebecca willingly assented. Anything interested her, even a
village missionary meeting, and the idea of representing the
family was rather intoxicating.

The service was held in the Sunday-School room, and although the Reverend Mr. Burch was on the platform when
Rebecca entered, there were only a dozen persons present. Feeling a little shy and considerably too young for this assemblage,
Rebecca sought the shelter of a friendly face, and seeing Mrs.
Robinson in one of the side seats near the front, she walked up
the aisle and sat beside her.

"Both my aunts had bad colds," she said softly, "and sent me
to represent the family."

"That's Mrs. Burch on the platform with her husband," whispered Mrs. Robinson. "She's awful tanned up, ain't she? If
you're goin' to save souls seems like you hev' to part with your
complexion. Eudoxy Morton ain't come yet; I hope to the land
she will, or Mis' Deacon Milliken 'll pitch the tunes where we
can't reach 'em with a ladder; can't you pitch, afore she gits her
breath and clears her throat?"

Mrs. Burch was a slim, frail little woman with dark hair, a
broad low forehead, and patient mouth. She was dressed in a
well-worn black silk, and looked so tired that Rebecca's heart
went out to her.

"They're poor as Job's turkey," whispered Mrs. Robinson;

"but if you give 'em anything they'd turn right round and give it to the heathen. His congregation up to Parsonsfield clubbed together and give him that gold watch he carries; I s'pose he'd 'a' handed that over too, only heathens always tell time by the sun 'n' don't need watches. Eudoxy ain't comin'; now for massy's sake, Rebecca, do git ahead of Mis' Deacon Milliken and pitch real low."

The meeting began with prayer and then the Reverend Mr. Burch announced, to the tune of "Mendon":

> "Church of our God! arise and shine,
> Bright with the beams of truth divine:
> Then shall thy radiance stream afar,
> Wide as the heathen nations are.
>
> Gentiles and kings thy light shall view,
> And shall admire and love thee too;
> They come, like clouds across the sky,
> As doves that to their windows fly."

"Is there anyone present who will assist us at the instrument?" he asked unexpectedly.

Everybody looked at everybody else, and nobody moved; then there came a voice out of a far corner saying informally, "Rebecca, why don't you?" It was Mrs. Cobb. Rebecca could have played "Mendon" in the dark, so she went to the melodeon and did so without any ado, no member of her family being present to give her self-consciousness.

The talk that ensued was much the usual sort of thing. Mr. Burch made impassioned appeals for the spreading of the gospel, and added his entreaties that all who were prevented from visiting in person the peoples who sat in darkness should contribute liberally to the support of others who could. But he did more than this. He was a pleasant, earnest speaker, and he interwove his discourse with stories of life in a foreign land,—of the manners, the customs, the speech, the point of view; even giving glimpses of the daily round, the common task, of his own household, the work of his devoted helpmate and their little group of children, all born under Syrian skies.

219

Rebecca sat entranced, having been given the key of another world. Riverboro had faded; the Sunday-School room, with Mrs. Robinson's red plaid shawl, and Deacon Milliken's wig, on crooked, the bare benches and torn hymnbooks, the hanging texts and maps, were no longer visible, and she saw blue skies and burning stars, white turbans and gay colors; Mr. Burch had not said so, but perhaps there were mosques and temples and minarets and date-palms. What stories they must know, those children born under Syrian skies! Then she was called upon to play "Jesus shall reign where'er the sun."

The contribution box was passed and Mr. Burch prayed. As he opened his eyes and gave out the last hymn he looked at the handful of people, at the scattered pennies and dimes in the contribution box, and reflected that his mission was not only to gather funds for the building of his church, but to keep alive, in all these remote and lonely neighborhoods, that love for the cause which was its only hope in the years to come.

"If any of the sisters will provide entertainment," he said, "Mrs. Burch and I will remain among you tonight and tomorrow. In that event we could hold a parlor meeting. My wife and one of my children would wear the native costume, we would display some specimens of Syrian handiwork, and give an account of our educational methods with the children. These informal parlor meetings, admitting of questions or conversation, are often the means of interesting those not commonly found at church services; so I repeat, if any member of the congregation desires it and offers her hospitality, we will gladly stay and tell you more of the Lord's work."

A pall of silence settled over the little assembly. There was some cogent reason why every "sister" there was disinclined for company. Some had no spare room, some had a larder less well stocked than usual, some had sickness in the family, some were "unequally yoked together with unbelievers" who disliked strange ministers. Mrs. Burch's thin hands fingered her black silk nervously. "Would no one speak!" thought Rebecca, her heart fluttering with sympathy. Mrs. Robinson leaned over and whispered significantly, "The missionaries always used to be

220

entertained at the brick house; your grandfather never would
let 'em sleep anywheres else when he was alive." She meant this
for a stab at Miss Miranda's parsimony, remembering the four
spare chambers, closed from January to December; but Rebecca
thought it was intended as a suggestion. If it had been a former
custom, perhaps her aunts would want her to do the right thing;
for what else was she representing the family? So, delighted
that duty lay in so pleasant a direction, she rose from her seat
and said in a pretty voice and with the quaint manner that so
separated her from all the other young people in the village,
"My aunts, Miss Miranda and Miss Jane Sawyer, would be very
happy to have you visit them at the brick house, as the ministers
always used to do when their father was alive. They sent their
respects by me." The "respects" might have been the freedom
of the city, or an equestrian statue, when presented in this way,
and the aunts would have shuddered could they have foreseen
the manner of delivery; but it was vastly impressive to the
audience, who concluded that Mirandy Sawyer must be making
her way uncommonly fast to mansions in the skies, else what
meant this abrupt change of heart?

Mr. Burch bowed courteously, accepted the invitation "in the
same spirit in which it was offered," and asked Brother Milliken
to lead in prayer.

If the Eternal Ear could ever tire it would have ceased long ere this to listen to Deacon Milliken, who had wafted to the throne of grace the same prayer, with very slight variations, for forty years. Mrs. Perkins followed; she had several petitions at her command, good sincere ones too, but a little cut and dried, made of Scripture texts laboriously woven together. Rebecca wondered why she always ended, at the most peaceful seasons, with the form, "Do Thou be with us, God of Battles, while we strive onward like Christian soldiers marching as to war." But everything sounded real to her today; she was in a devout mood, and many things Mr. Burch had said had moved her strangely. As she lifted her head the minister looked directly at her and said,—

"Will our young sister close the service by leading us in prayer?"

Every drop of blood in Rebecca's body seemed to stand still, and her heart almost stopped beating. Mrs. Cobb's excited breathing could be heard distinctly in the silence. There was nothing extraordinary in Mr. Burch's request. In his journeyings among country congregations he was constantly in the habit of meeting young members who had "experienced religion" and joined the church when nine or ten years old. Rebecca was now thirteen; she had played the melodeon, led the singing, delivered her aunts' invitation with an air of great worldly wisdom, and he, concluding that she must be a youthful pillar of the church, called upon her with the utmost simplicity.

Rebecca's plight was pathetic. How could she refuse; how could she explain she was not a "member"; how could she pray before all those elderly women! John Rogers at the stake hardly suffered more than this poor child for the moment as she rose to her feet, forgetting that ladies prayed sitting, while deacons stood in prayer. Her mind was a maze of pictures that the Reverend Mr. Burch had flung on the screen. She knew the conventional phraseology, of course; what New England child, accustomed to Wednesday evening meetings, does not? But her own secret prayers were different. However, she began slowly and tremulously,—

222

"Our Father who art in Heaven, . . . Thou art God in Syria just the same as in Maine; . . . over there today are blue skies and yellow stars and burning suns . . . the great trees are waving in the warm air, while here the snow lies thick under our feet, . . . but no distance is too far for God to travel and so He is with us here as He is with them there, . . . and our thoughts rise to Him 'as doves that to their windows fly.' . . .

"We cannot all be missionaries, teaching people to be good, . . . some of us have not learned yet how to be good ourselves, but if thy kingdom is to come and thy will is to be done on earth as it is in heaven, everybody must try and everybody must help, . . . those who are old and tired and those who are young and strong. . . . The little children of whom we have heard, those born under Syrian skies, have strange and interesting work to do for Thee, and some of us would like to travel in far lands and do wonderful brave things for the heathen and gently take away their idols of wood and stone. But perhaps we have to stay at home and do what is given us to do . . . sometimes even things we dislike, . . . but that must be what it means in the hymn we sang, when it talked about the sweet perfume that rises with every morning sacrifice. . . . This is the way that God teaches us to be meek and patient, and the thought that He has willed it so should rob us of our fears and help us bear the years. Amen."

Poor little ignorant, fantastic child! Her petition was simply a succession of lines from the various hymns, and images the minister had used in his sermon, but she had her own way of recombining and applying these things, even of using them in a new connection, so that they had a curious effect of belonging to her. The words of some people might generally be written with a minus sign after them, the minus meaning that the personality of the speaker subtracted from, rather than added to, their weight; but Rebecca's words might always have borne the plus sign.

The "Amen" said, she sat down, or presumed she sat down, on what she believed to be a bench, and there was a benediction. In a moment or two, when the room ceased spinning, she went up to Mrs. Burch, who kissed her affectionately and said, "My dear, how glad I am that we are going to stay with you. Will half-past five be too late for us to come? It is three now, and we have to go to the station for our valise and for our children. We left them there, being uncertain whether we should go back or stop here."

Rebecca said that half-past five was their supper hour, and then accepted an invitation to drive home with Mrs. Cobb. Her face was flushed and her lip quivered in a way that Aunt Sarah had learned to know, so the homeward drive was taken almost in silence. The bleak wind and Aunt Sarah's quieting presence brought her back to herself, however, and she entered the brick house cheerily. Being too full of news to wait in the side entry to take off her rubber boots, she carefully lifted a braided rug into the sitting room and stood on that while she opened her budget.

"There are your shoes warming by the fire," said Aunt Jane. "Slip them right on while you talk."

"It was a very small meeting, Aunt Miranda," began Rebecca, "and the missionary and his wife are lovely people, and they are coming here to stay all night and tomorrow with you. I hope you won't mind."

"Coming here!" exclaimed Miranda, letting her knitting fall in her lap, and taking her spectacles off, as she always did in moments of extreme excitement. "Did they invite themselves?"

"No," Rebecca answered. "I had to invite them for you; but I thought you'd like to have such interesting company. It was this way—"

"Stop your explainin', and tell me first when they'll be here. Right away?"

"No, not for two hours—about half-past five."

"Then you can explain, if you can, who gave you authority to invite a passel of strangers to stop here overnight, when you know we ain't had any company for twenty years, and don't intend to have any for another twenty,—or at any rate, while I'm the head of the house."

"Don't blame her, Miranda, till you've heard her story," said

224

Jane. "It was in my mind right along, if we went to the meeting, some such thing might happen, on account of Mr. Burch knowing father."

"The meeting was a small one," began Rebecca. "I gave all your messages, and everybody was disappointed you couldn't come, for the president wasn't there, and Mrs. Matthews took the chair, which was a pity, for the seat wasn't nearly big enough for her, and she reminded me of a line in a hymn we sang, 'Wide as the heathen nations are,' and she wore that kind of a beaver garden hat that always gets on one side. And Mr. Burch talked beautifully about the Syrian heathen, and the singing went real well, and there looked to be about forty cents in the basket that was passed on our side. And that wouldn't save even a heathen baby, would it? Then Mr. Burch said, if any sister would offer entertainment, they would pass the night, and have a parlor meeting in Riverboro tomorrow, with Mrs. Burch in Syrian costume, and lovely foreign things to show. Then he waited and waited, and nobody said a word. I was so mortified I didn't know what to do. And then he repeated what he said, and explained why he wanted to stay, and you could see he thought it was his duty. Just then Mrs. Robinson whispered to me and said the missionaries always used to go to the brick house when grandfather was alive, and that he never would let them sleep anywhere else. I didn't know you had

225

stopped having them, because no traveling ministers have been here, except just for a Sunday morning, since I came to Riverboro. So I thought I ought to invite them as you weren't there to do it for yourself, and you told me to represent the family."

"What did you do—go up and introduce yourself as folks was goin' out?"

"No; I stood right up in meeting. I had to, for Mr. Burch's feelings were getting hurt at nobody's speaking. So I said, 'My aunts, Miss Miranda and Miss Jane Sawyer, would be happy to have you visit at the brick house, just as the missionaries always did when their father was alive, and they sent their respects by me.' Then I sat down; and Mr. Burch prayed for Grandfather, and called him a man of God, and thanked our Heavenly Father that his spirit was still alive in his descendants (that was you), and that the good old house where so many of the brethren had been cheered and helped, and from which so many had gone out strengthened for the fight, was still hospitably open for the stranger and wayfarer."

Sometimes, nature seems to be the most perfect art. The word or the deed coming straight from the heart, without any thought of effect, seems inspired.

A certain gateway in Miranda Sawyer's soul had been closed for years; not all at once had it been done, but gradually, and without her full knowledge. If Rebecca had plotted for days, and with the utmost cunning, she could not have effected an entrance into that forbidden country, and now, unknown to both of them, the gate swung on its stiff and rusty hinges, and the favoring wind of opportunity opened it wider and wider as time went on. All things had worked together amazingly for good. The memory of old days had been evoked, and the daily life of a pious and venerated father called to mind; the Sawyer name had been publicly dignified and praised; Rebecca had comported herself as the granddaughter of Deacon Israel Sawyer should, and showed conclusively that she was not "all Randall," as had been supposed. Miranda was rather pleased with the turn of events, but she did not intend to show it, or give anybody any reason to expect that this expression of hospitality was to serve for a precedent on any subsequent occasion.

"Well, I see you did only what you was obliged to do, Re-becca," she said, "and you worded your invitation as nice as anybody could have done. I wish your Aunt Jane and me wasn't both so worthless with these colds; but it only shows the good of havin' a clean house, with every room in order, whether open or shut, and enough victuals cooked so 't you can't be surprised and belittled by anybody, whatever happens. There was half a dozen there that might have entertained the Burches as easy as not, if they hadn't 'a' been too mean or lazy. Why didn't your missionaries come right along with you?"

"They went to the station for their valise and their children."

"Are there children?" groaned Miranda.

"Yes, Aunt Miranda, all born under Syrian skies."

"Syrian grandmother!" ejaculated Miranda (and it was not a fact). "How many?"

"I didn't think to ask; but I will get two rooms ready, and if there are any over I'll take 'em into my bed," said Rebecca, secretly hoping that this would be the case. "Now, as you're both half sick, couldn't you trust me just once to get ready for the company? You can come up when I call. Will you?"

"I believe I will," sighed Miranda reluctantly. "I'll lay down side o' Jane in our bedroom and see if I can get strength to cook supper. It's half-past three—don't you let me lay a minute past five. I kep' a good fire in the kitchen stove. I don't know, I'm sure, why I should have baked a pot o' beans in the middle of the week, but they'll come in handy. Father used to say there was nothing that went right to the spot with returned mis-sionaries like pork 'n' beans 'n' brown bread. Fix up the two south chambers, Rebecca."

Rebecca, given a free hand for the only time in her life, dashed upstairs like a whirlwind. Every room in the brick house was as neat as wax, and she had only to pull up the shades, go over the floors with a whisk broom, and dust the furniture. The aunts could hear her scurrying to and fro, beating up pillows and featherbeds, flapping towels, jingling crockery, singing meanwhile in her clear voice:

227

"In vain with lavish kindness
The gifts of God are strown;
The heathen in his blindness
Bows down to wood and stone."

She had grown to be a handy little creature, and tasks she was capable of doing at all she did like a flash, so that when she called her aunts at five o'clock to pass judgment, she had accomplished wonders. There were fresh towels on bureaus and washstands, the beds were fair and smooth, the pitchers were filled, and soap and matches were laid out; newspaper, kindling, and wood were in the boxes, and a large stick burned slowly in each airtight stove. "I thought I'd better just take the chill off," she explained, "as they're right from Syria; and that reminds me, I must look it up in the geography right away."

There was nothing to disapprove, so the two sisters went downstairs to make some slight changes in their dress. As they passed the parlor door Miranda thought she heard a crackle and looked in. The shades were up, there was a cheerful blaze in the open stove in the front parlor, and a fire laid on the hearth in the back room. Rebecca's own lamp, her second Christmas present from Mr. Aladdin, stood on a marble-topped table in the corner, the light that came softly through its rose-colored shade transforming the stiff and gloomy ugliness of the room into a place where one could sit and love one's neighbor.

"For massy's sake, Rebecca," called Miss Miranda up the stairs, "did you think we'd better open the parlor?"

Rebecca came out on the landing braiding her hair.

"We did on Thanksgiving and Christmas, and I thought this was about as great an occasion," she said. "I moved the wax flowers off the mantelpiece so they wouldn't melt, and put the shells, the coral, and the green stuffed bird on top of the what-not, so the children wouldn't ask to play with them. Brother Milliken's coming over to see Mr. Burch about business, and I shouldn't wonder if Brother and Sister Cobb happened in. Don't go down cellar, I'll be there in a minute to do the running."

Miranda and Jane exchanged glances.

228

"Ain't she the beatin'est creetur ever!" exclaimed Miranda;
"but she can turn off work when she's got a mind to!"

At quarter-past five everything was ready, and the neighbors,
those at least who were within sight of the brick house, were
curious almost to desperation. Shades up in both parlors! Shades
up in the two south bedrooms! And fires—if human vision was
to be relied on—fires in about every room. If it had not been
for the kind offices of a lady who had been at the meeting, and
who charitably called in at one or two houses and explained
the reason of all this preparation, there would have been no
sleep in many families.

The missionary party arrived promptly, and there were but
two children, seven or eight having been left with the brethren
in Portland to diminish traveling expenses. Jane escorted them
all upstairs, while Miranda watched the cooking of the supper;
but Rebecca promptly took the two little girls away from their
mother, divested them of their wraps, smoothed their hair, and
brought them down to the kitchen to smell the beans.

There was a bountiful supper, and the presence of the young
people robbed it of all possible stiffness. Aunt Jane helped clear
the table and put away the food, while Miranda entertained in
the parlor; but Rebecca and the infant Burches washed the
dishes and held high carnival in the kitchen, doing only trifling
damage—breaking a cup and plate that had been cracked before, emptying a silver spoon with some dishwater out of the

back door (an act never permitted at the brick house), and putting coffee grounds in the sink. All evidences of crime having been removed by Rebecca, and damages repaired in all possible cases, the three entered the parlor, where Mr. and Mrs. Cobb and Deacon and Mrs. Milliken had already appeared.

It was such a pleasant evening! Occasionally they left the heathen in his blindness bowing down to wood and stone, and then the Burches told strange, beautiful, marvelous things. The two smaller children sang together, and Rebecca, at the urgent request of Mrs. Burch, seated herself at the tinkling old piano and gave "Wild roved an Indian girl, bright Alfarata" with considerable spirit and style.

At eight o'clock she crossed the room, handed a palm-leaf fan to her Aunt Miranda, ostensibly that she might shade her eyes from the lamplight; but it was a piece of strategy that gave her an opportunity to whisper, "How about cookies?"

"Do you think it's worth while?" Miss Miranda asked.

"The Perkinses always do."

"All right. You know where they be."

Rebecca moved quietly towards the door, and the young Burches cataracted after her as if they could not bear a second's separation. In five minutes they returned, the little ones bearing plates of thin caraway wafers,—hearts, diamonds, and circles daintily sugared, and flecked with caraway seed raised in the garden behind the house. These were a specialty of Miss Jane's, and Rebecca carried a tray with six tiny crystal glasses filled with dandelion wine. Old Deacon Israel had always had it passed, and he had bought the glasses himself in Boston. Miranda admired them greatly, not only for their beauty but because they held so little. Before their advent the dandelion wine had been served in sherry glasses.

As soon as these refreshments—commonly called a "colation" in Riverboro—had been genteelly partaken of, Rebecca looked at the clock, rose from her chair in the children's corner, and said cheerfully, "Come! time for little missionaries to be in bed!"

Everybody laughed at this, the big missionaries most of all, as the young people shook hands and disappeared with Rebecca.

John Ruskin

THE KING OF THE
GOLDEN RIVER

<small>ILLUSTRATED BY</small> *Fritz Kredel*

IN A secluded and mountainous part of
Styria there was, in old time, a valley of the most surprising and
luxuriant fertility. It was surrounded on all sides by steep and
rocky mountains, rising into peaks which were always covered
with snow, and from which a number of torrents descended in
constant cataracts. One of these fell westward, over the face of
a crag so high that, when the sun had set to everything else, and
all below was darkness, his beams still shone full upon this
waterfall, so that it looked like a shower of gold. It was therefore called by the people of the neighborhood the Golden River.
It was strange that none of these streams fell into the valley
itself. They all descended on the other side of the mountains
and wound away through broad plains and by populous cities.
But the clouds were drawn so constantly to the snowy hills, and
rested so softly in the circular hollow, that, in time of drought
and heat, when all the country round was burnt up, there was
still rain in the little valley; and its crops were so heavy, and its
hay so high, and its apples so red, and its grapes so blue, and
its wine so rich, and its honey so sweet, that it was a marvel to
everyone who beheld it, and was commonly called the Treasure
Valley.

The whole of this little valley belonged to three brothers,
called Schwartz, Hans, and Gluck. Schwartz and Hans, the two
elder brothers, were very ugly men, with overhanging eyebrows
and small, dull eyes, which were always half shut, so that you
couldn't see into them, and always fancied they saw very far

into you. They lived by farming the Treasure Valley, and very good farmers they were. They killed everything that did not pay for its eating. They shot the blackbirds, because they pecked the fruit; and killed the hedgehogs, lest they should suck the cows; they poisoned the crickets for eating the crumbs in the kitchen; and smothered the cicadas, which used to sing all summer in the lime trees. They worked their servants without any wages, till they would not work any more, and then quarreled with them and turned them out-of-doors without paying them. It would have been very odd if, with such a farm and such a system of farming, they hadn't got very rich; and very rich they did get. They generally contrived to keep their corn by them till it was very dear, and then sell it for twice its value; they had heaps of gold lying about on their floors, yet it was never known that they had given so much as a penny or a crust in charity; they never went to mass; grumbled perpetually at paying tithes; and were, in a word, of so cruel and grinding a temper as to receive from all those with whom they had any dealings, the nickname of the "Black Brothers."

The youngest brother, Gluck, was as completely opposed, in both appearance and character, to his seniors as could possibly be imagined or desired. He was not above twelve years old, fair, blue-eyed, and kind in temper to every living thing. He did not, of course, agree particularly well with his brothers, or, rather, they did not agree with him. He was usually appointed to the honorable office of turnspit, when there was anything to roast, which was not often; for, to do the brothers justice, they were hardly less sparing upon themselves than upon other people. At other times he used to clean the shoes, the floors, and sometimes the plates, occasionally getting what was left on them, by way of encouragement, and a wholesome quantity of dry blows, by way of education.

Things went on in this manner for a long time. At last came a very wet summer, and everything went wrong in the country round. The hay had hardly been got in, when the haystacks were floated bodily down to the sea by an inundation; the vines were cut to pieces with the hail; the corn was all killed by a

232

black blight; only in the Treasure Valley, as usual, all was safe. As it had rain when there was rain nowhere else, so it had sun when there was sun nowhere else. Everybody came to buy corn at the farm and went away pouring maledictions on the Black Brothers. They asked what they liked and got it, except from the poor people, who could only beg, and several of whom were starved at their very door, without the slightest regard or notice.

It was drawing toward winter, and very cold weather, when one day the two elder brothers had gone out, with their usual warning to little Gluck, who was left to mind the roast, that he was to let nobody in, and give nothing out. Gluck sat down quite close to the fire, for it was raining very hard, and the kitchen walls were by no means dry or comfortable looking. He turned and turned, and the roast got nice and brown. "What a pity," thought Gluck, "my brothers never ask anybody to dinner! I'm sure, when they've got such a nice piece of mutton as this, and nobody else has got so much as a piece of dry bread, it would do their hearts good to have somebody to eat it with them."

Just as he spoke there came a double knock at the house door, yet heavy and dull, as though the knocker had been tied up,—more like a puff than a knock.

"It must be the wind," said Gluck; "nobody else would venture to knock double knocks at our door."

No, it wasn't the wind; there it came again very hard, and—what was particularly astounding—the knocker seemed to be in a hurry and not in the least afraid of the consequences. Gluck went to the window and put his head out to see who it was.

It was the most extraordinary looking little gentleman he had ever seen in his life. He had a very large nose, slightly brass-colored; his cheeks were very round and very red, and might have warranted a supposition that he had been blowing a re-fractory fire for the last eight-and-forty hours; his eyes twinkled merrily through long silky eyelashes, his mustaches curled twice round like a corkscrew on each side of his mouth, and his hair, of a curious mixed pepper-and-salt color, descended far over

233

his shoulders. He was about four feet six in height, and wore a conical-pointed cap of nearly the same altitude, decorated with a black feather some three feet long. His doublet was prolonged behind into something resembling a violent exaggeration of what is now termed a "swallow-tail," but was much obscured by the swelling folds of an enormous black, glossy-looking cloak which must have been very much too long in calm weather, as the wind, whistling round the old house, carried it clear out from the wearer's shoulders to about four times his own length.

Gluck was so perfectly paralyzed by the singular appearance of his visitor that he remained fixed without uttering a word, until the old gentleman, having performed another and a more energetic concerto on the knocker, turned round to look after his fly-away cloak. In so doing he caught sight of Gluck's little yellow head jammed in the window, with its mouth and eyes very wide open indeed.

"Hello!" said the little gentleman, "that's not the way to answer the door; I'm wet, let me in."

To do the little gentleman justice, he was wet. His feather hung down between his legs like a beaten puppy's tail, dripping like an umbrella; and from the ends of his mustaches the water was running into his waistcoat-pockets, and out again like a millstream.

"I beg pardon, sir," said Gluck; "I'm very sorry, but I really can't."

"Can't what?" said the old gentleman.

"I can't let you in, sir,—I can't indeed; my brothers would beat me, sir, if I thought of such a thing. What do you want, sir?"

"Want?" said the old gentleman, petulantly, "I want fire and shelter; and there's your great fire there blazing, crackling, and dancing on the walls, with nobody to feel it. Let me in, I say; I only want to warm myself."

Gluck had had his head, by this time, so long out of the window that he began to feel it was really unpleasantly cold, and when he turned, and saw the beautiful fire rustling and roaring, and throwing long bright tongues up the chimney, as if it were licking its chops at the savory smell of the leg of mutton, his heart melted within him that it should be burning away for nothing. "He does look very wet," said little Gluck; "I'll just let him in for a quarter of an hour." Round he went to the door and opened it; and as the little gentleman walked in, through the house came a gust of wind that made the old chimneys totter.

"That's a good boy," said the little gentleman. "Never mind your brothers. I'll talk to them."

"Pray, sir, don't do any such thing," said Gluck. "I can't let you stay till they come; they'd be the death of me."

"Dear me," said the old gentleman, "I'm very sorry to hear that. How long may I stay?"

"Only till the mutton's done, sir," replied Gluck, "and it's very brown."

Then the old gentleman walked into the kitchen, and sat himself down on the hob, with the top of his cap accommodated up the chimney, for it was a great deal too high for the roof.

"You'll soon dry there, sir," said Gluck, and sat down again

to turn the mutton. But the old gentleman did *not* dry there, but went on drip, drip, dripping among the cinders, and the fire fizzed and sputtered and began to look very black and uncomfortable; never was such a cloak; every fold in it ran like a gutter.

"I beg your pardon, sir," said Gluck at length, after watching the water spreading in long quicksilver-like streams over the floor for a quarter of an hour; "mayn't I take your cloak?"

"No, thank you," said the old gentleman.

"Your cap, sir?"

"I'm all right, thank you," said the old gentleman, rather gruffly.

"But—sir—I'm very sorry," said Gluck, hesitatingly; "but—really, sir—you're putting the fire out."

"It'll take longer to do the mutton, then," replied his visitor, dryly.

Gluck was very puzzled by the behavior of his guest; it was such a strange mixture of coolness and humility. He turned away at the string meditatively for another five minutes.

"That mutton looks very nice," said the old gentleman, at length. "Can't you give me a little bit?"

"Impossible, sir," said Gluck.

"I'm very hungry," continued the old gentleman; "I've had nothing to eat yesterday, nor today. They surely couldn't miss a bit from the knuckle!"

He spoke in so very melancholy a tone that it quite melted Gluck's heart. "They promised me one slice today, sir," said he; "I can give you that, but not a bit more."

"That's a good boy," said the old gentleman again.

Then Gluck warmed a plate and sharpened a knife. "I don't care if I do get beaten for it," thought he. Just as he had cut a large slice out of the mutton, there came a tremendous rap at the door. The old gentleman jumped off the hob, as if it had suddenly become inconveniently warm. Gluck fitted the slice into the mutton again, with desperate efforts at exactitude, and ran up to open the door.

"What did you keep us waiting in the rain for?" said Schwartz, as he walked in, throwing his umbrella in Gluck's face.

"Ay! what for, indeed, you little vagabond?" said Hans, administering an educational box on the ear, as he followed his brother into the kitchen.

"Bless my soul!" said Schwartz, when he opened the door.

"Amen," said the little gentleman, who had taken his cap off, and was standing in the middle of the kitchen, bowing, with the utmost possible velocity.

"Who's that?" said Schwartz, catching up a rolling pin, and turning to Gluck with a fierce frown.

"I don't know, indeed, brother," said Gluck, in great terror.

"How did he get in?" roared Schwartz.

"My dear brother," said Gluck deprecatingly, "he was so very wet!"

The rolling pin was descending on Gluck's head; but, at the instant, the old gentleman interposed his conical cap, on which it crashed with a shock that shook the water out of it all over the room. What was very odd, the rolling pin no sooner touched

the cap, than it flew out of Schwartz's hand, spinning like a straw in a high wind, and fell into the corner at the further end of the room.

"Who are you, sir?" demanded Schwartz, turning upon him.

"What's your business?" snarled Hans.

"I'm a poor old man, sir," the little gentleman began very modestly, "and I saw your fire through the window and begged shelter for a quarter of an hour."

"Have the goodness to walk out again, then," said Schwartz. "We've quite enough water in our kitchen, without making it a drying-house."

"It is a cold day to turn an old man out in, sir; look at my gray hairs." They hung down to his shoulders, as I told you before.

"Ay!" said Hans, "there are enough of them to keep you warm. Walk!"

"I'm very, very hungry, sir; couldn't you spare me a bit of bread before I go?"

"Bread, indeed!" said Schwartz; "do you suppose we've nothing to do with our bread but to give it to such red-nosed fellows as you?"

238

"Why don't you sell your feather?" said Hans, sneeringly. "Out with you."

"A little bit," said the old gentleman.

"Be off!" said Schwartz.

"Pray, gentlemen."

"Off, and be hanged!" cried Hans, seizing him by the collar. But he had no sooner touched the old gentleman's collar, than away he went after the rolling pin, spinning round and round, till he fell into the corner on the top of it. Then Schwartz was very angry and ran at the old gentleman to turn him out; but he also had hardly touched him, when away he went after Hans and the rolling pin and hit his head against the wall as he tumbled into the corner. And so there they lay all three.

Then the old gentleman spun himself round with velocity in the opposite direction; continued to spin until his long cloak was all wound neatly about him; clapped his cap on his head, very much on one side (for it could not stand upright without going through the ceiling), gave an additional twist to his corkscrew mustaches, and replied with perfect coolness, "Gentlemen, I wish you a very good morning. At twelve o'clock to-night I'll call again; after such a refusal of hospitality as I have just experienced, you will not be surprised if that visit is the last I ever pay you."

"If ever I catch you here again," muttered Schwartz, coming, half frightened, out of the corner,—but before he could finish his sentence, the old gentleman had shut the house door behind him with a great bang, and past the window, at the same instant, drove a wreath of ragged cloud, that whirled and rolled away down the valley in all manner of shapes; turning over and over in the air; and melting away at last in a gush of rain.

"A very pretty business, indeed, Mr. Gluck!" said Schwartz. "Dish the mutton, sir. Bless me, why the mutton's been cut!"

"You promised me one slice, brother, you know," said Gluck.

"Oh! and you were cutting it hot, I suppose, and going to catch all the gravy. It'll be long before I promise you such a thing again. Leave the room, sir; and have the kindness to wait in the coal cellar till I call you."

Gluck left the room melancholy enough. The brothers ate as much mutton as they could and locked the rest in the cupboard. . . .

Such a night it was! Howling wind and rushing rain without intermission. The brothers put up all the shutters, and double-barred the door, before they went to bed. They usually slept in the same room. As the clock struck twelve, they were both awakened by a tremendous crash. Their door burst open with a violence that shook the house from top to bottom.

"What's that?" cried Schwartz, starting up in his bed.

"Only I," said the little gentleman.

The two brothers sat up on their bolster, and stared into the darkness. The room was full of water, and by a misty moonbeam, which found its way through a hole in the shutter, they could see, in the midst of it, an enormous foam globe, spinning round, and bobbing up and down like a cork, on which, as on a most luxurious cushion, reclined the little old gentleman, cap and all. There was plenty of room for it now, for the roof was off.

"Sorry to incommode you," said their visitor, ironically. "I'm afraid your beds are dampish; perhaps you had better go to your brother's room; I've left the ceiling on there."

They required no second admonition, but rushed into Gluck's room, wet through, and in an agony of terror.

"You'll find my card on the kitchen table," the old gentleman called after them. "Remember, the *last* visit."

"Pray Heaven it may be!" said Schwartz, shuddering. And the foam globe disappeared.

Dawn came at last, and the two brothers looked out of Gluck's little window in the morning. The Treasure Valley was one mass of ruin and desolation. The inundation had swept away trees, crops, and cattle, and left, in their stead, a waste of red sand and gray mud. The two brothers crept, shivering and horror-struck, into the kitchen. The water had gutted the whole first floor: corn, money, almost every movable thing had been swept away, and there was left only a small white card on the kitchen table. On it, in large, breezy, long-legged letters, were engraved the words:

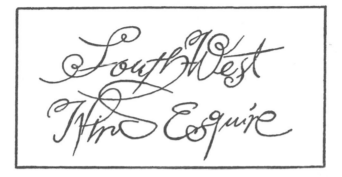

Southwest Wind, Esquire, was as good as his word. After the momentous visit above related, he entered the Treasure Valley no more; and, what was worse, he had so much influence with his relations, the West Winds in general, and used it so effectually, that they all adopted a similar line of conduct. So no rain fell in the valley from one year's end to another. Though everything remained green and flourishing in the plains below, the inheritance of the Three Brothers was a desert. What had once been the richest soil in the kingdom became a shifting heap of red sand; and the brothers, unable longer to contend with the adverse skies, abandoned their valueless patrimony in despair, to seek some means of gaining a livelihood among the cities and people of the plains. All their money was gone, and they had nothing left but some curious, old-fashioned pieces of gold plate, the last remnants of their ill-gotten wealth.

"Suppose we turn goldsmiths," said Schwartz to Hans, as they entered the large city. "It is a good knave's trade: we can put a great deal of copper into the gold, without any one's finding it out."

The thought was agreed to be a very good one; they hired a furnace, and turned goldsmiths. But two slight circumstances affected their trade: the first, that people did not approve of the coppered gold; the second, that the two elder brothers, whenever they had sold anything, used to leave little Gluck to mind the furnace, and go and drink out the money in the alehouse

241

next door. So they melted all their gold, without making money enough to buy more, and were at last reduced to one large drinking-mug, which an uncle of his had given to little Gluck, and which he was very fond of and would not have parted with for the world; though he never drank anything out of it but milk and water. The mug was a very odd mug to look at. The handle was formed of two wreaths of flowing golden hair, so finely spun that it looked more like silk than like metal, and these wreaths descended into, and mixed with, a beard and whiskers, of the same exquisite workmanship, which surrounded and decorated a very fierce little face, of the reddest gold imaginable, right in the front of the mug, with a pair of eyes in it which seemed to command its whole circumference. It was impossible to drink out of the mug without being subjected to an intense gaze out of the side of these eyes; and Schwartz positively averred that once, after emptying it full of Rhenish seventeen times, he had seen them wink! When it came to the mug's turn to be made into spoons, it half broke poor little Gluck's heart; but the brothers only laughed at him, tossed the mug into the melting-pot, and staggered out to the alehouse; leaving him, as usual, to pour the gold into bars, when it was all ready.

When they were gone, Gluck took a farewell look at his old friend in the melting-pot. The flowing hair was all gone; nothing remained but the red nose, and the sparkling eyes, which looked more malicious than ever. "And no wonder," thought Gluck, "after being treated in that way." He sauntered disconsolately to the window, and sat himself down to catch the fresh evening air, and escape the hot breath of the furnace. Now this window commanded a direct view of the range of mountains which, as I told you before, overhung the Treasure Valley, and more especially of the peak from which fell the Golden River. It was just at the close of the day, and when Gluck sat down at the window, he saw the rocks of the mountaintops all crimson and purple with the sunset; and there were bright tongues of fiery cloud burning and quivering about them; and the river, brighter than all, fell, in a waving

242

column of pure gold, from precipice to precipice, with the double arch of a broad purple rainbow stretched across it, flushing and fading alternately in the wreaths of spray.

"Ah!" said Gluck aloud, after he had looked at it for a little while, "if that river were really all gold, what a nice thing it would be!"

"No, it wouldn't, Gluck," said a clear, metallic voice, close at his ear.

"Bless me, what's that?" exclaimed Gluck, jumping up. There was nobody there. He looked round the room, and under the table, and a great many times behind him, but there was certainly nobody there, and he sat down again at the window. This time he didn't speak, but he couldn't help thinking again that it would be very convenient if the river were really all gold.

"Not at all, my boy," said the same voice, louder than before.

"Bless me!" said Gluck again, "what *is* that?" He looked again into all the corners and cupboards and then began turning round and round, as fast as he could, in the middle of the room, thinking there was somebody behind him, when the same voice struck again on his ear. It was singing now very merrily, "Lala-lira-la,"—no words, only a soft running effervescent melody, something like that of a kettle on the boil. Gluck looked out of the window. No, it was certainly in the house. Upstairs and downstairs. No, it was certainly in that very room, coming in quicker time and clearer notes every moment, "Lala-lira-la." All at once it struck Gluck that it sounded louder near the furnace. He ran to the opening and looked in. Yes, he saw right; it seemed to be coming, not only out of the furnace, but out of the pot. He uncovered it and ran back in a great fright, for the pot was certainly singing! He stood in the farthest corner of the room, with his hands up and his mouth open, for a minute or two, when the singing stopped, and the voice became clear and pronunciative.

"Hello!" said the voice.

Gluck made no answer.

"Hello, Gluck, my boy!" said the pot again.

Gluck summoned all his energies, walked straight up to the crucible, drew it out of the furnace, and looked in. The gold was all melted, and its surface as smooth and polished as a river; but instead of its reflecting little Gluck's head, as he looked in, he saw meeting his glance, from beneath the gold, the red nose and the sharp eyes of his old friend of the mug, a thousand times redder and sharper than ever he had seen them in his life.

"Come, Gluck, my boy," said the voice out of the pot again, "I'm all right; pour me out."

But Gluck was too much astonished to do anything of the kind.

"Pour me out, I say," said the voice rather gruffly.

Still Gluck couldn't move.

"*Will* you pour me out?" said the voice passionately. "I'm too hot!"

By a violent effort, Gluck recovered the use of his limbs, took hold of the crucible, and sloped it so as to pour out the gold. But instead of a liquid stream, there came out, first, a pair of

pretty little yellow legs, then some coat-tails, then a pair of arms
stuck akimbo, and, finally, the well-known head of his friend
the mug; all which articles, uniting as they rolled out, stood up
energetically on the floor, in the shape of a little golden dwarf,
about a foot and a half high.

"That's right!" said the dwarf, stretching out first his legs,
and then his arms, and then shaking his head up and down, and
as far round as it would go, for five minutes, without stopping,—
apparently with the view of ascertaining if he were quite cor-
rectly put together, while Gluck stood contemplating him in
speechless amazement. He was dressed in a slashed doublet of
spun gold, so fine in its texture that the prismatic colors gleamed
over it, as if on a surface of mother-of-pearl; and over this brilliant doublet his hair and beard fell full halfway to the ground,
in waving curls, so exquisitely delicate that Gluck could hardly
tell where they ended; they seemed to melt into air. The features of the face, however, were by no means finished with the
same delicacy; they were rather coarse, slightly inclining to
coppery in complexion, and indicative, in expression, of a very
pertinacious and intractable disposition in their small proprietor. When the dwarf had finished his self-examination, he
turned his small, sharp eyes full on Gluck, and stared at him

deliberately for a minute or two. "No, it wouldn't, Gluck, my boy," said the little man.

This was certainly rather an abrupt and unconnected mode of commencing conversation. It might indeed be supposed to refer to the course of Gluck's thoughts, which had first produced the dwarf's observations out of the pot; but whatever it referred to, Gluck had no inclination to dispute the dictum.

"Wouldn't it, sir?" said Gluck, very mildly and submissively indeed.

"No," said the dwarf conclusively. "No, it wouldn't." And with that, the dwarf pulled his cap hard over his brows and took two turns of three feet long, up and down the room, lifting his legs very high and setting them down very hard. This pause gave time for Gluck to collect his thoughts a little, and, seeing no great reason to view his diminutive visitor with dread and feeling his curiosity overcome his amazement, he ventured on a question of peculiar delicacy.

"Pray, sir," said Gluck, rather hesitatingly, "were you my mug?"

On which the little man turned sharp round, walked straight up to Gluck, and drew himself up to his full height. "I," said the little man, "am the King of the Golden River." Whereupon he turned about again, and took two more turns, some six feet long, in order to allow time for the consternation which this announcement produced in his auditor to evaporate. After which he again walked up to Gluck and stood still, as if expecting some comment on his communication.

Gluck determined to say something, at all events. "I hope Your Majesty is very well," said Gluck.

"Listen!" said the little man, deigning no reply to this polite inquiry. "I am the King of what you mortals call the Golden River. The shape you saw me in was owing to the malice of a stronger king, from whose enchantments you have this instant freed me. What I have seen of you, and your conduct to your wicked brothers, renders me willing to serve you; therefore attend to what I tell you. Whoever shall climb to the top of that mountain from which you see the Golden River issue and shall cast into the stream at its source three drops of holy water, for him, and for him only, the river shall turn to gold. But no one failing in his first can succeed in a second attempt; and if anyone shall cast unholy water into the river, it will overwhelm him, and he will become a black stone." So saying, the King of the Golden River turned away, and deliberately walked into the center of the hottest flame of the furnace. His figure became red, white, transparent, dazzling,—a blaze of intense light, —rose, trembled, and disappeared. The King of the Golden River had evaporated.

"Oh!" cried poor Gluck, running to look up the chimney after him; "oh dear, dear, dear me! My mug! my mug! my mug!"

The King of the Golden River had hardly made his extraordinary exit before Hans and Schwartz came roaring into the house, very savagely drunk. The discovery of the total loss of their last piece of plate had the effect of sobering them just enough to enable them to stand over Gluck, beating him very steadily for a quarter of an hour; at the expiration of which period they dropped into a couple of chairs, and requested to know what he had got to say for himself. Gluck told them his story, of which of course they did not believe a word. They beat him again, till their arms were tired, and staggered to bed. In the morning, however, the steadiness with which he adhered

247

to his story obtained him some degree of credence; the immediate consequence of which was that the two brothers, after wrangling a long time on the knotty question which of them should try his fortune first, drew their swords, and began fighting. The noise of the fray alarmed the neighbors, who, finding they could not pacify the combatants, sent for the constable.

Hans, on hearing this, contrived to escape, and hid himself; but Schwartz was taken before the magistrate, fined for breaking the peace, and having drunk out his last penny the evening before, was thrown into prison till he should pay.

When Hans heard this, he was much delighted, and determined to set out immediately for the Golden River. How to get the holy water was the question. He went to the priest, but the priest could not give any holy water to so abandoned a character. So Hans went to vespers in the evening for the first time in his life, and, under pretense of crossing himself, stole a cupful, and returned home in triumph.

Next morning he got up before the sun rose, put the holy water into a strong flask, and two bottles of wine and some meat in a basket, slung them over his back, took his alpine staff in his hand, and set off for the mountains.

On his way out of the town he had to pass the prison, and as he looked in at the windows, whom should he see but Schwartz himself peeping out of the bars and looking very disconsolate.

"Good morning, brother," said Hans; "have you any message for the King of the Golden River?"

Schwartz gnashed his teeth with rage and shook the bars with all his strength; but Hans only laughed at him, and advising him to make himself comfortable till he came back again, shouldered his basket, shook the bottle of holy water in Schwartz's face till it frothed again, and marched off in the highest spirits in the world.

It was, indeed, a morning that might have made any one happy, even with no Golden River to seek for. Level lines of dewy mist lay stretched along the valley, out of which rose the massy mountains,—their lower cliffs in pale gray shadow, hardly distinguishable from the floating vapor, but gradually ascend-

ing till they caught the sunlight, which ran in sharp touches of ruddy color along the angular crags, and pierced, in long level rays, through their fringes of spearlike pine. Far above shot up red splintered masses of castellated rock, jagged and shivered into myriads of fantastic forms, with here and there a streak of sunlit snow, traced down their chasms like a line of forked lightning; and, far beyond, and far above all these, fainter than the morning cloud, but purer and changeless, slept, in the blue sky, the utmost peaks of the eternal snow.

The Golden River, which sprang from one of the lower and snowless elevations, was now nearly in shadow; all but the uppermost jets of spray, which rose like slow smoke above the undulating line of the cataract, and floated away in feeble wreaths upon the morning wind.

On this object, and on this alone, Hans's eyes and thoughts were fixed; forgetting the distance he had to traverse, he set off at an imprudent rate of walking, which greatly exhausted him before he had scaled the first range of the green and low hills. He was, moreover, surprised, on surmounting them, to find that a large glacier, of whose existence, notwithstanding his previous knowledge of the mountains, he had been absolutely ignorant, lay between him and the source of the Golden River. He entered on it with the boldness of a practiced mountaineer; yet he thought he had never traversed so strange or so dangerous a glacier in his life. The ice was excessively slippery; and out of all its chasms came wild sounds of gushing water: not monotonous or low, but changeful and loud, rising occasionally into drifting passages of wild melody, then breaking off into short, melancholy tones, or sudden shrieks, resembling those of human voices in distress or pain. The ice was broken into thousands of confused shapes, but none, Hans thought, like the ordinary forms of splintered ice. There seemed a curious *expression* about all their outlines,—a perpetual resemblance to living features, distorted and scornful. Myriads of deceitful shadows and lurid lights played and floated about and through the pale blue pinnacles, dazzling and confusing the sight of the traveler; while his ears grew dull and his head giddy with the constant gush and roar of the concealed waters. These painful circumstances increased upon him as he advanced; the ice crashed and yawned into fresh chasms at his feet, tottering spires nodded around him, and fell thundering across his path; and though he had repeatedly faced these dangers on the most terrific glaciers, and in the wildest weather, it was with a new and oppressive feeling of panic-terror that he leaped the last chasm, and flung himself, exhausted and shuddering, on the firm turf of the mountain.

He had been compelled to abandon his basket of food, which became a perilous incumbrance on the glacier, and had now no means of refreshing himself but by breaking off and eating some of the pieces of ice. This, however, relieved his thirst; an hour's repose recruited his hardy frame, and, with the indomitable spirit of avarice, he resumed his laborious journey.

His way now lay straight up a ridge of bare, red rocks, without a blade of grass to ease the foot or a projecting angle to

afford an inch of shade from the south sun. It was past noon, and the rays beat intensely upon the steep path, while the whole atmosphere was motionless, and penetrated with heat. Intense thirst was soon added to the bodily fatigue with which Hans was now afflicted; glance after glance he cast on the flask of water which hung at his belt. "Three drops are enough," at last thought he; "I may, at least, cool my lips with it."

He opened the flask, and was raising it to his lips, when his eye fell on an object lying on the rock beside him; he thought it moved. It was a small dog, apparently in the last agony of death from thirst. Its tongue was out, its jaws dry, its limbs extended lifelessly. . . . Its eyes moved to the bottle which Hans held in his hand. He raised it, drank, spurned the animal with his foot, and passed on. And he did not know how it was, but he thought that a strange shadow had suddenly come across the blue sky.

The path became steeper and more rugged every moment; and the high hill air, instead of refreshing him, seemed to throw

his blood into a fever. The noise of the hill cataracts sounded like mockery in his ears; they were all distant, and his thirst increased every moment. Another hour passed, and he again looked down to the flask at his side; it was half empty, but there was much more than three drops in it. He stopped to open it, and again, as he did so, something moved in the path above him. It was a fair child, stretched nearly lifeless on the rock, its breast heaving with thirst, its eyes closed, and its lips parched and burning. Hans eyed it deliberately, drank, and passed on. And a dark gray cloud came over the sun, and long snakelike shadows crept up along the mountainsides. Hans struggled on. The sun was sinking, but its descent seemed to bring no coolness; the leaden weight of the dead air pressed upon his brow and heart, but the goal was near. He saw the cataract of the Golden River springing from the hillside, scarcely five hundred feet above him. He paused for a moment to breathe and sprang on to complete his task.

At this instant a faint cry fell on his ear. He turned and saw a gray-haired old man extended on the rocks. His eyes were sunk, his features deadly pale, and gathered into an expression of despair. "Water!"—He stretched his arms to Hans, and cried feebly,—"Water! I am dying."

"I have none," replied Hans; "thou hast had thy share of life." He strode over the prostrate body and darted on. And a flash of blue lightning rose out of the east, shaped like a sword; it shook thrice over the whole heaven, and left it dark with one heavy, impenetrable shade. The sun was setting; it plunged toward the horizon like a red-hot ball.

The roar of the Golden River rose on Hans's ear. He stood at the brink of the chasm through which it ran. Its waves were filled with the red glory of the sunset; they shook their crestlike tongues of fire, and flashes of bloody light gleamed along their foam. Their sound came mightier and mightier on his senses; his brain grew giddy with the prolonged thunder. Shuddering, he drew the flask from his girdle, and hurled it into the center of the torrent. As he did so, an icy chill shot through his limbs; he staggered, shrieked, and fell. The waters closed over his cry. And the moaning of the river rose wildly into the night, as it gushed over

The Black Stone.

Poor little Gluck waited very anxiously alone in the house for Hans's return. Finding he did not come back, he was terribly frightened and went and told Schwartz in the prison all that had happened. Then Schwartz was very much pleased and said that Hans must certainly have been turned into a black stone, and he should have all the gold to himself. But Gluck was very sorry and cried all night. When he got up in the morning there was no bread in the house, nor any money; so Gluck went and hired himself to another goldsmith, and he worked so hard, and so neatly, and so long every day, that he soon got money enough together to pay his brother's fine, and he went and gave it all to Schwartz, and Schwartz got out of prison. Then Schwartz was quite pleased and said he should have some of the gold of the river. But Gluck only begged he would go and see what had become of Hans.

Now when Schwartz had heard that Hans had stolen the holy water, he thought to himself that such a proceeding might not be considered altogether correct by the King of the Golden River, and determined to manage matters better. So he took more of Gluck's money and went to a druid priest, who gave him some holy water very readily for it. Then Schwartz was sure it was all quite right. So Schwartz got up early in the morning before the sun rose, and took some bread and wine in a basket, and put his holy water in a flask, and set off for the mountains. Like his brother, he was much surprised at the sight of the glacier and had great difficulty in crossing it, even after leaving his basket behind him. The day was cloudless, but not bright: a heavy purple haze was hanging over the sky, and the hills looked lowering and gloomy. And as Schwartz climbed the steep rock path, the thirst came upon him, as it had upon his brother, until he lifted his flask to his lips to drink. Then he saw the fair child lying near him on the rocks, and it cried to him, and moaned for water.

"Water, indeed!" said Schwartz. "I haven't half enough for myself," and passed on. And as he went he thought the sunbeams grew more dim, and he saw a low bank of black cloud rising out of the west; and when he had climbed for another hour the thirst overcame him again, and he would have drunk. Then he saw the old man lying before him on the path, and heard him cry out for water. "Water, indeed!" said Schwartz. "I haven't half enough for myself," and on he went.

Then again the light seemed to fade from before his eyes, and he looked up, and, behold, a mist of the color of blood had come over the sun; and the bank of black cloud had risen very high, and its edges were tossing and tumbling like the waves of the angry sea. And they cast long shadows, which flickered over Schwartz's path.

Then Schwartz climbed for another hour, and again his thirst returned; and as he lifted his flask to his lips, he thought he saw his brother Hans lying exhausted on the path before him, and as he gazed the figure stretched its arms to him, and cried for water. "Ha, ha," laughed Schwartz, "are you there? Remember the prison bars, my boy. Water, indeed! do you suppose I carried it all the way up here for *you?*" And he strode over the figure; yet, as he passed, he thought he saw a strange expression of mockery about its lips. And, when he had gone a few yards farther, he looked back; but the figure was not there.

And a sudden horror came over Schwartz, he knew not why; but the thirst for gold prevailed over his fear, and he rushed on. And the bank of black cloud rose to the zenith, and out of it came bursts of spiry lightning, and waves of darkness seemed

to heave and float between their flashes over the whole heavens. And the sky where the sun was setting was all level, and like a lake of blood; and a strong wind came out of that sky, tearing its crimson clouds into fragments, and scattering them far into the darkness. And when Schwartz stood by the brink of the Golden River, its waves were black like thunderclouds, but their foam was like fire; and the roar of the waters below and the thunder above met, as he cast the flask into the stream. And, as he did so, the lightning glared in his eyes, and the earth gave way beneath him, and the waters closed over his cry. And the moaning of the river rose wildly into the night, as it gushed over

The Two Black Stones.

When Gluck found that Schwartz did not come back, he was very sorry and did not know what to do. He had no money and was obliged to go and hire himself again to the goldsmith, who worked him very hard and gave him very little money. So, after a month or two, Gluck grew tired, and made up his mind to go and try his fortune with the Golden River. "The little king looked very kind," thought he. "I don't think he will turn me into a black stone." So he went to the priest, and the priest gave him some holy water as soon as he asked for it. Then Gluck took some bread in his basket, and the bottle of water, and set off very early for the mountains.

If the glacier had occasioned a great deal of fatigue to his brothers, it was twenty times worse for him, who was neither so strong nor so practiced on the mountains. He had several very bad falls, lost his basket and bread, and was very much frightened at the strange noises under the ice. He lay a long time to rest on the grass, after he had got over, and began to climb the hill just in the hottest part of the day. When he had climbed for an hour, he got dreadfully thirsty, and was going to drink like his brothers, when he saw an old man coming down the path above him, looking very feeble, and leaning on a staff. "My son," said the old man, "I am faint with thirst; give me some of that water." Then Gluck looked at him, and when

256

he saw that he was pale and weary, he gave him the water. "Only pray don't drink it all," said Gluck. But the old man drank a great deal, and gave him back the bottle two-thirds empty. Then he bade him good speed, and Gluck went on again merrily. And the path became easier to his feet, and two or three blades of grass appeared upon it, and some grasshoppers began singing on the bank beside it; and Gluck thought he had never heard such merry singing.

Then he went on for another hour, and the thirst increased on him so that he thought he should be forced to drink. But, as he raised the flask, he saw a little child lying panting by the roadside, and it cried out piteously for water. Then Gluck struggled with himself and determined to bear the thirst a little longer; and he put the bottle to the child's lips, and it drank it all but a few drops. Then it smiled on him and got up, and ran down the hill; and Gluck looked after it, till it became as small as a little star, and then turned, and began climbing again.

And then there were all kinds of sweet flowers growing on the rocks, bright green moss, with pale pink starry flowers, and soft-belled gentians, more blue than the sky at its deepest, and pure white transparent lilies. And crimson and purple butterflies darted hither and thither, and the sky sent down such pure light that Gluck had never felt so happy in his life.

Yet, when he had climbed for another hour, his thirst became intolerable again; and, when he looked at his bottle, he saw that there were only five or six drops left in it, and he could not venture to drink. And as he was hanging the flask to his belt again, he saw a little dog lying on the rocks, gasping for breath,—just as Hans had seen it on the day of his ascent. And Gluck stopped and looked at it, and then at the Golden River, not five hundred yards above him; and he thought of the dwarf's words, that no one could succeed, except in his first attempt; and he tried to pass the dog, but it whined piteously, and Gluck stopped again. "Poor beastie," said Gluck, "it'll be dead when I come down again, if I don't help it." Then he looked closer and closer at it, and its eye turned on him so mournfully that he could not stand it. "Confound the king and his gold, too!" said Gluck; and he opened the flask, and poured all the water into the dog's mouth.

The dog sprang up and stood on its hind legs. Its tail disappeared, its ears became long, longer, silky, golden; its nose became very red, its eyes became very twinkling; in three seconds the dog was gone, and before Gluck stood his old acquaintance, the King of the Golden River.

"Thank you," said the monarch; "but don't be frightened, it's all right"; for Gluck showed manifest symptoms of consternation at this unlooked-for reply to his last observation. "Why didn't you come before," continued the dwarf, "instead of sending me those rascally brothers of yours, for me to have the trouble of turning into stones? Very hard stones they make, too."

"Oh, dear me!" said Gluck, "have you really been so cruel?"

"Cruel?" said the dwarf. "They poured unholy water into my stream,—do you suppose I'm going to allow that?"

"Why," said Gluck, "I am sure, sir,—Your Majesty, I mean,—

258

they got the water out of the church font."

"Very probably," replied the dwarf; "but," and his countenance grew stern as he spoke, "the water which has been refused to the cry of the weary and dying is unholy, though it had been blessed by every saint in heaven; and the water which is found in the vessel of mercy is holy, though it had been defiled with corpses."

So saying, the dwarf stooped and plucked a lily that grew at his feet. On its white leaves hung three drops of clear dew, and the dwarf shook them into the flask which Gluck held in his hand. "Cast these into the river," he said, "and descend on the other side of the mountains into the Treasure Valley. And so good speed."

As he spoke, the figure of the dwarf became indistinct. The playing colors of his robe formed themselves into a prismatic mist of dewy light; he stood for an instant veiled with them as with the belt of a broad rainbow. The colors grew faint, the mist rose into the air; the monarch had evaporated.

And Gluck climbed to the brink of the Golden River, and its waves were as clear as crystal and as brilliant as the sun. And when he cast the three drops of dew into the stream, there opened where they fell a small circular whirlpool, into which the waters descended with a musical noise.

Gluck stood watching it for some time, very much disappointed, because not only the river was not turned into gold, but its waters seemed much diminished in quantity. Yet he obeyed his friend the dwarf and descended the other side of the mountains, toward the Treasure Valley; and, as he went, he thought he heard the noise of water working its way under the ground. And when he came in sight of the Treasure Valley, behold, a river like the Golden River was springing from a new cleft of the rocks above it, and was flowing in innumerable streams among the dry heaps of red sand.

And as Gluck gazed, fresh grass sprang beside the new streams, and creeping plants grew and climbed among the moistening soil. Young flowers opened suddenly along the river sides, as stars leap out when twilight is deepening, and thickets of myrtle and tendrils of vine cast lengthening shadows over the valley as they grew. And thus the Treasure Valley became a garden again, and the inheritance which had been lost by cruelty was regained by love.

And Gluck went and dwelt in the valley, and the poor were never driven from his door; so that his barns became full of corn, and his house of treasure. And, for him, the river had, according to the dwarf's promise, become a River of Gold.

And to this day the inhabitants of the valley point out the place where the three drops of holy dew were cast into the stream, and trace the course of the Golden River under the ground, until it emerges in the Treasure Valley. And at the top of the cataract of the Golden River are still to be seen two black stones, round which the waters howl mournfully every day at sunset; and these stones are still called, by the people of the valley, THE BLACK BROTHERS.

TEN YEARS before this story begins, Raff Brinker lost his memory when he was injured on the dikes. On that very day Raff gave a gold watch to his wife and asked her to keep it safely until he could return it to the owner. He also buried his life savings of a thousand guilders. He was injured before he could tell his wife the name of the owner of the watch, or where he had buried the money. Frau Brinker and the two children, Hans and Gretel, were very poor all this time.

As his father seemed to be getting worse, Hans persuaded the greatest surgeon in Holland, Dr. Boekman, to operate. The operation was successful, but Raff was very weak and needed special food. Hans sold his skates to provide it, even though it meant he would not be able to take part in the great skating race.

Mary Mapes Dodge

MYSTERY— AND THE RACE

ILLUSTRATED BY *Dorothy Short*

THE sun had gone down quite out of sight when Hans, with a happy heart but with something like a sneer on his countenance, as he jerked off the wooden "runners," trudged hopefully toward the tiny hutlike building, known of old as the "idiot's cottage."

Duller eyes than his would have discerned two slight figures moving near the doorway.

That gray, well-patched jacket and the dull blue skirt covered with an apron of still duller blue, that faded, close-fitting cap, and those quick little feet in their great boatlike shoes, they were Gretel's of course. He would have known them anywhere.

That bright, coquettish, red jacket, with its pretty skirt, bordered with black, that graceful cap bobbing over the gold earrings, that dainty apron, and those snug leather shoes that seemed to have grown with the feet, why if the Pope of Rome had sent them to him by express, Hans could have sworn they were Annie's.

The two girls were slowly pacing up and down in front of the cottage. Their arms were entwined, of course, and their heads were nodding and shaking as emphatically as if all the affairs of the kingdom were under discussion.

With a joyous shout, Hans hastened toward them.

"Huzza, girls, I've found work!"

This brought his mother to the cottage door.

She, too, had pleasant tidings. The father was still improving. He had been sitting up nearly all day, and was now sleeping as Dame Brinker declared, "just as quiet as a lamb."

"It is my turn now, Hans," said Annie, drawing him aside after he had told his mother the good word from Mynheer van Holp. "Your skates are sold and here's the money."

"Seven guilders!" cried Hans, counting the pieces in astonishment. "Why, that is three times as much as I paid for them."

"I cannot help that," said Annie. "If the buyer knew no better, it is not our fault."

Hans looked up quickly.

"Oh, Annie!"

"Oh, Hans!" she mimicked, pursing her lips, and trying to look desperately wicked and unprincipled.

"Now, Annie, I know you would never mean that! You must return some of this money."

"But I'll not do any such thing," insisted Annie. "They're sold, and that's an end of it." Then seeing that he looked really pained she added in a lower tone,—

"Will you believe me, Hans, when I say that there has been no mistake, that the person who bought your skates *insisted* upon paying seven guilders for them?"

"I will," he answered; and the light from his clear blue eyes seemed to settle and sparkle under Annie's lashes.

Dame Brinker was delighted at the sight of so much silver, but when she learned that Hans had parted with his treasures to obtain it, she sighed, as she exclaimed:

"Bless thee, child! That will be a sore loss for thee!"

"Here, Mother," said the boy, plunging his hands far into his pocket, "here is more; we shall be rich if we keep on!"

"Aye, indeed," she answered, eagerly reaching forth her hand. Then, lowering her voice, added, "We *should* be rich but for that Jan Kamphuisen. He was at the willow tree years ago, Hans, depend upon it!"

"Indeed, it seems likely," sighed Hans. "Well, Mother, we must give up the money bravely. It is certainly gone; the father has told us all he knows. Let us think no more about it."

"That's easy saying, Hans. I shall try, but it's hard, and my poor man wanting so many comforts. Bless me! How girls fly about! They were here but this instant. Where did they run to?"

"They slipped behind the cottage," said Hans, "like enough to hide from us. Hist! I'll catch them for you! They both can move quicker and softer than yonder rabbit, but I'll give them a good start first."

"Why, there *is* a rabbit, sure enough. Hold, Hans, the poor thing must have been in sore need to venture from its burrow this bitter weather. I'll get a few crumbs for it within."

So saying, the good woman bustled into the cottage. She soon came out again, but Hans had forgotten to wait, and the rabbit after taking a cool survey of the premises had scampered off to unknown quarters. Turning the corner of the cottage, Dame Brinker came upon the children. Hans and Gretel were standing before Annie who was seated carelessly upon a stump.

"That is as good as a picture!" cried Dame Brinker, halting in admiration of the group. "Many a painting have I seen at the grand house at Heidelberg not a whit prettier. My two are rough chubs, Annie, but *you* look like a fairy."

"Do I?" laughed Annie, sparkling with animation. "Well then, Gretel and Hans, imagine I'm your godmother just paying you a visit. Now I'll grant you each a wish. What will you have, Master Hans?"

A shade of earnestness passed over Annie's face as she looked up at him; perhaps it was because she wished from the depths of her heart that for once she could have a fairy's power.

Something whispered to Hans that, for the moment, she was more than mortal.

"I wish," said he, solemnly, "that I could find something I was searching for last night!"

Gretel laughed merrily. Dame Brinker moaned, "Shame on you, Hans!" and passed wearily into the cottage.

The fairy godmother sprang up and stamped her foot three times.

"Thou shalt have thy wish," said she, "let them say what they will." Then, with playful solemnity, she put her hand in her apron pocket and drew forth a large glass bead. "Bury this," said she, giving it to Hans, "where I have stamped, and ere moon-rise thy wish shall be granted."

Gretel laughed more merrily than ever.

The godmother pretended great displeasure.

"Naughty child," said she, scowling terribly. "In punishment for laughing at a fairy, *thy* wish shall not be granted."

"Ha!" cried Gretel in high glee. "Better wait till you're asked, godmother. I haven't made any wish!"

Annie acted her part well. Never smiling, through all their merry laughter, she stalked away, the embodiment of offended dignity.

"Good night, fairy!" they cried again and again.

"Good night, mortals!" she called out at last as she sprang over a frozen ditch, and ran quickly homeward.

"Oh, isn't she—just like flowers, so sweet and lovely!" cried Gretel, looking after her in great admiration. "And to think how many days she stays in that dark room with her grandmother. Why, Hans! What is the matter? What are you going to do?"

"Wait and see!" answered Hans as he plunged into the cottage and came out again, all in an instant, bearing the spade and ysbreeker in his hands. "I'm going to bury my magic bead!"

264

Raff Brinker still slept soundly; his wife took a small block of peat from her nearly exhausted store, and put it upon the embers. Then opening the door, she called gently: "Come in, children."

"Mother! Mother! See here!" shouted Hans.

"Holy St. Bavon!" exclaimed the dame, springing over the door step. "What ails the boy!"

"Come quick, Mother," he cried, in great excitement, working with all his might, and driving in the ysbreeker at each word. "Don't you see? *This* is the spot, right here on the south side of the stump. Why didn't we think of it last night? *The stump* is the old willow tree, the one you cut down last spring because it shaded the potatoes. That little tree wasn't here when father —Huzza!"

Dame Brinker could not speak. She dropped on her knees beside Hans just in time to see him drag forth—*the old stone pot!*

He thrust in his hand and took out—a piece of brick, then another, then another, then, the stocking and the pouch, black and moldy, but filled with the long-lost treasure!

Such a time! Such laughing! Such crying! Such counting, after they went into the cottage! It was a wonder that Raff did not waken. His dreams were pleasant, however, for he smiled in his sleep.

Dame Brinker and her children had a fine supper, I can assure you. No need of saving the delicacies now.

"We'll get Father some nice, fresh things tomorrow," said the dame, as she brought forth cold meat, wine, bread, and jelly, and placed them on the clean pine table. "Sit by, children, sit by."

That night Annie fell asleep wondering whether it was a knife Hans had lost, and thinking how funny it would be if he should find it, after all.

Hans had scarcely closed his eyes, before he found himself trudging through a thicket; pots of gold were lying all around, and watches and skates and glittering beads were swinging from every branch.

Strange to say, each tree, as he approached it, changed into a stump, and on the stump sat the prettiest fairy imaginable, clad in a scarlet jacket and a blue petticoat.

Something else than the missing guilders was brought to light on the day of the fairy godmother's visit. This was the story of the watch that for ten long years had been so jealously guarded by Raff's faithful vrouw. Through many an hour of sore temptation she had dreaded almost to look upon it, lest she might be tempted to disobey her husband's request. It had been hard to see her children hungry and to know that the watch, if sold, would enable the roses to bloom in their cheeks again. "But nay," she would exclaim, "Meitje Brinker is not one to forget her man's last bidding, come what may!"

"Take good care of this, mine vrouw," he had said, as he handed it to her: that was all. No explanation followed, for the words were scarcely spoken, when one of his fellow workmen rushed into the cottage, crying, "Come, man! The waters are rising! You're wanted on the dikes."

Raff had started at once, and that was the last she saw of him in his right mind.

On the day when Hans was in Amsterdam looking for work,

and Gretel, after performing her household labors, was wandering about in search of chips, twigs, anything that could be burned, Dame Brinker with suppressed excitement had laid the watch in her husband's hand.

"It wasn't in reason," as she afterwards said to Hans, "to wait any longer, when a word from the father would settle all; no woman living but would want to know how he came by that watch." Raff Brinker turned the bright, polished thing over and over in his hand—then he examined the bit of smoothly ironed black ribbon fastened to it; he seemed hardly to recognize it. At last he said, "Ah, I remember this! Why, you've been rubbing it, vrouw, till it shines like a new guilder."

"Aye," said Dame Brinker, nodding her head complacently.

Raff looked at it again. "Poor boy!" he murmured, then fell into a brown study.

This was too much for the dame. "'Poor boy!'" she echoed, somewhat tartly. "What do you think I'm standing here for, Raff Brinker, and my spinning a-waiting, if not to hear more than that?"

"I told ye all, long since," said Raff, positively, as he looked up in surprise.

"Indeed, and you never did!" retorted the vrouw.

"Well, if not, since it's no affair of ours, we'll say no more about it," said Raff, shaking his head sadly; "like enough while I've been dead on the earth, all this time, the poor boy's died and been in heaven. He looked near enough to it, poor lad!"

"Raff Brinker! If you're going to treat me this way, and I nursing you and bearing with you since I was twenty-two years old; it's a shame; aye, and a disgrace!" cried the vrouw growing quite red and scant of breath.

Raff's voice was feeble yet, "Treat you *what* way, Meitje?"

"What way," said Dame Brinker, mimicking his voice and manner, "what way? Why just as every woman in the world is treated after she's stood by a man through the worst, like a—"

"Meitje!"

Raff was leaning forward with outstretched arms. His eyes were full of tears.

In an instant Dame Brinker was at his feet, clasping his hands in hers.

"Oh, what have I done! Made my good man cry, and he not back with me four days! Look up, Raff! Nay, Raff, my own boy, I'm sorry I hurt thee. It's hard not to be told about the watch after waiting ten years to know; but I'll ask thee no more, Raff. Here, we'll put the thing away that's made the first trouble between us, after God just gave thee back to me."

"I was a fool to cry, Meitje," he said, kissing her, "and it's no more than right that ye should know the truth. But it seemed as if it might be telling the secrets of the dead to talk about the matter."

"Is the man—the lad—thou wert talking of dead, think thee?" asked the vrouw, hiding the watch in her hand, but seating herself expectantly on the end of his long foot bench.

"It's hard telling," he answered.

"Was he so sick, Raff?"

"No, not sick, I may say; but troubled, vrouw, very troubled."

"Had he done any wrong, think ye?" she asked, lowering her voice.

Raff nodded.

"*Murder?*" whispered the wife, not daring to look up.

"He said it was like to that, indeed."

"Oh! Raff, you frighten me. Tell me more, you speak so strange, and you tremble. I must know all."

"If I tremble, mine vrouw, it must be from the fever. There is no guilt on my soul, thank God!"

"Take a sip of this wine, Raff. There, now you are better. It was like to a crime you were saying."

"Aye, Meitje, like to murder; *that* he told me himself. But I'll never believe it. A likely lad, fresh and honest looking as our own youngster, but with something not so bold and straight about him."

"Aye, I know," said the dame, gently, fearing to interrupt the story.

"He came upon me quite sudden," continued Raff. "I had never seen his face before, the palest, frightenedest face that

268

ever was. He caught me by the arm, 'You look like an honest man,' says he."

"Aye, he was right in that," interrupted the dame, emphatically.

Raff looked somewhat bewildered.

"Where was I, mine vrouw?"

"The lad took hold of your arm, Raff," she said, gazing at him anxiously.

"Aye, so. The words come awkward to me, and everything is half like a dream, ye see."

"S-stut! What wonder, poor man," sighed the dame, stroking his hand. "If ye had not had enough for a dozen, the wit would never have come to ye again. Well, the lad caught ye by the arm and said ye looked honest. (Well he might!) What then? Was it noontime?"

"Nay; before daylight, long before early chimes."

"It was the same day you were hurt," said the dame. "I know it seemed that you went to your work in the middle of the night. You left off where he caught your arm, Raff."

"Yes," resumed her husband, "and I can see his face this minute—so white and wild looking. 'Take me down the river a way,' says he. I was working then, you'll remember, far down on the line, across from Amsterdam. I told him I was no boatman. 'It's an affair of life and death,' says he. 'Take me on a few miles. Yonder skiff is not locked, but it may be a poor man's boat and I'd be loath to rob him!' (The words might differ some, vrouw, for it's all like a dream.) Well, I took him down, it might be six or eight miles, and then he said he could run the rest of the way on shore. I was in haste to get the boat back. Before he jumped out, he says, sobbing-like, 'I can trust you. I've done a thing—God knows I never intended it—but the man is dead. I must fly from Holland.' "

"What was it, did he say, Raff? Had he been shooting at a comrade, as they do down at the University at Gottingen?"

"I can't recall that. Mayhap he told me; but it's all like a dream. I said it wasn't for me, a good Hollander, to cheat the laws of my country by helping him off that way; but he kept saying, 'God knows I am innocent!' and looked at me in the starlight as fair, now, and clear-eyed as our little Hans might—and I just pulled away faster."

"It must have been Jan Kamphuisen's boat," remarked Dame Brinker, dryly. "None other would have left his oars out that careless."

"Aye, it was Jan's boat sure enough. The man will be coming in to see me Sunday, likely, if he's heard; and young Hoogsvliet too. Where was I?"

"Where were you? Why not very far, forsooth—the lad hadn't yet given ye the watch—alack I misgive whether he came by it honestly!"

"Why, vrouw!" exclaimed Raff in an injured tone. "He was dressed soft and fine as the prince himself. The watch was his own, clear enough."

"How came he to give it up?" asked the dame, looking uneasily at the fire, for it needed another block of peat.

"I told ye just now," he answered with a puzzled air.

"Tell me again," said Dame Brinker, wisely warding off another digression.

"Well, just before jumping from the boat, he says, handing me the watch, 'I'm flying from my country as I never thought I could. I'll trust you because you look honest. Will you take this to my father, not today, but in a week, and tell him his unhappy boy sent it; and tell him if ever the time comes that he wants me to come back to him, I'll brave everything and come. Tell him to send a letter to—to'— There, the rest is all gone from me. I *can't* remember where the letter was to go. Poor lad, poor lad!" resumed Raff, sorrowfully, taking the watch from his vrouw's lap, as he spoke. "And it's never been sent to his father to this day."

"I'll take it, Raff, never fear, the moment Gretel gets back. She will be in soon. What was the father's name, did you say? Where were you to find him?"

"Alack!" answered Raff, speaking very slowly. "It's all slipped me. I can see the lad's face, and his great eyes, just as plain! And I remember his opening the watch, and snatching something from it and kissing it. But no more. All the rest whirls past me; there's a kind of sound like rushing waters comes over me when I try to think."

"Aye. That's plain to see, Raff; but I've had the same feeling after a fever. You're tired now; I must get ye straight on the bed again. Where *is* the child, I wonder?"

Dame Brinker opened the door, and called, "Gretel! Gretel!"

"Stand aside, vrouw," said Raff, feebly, as he leaned forward and endeavored to look out upon the bare landscape. "I've half a mind to stand beyond the door just once."

"Nay, nay," she laughed. "I'll tell the meester how ye tease and fidget and bother to be let out in the air; and, if he says it, I'll bundle ye warm tomorrow, and give ye a turn on your feet. But I'm freezing you with this door open. I declare if there isn't Gretel with her apron full, skating on the canal, like wild. Why, man," she continued almost in a scream, as she slammed the door, "thou'rt walking to the bed without my touching thee! Thou'lt fall!"

The dame's "thee" proved her mingled fear and delight, even more than the rush which she made toward her husband. Soon he was comfortably settled under the new cover, declaring as his vrouw tucked him in snug and warm, that it was the last daylight that should see him abed.

271

"Aye! I can hope it myself," laughed Dame Brinker, "now you have been frisking about at that rate." As Raff closed his eyes, the dame hastened to revive her fire, or rather to dull it, for Dutch peat is like a Dutchman, slow to kindle, but very good at a blaze when once started. Then putting her neglected spinning wheel away, she drew forth her knitting from some invisible pocket and seated herself by the bedside.

"If you could remember that man's name, Raff," she began cautiously, "I might take the watch to him, while you're sleeping; Gretel can't but be in soon."

Raff tried to think, but in vain.

"Could it be Boomphoffen?" suggested the dame. "I've heard how they've had two sons turn out bad—Gerard and Lambert."

"It might be," said Raff. "Look if there's letters on the watch, that'll guide us some."

"Bless thee, man," cried the happy dame, eagerly lifting the watch, "why thou'rt sharper than ever! Sure enough. Here's letters! L.J.B. That's Lambert Boomphoffen you may depend. What the J. is for I can't say; but they used to be grand kind o' people, high-feathered as fancy fowl—just the kind to give their children all double names, which isn't Scripture anyway."

"I don't know about that, vrouw. Seems to me there's long, mixed names in the Holy Book, hard enough to make out. But you've got the right guess at a jump. It was your way always," said Raff, closing his eyes. "Take the watch to Boompkinks and try."

"Not Boompkinks, I know no such name; it's Boomphoffen."

"Aye, take it there."

"Take it there, man! Why the whole brood of 'em's been gone to America these four years. But go to sleep, Raff; you look pale and out of strength. It'll all come to you, what's best to do, in the morning.

"So, Mistress Gretel! Here you are at last!"

Before Raff awoke that evening, the fairy godmother, as we know, had been at the cottage, the guilders were once more safely locked in the big chest, and Dame Brinker and the children were faring sumptuously on meat and white bread and wine.

So the mother, in the joy of her heart, told them the story of the watch as far as she deemed it prudent to divulge it. It was no more than fair, she thought, that the poor things should know, after keeping the secret so safe ever since they had been old enough to know anything.

The next sun brought a busy day to the Brinkers. In the first place the news of the thousand guilders had, of course, to be told to the father. Such tidings as that surely could not harm him. Then while Gretel was diligently obeying her mother's injunction to "clean the place fresh as a new brewing," Hans and the dame sallied forth to revel in the purchasing of peat and provisions.

Hans was careless and contented; the dame was filled with delightful anxieties caused by the unreasonable demands of ten thousand guilders' worth of new wants that had sprung up like mushrooms in a single night. The happy woman talked so largely to Hans on their way to Amsterdam, and brought back such little bundles after all, that he scratched his bewildered head as he leaned against the chimney piece, wondering whether, "bigger the pouch, tighter the string" was in Jacob Cats, and therefore true, or whether he had dreamed it when he lay in a fever.

"What thinking on, Big-eyes?" chirruped his mother, half reading his thoughts as she bustled about, preparing the dinner. "What thinking on? Why, Raff, would ye believe it, the child thought to carry half Amsterdam back on his head. Bless us! He would have bought as much coffee as would have filled this fire pot. 'No, no, my lad!' says I, 'no time for leaks when the ship is rich laden'; and then how he stared! Aye, just as he stares this minute. Hoot, lad! Fly around a mite. Ye'll grow to the chimney place with your staring and wondering. Now, Raff, here's your chair at the head of the table, where it should be, for there's a man to the house now—I'd say it to the king's face. Aye, that's the way—lean on Hans; there's a strong staff for you! Growing like a weed, too, and it seems only yesterday since he was toddling. Sit by, my man, sit by."

"Can you call to mind, vrouw," said Raff, settling himself cautiously in the big chair, "the wonderful music box that cheered your working in the big house at Heidelberg?"

"Aye, that I can," answered the dame. "Three turns of a brass key, and the witchy thing would send the music fairly running up and down one's back. I remember it well. But, Raff" (growing solemn in an instant), "you would never throw our guilders away for a thing like that?"

"No, no, not I, vrouw; for the good Lord has already given me a music box without pay."

All three cast quick, frightened glances at one another and at Raff. Were his wits on the wing again?

"Aye, and a music box that fifty pouchfull would not buy from me," insisted Raff. "And it's set going by the turn of a mop handle, and it slips and glides around the room, everywhere in a flash, carrying the music about till you'd swear the birds were back again."

"Holy St. Bavon!" screeched the dame. "What's in the man?"

"Comfort and joy, vrouw, that's what's in him! Ask Gretel, ask my little music box Gretel, if your man has lacked comfort and joy this day."

"Not he, Mother," laughed Gretel. "He's been *my* music box, too. We sang together half the time you were gone."

After dinner the affair of the watch was talked over, and the mysterious initials duly discussed.

Hans had just pushed back his stool, intending to start at once for Mynheer Van Holp's, and his mother had risen to put the watch away in its old hiding place, when they heard the sound of wheels upon the frozen ground.

Someone knocked at the door, opening it at the same time.

"Come in," stammered Dame Brinker hastily trying to hide the watch in her bosom. "Oh! is it you, mynheer? Good day, the father is nearly well, as you see. It's a poor place to greet you in, mynheer, and the dinner not cleared away."

Dr. Boekman scarcely noticed the dame's apology. He was evidently in haste.

274

"Ahem!" he exclaimed. "Not needed here, I perceive. The patient is mending fast."

"Well he may, mynheer," cried the dame, "for only last night we found a thousand guilders that's been lost to us these ten years."

Dr. Boekman opened his eyes.

"Yes, mynheer," said Raff. "I bid the vrouw tell you, though it's to be held a secret among us, for I see you can keep your lips closed as well as any man."

The doctor scowled. He never liked personal remarks.

"Now, mynheer," continued Raff, "you can take your rightful pay. God knows you have earned it, if bringing such a poor tool back to the world and his family can be called a service. Tell the vrouw what's to pay, mynheer; she will hand out the sum right willingly."

"Tut! Tut!" said the doctor kindly. "Say nothing about money. I can find plenty of such pay any time, but gratitude comes seldom. That boy's 'thank you,'" he added, nodding sidewise toward Hans, "was pay enough for me."

"Like enough ye have a boy of your own," said Dame Brinker, quite delighted to see the great man becoming so sociable.

Dr. Boekman's good nature vanished at once. He gave a growl (at least, it seemed so to Gretel), but made no actual reply.

"Do not think the vrouw meddlesome, mynheer," said Raff. "She has been sore touched of late about a lad whose folks have gone away, none know where; and I had a message for them from the young gentleman."

"The name was Boomphoffen," said the dame eagerly. "Do you know aught of the family, mynheer?"

The doctor's reply was brief and gruff.

"Yes. A troublesome set. They went long since to America."

"It might be, Raff," persisted Dame Brinker, timidly, "that the meester knows somebody in that country, though I'm told they are mostly savages over there. If he could get the watch to the Boomphoffens with the poor lad's message, it would be a most blessed thing."

275

"Tut, vrouw, why pester the good meester and dying men and women wanting him everywhere? How do ye know ye have the true name?"

"I'm sure of it," she replied. "They had a son Lambert, and there's an L. for Lambert and a B. for Boomphoffen, on the back; though to be sure there's an odd J. too, but the meester can look for himself."

So saying, she drew forth the watch.

"L.J.B.!" cried Dr. Boekman, springing toward her.

Why attempt to describe the scene that followed? I need only say that the lad's message was delivered to his father at last, delivered while the great surgeon was sobbing like a little child.

"Laurens! My Laurens!" he cried, gazing with yearning eyes at the watch as he held it tenderly in his palm. "Ah, if I had but known sooner! Laurens a homeless wanderer! Great Heaven! He may be suffering, dying at this moment! Think, man, where is he? Where did my boy say that the letter must be sent?"

Raff shook his head sadly.

"Think!" implored the doctor. Surely the memory so lately awakened through his aid could not refuse to serve him in a moment like this.

"It is all gone, mynheer," sighed Raff.

Hans, forgetting distinctions of rank and station, forgetting everything but that his good friend was in trouble, threw his arms around the doctor's neck.

"I can find your son, mynheer. If alive, he is *somewhere*. The earth is not so very large; I will devote every day of my life to the search. Mother can spare me, now. You are rich, mynheer; send me where you will."

Gretel began to cry. It was right for Hans to go; but how could they ever live without him?

Dr. Boekman made no reply, neither did he push Hans away. His eyes were fixed anxiously upon Raff Brinker. Suddenly he lifted the watch, and with trembling eagerness attempted to open it. Its stiffened spring yielded at last; the case flew open, disclosing a watchpaper in the back bearing a group of blue forget-me-nots. Raff, seeing a shade of intense disappointment pass over the doctor's face, hastened to say,—

"There was something else in it, mynheer, but the young gentleman tore it out before he handed it to me. I saw him kiss it as he put it away."

"It was his mother's picture," moaned the doctor. "She died when he was ten years old. Thank God, the boy had not forgotten! Both dead? It is impossible!" he cried, starting up. "My boy is alive. You shall hear his story. Laurens acted as my assistant. By mistake he portioned out the wrong medicine for one of my patients—a deadly poison; but it was never administered, for I discovered the error in time. The man died that day. I was detained with other bad cases until the next evening. When I reached home my boy was gone. Poor Laurens!" sobbed the doctor, breaking down completely. "Never to hear from me through all these years. His message disregarded. Oh, what must he have suffered!"

Dame Brinker ventured to speak. Anything was better than to see the meester cry.

277

"It is a mercy to know the young gentleman was innocent. Ah! How he fretted! Telling you, Raff, that his crime was like unto murder. It was sending the wrong physic he meant. Crime, indeed! Why our own Gretel might have done that! Like enough the poor young gentleman heard that the man was dead. That's why he ran, mynheer. He said, you know, Raff, that he never could come back to Holland again, unless—" she hesitated—"ah, your honor, ten years is a dreary time to be waiting to hear from—"

"Hist, vrouw!" said Raff sharply.

"Waiting to hear," groaned the doctor, "and I, like a fool, sitting stubbornly at home, thinking that he had abandoned me. I never dreamed, Brinker, that the boy had discovered the mistake. I believed it was youthful folly, ingratitude, love of adventure, that sent him away. My poor, poor Laurens!"

"But you know all, now, mynheer," whispered Hans. "You know he was innocent of wrong, that he loved you and his dead mother. We will find him. You shall see him again, dear meester."

"God bless you!" said Dr. Boekman, seizing the boy's hand. "It may be as you say. I shall try, I shall try—and, Brinker, if ever the faintest gleam of recollection concerning him should come to you, you will send me word at once?"

"Indeed we will!" cried all but Hans, whose silent promise would have satisfied the doctor even had the others not spoken.

"Your boy's eyes," he said, turning to Dame Brinker, "are strangely like my son's. The first time I met him it seemed that Laurens himself was looking at me."

"Aye, mynheer," replied the mother proudly. "I have marked that you were much drawn to the child."

For a few moments the meester seemed lost in thought; then, arousing himself, he spoke in a new voice,—

"Forgive me, Raff Brinker, for this tumult. Do not feel distressed on my account. I leave your house today a happier man than I have been for many a long year. Shall I take the watch?"

"Certainly you must, mynheer. It was your son's wish."

"Even so," responded the doctor, regarding his treasure with a queer frown, for his face could not throw off its bad habits in an hour, "even so. And now I must be gone. No medicine is needed by my patient; only peace and cheerfulness, and both are here in plenty. Heaven bless you, my good friends! I shall ever be grateful to you."

"May Heaven bless you, too, mynheer, and may you soon find the dear young gentleman," said Dame Brinker earnestly, after hurriedly wiping her eyes upon the corner of her apron.

Raff uttered a hearty "Amen!" and Gretel threw such a wistful, eager glance at the doctor, that he patted her head as he turned to leave the cottage.

Hans went out also.

"When I can serve you, mynheer, I am ready."

"Very well, boy," replied Dr. Boekman with peculiar mildness. "Tell them, within, to say nothing of what has just happened. Meantime, Hans, when you are with your father, watch his mood. You have tact. At any moment he may suddenly be able to tell us more."

"Trust me for that, mynheer."

"Good day, my boy!" cried the doctor, as he sprang into his stately coach.

"Aha!" thought Hans, as it rolled away, "the meester has more life in him than I thought."

The twentieth of December came at last, bringing with it the perfection of winter weather. All over the level landscape lay the warm sunlight. It tried its power on lake, canal, and river; but the ice flashed defiance and showed no sign of melting. The very weathercocks stood still to enjoy the sight. This gave the windmills a holiday. Nearly all the past week they had been whirling briskly; now, being rather out of breath, they rocked lazily in the clear, still air. Catch a windmill working when the weathercocks have nothing to do!

There was an end to grinding, crushing, and sawing for that day. It was a good thing for the millers near Broek. Long before noon they concluded to take in their sails, and go to the race Everybody would be there. Already the north side of the frozen Y was bordered with eager spectators; the news of the great

279

skating match had traveled far and wide. Men, women, and children in holiday attire were flocking toward the spot. Some wore furs and wintry cloaks or shawls; but many, consulting their feelings rather than the almanac, were dressed as for an October day.

The site selected for the race was a faultless plain of ice near Amsterdam, on that great arm of the Zuyder Zee which Dutchmen, of course, must call the Eye. The townspeople turned out in large numbers. Strangers in the city deemed it a fine chance to see what was to be seen. Many a peasant from the northward had wisely chosen the twentieth as the day for the next city trading. It seemed that everybody, young and old, who had wheels, skates, or feet at command, had hastened to the scene.

There were the gentry in their coaches, dressed like Parisians, fresh from the Boulevards; Amsterdam children in charity uniforms; girls from the Roman Catholic orphan house, in sable gowns and white headbands; boys from the Burgher Asylum, with their black tights and short-skirted, harlequin coats. There were old-fashioned gentlemen in cocked hats and velvet knee breeches; old-fashioned ladies, too, in stiff, quilted skirts and bodices of dazzling brocade. These were accompanied by servants bearing foot stoves and cloaks. There were the peasant folk arrayed in every possible Dutch costume, shy young rustics in brazen buckles; simple village maidens concealing their flaxen hair under fillets of gold; women whose long, narrow aprons were stiff with embroidery; women with short, corkscrew curls hanging over their foreheads; women with shaved heads and close-fitting caps, and women in striped skirts and windmill bonnets; men in leather, in homespun, in velvet, and in broadcloth; burghers in model European attire, and burghers in short jackets, wide trousers, and steeple-crowned hats.

There were beautiful Friesland girls in wooden shoes and coarse petticoats, with solid gold crescents encircling their heads, finished at each temple with a golden rosette, and hung with lace a century old. Some wore necklaces, pendants, and earrings of the purest gold. Many were content with gilt or even with brass, but it is not an uncommon thing for a Friesland woman to have all the family treasure in her headgear. More than one rustic lass displayed the value of two thousand guilders upon her head that day.

Scattered throughout the crowd were peasants from the Island of Marken, with sabots, black stockings, and the widest of breeches; also women from Marken with short, blue petticoats, and black jackets, gaily figured in front. They wore red sleeves, white aprons, and a cap like a bishop's miter over their golden hair.

The children often were as quaint and odd-looking as their elders. In short, one-third of the crowd seemed to have stepped bodily from a collection of Dutch paintings.

Everywhere could be seen tall women and stumpy men, lively-faced girls and youths whose expression never changed from sunrise to sunset.

There seemed to be at least one specimen from every known town in Holland. There were Utrecht water-bearers, Gouda cheese-makers, Delft pottery-men, Schiedam distillers, Amsterdam diamond-cutters, Rotterdam merchants, dried-up herring-packers, and two sleepy-eyed shepherds from Texel. Every man of them had his pipe and tobacco pouch. Some carried what might be called the smoker's complete outfit—a pipe, tobacco, a pricker with which to clean the tube, a silver net for protecting the bowl, and a box of the strongest of brimstone matches.

A true Dutchman, you must remember, is rarely without his pipe on any possible occasion. He may for a moment neglect to breathe, but when the pipe is forgotten, he must be dying, indeed. There were no such sad cases here. Wreaths of smoke were rising from every possible quarter. The more fantastic the smoke wreath, the more placid and solemn the smoker.

Look at those boys and girls on stilts! That is a good idea. They can see over the heads of the tallest. It is strange to see those little bodies high in the air, carried about on mysterious legs. They have such a resolute look on their round faces, what wonder that nervous old gentlemen, with tender feet, wince and tremble while the long-legged little monsters stride past them.

You will read in certain books that the Dutch are a quiet

people: so they are generally. But listen! Did ever you hear such a din? All made up of human voices—no, the horses are helping somewhat, and the fiddles are squeaking pitifully (how it must pain fiddles to be tuned!), but the mass of the sound comes from the great *vox humana* that belongs to a crowd.

That queer little dwarf going about with a heavy basket, winding in and out among the people, helps not a little. You can hear his shrill cry above all the other sounds, *"Pypen en tabac! Pypen en tabac!"*

Another, his big brother, though evidently some years younger, is selling doughnuts and bonbons. He is calling on all pretty children far and near to come quickly or the cakes will be gone.

You know quite a number among the spectators. High up in the center of yonder pavilion, erected upon the border of the ice, is Madame van Gleck. It is her birthday; she has the post of honor. There is Mynheer van Gleck, whose meerschaum has not really grown fast to his lips; it only appears so. There are Grandfather and Grandmother too. All the children are with them. It is so mild they have brought even the baby. The poor little creature is swaddled very much after the manner of an Egyptian mummy, but it can crow with delight, and when the band is playing, open and shut its animated mittens in perfect time to the music.

Grandfather, with his pipe and spectacles and fur cap, makes quite a picture as he holds baby upon his knee. Perched high upon their canopied platforms, the party can see all that is going on. No wonder the ladies look complacently at the glassy ice; with a stove for a footstool one might sit cozily beside the north pole.

There is a gentleman with them who somewhat resembles St. Nicholas as he appeared to the young van Glecks, on the fifth of December. But the saint had a flowing white beard, and this face is as smooth as a pippin. His saintship was larger around the body, too, and (between ourselves) he had a pair of thimbles in his mouth, which this gentleman certainly has not. It cannot be St. Nicholas after all.

Near by, in the next pavilion, sit the Van Holps with their son and daughter (the Van Gends) from The Hague. Peter's sister is not one to forget her promises. She has brought bouquets of exquisite hothouse flowers for the winners.

These pavilions, and there are others beside, have all been erected since daylight. That semicircular one, containing Mynheer Korbes' family, is very pretty, and proves that the Hollanders are quite skilled at tent-making, but I like the Van Gleck's best, the center one, striped red and white, and hung with evergreens.

The one with the blue flags contains the musicians. Those pagoda-like affairs, decked with sea shells and streamers of every possible hue, are the judges' stands, and those columns and flagstaffs upon the ice mark the limit of the racecourse. The two white columns twined with green, connected at the top by that long, floating strip of drapery, form the starting-point. Those flagstaffs, half a mile off, stand at each end of the boundary line, which is cut sufficiently deep to be distinct to the skaters, though not deep enough to trip them when they turn to come back to the starting-point.

283

The air is so clear that it seems scarcely possible that the columns and flagstaffs are so far apart. Of course the judges' stands are but little nearer together.

Half a mile on the ice, when the atmosphere is like this, is but a short distance after all, especially when fenced with a living chain of spectators.

The music has commenced. How melody seems to enjoy itself in the open air! The fiddles have forgotten their agony, and everything is harmonious. Until you look at the blue tent it seems that the music springs from the sunshine, it is so boundless, so joyous. Only the musicians are solemn.

Where are the racers? All assembled together near the white columns. It is a beautiful sight. Forty boys and girls in picturesque attire darting with electric swiftness in and out among each other, or sailing in pairs and triplets, beckoning, chatting, whispering, in the fullness of youthful glee.

A few careful ones are soberly tightening their straps; others, halting on one leg, with flushed, eager faces, suddenly cross the suspected skate over their knee, give it an examining shake, and dart off again. One and all are possessed with the spirit of motion. They cannot stand still. Their skates are a part of them, and every runner seems bewitched.

Holland is the place for skaters, after all. Where else can nearly every boy and girl perform feats on the ice that would attract a crowd if seen in Central Park? Look at Ben! He is really astonishing the natives; no easy thing to do in the Netherlands. Save your strength, Ben, you will need it soon. Now other boys are trying! Ben is surpassed already. Such jumping, such poising, such spinning, such india-rubber exploits generally! That boy with a red cap is the lion now; his back is a watch spring, his body is cork—no, it is iron, or it would snap at that! He's a bird, a top, a rabbit, a corkscrew, a sprite, a flesh-ball, all in an instant. When you think he is erect he is down; and when you think he is down he is up. He drops his glove on the ice and turns a somersault as he picks it up. Without stopping, he snatches the cap from Jacob Poot's astonished head and claps it back again "hind side before." Lookers-on hurrah and laugh.

Foolish boy! It is arctic weather under your feet, but more than temperate overhead. Big drops already are rolling down your forehead. Superb skater as you are, you may lose the race.

A French traveler, standing with a notebook in his hand, sees our English friend, Ben, buy a doughnut of the dwarf's brother, and eat it. Thereupon he writes in his notebook, that the Dutch take enormous mouthfuls, and universally are fond of potatoes boiled in molasses.

There are some familiar faces near the white columns. Lambert, Ludwig, Peter, and Carl are all there, cool and in good skating order. Hans is not far off. Evidently he is going to join in the race, for his skates are on, the very pair that he sold for seven guilders! He had soon suspected that his fairy godmother was the mysterious "friend" who bought them. This settled, he had boldly charged her with the deed, and she knowing well that all her little savings had been spent in the purchase, had not had the face to deny it. Through the fairy godmother, too, he had been rendered amply able to buy them back again. Therefore Hans is to be in the race. Carl is more indignant than ever about it, but as three other peasant boys have entered, Hans is not alone.

Twenty boys and twenty girls. The latter by this time are standing in front, braced for the start, for they are to have the first "run." Hilda, Rychie, and Katrinka are among them. Two or three bend hastily to give a last pull at their skate straps. It is pretty to see them stamp, to be sure that all is firm. Hilda is speaking pleasantly to a graceful little creature in a red jacket and a new brown petticoat. Why, it is Gretel! What a difference those pretty shoes make, and the skirt, and the new cap. Annie Bouman is there, too. Even Janzoon Kolp's sister has been admitted; but Janzoon himself has been voted out by the directors, because he killed the stork, and only last summer was caught in the act of robbing a bird's nest, a legal offence in Holland.

The race is about to commence. Twenty girls are formed in a line. The music has ceased.

A man, whom we shall call the crier, stands between the columns and the first judges' stand. He reads the rules.

285

"The girls and boys are to race in turn, until one girl and one boy have beaten twice. They are to start in a line from the united columns, skate to the flagstaff line, turn, and then come back to the starting-point, thus making a mile at each run."

A flag is waved from the judges' stand. Madame van Gleck rises in her pavilion. She leans forward with a white handkerchief in her hand. When she drops it, a bugler is to give the signal for them to start.

The handkerchief is fluttering to the ground! Hark!

They are off!

No. Back again. Their line was not true in passing the judges' stand.

The signal is repeated.

Off again. No mistake this time. Whew! How fast they go!

The multitude is quiet for an instant, absorbed in eager, breathless watching.

Cheers spring up along the line of spectators. Huzza! Five girls are ahead. Who comes flying back from the boundary mark? We cannot tell. Something red, that is all. There is a blue spot flitting near it, and a dash of yellow nearer still. Spectators at this end of the line strain their eyes and wish that they had taken their post nearer the flagstaff.

The wave of cheers is coming back again. Now we can see. Katrinka is ahead!

She passes the Van Holp pavilion. The next is Madame van Gleck's. That leaning figure gazing from it is a magnet. Hilda shoots past Katrinka, waving her hand to her mother as she passes. Two others are close now, whizzing on like arrows. What is that flash of red and gray? Hurrah, it is Gretel! She too waves her hand, but toward no gay pavilion. The crowd is cheering, but she hears only her father's voice, "Well done, little Gretel!" Soon Katrinka, with a quick, merry laugh shoots past Hilda. The girl in yellow is gaining now. She passes them all, all except Gretel. The judges lean forward without seeming to lift their eyes from their watches. Cheer after cheer fills the air; the very columns seem rocking. Gretel has passed them. She has won.

"Gretel Brinker, one mile!" shouts the crier.

The judges nod. They write something upon a tablet which each holds in his hand.

While the girls are resting, some crowding eagerly around our frightened little Gretel, some standing aside in high disdain, the boys form in a line.

Mynheer van Gleck drops the handkerchief this time. The buglers give a vigorous blast.

The boys have started!

Halfway already! Did ever you see the like!

Three hundred legs flashing by in an instant. But there are only twenty boys. No matter, there were hundreds of legs I am sure! Where are they now? There is such a noise one gets bewildered. What are the people laughing at? Oh, at that fat boy in the rear. See him go! See him! He'll be down in an instant, no, he won't. I wonder if he knows he is all alone; the other boys are nearly at the boundary line. Yes, he knows it. He stops. He wipes his hot face. He takes off his cap and looks about him. Better to give up with a good grace. He has made a hundred friends by that hearty, astonished laugh. Good Jacob Poot!

The fine fellow is already among the spectators, gazing as eagerly as the rest.

A cloud of feathery ice flies from the heels of the skaters as they "bring to" and turn at the flagstaffs.

Something black is coming now, one of the boys: it is all we know. He has touched the *vox humana* stop of the crowd; it fairly roars. Now they come nearer—we can see the red cap. There's Ben—there's Peter—there's Hans!

Hans is ahead! Young Madame Van Gend almost crushes the flowers in her hand; she had been quite sure that Peter would be first. Carl Schummel is next, then Ben, and the youth with the red cap. The others are pressing close. A tall figure darts from among them. He passes the red cap, he passes Ben, then Carl. Now it is an even race between him and Hans. Madame Van Gend catches her breath.

It is Peter! He is ahead! Hans shoots past him. Hilda's eyes fill with tears; Peter *must* beat. Annie's eyes flash proudly. Gretel gazes with clasped hands; four strokes more will take her brother to the columns.

He is there! Yes, but so was young Schummel just a second before. At the last instant, Carl, gathering his powers, had whizzed between them and passed the goal.

"Carl Schummel, one mile!" shouts the crier.

Soon Madame van Gleck rises again. The falling handkerchief starts the bugle; and the bugle, using its voice as a bowstring, shoots off twenty girls like so many arrows.

It is a beautiful sight, but one has not long to look; before we can fairly distinguish them they are far in the distance. This time they are close upon one another; it is hard to say as they come speeding back from the flagstaff which will reach the columns first. There are new faces among the foremost—eager, glowing faces, unnoticed before. Katrinka is there, and Hilda, but Gretel and Rychie are in the rear. Gretel is wavering, but when Rychie passes her, she starts forward afresh. Now they are nearly beside Katrinka. Hilda is still in advance, she is almost "home." She has not faltered since that bugle note sent her flying; like an arrow still she is speeding toward the goal. Cheer after cheer rises in the air. Peter is silent, but his eyes shine like stars. "Huzza! Huzza!"

The crier's voice is heard again.

"Hilda van Gleck, one mile!"

A loud murmur of approval runs through the crowd, catching the music in its course, till all seems one sound, with a glad rhythmic throbbing in its depths. When the flag waves all is still.

Once more the bugle blows a terrific blast. It sends off the boys like chaff before the wind, dark chaff I admit, and in big pieces.

It is whisked around at the flagstaff, driven faster yet by the cheers and shouts along the line. We begin to see what is coming. There are three boys in advance this time, and all abreast—Hans, Peter, and Lambert. Carl soon breaks the ranks, rushing through with a whiff. Fly, Hans, fly, Peter, don't let Carl beat again—Carl the bitter, Carl the insolent! Van Mounen is flagging; but you are strong as ever. Hans and Peter, Peter and Hans; which is foremost? We love them both. We scarcely care which is the fleeter.

Hilda, Annie, and Gretel, seated upon the long crimson bench, can remain quiet no longer. They spring to their feet, so different, and yet one in eagerness. Hilda instantly reseats herself; none shall know how interested she is, none shall know how anxious, how filled with one hope. Shut your eyes then, Hilda, hide your face rippling with joy. Peter has beaten.

"Peter Van Holp, one mile!" calls the crier.

The same buzz of excitement as before, while the judges take notes, the same throbbing of music through the din; but something is different. A little crowd presses close about some object, near the column. Carl has fallen. He is not hurt, though somewhat stunned. If he were less sullen he would find more sympathy in these warm young hearts. As it is, they forget him as soon as he is fairly on his feet again.

The girls are to skate their third mile.

How resolute the little maidens look as they stand in a line! Some are solemn with a sense of responsibility, some wear a smile half bashful, half provoked, but one air of determination pervades them all.

This third mile may decide the race. Still if neither Gretel nor Hilda wins, there is yet a chance among the rest for the silver skates.

Each girl feels sure that this time she will accomplish the distance in one-half the time. How they stamp to try their runners, how nervously they examine each strap, how erect they stand at last, every eye upon Madame van Gleck.

The bugle thrills through them again. With quivering eagerness they spring forward, bending, but in perfect balance. Each flashing stroke seems longer than the last.

Now they are skimming off in the distance.

Again the eager straining of eyes, again the shouts and cheering, again the thrill of excitement as, after a few moments, four or five, in advance of the rest, come speeding back, nearer, nearer to the white columns.

Who is first? Not Rychie, Katrinka, Annie, nor Hilda, nor the girl in yellow, but Gretel, Gretel, the fleetest sprite of a girl that ever skated. She was but playing in the earlier races, *now* she is in earnest, or rather something within her has determined to win. That lithe little form makes no effort; but it cannot stop, not until the goal is passed!

In vain the crier lifts his voice; he cannot be heard. He has no news to tell; it is already ringing through the crowd. *Gretel has won the silver skates!*

Like a bird she has flown over the ice, like a bird she looks about her in a timid, startled way. She longs to dart to the sheltered nook where her father and mother stand. But Hans is beside her, the girls are crowding round. Hilda's kind, joyous voice breathes in her ear. From that hour, none will despise her. Goose-girl or not, Gretel stands acknowledged Queen of the Skaters!

With natural pride Hans turns to see if Peter Van Holp is witnessing his sister's triumph. Peter is not looking toward them at all. He is kneeling, bending his troubled face low, and working hastily at his skate strap. Hans is beside him at once.

"Are you in trouble, mynheer?"

"Ah, Hans! that you? Yes, my fun is over. I tried to tighten my strap, to make a new hole, and this botheration of a knife has cut it nearly in two."

"Mynheer," said Hans, at the same time pulling off a skate, "you must use my strap!"

"Not I, indeed, Hans Brinker," cried Peter, looking up, "though I thank you warmly. Go to your post, my friend, the bugle will be sounding in another minute."

"Mynheer," pleaded Hans in a husky voice. "You have called me your friend. Take this strap, quick! There is not an instant to lose. I shall not skate this time. Indeed I am out of practice. Mynheer, you *must* take it"—and Hans blind and deaf to any remonstrance, slipped his strap into Peter's skate and implored him to put it on.

"Come, Peter!" cried Lambert, from the line. "We are waiting for you."

"For madame's sake," pleaded Hans, "be quick. She is motioning to you to join the racers. There, the skate is almost on; quick, mynheer; fasten it. I could not possibly win. The race lies between Master Schummel and yourself."

"You are a noble fellow, Hans!" cried Peter yielding at last. He sprang to his post just as the white handkerchief fell to the ground. The bugle sends forth its blast, loud, clear, and ringing.

Off go the boys!

"Mine Gott," cries a tough old fellow from Delft. "They beat everything, these Amsterdam youngsters. See them!"

See them, indeed! They are winged Mercuries every one of them. What mad errand are they on? Ah, I know; they are hunting Peter Van Holp. He is some fleet-footed runaway from Olympus. Mercury and his troop of winged cousins are in full chase. They will catch him! Now Carl is the runaway. The pursuit grows furious. Ben is foremost!

The chase turns in a cloud of mist. It is coming this way. Who is hunted now? Mercury himself. It is Peter, Peter Van Holp! Fly, Peter! Hans is watching you. He is sending all his fleetness, all his strength into your feet. Your mother and sister are pale with eagerness. Hilda is trembling and dares not look up. Fly, Peter; the crowd has not gone deranged, it is only cheering. The pursuers are close upon you! Touch the white column! It beckons; it is reeling before you—it——

"Huzza, Huzza! Peter has won the silver skates!"

"Peter Van Holp!" shouted the crier. But who heard him? "Peter Van Holp!" shouted a hundred voices, for he was the favorite boy of the place. "Huzza! Huzza!"

Now the music was resolved to be heard. It struck up a lively air, then a tremendous march. The spectators, thinking something new was about to happen, deigned to listen and to look.

The racers formed in single file. Peter, being tallest, stood first. Gretel, the smallest of all, took her place at the end. Hans, who had borrowed a strap from the cake boy, was near the head.

Three gaily twined arches were placed at intervals upon the river facing the Van Gleck pavilion.

Skating slowly, and in perfect time to the music, the boys and girls moved forward, led on by Peter. It was beautiful to see the bright procession glide along like a living creature. It curved and doubled, and drew its graceful length in and out among the arches. Whichever way Peter the head went, the body was sure to follow. Sometimes it steered direct for the center arch; then, as if seized with a new impulse, turned away and curled itself about the first one; then unwound slowly and bending low, with quick, snakelike curvings, crossed the river, passing at length through the furthest arch.

When the music was slow, the procession seemed to crawl like a thing afraid; it grew livelier, and the creature darted forward with a spring, gliding rapidly among the arches, in and out, curling, twisting, turning, never losing form until, at the shrill call of the bugle rising above the music, it suddenly resolved itself into boys and girls standing in double semicircle before Madame van Gleck's pavilion.

Peter and Gretel stand in the center in advance of the others. Madame van Gleck rises majestically. Gretel trembles, but feels that she must look at the beautiful lady. She cannot hear what is said, there is such a buzzing all around her. She is thinking that she ought to try and make a courtesy, such as her mother makes to the meester, when suddenly something so dazzling is placed in her hand that she gives a cry of joy.

Then she ventures to look about her. Peter, too, has something in his hands. "Oh! oh! how splendid!" she cries, and "Oh! how splendid!" is echoed as far as people can see.

Meantime the silver skates flash in the sunshine, throwing dashes of light upon those two happy faces.

Mevrouw Van Gend sends a little messenger with her bouquets—one for Hilda, one for Carl, and others for Peter and Gretel.

At sight of the flowers the Queen of the Skaters becomes uncontrollable. With a bright stare of gratitude, she gathers skates and bouquet in her apron, hugs them to her bosom, and darts off to search for her father and mother in the scattering crowd.

Perhaps you were surprised to learn that Raff and his vrouw

were at the skating race; you would have been more so had you been with them on the evening of that merry twentieth of December. To see the Brinker cottage standing sulkily alone on the frozen marsh, with its bulgy, rheumatic-looking walls, and its slouched hat of a roof pulled far over its eyes, one would never suspect that a lively scene was passing within. Without, nothing was left of the day but a low line of blaze at the horizon. A few venturesome clouds had already taken fire, and others, with their edges burning, were lost in the gathering smoke.

A stray gleam of sunshine slipping down from the willow stump, crept stealthily under the cottage. It seemed to feel that the inmates would give it welcome if it could only get near them. The room under which it hid was as clean as clean could be. The very cracks in the rafters were polished. Delicious odors filled the air. A huge peat fire upon the hearth sent flashes of harmless lightning at the somber walls. It played in turn upon the great leather Bible, upon Gretel's closet-bed, the household things on their pegs, and the beautiful silver skates and the flowers upon the table. Dame Brinker's honest face shone and twinkled in the changing light. Gretel and Hans, with arms entwined, were leaning against the fireplace, laughing merrily, and Raff Brinker was dancing!

I do not mean that he was pirouetting or cutting a pigeon-wing, either of which would have been entirely too undignified for the father of a family; I simply affirm that while they were chatting pleasantly together Raff suddenly sprang from his seat, snapped his fingers and performed two or three flourishes very much like the climax of a Highland fling. Next he caught his vrouw in his arms and lifted her from the ground in his delight.

"Huzza!" he cried, "I have it! I have it! It's Thomas Higgs. That's the name! It came upon me like a flash. Write it down, lad, write it down!"

Someone knocked at the door.

"It's the meester," cried the delighted dame. "*Goede Gunst,* how things come to pass!"

Mother and children came in merry collision as they rushed to open the door.

It was not the doctor, after all, but three boys, Peter Van Holp, Lambert, and Ben.

"Good evening, young gentlemen," said Dame Brinker, so happy and proud that she would scarcely have been surprised at a visit from the king himself.

"Good evening, jufrouw," said the trio, making magnificent bows.

"Dear me," thought Dame Brinker as she bobbed up and down like a churn dasher, "it's lucky I learned to courtesy at Heidelberg!"

Raff was content to return the boys' salutations with a respectful nod.

"Pray be seated, young masters," said the dame, as Gretel bashfully thrust a stool toward them. "There's a lack of chairs as you see, but this one by the fire is at your service, and if you don't mind the hardness, that oak chest is as good a seat as the best. That's right, Hans, pull it out."

By the time the boys were seated to the dame's satisfaction, Peter, acting as spokesman, had explained that they were going to attend a lecture at Amsterdam, and had stopped on the way to return Hans' strap.

"Oh, mynheer," cried Hans, earnestly, "it is too much trouble. I am very sorry."

"No trouble at all, Hans, I could have waited for you to come to your work tomorrow, had I not wished to call. And, Hans, talking of your work, my father is much pleased with it; a carver by trade could not have done it better. He would like to have the south arbor ornamented also, but I told him you were going to school again."

"Aye!" put in Raff Brinker, emphatically. "Hans must go to school at once, and Gretel as well; that is true."

"I am glad to hear you say so," responded Peter, turning toward the father, "and very glad to know that you are again a well man."

"Yes, young master, a well man, and able to work as steady as ever, thank God!"

(Here Hans hastily wrote something on the edge of a time-

295

worn almanac that hung by the chimney place.) "Aye, that's right lad, set it down. Figgs! Wiggs! Alack! Alack!" added Raff in great dismay, "it's gone again!"

"All right, Father," said Hans, "the name's down now in black and white. Here, look at it, Father; mayhap the rest will come to you. If we had the place as well, it would be complete!" Then turning to Peter, he said in a low tone, "I have an important errand in town, mynheer, and if——"

"Wist!" exclaimed the dame, lifting her hands, "not to Amsterdam tonight, and you've owned your legs were aching under you. Nay, nay, it'll be soon enough to go at early daylight."

"Daylight indeed!" echoed Raff. "That would never do. Nay, Meitje, he must go this hour."

The vrouw looked for an instant as if Raff's recovery was becoming rather a doubtful benefit; her word was no longer sole law in the house. Fortunately, the proverb, "Humble wife is husband's boss" had taken deep root in her mind; even as the dame pondered, it bloomed.

"Very well, Raff," she said smilingly, "it is thy boy as well as mine. Ah! I've a troublesome house, young masters."

Just then Peter drew a long strap from his pocket.

Handing it to Hans he said in an undertone, "I need not thank you for lending me this, Hans Brinker. Such boys as you do not ask for thanks; but I must say you did me a great kindness, and I am proud to acknowledge it. I did not know," he added, laughingly, "until fairly in the race, how anxious I was to win."

Hans was glad to join in Peter's laugh: it covered his embarrassment and gave his face a chance to cool off a little. Honest, generous boys like Hans have such a stupid way of blushing when you least expect it.

"It was nothing, mynheer," said the dame, hastening to her son's relief. "The lad's whole soul was in having you win the race, I know it was!"

This helped matters, beautifully.

"Ah, mynheer," Hans hurried to say, "from the first start I felt stiff and strange on my feet; I was well out of it so long as I had no chance of winning."

Peter looked rather distressed.

"We may hold different opinions there. That part of the business troubles me. It is too late to mend it now, but it would be really a kindness to me if——"

The rest of Peter's speech was uttered so confidentially that I cannot record it. Enough to say, Hans soon started back in dismay, and Peter, looking very much ashamed, stammered out something to the effect that he would keep them, since he won the race, but it was "all wrong."

Here Van Mounen coughed, as if to remind Peter that lecture hour was approaching fast. At the same moment Ben laid something upon the table.

"Ah," exclaimed Peter, "I forgot my other errand. Your sister ran off so quickly today that Madame van Gleck had no opportunity to give her the case for her skates."

"S-s-t!" said Dame Brinker, shaking her head reproachfully at Gretel. "She was a very rude girl I'm sure." (Secretly, she was thinking that very few women had such a fine little daughter.)

"No, indeed," laughed Peter, "she did exactly the right thing, ran home with her richly won treasures. Who would not? Don't let us detain you, Hans," he continued turning around as he spoke; but Hans, who was eagerly watching his father, seemed to have forgotten their presence.

Meantime, Raff, lost in thought, was repeating, under his breath, "Thomas Higgs, Thomas Higgs, aye, that's the name. Alack! if I could but tell the place as well."

The skate case was elegantly made of crimson morocco, ornamented with silver. If a fairy had breathed upon its tiny key, or Jack Frost himself had designed its delicate tracery, they could not have been more daintily beautiful. *For the Fleetest* was written upon the cover in sparkling letters. It was lined with velvet, and in one corner was stamped the name and address of the maker.

Gretel thanked Peter in her own simple way; then, being quite delighted and confused, and not knowing what else to do, she lifted the case, carefully examining it in every part. "It's made by Mynheer Birmingham," she said after a while, still blushing

297

and holding it before her eyes.

"Birmingham!" replied Lambert Van Mounen, "that's the name of a place in England. Let me see it."

"Ha! ha!" he laughed, holding the open case toward the fire-light. "No wonder you thought so; but it's a slight mistake. The case was made at Birmingham, but the maker's name is in smaller letters. Humph! They're so small, I can't read them."

"Let me try," said Peter, leaning over his shoulder. "Why, man, it's perfectly distinct. It's T—H—it's T——"

"Well!" exclaimed Lambert, triumphantly, "if you can read it so easily, let's hear it, T—H, what?"

"T. H.—T. H. Oh! why, Thomas Higgs, to be sure," replied Peter, pleased to be able to decipher it at last. Then, feeling they had been behaving rather unceremoniously, he turned toward Hans.

Peter turned pale! What was the matter with the people? Raff and Hans had started up, and were staring at him, in glad amazement. Gretel looked wild. Dame Brinker, with an unlighted candle in her hand, was rushing about the room, crying, "Hans! Hans! Where's your hat? Oh, the meester! Oh, the meester!"

"Birmingham Higgs!" exclaimed Hans. "Did you say Higgs? We've found him! I must be off."

"You see, young masters," panted the dame, at the same time snatching Hans' hat from the bed, "you see—we know him. He's our—no, he isn't—I mean—oh, Hans, you must go to Amsterdam this minute!"

"Good night, mynheer," panted Hans, radiant with sudden joy. "Good night—you will excuse me, I must go. Birmingham—Higgs—Higgs—Birmingham," and seizing his hat from his mother, and his skates from Gretel, he rushed from the cottage.

What could the boys think, but that the entire Brinker family had suddenly gone crazy!

They bade an embarrassed "Good evening," and turned to go. But Raff stopped them.

"This Thomas Higgs, young masters, is a—a person."

"Ah!" exclaimed Peter, quite sure that Raff was the most crazy of all.

"Yes—a person—a—ahem!—a friend. We thought him dead. I hope it is the same man. In England, did you say?"

"Yes, Birmingham," answered Peter. "It must be Birmingham in England."

"I know the man," said Ben, addressing Lambert. "His factory is not four miles from our place. A queer fellow, still as an oyster, doesn't seem at all like an Englishman. I've often seen him, a solemn looking chap, with magnificent eyes. He made a writing case once for me to give Jenny on her birthday. Makes pocketbooks, telescope cases, and all kinds of leather work."

As this was said in English, Van Mounen of course translated it for the benefit of all concerned, noticing meanwhile that neither Raff nor his vrouw looked very miserable, though Raff was trembling, and the dame's eyes were swimming with tears.

You may believe that the doctor heard every word of the story, when later in the evening he came driving back with Hans. "The three young gentlemen had been gone some time," Dame Brinker said, "but like enough by hurrying, it would be easy to find them coming out from the lecture, wherever that was."

"True," said Raff, nodding his head. "The vrouw always hits upon the right thing. It would be well to see the young English gentleman, mynheer, before he forgets all about Thomas Higgs. It's a slippery name, d'ye see? One can't hold it safe a minute. It come upon me sudden and strong as a pile driver, and my boy writ it down. Aye, mynheer, I'd haste to talk with the English lad; he's seen your son many a time—only to think on't!"

Dame Brinker took up the thread of the discourse.

"You'll pick out the lad quick enough, mynheer, because he's in company with Master Peter Van Holp; and his hair curls up over his forehead like foreign folk's, and, if you hear him speak, he talks kind of big and fast, only it's English; but that wouldn't be any hindrance to your honor."

The doctor had already lifted his hat to go. With a beaming face, he muttered something about its being just like the young scamp to give himself a rascally English name; called Hans "my son," thereby making that young gentleman happy as a lord, and left the cottage with very little ceremony, considering what a great meester he was.

The grumbling coachman comforted himself by speaking his mind as he drove back to Amsterdam. Since the doctor was safely stowed away in the coach and could not hear a word, it was a fine time to say terrible things of folks who hadn't no manner of feeling for nobody, and who were always wanting the horses a dozen times of a night.

300

Higgs' factory was a mine of delight for the gossips of Birmingham. It was a small building, but quite large enough to hold a mystery. Who the proprietor was, or where he came from, none could tell. He looked like a gentleman, that was certain, though everybody knew he had risen from an apprenticeship, and he could handle his pen like a writing master.

Years ago he had suddenly appeared in the place, a lad of eighteen; learned his trade faithfully, and risen in the confidence of his employer; been taken in as a partner soon after his time was up; and, finally, when old Willett died, had assumed the business on his own hands. This was all that was known of his affairs. It was a common remark among some of the good people that he never had a word to say to a Christian soul; while others declared that though he spoke beautifully, when he chose to, there was something wrong in his accent. A tidy man, too, they called him, all but for having that scandalous green pond alongside his factory, which wasn't deep enough for an eel, and was "just a fever nest, as sure as you live."

His nationality was a great puzzle. The English name spoke plain enough for one side of his house, but of what manner of nation was his mother? If she'd been an American, he'd certainly have had high cheekbones and reddish skin; if a German, he would have known the language, and Squire Smith declared he didn't; if French (and his having that frog-pond made it seem likely) it would come out in his speech. No, there was nothing he could be but Dutch. And strangest of all, though the man always pricked up his ears when you talked of Holland, he didn't seem to know the first thing about the country when you put him to the point.

Anyhow, as no letters ever came to him from his mother's family in Holland, and as nobody living had ever seen old Higgs, the family couldn't be anything much. Probably Thomas Higgs himself was no better than he should be, for all he pretended to carry himself so straight; and for their parts, the gossips declared, they were not going to trouble their heads about him. Consequently Thomas Higgs and his affairs were never-failing subjects of discussion.

301

Picture, then, the consternation among all the good people, when it was announced by "somebody who was there and ought to know," that the postboy had that very morning handed Higgs a foreign-looking letter, and the man had "turned as white as the wall; rushed to his factory, talked a bit with one of the head workmen, and without bidding a creature good-bye, was off bag and baggage before you could wink, ma'am." Mistress Scrubbs, his landlady, was in deep affliction. The dear soul became quite out of breath while speaking of him. "To leave lodgin's in that suddent way without never so much as a day's warnin' which was what every woman who didn't wish to be trodden under foot, (which, thank Hevving, wasn't *her* way,) had a perfect right to expect; yes, and a week's warnin' now you mention it, and without even so much as sayin', 'Many thanks to you, Mistress Scrubbs, for all past kindnesses,' which was most numerous, though she said it who shouldn't say it; leastwise she wasn't never no kind of a person to be lookin' for thanks every minute. It was really scanderlous, though to be sure Mister 'iggs paid up everythin' to the last farthin' and it fairly brought tears to her eyes to see his dear empty boots lyin' there in the corner of his room, which alone showed trouble of mind for he always stood 'em up straight as solgers, though bein' half-soled twice they hadn't, of course, been worth takin' away."

Whereupon her dearest friend, Miss Scrumpkins, ran home to tell all about it. And, as everybody knew the Scrumpkinses, a shining gossamer of news was soon woven from one end of the street to the other.

An investigating committee met that evening at Mrs. Snigham's, sitting, in secret session, over her best china. Though invited only to a quiet "tea," the amount of judicial business they transacted on the occasion was prodigious. The biscuits were actually cold before the committee had a chance to eat anything. There was so much to talk over, and it was so important that it should be firmly established that each member had always been "certain sure that something extraordinary would be happening to that man yet," that it was nearly eight o'clock before Mrs. Snigham gave anybody a second cup.

One snowy day in January, Laurens Boekman went with his father to pay his respects to the Brinker family.

Raff was resting after the labors of the day; Gretel, having filled and lighted his pipe, was brushing every speck of ash from the hearth; the dame was spinning; and Hans, perched upon a stool by the window, was diligently studying his lessons. It was a peaceful, happy household whose main excitement during the past week had been the looking forward to this possible visit from Thomas Higgs.

As soon as the grand presentation was over, Dame Brinker insisted upon giving her guests some hot tea; it was enough to freeze anyone, she said, to be out in such crazy, blustering weather. While they were talking with her husband she whispered to Gretel that the young gentleman's eyes and her boy's were certainly as much alike as four beans, to say nothing of a way they both had of looking as if they were stupid and yet knew as much as a body's grandfather.

Gretel was disappointed. She had looked forward to a tragic scene, such as Annie Bouman had often described to her, from story books; and here was the gentleman who came so near being a murderer, who for ten years had been wandering over the face of the earth, who believed himself deserted and scorned by his father, the very young gentleman who had fled from his country in such magnificent trouble, sitting by the fire just as pleasant and natural as could be!

To be sure his voice had trembled when he talked with her parents, and he had met his father's look with a bright kind of smile that would have suited a dragon-killer bringing the waters of perpetual youth to his king; but after all he wasn't at all like the conquered hero in Annie's book. He did not say, lifting his hand toward heaven, "I hereby swear to be forever faithful to my home, my God, and my country!" which would have been only right and proper under the circumstances.

All things considered, Gretel was disappointed. Raff, however, was perfectly satisfied. The message was delivered; Dr. Boekman had his son safe and sound; and the poor lad had done nothing sinful after all, except in thinking that his father would

303

have abandoned him for an accident. To be sure, the graceful stripling had become rather a heavy man. Raff had unconsciously hoped to clasp that same boyish hand again; but all things were changed to Raff, for that matter. So he pushed back every feeling but joy, as he saw father and son sitting side by side at his hearthstone. Meantime, Hans was wholly occupied in the thought of Thomas Higgs' happiness in being able to be the meester's assistant again; and Dame Brinker was sighing softly to herself, wishing that the lad's mother were alive to see him, such a fine young gentleman as he was, and wondering how Dr. Boekman could bear to see the silver watch getting so dull. He had worn it ever since Raff handed it over, that was evident. What had he done with the gold one he used to wear?

The light was shining full upon Dr. Boekman's face. How contented he looked! How much younger and brighter than formerly! The hard lines were quite melting away. He was laughing, as he said to his father,—

"Am I not a happy man, Raff Brinker? My son will sell out his factory this month and open a warehouse in Amsterdam. I shall have all my spectacle cases for nothing."

Hans started from his reverie. "A warehouse, mynheer! And will Thomas Higgs—I mean is your son not to be your assistant again?"

A shade passed over the meester's face, but he brightened with an effort, as he replied,—

"Oh, no, Laurens has had quite enough of that. He wishes to be a merchant."

Hans appeared so surprised and disappointed that his friend asked good-naturedly,—

"Why so silent, boy? Is it any disgrace to be a merchant?"

"N—not a disgrace, mynheer," stammered Hans, "but——"

"But what?"

"Why, the other calling is so much better," answered Hans, "so much nobler. I think, mynheer," he added, kindling with enthusiasm, "that to be a surgeon, to cure the sick and crippled, to save human life, to be able to do what you have done for my father, is the grandest thing on earth."

The doctor was regarding him sternly. Hans felt rebuked. His cheeks were flushed; hot tears were gathering under his lashes.

"It is an ugly business, boy, this surgery," said the doctor, still frowning at Hans. "It requires great patience, self-denial, and perseverance."

"I am sure that it does," cried Hans, kindling again. "It calls for wisdom, too, and a reverence for God's work. Ah, mynheer, it may have its trials and drawbacks—but you do not mean what you say. It is great and noble, not ugly! Pardon me, mynheer. It is not for me to speak so boldly."

Dr. Boekman was evidently displeased. He turned his back on the boy and conferred aside with Laurens. Meanwhile the dame scowled a terrible warning at Hans. These great people, she knew well enough, never like to hear poor folk speak up so pert.

The meester turned around.

"How old are you, Hans Brinker?"

"Fifteen, mynheer," was the startled reply.

"Would you like to become a physician?"

"Yes, mynheer," answered Hans, quivering with excitement.

"Would you be willing with your parents' consent, to devote yourself to study, to go to the University, and, in time, be a student in my office?"

"YES, mynheer."

"You would not grow restless, think you, and change your mind just as I had set my heart upon preparing you to be my successor?"

Hans' eyes flashed.

"No, mynheer, I would not change."

"You may believe him, there," cried the dame, who could remain quiet no longer. "Hans is like a rock, when once he decides; and as for study, mynheer, the child has almost grown fast to his books of late. He can jumble off Latin already, like any priest!"

The doctor smiled. "Well, Hans, I see nothing to prevent us from carrying out this plan, if your father agrees."

"Ahem," said Raff, too proud of his boy to be very meek, "the fact is, mynheer, I prefer an active, out-of-door life, myself. But if the lad's inclined to study for a meester, and he'd have the benefit of your good word to push him on in the world, it's all one to me. The money's all that's wanting, but it mightn't be long, with two strong pair of arms to earn it, before we——"

"Tut! tut!" interrupted the doctor. "If I take your right-hand man away, I must pay the cost, and glad enough will I be to do it. It will be like having *two* sons, eh, Laurens? One a merchant and the other a surgeon. I shall be the happiest man in Holland! Come to me in the morning, Hans, and we will arrange matters at once."

Hans bowed assent. He dared not trust himself to speak.

"And, Brinker," continued the doctor, "my son Laurens will need a trusty, ready man like you, when he opens his warehouse in Amsterdam; someone to oversee matters, and see that the lazy clowns round about the place do their duty. Someone to——Why don't you tell him yourself, you rascal!"

This last was addressed to the son, and did not sound half as fierce as it looks in print. The rascal and Raff soon under-

306

stood each other perfectly.

"I'm loath to leave the dikes," said the latter, after they had talked together awhile, "but you have made me such a good offer, mynheer, I'd be robbing my family if I let it go past me."

Take a long look at Hans as he sits there staring gratefully at the meester.

And Gretel—ah, what a vista of puzzling work suddenly opens before her! Yes, for dear Hans' sake she will study now. If he really is to be a meester, his sister must not shame his greatness.

How faithfully those glancing eyes shall yet seek for the jewels that lie hidden in rocky schoolbooks! And how they shall yet brighten and droop at the coming of one whom she knows of now only as the boy who wore a red cap on that wonderful day when she found the silver skates in her apron!

But the doctor and Laurens are going. Dame Brinker is making her best courtesy. Raff stands beside her, looking every inch a man as he grasps the meester's hand. Through the open cottage door we can look out upon the level Dutch landscape all alive with the falling snow.

Samuel Clemens

TOM AND BECKY IN THE CAVE

ANOTHER ADVENTURE OF TOM SAWYER

ILLUSTRATED BY *Walter R. Sabel*

THE first thing Tom heard on Friday morning was a glad piece of news—Judge Thatcher's family had come back to town the night before. Becky took the chief place in the boy's interest. He saw her, and they had an exhausting good time playing "hi-spy" and "gully-keeper" with a crowd of their schoolmates. The day was completed and crowned in a peculiarly satisfactory way: Becky teased her mother to appoint the next day for the long-promised and long-delayed picnic, and she consented. The child's delight was boundless; and Tom's not more moderate. The invitations were sent out before sunset, and straightway the young folks of the village were thrown into a fever of preparation and pleasurable anticipation. Tom's excitement enabled him to keep awake until a pretty late hour, and he had good hopes of hearing Huck's "meow," and of having his treasure to astonish Becky and the picnickers with, next day; but he was disappointed. No signal came that night.

Morning came, eventually, and by ten or eleven o'clock a giddy and rollicking company were gathered at Judge Thatcher's, and everything was ready for a start. It was not the custom for elderly people to mar picnics with their presence. The children were considered safe enough under the wings of a few young ladies of eighteen and a few young gentlemen of twenty-three or thereabouts. The old steam-ferryboat was chartered for the occasion; presently the gay throng filed up the main street laden with provision-baskets. Sid was sick and had to miss the fun; Mary remained at home to entertain him. The last thing Mrs. Thatcher said to Becky was,—

"You'll not get back till late. Perhaps you'd better stay all night with some of the girls that live near the ferry landing, child."

"Then I'll stay with Susy Harper, mamma."

"Very well. And mind and behave yourself and don't be any trouble."

Presently, as they tripped along, Tom said to Becky,—

"Say—I'll tell you what we'll do. 'Stead of going to Joe Harper's we'll climb right up the hill and stop at the Widow Douglas's. She'll have ice cream! She has it most every day—dead loads of it. And she'll be awful glad to have us."

"Oh, that will be fun!"

Then Becky reflected a moment and said,—

"But what will mamma say?"

"How'll she ever know?"

The girl turned the idea over in her mind, and said reluctantly,—

"I reckon it's wrong—but—"

"But shucks! Your mother won't know, and so what's the harm? All she wants is that you'll be safe; and I bet you she'd 'a' said go there if she'd 'a' thought of it. I know she would!"

The Widow Douglas's splendid hospitality was a tempting bait. It and Tom's persuasions presently carried the day. So it was decided to say nothing to anybody about the night's program.

Three miles below town the ferryboat stopped at the mouth of a woody hollow and tied up. The crowd swarmed ashore and soon the forest distances and craggy heights echoed far and near with shoutings and laughter. All the different ways of getting hot and tired were gone through with, and by and by the rovers straggled back to camp fortified with responsible appetites, and then the destruction of the good things began. After the feast there was a refreshing season of rest and chat in the shade of spreading oaks. By and by somebody shouted,—

"Who's ready for the cave?"

Everybody was. Bundles of candles were procured, and straightway there was a general scamper up the hill. The mouth of the cave was up the hillside—an opening shaped like a letter A. Its massive oaken door stood unbarred. Within was a small chamber, chilly as an icehouse, and walled by Nature with solid limestone that was dewy with a cold sweat. It was romantic and mysterious to stand here in the deep gloom and look out upon the green valley shining in the sun. But the impressiveness of the situation quickly wore off, and the romping began again. The moment a candle was lighted there was a general rush upon the owner of it; a struggle and a gallant defense followed, but the candle was soon knocked down or blown out, and then there was a glad clamor of laughter and a new chase. But all things have an end. By and by the procession went filing down the steep descent of the main avenue, the flickering rank of lights dimly revealing the lofty walls of rock almost to their point of junction sixty feet overhead. This main avenue was not more than eight or ten feet wide. Every few steps other lofty and still narrower crevices branched from it on either hand—for McDougal's cave was but a vast labyrinth of crooked aisles that ran into each other and out again and led nowhere. It was said that one might wander days and nights together through its intricate tangle of rifts and chasms, and never find the end of the cave; and that he might go down and down, and still down, into the earth, and it was just the same—labyrinth underneath labyrinth, and no end to any of them. No man "knew" the cave. That was an impossible thing. Most of the young men knew a portion of it, and it was not customary to venture much beyond this known portion. Tom Sawyer knew as much of the cave as anyone.

The procession moved along the main avenue some three-quarters of a mile, and then groups and couples began to slip aside into branch avenues, fly along the dismal corridors, and take each other by surprise at points where the corridors joined again. Parties were able to elude each other for the space of half an hour without going beyond the "known" ground.

By and by, one group after another came straggling back to the mouth of the cave, panting, hilarious, smeared from head to foot with tallow drippings, daubed with clay, and entirely delighted with the success of the day. Then they were astonished to find that they had been taking no note of time and that night was about at hand. The clanging bell had been calling for half an hour. However, this sort of close to the day's adventures was romantic and therefore satisfactory. When the ferryboat with her wild freight pushed into the stream, nobody cared sixpence for the wasted time but the captain of the craft. . . .

There was no Sabbath-school during day-school vacation, but everybody was early at church. . . . When the sermon was finished, Judge Thatcher's wife dropped alongside of Mrs. Harper as she moved down the aisle with the crowd and said,—

"Is my Becky going to sleep all day? I just expected she would be tired to death."

"Your Becky?"

"Yes," with a startled look—"didn't she stay with you last night?"

"Why, no."

Mrs. Thatcher turned pale, and sank into a pew, just as Aunt Polly, talking briskly with a friend, passed by. Aunt Polly said,—

"Good morning, Mrs. Thatcher. Good morning, Mrs. Harper. I've got a boy that's turned up missing. I reckon my Tom stayed at your house last night—one of you. And now he's afraid to come to church. I've got to settle with him."

Mrs. Thatcher shook her head feebly and turned paler than ever.

"He didn't stay with us," said Mrs. Harper, beginning to look uneasy. A marked anxiety came into Aunt Polly's face.

"Joe Harper, have you seen my Tom this morning?"

"No'm."

"When did you see him last?"

Joe tried to remember, but was not sure he could say. The people had stopped moving out of church. Whispers passed along, and a boding uneasiness took possession of every countenance. Children were anxiously questioned, and young teachers. They all said they had not noticed whether Tom and Becky were on board the ferryboat on the homeward trip; it was dark; no one thought of inquiring if anyone was missing. One young man finally blurted out his fear that they were still in the cave! Mrs. Thatcher swooned away. Aunt Polly fell to crying and wringing her hands.

The alarm swept from lip to lip, from group to group, from street to street, and within five minutes the bells were wildly clanging and the whole town was up! Horses were saddled, skiffs were manned, the ferryboat ordered out, and before the horror was half an hour old two hundred men were pouring down highroad and river toward the cave.

All the long afternoon the village seemed empty and dead. Many women visited Aunt Polly and Mrs. Thatcher and tried

312

to comfort them. They cried with them, too, and that was still better than words. All the tedious night the town waited for news; but when the morning dawned at last, all the word that came was, "Send more candles—and send food." Mrs. Thatcher was almost crazed.

Early in the forenoon parties of jaded men began to straggle into the village, but the strongest of the citizens continued searching. All the news that could be gained was that remotenesses of the cavern were being ransacked that had never been visited before; that every corner and crevice was going to be be thoroughly searched; that wherever one wandered through the maze of passages, lights were to be seen flitting hither and thither in the distance, and shoutings and pistol-shots sent their hollow reverberations to the ear down the somber aisles. In one place, far from the section usually traversed by tourists, the names "BECKY & TOM" had been found traced upon the rocky wall with candle-smoke, and near at hand a grease-soiled bit of ribbon. Mrs. Thatcher recognized the ribbon and cried over it. She said it was the last relic she should ever have of her child; and that no other memorial of her could ever be so precious, because this one parted latest from the living body before the awful death came. Some said that now and then, in the cave, a far-away speck of light would glimmer, and then a glorious shout would burst forth and a score of men go trooping down the echoing aisle—and then a sickening disappointment always followed; the children were not there; it was only a searcher's light.

Three dreadful days and nights dragged their tedious hours along, and the village sank into a hopeless stupor. No one had heart for anything.

Now to return to Tom and Becky's share in the picnic. They tripped along the murky aisles with the rest of the company, visiting the familiar wonders of the cave—wonders dubbed with rather overdescriptive names, such as "The Drawing-Room," "The Cathedral," "Aladdin's Palace," and so on. Presently the hide-and-seek frolicking began, and Tom and Becky engaged in it with zeal until the exertion began to grow a trifle wearisome; then they wandered down a sinuous avenue holding their candles aloft and reading the tangled webwork of names, dates, post-office addresses, and mottoes with which the rocky walls had been frescoed (in candle-smoke). Still drifting along and talking, they scarcely noticed that they were now in a part of the cave whose walls were not frescoed. They smoked their own names under an overhanging shelf and moved on. Presently they came to a place where a little stream of water, trickling over a ledge and carrying a limestone sediment with it, had, in the slow-dragging ages, formed a laced and ruffled Niagara in gleaming and imperishable stone. Tom squeezed his small body behind it in order to illuminate it for Becky's gratification. He found that it curtained a sort of steep natural stairway which was inclosed between narrow walls, and at once the ambition to be a discoverer seized him. Becky responded to his call, and they made a smoke-mark for future guidance and started upon their quest. They wound this way and that, far down into the secret depths of the cave, made another mark, and branched off in search of novelties to tell the upper world about. In one place they found a spacious cavern, from whose ceiling depended a multitude of shining stalactites of the length and circumference of a man's leg; they walked all about it, wondering and admiring, and presently left it by one of the numerous passages that opened into it. This shortly brought them to a bewitching spring, whose basin was incrusted with a frostwork of glittering crystals; it was in the midst of a cavern whose walls were supported by many fantastic pillars which had been formed by the joining of great stalactites and stalagmites together, the result of the ceaseless water-drip of centuries. Under the roof vast knots of bats had packed themselves together, thousands in a bunch; the lights disturbed the creatures, and they came flocking down by hundreds, squeaking and darting furiously at the candles. Tom knew their ways and the danger of this sort of conduct. He seized Becky's hand and hurried her into the first corridor that offered; and none too soon, for a bat struck Becky's light out with its wing while she was passing out of the cavern. The bats chased the children a good distance; but the fugitives plunged into

314

every new passage that offered, and at last got rid of the perilous things. Tom found a subterranean lake, shortly, which stretched its dim length away until its shape was lost in the shadows. He wanted to explore its borders, but concluded that it would be best to sit down and rest awhile, first. Now, for the first time, the deep stillness of the place laid a clammy hand upon the spirits of the children. Becky said,—

"Why, I didn't notice, but it seems ever so long since I heard of any of the others."

"Come to think, Becky, we are away down below them—and I don't know how far away north, or south, or east, or whichever it is. We couldn't hear them here."

Becky grew apprehensive.

"I wonder how long we've been down here, Tom. We better start back."

"Yes, I reckon we better. P'raps we better."

"Can you find the way, Tom? It's all a mixed-up crookedness to me."

"I reckon I could find it—but then the bats. If they put both our candles out it will be an awful fix. Let's try some other way, so as not to go through there."

"Well. But I hope we won't get lost. It would be so awful!" and the girl shuddered at the thought of the dreadful possibilities.

They started through a corridor, and traversed it in silence a long way, glancing at each new opening to see if there was anything familiar about the look of it; but they were all strange. Every time Tom made an examination, Becky would watch his face for an encouraging sign, and he would say cheerily,—

"Oh, it's all right. This ain't the one, but we'll come to it right away!"

But he felt less and less hopeful with each failure, and presently began to turn off into diverging avenues at sheer random, in desperate hope of finding the one that was wanted. He still said it was "all right," but there was such a leaden dread at his heart that the words had lost their ring and sounded just as if he had said, "All is lost!" Becky clung to his side in an anguish

315

of fear, and tried hard to keep back the tears, but they would come. At last she said,—

"Oh, Tom, never mind the bats, let's go back that way! We seem to get worse and worse off all the time."

Tom stopped.

"Listen!" said he.

Profound silence; silence so deep that even their breathings were conspicuous in the hush. Tom shouted. The call went echoing down the empty aisles and died out in the distance in a faint sound that resembled a ripple of mocking laughter.

"Oh, don't do it again, Tom, it is too horrid," said Becky.

"It is horrid, but I better, Becky; they *might* hear us, you know," and he shouted again.

The "might" was even a chillier horror than the ghostly laughter, it so confessed a perishing hope. The children stood still and listened; but there was no result. Tom turned upon the back track at once, and hurried his steps. It was but a little while before a certain indecision in his manner revealed another fearful fact to Becky—he could not find his way back!

"Oh, Tom, you didn't make any marks!"

"Becky, I was such a fool! Such a fool! I never thought we might want to come back! No—I can't find the way. It's all mixed up."

"Tom, Tom, we're lost! we're lost! We never can get out of this awful place! Oh, why *did* we ever leave the others!"

She sank to the ground and burst into such a frenzy of crying that Tom was appalled with the idea that she might die, or lose her reason. He sat down by her and put his arms around her; she buried her face in his bosom, she clung to him, she poured out her terrors, her unavailing regrets, and the far echoes turned them all to jeering laughter. Tom begged her to pluck up hope again, and she said she could not. He fell to blaming and abusing himself for getting her into this miserable situation; this had a better effect. She said she would try to hope again, she would get up and follow wherever he might lead if only he would not talk like that any more. For he was no more to blame than she, she said.

So they moved on again—aimlessly—simply at random—all they could do was to move, keep moving. For a little while, hope made a show of reviving—not with any reason to back it, but only because it is its nature to revive when the spring has not been taken out of it by age and familiarity with failure.

By and by Tom took Becky's candle and blew it out. This economy meant so much! Words were not needed. Becky understood, and her hope died again. She knew that Tom had a whole candle and three or four pieces in his pockets—yet he must economize.

By and by, fatigue began to assert its claims; the children tried to pay no attention, for it was dreadful to think of sitting down when time was grown to be so precious; moving, in some direction, in any direction, was at least progress and might bear fruit; but to sit down was to invite death and shorten its pursuit.

At last Becky's frail limbs refused to carry her farther. She sat down. Tom rested with her, and they talked of home, and the friends there, and the comfortable beds and, above all, the light! Becky cried, and Tom tried to think of some way of comforting her, but all his encouragements were grown threadbare with use, and sounded like sarcasms. Fatigue bore so heavily upon Becky that she drowsed off to sleep. Tom was grateful. He sat looking into her drawn face and saw it grow smooth and natural under the influence of pleasant dreams; and by and by a smile dawned and rested there. The peaceful face reflected somewhat of peace and healing into his own spirit, and his thoughts wandered away to bygone times and dreamy memories. While he was deep in his musings, Becky woke up with a breezy little laugh—but it was stricken dead upon her lips, and a groan followed it.

"Oh, how *could* I sleep! I wish I never, never had waked! No! No, I don't, Tom! Don't look so! I won't say it again."

"I'm glad you've slept, Becky; you'll feel rested, now, and we'll find the way out."

"We can try, Tom; but I've seen such a beautiful country in my dream. I reckon we are going there."

"Maybe not. Cheer up, Becky, and let's go on trying."

They rose up and wandered along, hand in hand and hopeless. They tried to estimate how long they had been in the cave, but all they knew was that it seemed days and weeks, and yet it was plain that this could not be, for their candles were not gone yet. A long time after this—they could not tell how long—Tom said they must go softly and listen for dripping water—they must find a spring. They found one presently, and Tom said it was time to rest again. Both were cruelly tired, yet Becky said she thought she could go on a little farther. She was surprised to hear Tom dissent. She could not understand it. They sat down, and Tom fastened his candle to the wall in front of them with some clay. Thought was soon busy; nothing was said for some time. Then Becky broke the silence,—

"Tom, I am so hungry!"

Tom took something out of his pocket.

"Do you remember this?" said he.

Becky almost smiled.

"It's our wedding cake, Tom."

"Yes—I wish it was as big as a barrel, for it's all we've got."

"I saved it from the picnic for us to dream on, Tom, the way grown-up people do with wedding cake—but it'll be our—"

She dropped the sentence where it was. Tom divided the cake and Becky ate with good appetite, while Tom nibbled at his moiety. There was abundance of cold water to finish the feast with. By and by Becky suggested that they move on again. Tom was silent a moment. Then he said,—

"Becky, can you bear it if I tell you something?"

Becky's face paled, but she thought she could.

"Well, then, Becky, we must stay here, where there's water to drink. That little piece is our last candle!"

Becky gave loose to tears and wailings. Tom did what he could to comfort her, but with little effect. At length Becky said,—

"Tom!"

"Well, Becky?"

"They'll miss us and hunt for us!"

"Yes, they will! Certainly they will!"

319

"Maybe they're hunting for us now, Tom."

"Why, I reckon maybe they are. I hope they are."

"When would they miss us, Tom?"

"When they get back to the boat, I reckon."

"Tom, it might be dark then—would they notice we hadn't come?"

"I don't know. But anyway, your mother would miss you as soon as they got home."

A frightened look in Becky's face brought Tom to his senses, and he saw that he had made a blunder. Becky was not to have gone home that night! The children became silent and thoughtful. In a moment a new burst of grief from Becky showed Tom that the thing in his mind had struck hers also—that the Sabbath morning might be half spent before Mrs. Thatcher discovered that Becky was not at Mrs. Harper's.

The children fastened their eyes upon their bit of candle and watched it melt slowly and pitilessly away; saw the half-inch of wick stand alone at last; saw the feeble flame rise and fall, climb the thin column of smoke, linger at its top a moment, and then— the horror of utter darkness reigned!

How long afterward it was that Becky came to a slow consciousness that she was crying in Tom's arms, neither could tell. All that they knew was, that after what seemed a mighty stretch of time, both awoke out of a dead stupor of sleep and resumed their miseries once more. Tom said it might be Sunday, now— maybe Monday. He tried to get Becky to talk, but her sorrows were too oppressive, all her hopes were gone. Tom said that they must have been missed long ago, and no doubt the search was going on. He would shout and maybe someone would come. He tried it; but in the darkness the distant echoes sounded so hideously that he tried it no more.

The hours wasted away, and hunger came to torment the captives again. A portion of Tom's half of the cake was left; they divided and ate it. But they seemed hungrier than before. The poor morsel of food only whetted desire.

By and by Tom said,—

"'Sh! Did you hear that?"

320

Both held their breath and listened. There was a sound like the faintest, far-off shout. Instantly Tom answered it, and, leading Becky by the hand, started groping down the corridor in its direction. Presently he listened again; again the sound was heard, and apparently a little nearer.

"It's them!" said Tom; "they're coming! Come along, Becky— we're all right now!"

The joy of the prisoners was almost overwhelming. Their speed was slow, however, because pitfalls were somewhat common and had to be guarded against. They shortly came to one and had to stop. It might be three feet deep, it might be a hundred—there was no passing it, at any rate. Tom got down on his breast and reached as far down as he could. No bottom. They must stay there and wait until the searchers came. They listened; evidently the distant shoutings were growing more distant! a moment or two more and they had gone altogether. The heart-sinking misery of it! Tom whooped until he was hoarse, but it was of no use. He talked hopefully to Becky; but an age of anxious waiting passed and no sounds came again.

The children groped their way back to the spring. The weary time dragged on; they slept again, and awoke famished and woe-stricken. Tom believed it must be Tuesday by this time.

Now an idea struck him. There were some side passages near at hand. It would be better to explore some of these than bear the weight of the heavy time in idleness. He took a kite-line from his pocket, tied it to a projection, and he and Becky started, Tom in the lead, unwinding the line as he groped along. At the end of twenty steps the corridor ended in a "jumping-off place." Tom got down on his knees and felt below, and then as far around the corner as he could reach with his hands conveniently; he made an effort to stretch yet a little farther to the right, and at that moment, not twenty yards away, a human hand, holding a candle, appeared from behind a rock! Tom lifted up a glorious shout, and instantly that hand was followed by the body it belonged to—Injun Joe's! Tom was paralyzed; he could not move. He was vastly gratified the next moment to see the "Spaniard" take to his heels and get himself out of sight. Tom wondered that Joe had not recognized his voice and come over and killed him for testifying in court. But the echoes must have disguised the voice. Without doubt, that was it, he reasoned. Tom's fright weakened every muscle in his body. He said to himself that if he had strength enough to get back to the spring he would stay there, and nothing should tempt him to run the risk of meeting Injun Joe again. He was careful to keep from Becky what it was he had seen. He told her he had only shouted "for luck."

But hunger and wretchedness rise superior to fears in the long run. Another tedious wait at the spring and another long sleep brought changes. The children awoke tortured with a raging hunger. Tom believed that it must be Wednesday or Thursday or even Friday or Saturday, now, and that the search had been given over. He proposed to explore another passage. He felt willing to risk Injun Joe and all other terrors. But Becky was very weak. She had sunk into a dreary apathy and would not be roused. She said she would wait, now, where she was, and die—it would not be long. She told Tom to go with the kite-line and explore if he chose; but she implored him to come back every little while and speak to her; and she made him promise that when the awful time came, he would stay by her and hold her hand until all was over.

Tom kissed her, with a choking sensation in his throat, and made a show of being confident of finding the searchers or an escape from the cave; then he took the kite-line in his hand and went groping down one of the passages on his hands and knees, distressed with hunger and sick with bodings of coming doom.

Tuesday afternoon came and waned to the twilight. The village of St. Petersburg still mourned. The lost children had not been found. Public prayers had been offered up for them, and many and many a private prayer that had the petitioner's whole heart in it; but still no good news came from the cave. The majority of the searchers had given up the quest and gone back to their daily vocations, saying that it was plain the children could never be found. Mrs. Thatcher was very ill, and a great part of the time delirious. People said it was heartbreak-

ing to hear her call her child, and raise her head and listen a
whole minute at a time, then lay it wearily down again with a
moan. Aunt Polly had drooped into a settled melancholy, and
her gray hair had grown almost white. The village went to its
rest on Tuesday night, sad and forlorn.

Away in the middle of the night a wild peal burst from the
village bells, and in a moment the streets were swarming with
frantic half-clad people, who shouted, "Turn out! turn out!
they're found! they're found!" Tin pans and horns were added
to the din, the population massed itself and moved toward the
river, met the children coming in an open carriage drawn by
shouting citizens, thronged around it, joined its homeward
march, and swept magnificently up the main street roaring
huzzah after huzzah!

The village was illuminated; nobody went to bed again; it was
the greatest night the little town had ever seen. During the first
half-hour a procession of villagers filed through Judge Thatcher's
house, seized the saved ones and kissed them, squeezed Mrs.
Thatcher's hand, tried to speak but couldn't—and drifted out
raining tears all over the place.

Aunt Polly's happiness was complete, and Mrs. Thatcher's
nearly so. It would be complete, however, as soon as the mes-

323

senger despatched with the great news to the cave should get the word to her husband. Tom lay upon a sofa with an eager auditory about him and told the history of the wonderful adventure, putting in many striking additions to adorn it withal; and closed with a description of how he left Becky and went on an exploring expedition; how he followed two avenues as far as his kite-line would reach; how he followed a third to the fullest stretch of the kite-line, and was about to turn back when he glimpsed a far-off speck that looked like daylight; dropped the line and groped toward it, pushed his head and shoulders through a small hole and saw the broad Mississippi rolling by! And if it had only happened to be night he would not have seen that speck of daylight and would not have explored that passage any more! He told how he went back for Becky and broke the good news, and she told him not to fret her with such stuff, for she was tired, and knew she was going to die, and wanted to. He described how he labored with her and convinced her; and how she almost died for joy when she had groped to where she actually saw the blue speck of daylight; how he pushed his way out at the hole and then helped her out; how they sat there and cried for gladness; how some men came along in a skiff and Tom hailed them and told them their situation and their famished condition; how the men didn't believe the wild tale at first, "because," said they, "you are five miles down the river below the valley the cave is in"—then took them aboard, rowed to a house, gave them supper, made them rest till two or three hours after dark, and then brought them home.

Before day-dawn, Judge Thatcher and the handful of searchers with him were tracked out, in the cave, by the twine clews they had strung behind them, and informed of the great news.

Frances Hodgson Burnett

SARA CREWE

ILLUSTRATED BY *Janet Smalley*

IN THE first place, Miss Minchin lived in London. Her home was a large, dull, tall one in a large, dull square, where all the houses were alike, and all the sparrows were alike, and where all the door-knockers made the same heavy sound, and on still days—and nearly all the days were still—seemed to resound through the entire row in which the knock was knocked. On Miss Minchin's door there was a brass plate. On the brass plate there was inscribed in black letters:

MISS MINCHIN'S SELECT SEMINARY
FOR YOUNG LADIES

Little Sara Crewe never went in or out of the house without reading that doorplate and reflecting upon it. By the time she was twelve, she had decided that all her trouble arose because, in the first place, she was not "Select," and in the second, she was not a "Young Lady." When she was eight years old, she had

325

been brought to Miss Minchin as a pupil and left with her. Her papa had brought her all the way from India. Her mamma had died when she was a baby, and her papa had kept her with him as long as he could. And then, finding the hot climate was making her very delicate, he had brought her to England and left her with Miss Minchin, to be part of the Select Seminary for Young Ladies. Sara, who had always been a sharp little child, who remembered things, recollected hearing him say that he had not a relative in the world whom he knew of, and so he was obliged to place her at a boarding school, and he had heard Miss Minchin's establishment spoken of very highly. The same day, he took Sara out and bought her a great many beautiful clothes—clothes so grand and rich that only a very young and inexperienced man would have bought them for a mite of a child who was to be brought up in a boarding school. But the fact was that he was a rash, innocent young man, and very sad at the thought of parting with his little girl, who was all he had left to remind him of her beautiful mother, whom he had dearly loved. And he wished her to have everything the most fortunate little girl could have; and so, when the polite saleswomen in the shops said, "Here is our very latest thing in hats, the plumes are exactly the same as those we sold to Lady Diana Sinclair yesterday," he immediately bought what was offered to him and paid whatever was asked. The consequence was that Sara had a most extraordinary wardrobe. Her dresses were silk and velvet and India cashmere, her hats and bonnets were covered with bows and plumes, her small undergarments were adorned with real lace, and she returned in the cab to Miss Minchin's with a doll almost as large as herself, dressed quite as grandly as herself, too.

Then her papa gave Miss Minchin some money and went away, and for several days Sara would neither touch the doll, nor her breakfast, nor her dinner, nor her tea, and would do nothing but crouch in a small corner by the window and cry. She cried so much, indeed, that she made herself ill. She was a queer little child, with old-fashioned ways and strong feelings, and she had adored her papa and could not be made to think that India and an interesting bungalow were not better for her than London and Miss Minchin's Select Seminary. The instant she had entered the house, she had begun promptly to hate Miss Minchin, and to think little of Miss Amelia Minchin, who was smooth and dumpy, and lisped, and was evidently afraid of her older sister. Miss Minchin was tall and had large, cold, fishy eyes, and large, cold hands, which seemed fishy, too, because they were damp and made chills run down Sara's back when they touched her, as Miss Minchin pushed her hair off her forehead and said,—

"A most beautiful and promising little girl, Captain Crewe. She will be a favorite pupil; *quite* a favorite pupil, I see."

For the first year she was a favorite pupil; at least she was indulged a great deal more than was good for her. And when the Select Seminary went walking, two by two, she was always decked out in her grandest clothes and led by the hand, at the head of the genteel procession, by Miss Minchin herself. And when the parents of any of the pupils came, she was always dressed and called into the parlor with her doll; and she used to hear Miss Minchin say that her father was a distinguished Indian officer, and she would be heiress to a great fortune. That her father had inherited a great deal of money, Sara had heard before; and also that some day it would be hers, and that he would not remain long in the army, but would come to live in London. And every time a letter came, she hoped it would say he was coming, and they were to live together again.

But about the middle of the third year a letter came bringing very different news. Because he was not a business man himself, her papa had given his affairs into the hands of a friend he trusted. The friend had deceived and robbed him. All the money was gone, no one knew exactly where, and the shock was so great to the poor, rash young officer, that, being attacked by jungle fever shortly afterward, he had no strength to rally, and so died, leaving Sara with no one to take care of her.

Miss Minchin's cold and fishy eyes had never looked so cold and fishy as they did when Sara went into the parlor, on being sent for, a few days after the letter was received.

No one had said anything to the child about mourning, so, in her old-fashioned way, she had decided to find a black dress for herself, and had picked out a black velvet she had outgrown, and came into the room in it, looking the queerest little figure in the world, and a sad little figure too. The dress was too short and too tight, her face was white, her eyes had dark rings around them, and her doll, wrapped in a piece of old black crape, was held under her arm. She was not a pretty child. She was thin, and had a weird, interesting little face, black hair, and very large, green-gray eyes fringed all around with heavy black lashes.

"I am the ugliest child in the school," she had said once, after staring at herself in the glass for some minutes.

But there had been a clever, good-natured little French teacher who had said to the music-master,—

"Zat leetle Crewe. Vat a child! A so ogly beauty! Ze so large eyes! ze so little spirituelle face. Waid till she grow up. You shall see!"

This morning, however, in the tight, small black frock, she looked thinner and odder than ever, and her eyes were fixed on Miss Minchin with a queer steadiness as she slowly advanced into the parlor, clutching her doll.

"Put your doll down!" said Miss Minchin.

"No," said the child, "I won't put her down; I want her with me. She is all I have. She has stayed with me all the time since my papa died."

She had never been an obedient child. She had had her own way ever since she was born, and there was about her an air of silent determination under which Miss Minchin had always felt secretly uncomfortable. And that lady felt even now that perhaps it would be as well not to insist on her point. So she looked at her as severely as possible.

"You will have no time for dolls in future," she said. "You will have to work and improve yourself, and make yourself useful."

Sara kept the big odd eyes fixed on her teacher and said nothing.

"Everything will be very different now," Miss Minchin went on. "I sent for you to talk to you and make you understand. Your father is dead. You have no friends. You have no money. You have no home and no one to take care of you."

The little pale olive face twitched nervously, but the green-gray eyes did not move from Miss Minchin's, and still Sara said nothing.

"What are you staring at?" demanded Miss Minchin sharply. "Are you so stupid you don't understand what I mean? I tell you that you are quite alone in the world, and have no one to do anything for you, unless I choose to keep you here."

The truth was, Miss Minchin was in her worst mood. To be suddenly deprived of a large sum of money yearly and a show pupil, and to find herself with a little beggar on her hands, was more than she could bear with any degree of calmness.

"Now listen to me," she went on, "and remember what I say. If you work hard and prepare to make yourself useful in a few years, I shall let you stay here. You are only a child, but you are a sharp child, and you pick up things almost without being taught. You speak French very well, and in a year or so you can begin to help with the younger pupils. By the time you are fifteen you ought to be able to do that much at least."

"I can speak French better than you, now," said Sara; "I always spoke it with my papa in India." Which was not at all polite, but was painfully true; because Miss Minchin could not speak French at all, and, indeed, was not in the least a clever person. But she was a hard, grasping business woman; and, after the first shock of disappointment, had seen that at very little expense to herself she might prepare this clever, determined child to be very useful to her and save her the necessity of paying large salaries to teachers of languages.

"Don't be impudent, or you will be punished," she said. "You will have to improve your manners if you expect to earn your bread. You are not a parlor-boarder now. Remember that if you don't please me, and I send you away, you have no home but the street. You can go now."

Sara turned away.

"Stay," commanded Miss Minchin, "don't you intend to thank me?"

Sara turned toward her. The nervous twitch was to be seen again in her face, and she seemed to be trying to control it.

"What for?" she said.

"For my kindness to you," replied Miss Minchin. "For my kindness in giving you a home."

Sara went two or three steps nearer to her. Her thin little chest was heaving up and down, and she spoke in a strange, unchildish voice.

"You are not kind," she said. "You are not kind." And she turned again and went out of the room, leaving Miss Minchin staring after her strange, small figure in stony anger.

The child walked up the staircase, holding tightly to her doll; she meant to go to her bedroom, but at the door she was met by Miss Amelia.

"You are not to go in there," she said. "That is not your room now."

"Where is my room?" asked Sara.

"You are to sleep in the attic next to the cook."

Sara walked on. She mounted two flights more, and reached the door of the attic room, opened it and went in, shutting it behind her. She stood against it and looked about her. The room was slanting-roofed and whitewashed; there was a rusty grate, an iron bedstead, and some odd articles of furniture, sent up from better rooms below, where they had been used until they were considered to be worn out. Under the skylight in the roof, which showed nothing but an oblong piece of dull gray sky, there was a battered old red footstool.

Sara went to it and sat down. She was a queer child, as I have said before, and quite unlike other children. She seldom cried. She did not cry now. She laid her doll, Emily, across her knees, and put her face down upon her, and her arms around her, and sat there, her little black head resting on the black crape, not saying one word, not making one sound.

From that day her life changed entirely. Sometimes she used to feel as if it must be another life altogether, the life of some

330

other child. She was a little drudge and outcast; she was given her lessons at odd times and expected to learn without being taught; she was sent on errands by Miss Minchin, Miss Amelia, and the cook. Nobody took any notice of her except when they ordered her about. She was often kept busy all day and then sent into the deserted schoolroom with a pile of books to learn her lessons or practice at night. She had never been intimate with the other pupils, and soon she became so shabby that, taking her queer clothes together with her queer little ways, they began to look upon her as a being of another world than their own. The fact was that, as a rule, Miss Minchin's pupils were rather dull, matter-of-fact young people, accustomed to being rich and comfortable; and Sara, with her elfish cleverness, her desolate life, and her odd habit of fixing her eyes upon them and staring them out of countenance, was too much for them.

"She always looks as if she was finding you out," said one girl, who was sly and given to making mischief.

"I am," said Sara promptly, when she heard of it. "That's what I look at them for. I like to know about people. I think them over afterward."

She never made any mischief herself or interfered with any one. She talked very little, did as she was told, and thought a great deal. Nobody knew, and in fact nobody cared, whether she was unhappy or happy, unless, perhaps, it was Emily, who lived in the attic and slept on the iron bedstead at night. Sara thought Emily understood her feelings, though she was only wax and had a habit of staring herself. Sara used to talk to her at night.

"You are the only friend I have in the world," she would say to her. "Why don't you say something? Why don't you speak? Sometimes I am sure you could, if you would try. It ought to make you try, to know you are the only thing I have. If I were you, I should try. Why don't you try?"

It really was a very strange feeling she had about Emily. It arose from her being so desolate. She did not like to own to herself that her only friend, her only companion, could feel and hear nothing. She wanted to believe, or to pretend to believe,

331

that Emily understood and sympathized with her, that she heard her even though she did not speak in answer. She used to put her in a chair sometimes and sit opposite to her on the old red footstool, and stare at her and think and pretend about her until her own eyes would grow large with something which was almost like fear, particularly at night, when the garret was so still, when the only sound that was to be heard was the occasional squeak and scurry of rats in the wainscot. There were rat-holes in the garret, and Sara detested rats, and was always glad Emily was with her when she heard their hateful squeak and rush and scratching. One of her "pretends" was that Emily was a kind of good witch and could protect her. Poor little Sara! everything was "pretend" with her. She had a strong imagination; there was almost more imagination than there was Sara, and her whole forlorn, uncared-for childlife was made up of imaginings. She imagined and pretended things until she almost believed them, and she would scarcely have been surprised at any remarkable thing that could have happened. So she insisted to herself that Emily understood all about her troubles and was really her friend.

"As to answering," she used to say, "I don't answer very often. I never answer when I can help it. When people are insulting you, there is nothing so good for them as not to say a word— just to look at them and *think*. Miss Minchin turns pale with rage when I do it. Miss Amelia looks frightened, so do the girls. They know you are stronger than they are, because you are strong enough to hold in your rage and they are not, and they say stupid things they wish they hadn't said afterward. There's nothing so strong as rage, except what makes you hold it in— that's stronger. It's a good thing not to answer your enemies. I scarcely ever do. Perhaps Emily is more like me than I am like myself. Perhaps she would rather not answer her friends, even. She keeps it all in her heart."

But though she tried to satisfy herself with these arguments, Sara did not find it easy. When, after a long, hard day, in which she had been sent here and there, sometimes on long errands, through wind and cold and rain; and, when she came in wet and hungry, had been sent out again because nobody chose to remember that she was only a child, and that her thin little legs might be tired, and her small body, clad in its forlorn, too small finery, all too short and too tight, might be chilled; when she had been given only harsh words and cold, slighting looks for thanks; when the cook had been vulgar and insolent; when Miss Minchin had been in her worst moods, and when she had seen the girls sneering at her among themselves and making fun of her poor, outgrown clothes—then Sara did not find Emily quite all that her sore, proud, desolate little heart needed as the doll sat in her little old chair and stared.

One of these nights, when she came up to the garret cold, hungry, tired, and with a tempest raging in her small breast, Emily's stare seemed so vacant, her sawdust legs and arms so limp and inexpressive, that Sara lost all control over herself.

"I shall die presently!" she said at first.

Emily stared.

"I can't bear this!" said the poor child, trembling. "I know I shall die. I'm cold, I'm wet, I'm starving to death. I've walked a thousand miles today, and they have done nothing but scold me from morning until night. And because I could not find that last thing they sent me for, they would not give me any supper. Some men laughed at me because my old shoes made me slip down in the mud. I'm covered with mud now. And they laughed! Do you *hear!*"

She looked at the staring glass eyes and complacent wax face, and suddenly a sort of heart-broken rage seized her. She lifted her little savage hand and knocked Emily off the chair, bursting into a passion of sobbing.

"You are nothing but a doll!" she cried. "Nothing but a doll—doll—doll! You care for nothing. You are stuffed with sawdust. You never had a heart. Nothing could ever make you feel. You are a *doll!*"

Emily lay upon the floor, with her legs ignominiously doubled up over her head, and a new flat place on the end of her nose; but she was still calm, even dignified.

Sara hid her face on her arms and sobbed. Some rats in

333

the wall began to fight and bite each other, and squeak and scramble. But, as I have already intimated, Sara was not in the habit of crying. After a while she stopped, and when she stopped she looked at Emily, who seemed to be gazing at her around the side of one ankle, and actually with a kind of glassy-eyed sympathy. Sara bent and picked her up. Remorse overtook her.

"You can't help being a doll," she said, with a resigned sigh, "any more than those girls downstairs can help not having any sense. We are not all alike. Perhaps you do your sawdust best."

None of Miss Minchin's young ladies were very remarkable for being brilliant; they were select, but some of them were very dull, and some of them were fond of applying themselves to their lessons. Sara, who snatched her lessons at all sorts of untimely hours from tattered and discarded books, and who had a hungry craving for everything readable, was often severe upon them in her small mind. They had books they never read; she had no books at all. If she had always had something to read, she would not have been so lonely. She liked romances and history and poetry; she would read anything. There was a sentimental housemaid in the establishment who bought the weekly penny papers, and subscribed to a circulating library, from which she got greasy volumes containing stories of marquises and dukes who invariably fell in love with orange-girls and gypsies and servant-maids, and made them the proud brides of coronets; and Sara often did parts of this maid's work so that she might earn the privilege of reading these romantic histories. There was also a fat, dull pupil, whose name was Ermengarde St. John, who was one of her resources. Ermengarde had an intellectual father who, in his despairing desire to encourage his daughter, constantly sent her valuable and interesting books, which were a continual source of grief to her. Sara had once actually found her crying over a big package of them.

"What is the matter with you?" she asked her disdainfully.

And it is just possible she would not have spoken to her, if she had not seen the books. The sight of books always gave Sara a hungry feeling, and she could not help drawing near to them if only to read their titles.

"What is the matter with you?" she asked.

"My papa has sent me some more books," answered Ermengarde woefully, "and he expects me to read them."

"Don't you like reading?" said Sara.

"I hate it!" replied Miss Ermengarde St. John. "And he will ask me questions when he sees me: he will want to know how much I remember; how would *you* like to have to read all those?"

"I'd like it better than anything else in the world," said Sara.

Ermengarde wiped her eyes to look at such a prodigy.

"Oh, gracious!" she exclaimed.

Sara returned the look with interest. A sudden plan formed itself in her sharp mind.

"Look here!" she said. "If you'll lend me those books, I'll read them and tell you everything that's in them afterward, and I'll tell it to you so that you will remember it. I know I can. The A B C children always remember what I tell them."

"Oh, goodness!" said Ermengarde. "Do you think you could?"

"I know I could," answered Sara. "I like to read, and I always remember. I'll take care of the books, too; they will look just as new as they do now, when I give them back to you."

Ermengarde put her handkerchief in her pocket.

"If you'll do that," she said, "and if you'll make me remember, I'll give you—I'll give you some money."

"I don't want your money," said Sara. "I want your books—I want them." And her eyes grew big and queer, and her chest heaved once.

"Take them, then," said Ermengarde; "I wish I wanted them, but I am not clever, and my father is, and he thinks I ought to be."

Sara picked up the books and marched off with them. But when she was at the door, she stopped and turned around.

"What are you going to tell your father?" she asked.

"Oh," said Ermengarde, "he needn't know; he'll think I've read them."

Sara looked down at the books; her heart really began to beat fast.

"I won't do it," she said rather slowly, "if you are going to tell him lies about it—I don't like lies. Why can't you tell him I read them and then told you about them?"

"But he wants me to read them," said Ermengarde.

"He wants you to know what is in them," said Sara; "and if I can tell it to you in an easy way and make you remember, I should think he would like that."

"He would like it better if I read them myself," replied Ermengarde.

"He will like it, I dare say, if you learn anything in any way," said Sara. "I should, if I were your father."

And though this was not a flattering way of stating the case, Ermengarde was obliged to admit it was true, and, after a little more argument, gave in. And so she used afterward always to hand over her books to Sara, and Sara would carry them to her garret and devour them; and after she had read each volume, she would return it and tell Ermengarde about it in a way of her own. She had a gift for making things interesting. Her imagination helped her to make everything rather like a story, and she managed this matter so well that Miss St. John gained more information from her books than she would have gained if she had read them three times over by her poor stupid little self. When Sara sat down by her and began to tell some story of travel or history, she made the travelers and historical people seem real; and Ermengarde used to sit and regard her dramatic gesticulations, her thin little flushed cheeks, and her shining, odd eyes with amazement.

"It sounds nicer than it seems in the book," she would say. "I never cared about Mary, Queen of Scots, before, and I always hated the French Revolution, but you make it seem like a story."

"It is a story," Sara would answer. "They are all stories. Everything is a story—everything in this world. You are a story—I am a story—Miss Minchin is a story. You can make a story out of anything."

"I can't," said Ermengarde.

Sara stared at her a minute reflectively.

"No," she said at last. "I suppose you couldn't. You are a little like Emily."

"Who is Emily?"

Sara recollected herself. She knew she was sometimes rather impolite in the candor of her remarks, and she did not want to be impolite to a girl who was not unkind—only stupid. Notwithstanding all her sharp little ways she had the sense to wish to be just to everybody. In the hours she spent alone, she used to argue out a great many curious questions with herself. One thing she had decided upon was, that a person who was clever ought to be clever enough not to be unjust or deliberately unkind to anyone. Miss Minchin was unjust and cruel, Miss Amelia was unkind and spiteful, the cook was malicious and hasty-tempered—they all were stupid, and made her despise them, and she desired to be as unlike them as possible. So she would be as polite as she could to people who in the least deserved politeness.

"Emily is—a person—I know," she replied.

"Do you like her?" asked Ermengarde.

"Yes, I do," said Sara.

Ermengarde examined her queer little face and figure again. She did look odd. She had on, that day, a faded blue plush skirt, which barely covered her knees, a brown cloth sacque, and a pair of olive-green stockings which Miss Minchin had made her piece out with black ones, so that they would be long enough to be kept on. And yet Ermengarde was beginning slowly to admire her. Such a forlorn, thin, neglected little thing as that, who could read and read and remember and tell you things so that they did not tire you all out! A child who could speak French, and who had learned German, no one knew how! One could not help staring at her and feeling interested, particularly one to whom the simplest lesson was a trouble and a woe.

"Do you like *me?*" said Ermengarde, finally, at the end of her scrutiny.

Sara hesitated one second, then she answered,—

"I like you because you are not ill-natured—I like you for letting me read your books—I like you because you don't make spiteful fun of me for what I can't help. It's not your fault that——"

She pulled herself up quickly. She had been going to say, "that you are stupid."

"That what?" asked Ermengarde.

"That you can't learn things quickly. If you can't, you can't. If I can, why, I can—that's all." She paused a minute, looking at the plump face before her, and then, rather slowly, one of her wise, old-fashioned thoughts came to her.

"Perhaps," she said, "to be able to learn things quickly isn't everything. To be kind is worth a good deal to other people. If Miss Minchin knew everything on earth, which she doesn't, and if she was like what she is now, she'd still be a detestable thing, and everybody would hate her. Lots of clever people have done harm and been wicked. Look at Robespierre——"

She stopped again and examined her companion's countenance.

"Do you remember about him?" she demanded. "I believe you've forgotten."

"Well, I don't remember *all* of it," admitted Ermengarde.

"Well," said Sara, with courage and determination, "I'll tell it to you over again."

And she plunged once more into the gory records of the

French Revolution, and told such stories of it, and made such vivid pictures of its horrors, that Miss St. John was afraid to go to bed afterward, and hid her head under the blankets when she did go, and shivered until she fell asleep. But afterward she preserved lively recollections of the character of Robespierre, and did not even forget Marie Antoinette and the Princess de Lamballe.

"You know they put her head on a pike and danced around it," Sara had said; "and she had beautiful blonde hair; and when I think of her, I never see her head on her body, but always on a pike, with those furious people dancing and howling."

Yes, it was true; to this imaginative child everything was a story; and the more books she read, the more imaginative she became. One of her chief entertainments was to sit in her garret, or walk about it, and "suppose" things. On a cold night, when she had not had enough to eat, she would draw the red foot-stool up before the empty grate, and say in the most intense voice,—

"Suppose there was a great, wide steel grate here, and a great glowing fire—a *glowing* fire—with beds of red-hot coal and lots of little dancing, flickering flames. Suppose there was a soft, deep rug, and this was a comfortable chair, all cushions and crimson velvet; and suppose I had a crimson velvet frock on, and a deep lace collar, like a child in a picture; and suppose all the rest of the room was furnished in lovely colors, and there were bookshelves full of books, which changed by magic as soon as you had read them; and suppose there was a little table here, with a snow-white cover on it, and little silver dishes, and in one there was hot, hot soup, and in another a roast chicken, and in another some raspberry-jam tarts with crisscross on them, and in another some grapes; and suppose Emily could speak, and we could sit and eat our supper, and then talk and read; and then suppose there was a soft, warm bed in the corner, and when we were tired we could go to sleep, and sleep as long as we liked."

Sometimes, after she had supposed things like these for half an hour, she would feel almost warm, and would creep into bed with Emily and fall asleep with a smile on her face.

"What large, downy pillows!" she would whisper. "What white sheets and fleecy blankets!" And she almost forgot that her real pillows had scarcely any feathers in them at all, and smelled musty, and that her blankets and coverlid were thin and full of holes.

At another time she would "suppose" she was a princess, and then she would go about the house with an expression on her face which was a source of great secret annoyance to Miss Minchin, because it seemed as if the child scarcely heard the spiteful, insulting things said to her, or, if she heard them, did not care for them at all. Sometimes, while she was in the midst of some harsh and cruel speech, Miss Minchin would find the odd, unchildish eyes fixed upon her with something like a proud smile in them. At such times she did not know that Sara was saying to herself,—

"You don't know that you are saying these things to a princess, and that if I chose I could wave my hand and order you to execution. I only spare you because I *am* a princess, and you are a poor, stupid, old, vulgar thing, and don't know any better."

This used to please and amuse her more than anything else; and queer and fanciful as it was, she found comfort in it, and it was not a bad thing for her. It really kept her from being made rude and malicious by the rudeness and malice of those about her.

"A princess must be polite," she said to herself. And so when the servants, who took their tone from their mistress, were insolent and ordered her about, she would hold her head erect and reply to them sometimes in a way which made them stare at her, it was so quaintly civil.

"I am a princess in rags and tatters," she would think, "but I am a princess, inside. It would be easy to be a princess if I were dressed in cloth-of-gold; it is a great deal more of a triumph to be one all the time when no one knows it. There was Marie Antoinette: when she was in prison, and her throne was gone, and she had only a black gown on, and her hair was white, and they insulted her and called her the Widow Capet,—she was a

great deal more like a queen then than when she was so gay and had everything grand. I like her best then. Those howling mobs of people did not frighten her. She was stronger than they were even when they cut her head off."

Once when such thoughts were passing through her mind the look in her eyes so enraged Miss Minchin that she flew at Sara and boxed her ears.

Sara awakened from her dream, started a little, and then broke into a laugh.

"What are you laughing at, you bold, impudent child!" exclaimed Miss Minchin.

It took Sara a few seconds to remember she was a princess. Her cheeks were red and smarting from the blows she had received.

"I was thinking," she said.

"Beg my pardon immediately," said Miss Minchin.

"I will beg your pardon for laughing, if it was rude," said Sara; "but I won't beg your pardon for thinking."

"What were you thinking?" demanded Miss Minchin. "How dare you think? What were you thinking?"

This occurred in the schoolroom, and all the girls looked up from their books to listen. It always interested them when Miss Minchin flew at Sara, because Sara always said something queer, and never seemed in the least frightened. She was not in the least frightened now, though her boxed ears were scarlet, and her eyes were as bright as stars.

"I was thinking," she answered gravely and quite politely, "that you did not know what you were doing."

"That I did not know what I was doing!" Miss Minchin fairly gasped.

"Yes," said Sara, "and I was thinking what would happen, if I were a princess and you boxed my ears—what I should do to you. And I was thinking that if I were one, you would never dare to do it, whatever I said or did. And I was thinking how surprised and frightened you would be if you suddenly found out——"

She had the imagined picture so clearly before her eyes, that she spoke in a manner which had an effect even on Miss Minchin. It almost seemed for the moment to her narrow, unimaginative mind that there must be some real power behind this candid daring.

"What!" she exclaimed, "found out what?"

"That I really was a princess," said Sara, "and could do anything—anything I liked."

"Go to your room," cried Miss Minchin breathlessly, "this instant. Leave the schoolroom. Attend to your lessons, young ladies."

Sara made a little bow.

"Excuse me for laughing, if it was impolite," she said, and walked out of the room, leaving Miss Minchin in a rage and the girls whispering over their books.

"I shouldn't be at all surprised if she did turn out to be something," said one of them. "Suppose she should!"

That very afternoon Sara had an opportunity of proving to herself whether she was really a princess or not. It was a dreadful afternoon. For several days it had rained continuously, the streets were chilly and sloppy; there was mud everywhere—sticky London mud—and over everything a pall of fog and drizzle. Of course there were several long and tiresome errands to be done,—there always were on days like this,—and Sara was sent out again and again, until her shabby clothes were damp through. The absurd old feathers on her forlorn hat were more draggled and absurd than ever, and her downtrodden shoes were so wet they could not hold any more water. Added to this, she had been deprived of her dinner, because Miss Minchin wished to punish her. She was very hungry. She was so cold and hungry and tired that her little face had a pinched look, and now and then some kind-hearted person passing her in the crowded street glanced at her with sympathy. But she did not know that. She hurried on, trying to comfort herself in that queer way of hers by pretending and "supposing,"—but really this time it was harder than she had ever found it, and once or twice she thought it almost made her more cold and hungry instead of less so. But she persevered obstinately. "Suppose I had dry clothes on," she thought. "Suppose I had good shoes and a long, thick coat and merino stockings and a whole umbrella. And suppose—suppose, just when I was near a baker's where they sold hot buns, I should find sixpence—which belonged to nobody. Suppose, if I did, I should go into the shop and buy six of the hottest buns, and should eat them all without stopping."

Some very odd things happen in this world sometimes. It certainly was an odd thing which happened to Sara. She had to cross the street just as she was saying this to herself—the mud was dreadful—she almost had to wade. She picked her way as carefully as she could, but she could not save herself much, only, in picking her way she had to look down at her feet and the mud, and in looking down—just as she reached the pavement—she saw something shining in the gutter. A piece of silver—a tiny piece trodden upon by many feet, but still with spirit enough left to shine a little. Not quite a sixpence, but the next thing to it—a four-penny piece! In one second it was in her cold, little red and blue hand.

"Oh!" she gasped. "It is true!"

And then, if you will believe me, she looked straight before her at the shop directly facing her. And it was a baker's, and a cheerful, stout, motherly woman, with rosy cheeks, was just putting into the window a tray of delicious hot buns,—large, plump, shiny buns, with currants in them.

It almost made Sara feel faint for a few seconds—the shock and the sight of the buns and the delightful odors of warm bread floating up through the baker's cellar-window.

She knew that she need not hesitate to use the little piece of money. It had evidently been lying in the mud for some time, and its owner was completely lost in the streams of passing people who crowded and jostled each other all through the day.

"But I'll go and ask the baker's woman if she has lost a piece of money," she said to herself, rather faintly.

So she crossed the pavement and put her wet foot on the step of the shop; and as she did so she saw something which made her stop.

It was a little figure more forlorn than her own—a little figure which was not much more than a bundle of rags, from which small, bare, red, and muddy feet peeped out—only because the rags with which the wearer was trying to cover them were not long enough. Above the rags appeared a shock head of tangled hair and a dirty face, with big, hollow, hungry eyes.

Sara knew they were hungry eyes the moment she saw them, and she felt a sudden sympathy.

"This," she said to herself, with a little sigh, "is one of the Populace—and she is hungrier than I am."

The child—this "one of the Populace"—stared up at Sara, and shuffled herself aside a little, so as to give her more room. She was used to being made to give room to everybody. She knew that if a policeman chanced to see her, he would tell her to "move on."

Sara clutched her little four-penny piece, and hesitated a few seconds. Then she spoke to her.

"Are you hungry?" she asked.

The child shuffled herself and her rags a little more.

"Ain't I jist!" she said, in a hoarse voice. "Jist ain't I!"

344

"Haven't you had any dinner?" said Sara.

"No dinner," more hoarsely still and with more shuffling, "nor yet no bre'fast—nor yet no supper—nor nothin'."

"Since when?" asked Sara.

"Dun'no. Never got nothin' today—nowhere. I've axed and axed."

Just to look at her made Sara more hungry and faint. But those queer little thoughts were at work in her brain, and she was talking to herself though she was sick at heart.

"If I'm a princess," she was saying—"if I'm a princess—! When they were poor and driven from their thrones—they always shared—with the Populace—if they met one poorer and hungrier. They always shared. Buns are a penny each. If it had been sixpence! I could have eaten six. It won't be enough for either of us—but it will be better than nothing."

"Wait a minute," she said to the beggar-child. She went into the shop. It was warm and smelled delightfully. The woman was just going to put more hot buns in the window.

"If you please," said Sara, "have you lost fourpence—a silver fourpence?" And she held the forlorn little piece of money out to her.

The woman looked at it and at her—at her intense little face and draggled, once-fine clothes.

"Bless us—no," she answered. "Did you find it?"

"In the gutter," said Sara.

"Keep it, then," said the woman. "It may have been there a week, and goodness knows who lost it. *You* could never find out."

"I know that," said Sara, "but I thought I'd ask you."

"Not many would," said the woman, looking puzzled and interested and good-natured all at once. "Do you want to buy something?" she added, as she saw Sara glance toward the buns.

"Four buns, if you please," said Sara; "those at a penny each."

The woman went to the window and put some in a paper bag. Sara noticed that she put in six.

"I said four, if you please," she explained. "I have only the fourpence."

345

"I'll throw in two for make-weight," said the woman, with her good-natured look. "I dare say you can eat them some time. Aren't you hungry?"

A mist rose before Sara's eyes.

"Yes," she answered. "I am very hungry, and I am much obliged to you for your kindness, and," she was going to add, "there is a child outside who is hungrier than I am." But just at that moment two or three customers came in at once and each one seemed in a hurry, so she could only thank the woman again and go out.

The child was still huddled up on the corner of the steps. She looked frightful in her wet and dirty rags. She was staring with a stupid look of suffering straight before her, and Sara saw her suddenly draw the back of her roughened, black hand across her eyes to rub away the tears which seemed to have surprised her by forcing their way from under her lids. She was muttering to herself.

Sara opened the paper bag and took out one of the hot buns, which had already warmed her cold hands a little.

"See," she said, putting the bun on the ragged lap, "that is nice and hot. Eat it, and you will not be so hungry."

The child started and stared up at her; then she snatched up the bun and began to cram it into her mouth with great wolfish bites.

"Oh, my! Oh, my!" Sara heard her say hoarsely, in wild delight.

"*Oh, my!*"

Sara took out three more buns and put them down.

"She is hungrier than I am," she said to herself. "She's starving." But her hand trembled when she put down the fourth bun. "I'm not starving," she said—and she put down the fifth.

The little starving London savage was still snatching and devouring when she turned away. She was too ravenous to give any thanks, even if she had been taught politeness—which she had not. She was only a poor little wild animal.

"Good-bye," said Sara.

When she reached the other side of the street she looked

back. The child had a bun in both hands, and had stopped in
the middle of a bite to watch her. Sara gave her a little nod, and
the child, after another stare,—a curious, longing stare,—jerked
her shaggy head in response, and until Sara was out of sight she
did not take another bite or even finish the one she had begun.

At that moment the baker-woman glanced out of her shop-
window.

"Well, I never!" she exclaimed. "If that young 'un hasn't
given her buns to a beggar-child! It wasn't because she didn't
want them, either—well, well, she looked hungry enough. I'd
give something to know what she did it for." She stood behind
her window for a few moments and pondered. Then her curiosity got the better of her. She went to the door and spoke to
the beggar-child.

"Who gave you those buns?" she asked her.

The child nodded her head toward Sara's vanishing figure.

"What did she say?" inquired the woman.

"Axed me if I was 'ungry," replied the hoarse voice.

"What did you say?"

"Said I was jist!"

"And then she came in and got buns and came out and gave
them to you, did she?"

The child nodded.

347

"How many?"

"Five."

The woman thought it over. "Left just one for herself," she said, in a low voice. "And she could have eaten the whole six— I saw it in her eyes."

She looked after the little, draggled, far-away figure, and felt more disturbed in her usually comfortable mind than she had felt for many a day.

"I wish she hadn't gone so quick," she said. "I'm blest if she shouldn't have had a dozen."

Then she turned to the child.

"Are you hungry, yet?" she asked.

"I'm allus 'ungry," was the answer; "but 'tain't so bad as it was."

"Come in here," said the woman, and she held open the shop-door.

The child got up and shuffled in. To be invited into a warm place full of bread seemed an incredible thing. She did not know what was going to happen; she did not care, even.

"Get yourself warm," said the woman, pointing to a fire in a tiny back room. "And, look here,—when you're hard up for a bite of bread, you can come here and ask for it. I'm blest if I won't give it to you for that young un's sake."

Sara found some comfort in her remaining bun. It was hot; and it was a great deal better than nothing. She broke off small pieces and ate them slowly to make it last longer.

"Suppose it was a magic bun," she said, "and a bite was as much as a whole dinner. I should be overeating myself if I went on like this."

It was dark when she reached the square in which Miss Minchin's Select Seminary was situated; the lamps were lighted, and in most of the windows gleams of light were to be seen. It always interested Sara to catch glimpses of the rooms before the shutters were closed. She liked to imagine things about people who sat before the fires in the houses, or who bent over books at the tables. There was, for instance, the Large Family opposite. She called these people the Large Family—not because they were large, for indeed most of them were little,—but because there were so many of them. There were eight children in the Large Family, and a stout, rosy mother, and a stout, rosy father, and a stout, rosy grandmamma, and any number of servants. The eight children were always either being taken out to walk, or to ride in perambulators, by comfortable nurses; or they were going to drive with their mamma; or they were flying to the door in the evening to kiss their papa and dance around him and drag off his overcoat and look for packages in the pockets of it; or they were crowding about the nursery windows and looking out and pushing each other and laughing,—in fact they were always doing something which seemed enjoyable and suited to the tastes of a large family. Sara was quite attached to them, and had given them all names out of books. She called them the Montmorencys, when she did not call them the Large Family. The fat, fair baby with the lace cap was Ethelberta Beauchamp Montmorency; the next baby was Violet Cholmondely Montmorency; the little boy who could just stagger, and who had such round legs, was Sydney Cecil Vivian Montmorency; and then came Lilian Evangeline, Guy Clarence, Maud Marian, Rosalind Gladys Veronica Eustacia, and Claude Harold Hector.

Next door to the Large Family lived the Maiden Lady, who had a companion, and two parrots, and a King Charles spaniel; but Sara was not so very fond of her, because she did nothing in particular but talk to the parrots and drive out with the spaniel. The most interesting person of all lived next door to Miss Minchin herself. Sara called him the Indian Gentleman. He was an elderly gentleman who was said to have lived in the East Indies, and to be immensely rich and to have something the matter with his liver,—in fact, it had been rumored that he had no liver at all, and was much inconvenienced by the fact. At any rate, he was very yellow and he did not look happy; and when he went out to his carriage, he was almost always wrapped up in shawls and overcoats, as if he were cold. He had a native servant who looked even colder than himself, and he had a monkey who looked colder than the native servant. Sara had seen the monkey sitting on a table, in the sun, in the parlor window, and he always wore such a mournful expression that she sympathized with him deeply.

"I dare say," she used sometimes to remark to herself, "he is thinking all the time of coconut trees and of swinging by his tail under a tropical sun. He might have had a family dependent on him too, poor thing!"

The native servant, whom she called the Lascar, looked mournful too, but he was evidently very faithful to his master.

"Perhaps he saved his master's life in the Sepoy rebellion," she thought. "They look as if they might have had all sorts of adventures. I wish I could speak to the Lascar. I remember a little Hindustani."

And one day she actually did speak to him, and his start at the sound of his own language expressed a great deal of surprise and delight. He was waiting for his master to come out to the carriage, and Sara, who was going on an errand as usual, stopped and spoke a few words. She had a special gift for languages and had remembered enough Hindustani to make herself understood by him. When his master came out, the Lascar spoke to him quickly, and the Indian Gentleman turned and looked at her curiously. And afterward the Lascar always greeted her with salaams of the most profound description. And occasionally they exchanged a few words. She learned that it was true that the Sahib was very rich—that he was ill—and also that he had no wife nor children, and that England did not agree with the monkey.

"He must be as lonely as I am," thought Sara. "Being rich does not seem to make him happy."

That evening, as she passed the windows, the Lascar was closing the shutters, and she caught a glimpse of the room inside. There was a bright fire glowing in the grate, and the Indian Gentleman was sitting before it, in a luxurious chair. The room was richly furnished, and looked delightfully comfortable, but the Indian Gentleman sat with his head resting on his hand and looked as lonely and unhappy as ever.

"Poor man!" said Sara; "I wonder what *you* are 'supposing'?"

When she went into the house she met Miss Minchin in the hall.

"Where have you wasted your time?" said Miss Minchin. "You have been out for hours!"

"It was so wet and muddy," Sara answered. "It was hard to walk, because my shoes were so bad and slipped about so."

"Make no excuses," said Miss Minchin, "and tell no falsehoods."

Sara went downstairs to the kitchen.

"Why didn't you stay all night?" said the cook.

"Here are the things," said Sara, and laid her purchases on the table.

The cook looked over them, grumbling. She was in a very bad temper indeed.

"May I have something to eat?" Sara asked rather faintly.

"Tea's over and done with," was the answer. "Did you expect me to keep it hot for you?"

Sara was silent a second.

"I had no dinner," she said, and her voice was quite low. She made it low, because she was afraid it would tremble.

"There's some bread in the pantry," said the cook. "That's all you'll get at this time of day."

Sara went and found the bread. It was old and hard and dry. The cook was in too bad a humor to give her anything to eat with it. She had just been scolded by Miss Minchin, and it was always safe and easy to vent her own spite on Sara.

Really it was hard for the child to climb the three long flights of stairs leading to her garret. She often found them long and steep when she was tired, but tonight it seemed as if she would never reach the top. Several times a lump rose in her throat and she was obliged to stop to rest.

"I can't pretend anything more tonight," she said wearily to herself. "I'm sure I can't. I'll eat my bread and drink some water and then go to sleep, and perhaps a dream will come and pretend for me. I wonder what dreams are."

Yes, when she reached the top landing there were tears in

351

her eyes, and she did not feel like a princess—only like a tired, hungry, lonely, lonely child.

"If my papa had lived," she said, "they would not have treated me like this. If my papa had lived, he would have taken care of me."

Then she turned the handle and opened the garret-door.

Can you imagine it—can you believe it? I find it hard to believe it myself. And Sara found it impossible; for the first few moments she thought something strange had happened to her eyes—to her mind—that the dream had come before she had had time to fall asleep.

"Oh!" she exclaimed breathlessly. "Oh! It isn't true! I know, I know it isn't true!" And she slipped into the room and closed the door and locked it, and stood with her back against it, staring straight before her.

Do you wonder? In the grate, which had been empty and rusty and cold when she left it, but which now was blackened and polished up quite respectably, there was a glowing, blazing fire. On the hob was a little brass kettle, hissing and boiling; spread upon the floor was a warm, thick rug; before the fire was a folding-chair, unfolded and with cushions on it; by the chair was a small folding-table, unfolded, covered with a white cloth, and upon it were spread small covered dishes, a cup and saucer, and a teapot; on the bed were new, warm coverings, a curious wadded silk robe, and some books. The little, cold, miserable room seemed changed into Fairyland. It was actually warm and glowing.

"It is bewitched!" said Sara. "Or I am bewitched. I only *think* I see it all; but if I can only keep on thinking it, I don't care— I don't care—if I can only keep it up!"

She was afraid to move, for fear it would melt away. She stood with her back against the door and looked and looked. But soon she began to feel warm, and then she moved forward.

"A fire that I only *thought* I saw surely wouldn't *feel* warm," she said. "It feels real—real."

She went to it and knelt before it. She touched the chair, the table; she lifted the cover of one of the dishes. There was some-

352

thing hot and savory in it—something delicious. The teapot had tea in it, ready for the boiling water from the little kettle; one plate had toast on it, another, muffins.

"It is real," said Sara. "The fire is real enough to warm me; I can sit in the chair; the things are real enough to eat."

It was like a fairy story come true—it was heavenly. She went to the bed and touched the blankets and the wrap. They were real too. She opened one book, and on the title page was written in a strange hand, "The little girl in the attic."

Suddenly—was it a strange thing for her to do?—Sara put her face down on the queer, foreign-looking quilted robe and burst into tears.

"I don't know who it is," she said, "but somebody cares about me a little—somebody is my friend."

Somehow that thought warmed her more than the fire. She had never had a friend since those happy, luxurious days when she had had everything; and those days had seemed such a long way off—so far away as to be only like dreams—during these last years at Miss Minchin's.

She really cried more at this strange thought of having a friend —even though an unknown one—than she had cried over many of her worst troubles.

But these tears seemed different from the others, for when she had wiped them away they did not seem to leave her eyes and her heart hot and smarting.

And then imagine, if you can, what the rest of the evening was like. The delicious comfort of taking off the damp clothes and putting on the soft, warm, quilted robe before the glowing fire—of slipping her cold feet into the luscious little wool-lined slippers she found near her chair. And then the hot tea and savory dishes, the cushioned chair and the books!

It was just like Sara, that, once having found the things real, she should give herself up to the enjoyment of them to the very utmost. She had lived such a life of imagining, and had found her pleasure so long in improbabilities, that she was quite equal to accepting any wonderful thing that happened. After she was quite warm and had eaten her supper and enjoyed herself for an hour or so, it had almost ceased to be surprising to her that such magical surroundings should be hers. As to finding out who had done all this, she knew that it was out of the question. She did not know a human soul by whom it could seem in the least degree probable that it could have been done.

"There is nobody," she said to herself, "nobody." She discussed the matter with Emily, it is true, but more because it was delightful to talk about it than with a view to making any discoveries.

"But we have a friend, Emily," she said; "we have a friend."

Sara could not even imagine a being charming enough to fill her grand ideal of her mysterious benefactor. If she tried to make in her mind a picture of him or her, it ended by being something glittering and strange—not at all like a real person, but bearing resemblance to a sort of Eastern magician, with long robes and a wand. And when she fell asleep, beneath the soft white blanket, she dreamed all night of this magnificent personage, and talked to him in Hindustani, and made salaams to him.

Upon one thing she was determined. She would not speak to anyone of her good fortune—it should be her own secret; in fact, she was rather inclined to think that if Miss Minchin knew, she would take her treasures from her or in some way spoil her pleasure. So, when she went down the next morning, she shut her door very tight and did her best to look as if nothing unusual had occurred. And yet this was rather hard, because she could not help remembering, every now and then, with a sort of start, and her heart would beat quickly every time she repeated to herself, "I have a friend!"

It was a friend who evidently meant to continue to be kind, for when she went to her garret the next night—and she opened the door, it must be confessed, with rather an excited feeling— she found that the same hands had been again at work and had done even more than before. The fire and the supper were again there, and beside them a number of other things which so altered the look of the garret that Sara quite lost her breath. A piece of bright, strange, heavy cloth covered the battered mantel, and on it some ornaments had been placed. All the bare, ugly things which could be covered with draperies had been concealed and made to look quite pretty. Some odd materials in rich colors had been fastened against the walls with sharp, fine tacks—so sharp that they could be pressed into the wood without hammering. Some brilliant fans were pinned up, and there were several large cushions. A long, old wooden box was covered with a rug, and some cushions lay on it, so that it wore quite the air of a sofa.

Sara simply sat down, and looked, and looked again.

"It is exactly like something fairy come true," she said. "There isn't the least difference. I feel as if I might wish for anything—diamonds and bags of gold—and they would appear! *That* couldn't be any stranger than this. Is this my garret? Am I the same cold, ragged, damp Sara? And to think how I used to pretend, and pretend, and wish there were fairies! The one thing I always wanted was to see a fairy story come true. I am *living* in a fairy story! I feel as if I might be a fairy myself, and be able to turn things into anything else!"

It was like a fairy story, and, what was best of all, it continued. Almost every day something new was done to the garret. Some new comfort or ornament appeared in it when Sara opened her door at night, until actually, in a short time, it was a bright little room, full of all sorts of odd and luxurious things. And the magician had taken care that the child should not be hungry, and that she should have as many books as she could read. When she left the room in the morning, the remains of her supper were on the table, and when she returned in the evening, the magician had removed them, and left another nice little meal. Downstairs Miss Minchin was as cruel and insulting as ever, Miss Amelia was as peevish, and the servants were as vulgar. Sara was sent on errands, and scolded, and driven hither and thither, but somehow it seemed as if she could bear it all. The delightful sense of romance and mystery lifted her above the cook's temper and malice. The comfort she enjoyed and could always look forward to was making her stronger. If she came home from her errands wet and tired, she knew she would soon be warm, after she had climbed the stairs. In a few weeks she began to look less thin. A little color came into her cheeks, and her eyes did not seem much too big for her face.

It was just when this was beginning to be so apparent that Miss Minchin sometimes stared at her questioningly, that another wonderful thing happened. A man came to the door and left several parcels. All were addressed (in large letters) to "the little girl in the attic." Sara herself was sent to open the door, and she took them in. She laid the two largest parcels down on the hall-table and was looking at the address, when Miss Minchin came down the stairs.

"Take the things upstairs to the young lady to whom they belong," she said. "Don't stand there staring at them."

"They belong to me," answered Sara, quietly.

"To you!" exclaimed Miss Minchin. "What do you mean?"

"I don't know where they came from," said Sara, "but they're addressed to me."

Miss Minchin came to her side and looked at them with an excited expression.

"What is in them?" she demanded.

"I don't know," said Sara.

"Open them!" she demanded, still more excitedly.

Sara did as she was told. They contained pretty and comfortable clothing,—clothing of different kinds; shoes and stockings and gloves, a warm coat, and even an umbrella. On the pocket of the coat was pinned a paper on which was written, "To be worn every day—will be replaced by others when necessary."

Miss Minchin was quite agitated. This was an incident which suggested strange things to her sordid mind. Could it be that she had made a mistake after all, and that the child so neglected and so unkindly treated by her had some powerful friend in the background? It would not be very pleasant if there should be such a friend, and he or she should learn all the truth about the thin, shabby clothes, the scant food, the hard work. She felt queer indeed and uncertain, and she gave a side-glance at Sara.

"Well," she said, in a voice such as she had never used since the day the child lost her father—"well, someone is very kind to you. As you have the things and are to have new ones when they are worn out, you may as well go and put them on and look respectable; and after you are dressed, you may come downstairs and learn your lessons in the schoolroom."

So it happened that, about half an hour afterward, Sara struck the entire schoolroom of pupils dumb with amazement, by making her appearance in a costume such as she had never worn since the change of fortune whereby she ceased to be a show-pupil and a parlor-boarder. She scarcely seemed to be the same Sara. She was neatly dressed in a pretty gown of warm browns and reds, and even her stockings and slippers were nice and dainty.

"Perhaps someone has left her a fortune," one of the girls whispered. "I always thought something would happen to her, she is so queer."

That night when Sara went to her room she carried out a plan she had been devising for some time. She wrote a note to her unknown friend. It ran as follows:

"I hope you will not think it is not polite that I should write this note to you when you wish to keep yourself a secret, but I do not mean to be impolite, or to try to find out at all, only I want to thank you for being so kind to me—so beautiful kind, and making everything like a fairy story. I am so grateful to you and I am so happy! I used to be so lonely and cold and, hungry, and now, oh, just think what you have done for me! Please let me say just these words. It seems as if I ought to say them. *Thank you—thank you—thank you!*

THE LITTLE GIRL IN THE ATTIC."

The next morning she left this on the little table, and it was taken away with the other things; so she felt sure the magician had received it, and she was happier for the thought.

A few nights later a very odd thing happened. She found something in the room which she certainly would never have expected. When she came in as usual she saw something small and dark in her chair,—an odd, tiny figure, which turned toward her a little, weird-looking, wistful face.

358

"Why, it's the monkey!" she cried. "It is the Indian Gentleman's monkey! Where can he have come from?"

It *was* the monkey, sitting up and looking so like a mite of a child that it really was quite pathetic; and very soon Sara found out how he happened to be in her room. The skylight was open, and it was easy to guess that he had crept out of his master's garret-window, which was only a few feet away and perfectly easy to get in and out of, even for a climber less agile than a monkey. He had probably climbed to the garret on a tour of investigation, and getting out upon the roof, and being attracted by the light in Sara's attic, had crept in. At all events this seemed quite reasonable, and there he was; and when Sara went to him, he actually put out his queer, elfish little hands, caught her dress, and jumped into her arms.

"Oh, you queer, poor, ugly, foreign little thing!" said Sara, caressing him. "I can't help liking you. You look like a sort of baby, but I am so glad you are not, because your mother could *not* be proud of you, and nobody would dare to say you were like any of your relations. But I do like you; you have such a forlorn little look in your face. Perhaps you are sorry you are so ugly, and it's always on your mind. I wonder if you have a mind?"

The monkey sat and looked at her while she talked, and seemed much interested in her remarks, if one could judge by his eyes and his forehead, and the way he moved his head up and down, and held it sideways and scratched it with his little hand. He examined Sara quite seriously, and anxiously, too.

He felt the stuff of her dress, touched her hands, climbed up and examined her ears, and then sat on her shoulder holding a lock of her hair, looking mournful but not at all agitated. Upon the whole, he seemed pleased with Sara.

"But I must take you back," she said to him, "though I'm sorry to have to do it. Oh, the company you *would* be to a person!"

She lifted him from her shoulder, set him on her knee, and gave him a bit of cake. He sat and nibbled it, and then put his head on one side, looked at her, wrinkled his forehead, and then nibbled again, in the most companionable manner.

"But you must go home," said Sara at last; and she took him in her arms to carry him downstairs. Evidently he did not want to leave the room, for as they reached the door he clung to her neck and gave a little scream of anger.

"You mustn't be an ungrateful monkey," said Sara. "You ought to be fondest of your own family. I am sure the Lascar is good to you."

Nobody saw her on her way out, and very soon she was standing on the Indian Gentleman's front steps, and the Lascar had opened the door for her.

"I found your monkey in my room," she said in Hindustani. "I think he got in through the window."

The man began a rapid outpouring of thanks; but, just as he was in the midst of them, a fretful, hollow voice was heard through the open door of the nearest room. The instant he heard it the Lascar disappeared and left Sara still holding the monkey.

It was not many moments, however, before he came back bringing a message. His master had told him to bring Missy into the library. The Sahib was very ill, but he wished to see Missy.

Sara thought this odd, but she remembered reading stories of Indian gentlemen who, having no constitutions, were extremely cross and full of whims, and who must have their own way. So she followed the Lascar.

When she entered the room the Indian Gentleman was lying on an easy chair, propped up with pillows. He looked frightfully ill. His yellow face was thin, and his eyes were hollow. He gave Sara a rather curious look—it was as if she wakened in him some anxious interest.

"You live next door?" he said.

"Yes," answered Sara. "I live at Miss Minchin's."

"She keeps a boarding school?"

"Yes," said Sara.

"And you are one of her pupils?"

Sara hesitated a moment.

"I don't know exactly what I am," she replied.

"Why not?" asked the Indian Gentleman.

The monkey gave a tiny squeak, and Sara stroked him.

"At first," she said, "I was a pupil and a parlor-boarder; but now——"

"What do you mean by 'at first'?" asked the Indian Gentleman.

"When I was first taken there by my papa."

"Well, what has happened since then?" said the invalid, staring at her and knitting his brows with a puzzled expression.

"My papa died," said Sara. "He lost all his money, and there was none left for me—and there was no one to take care of me or pay Miss Minchin, so——"

"So you were sent up into the garret and neglected, and made into a half-starved little drudge!" put in the Indian Gentleman. "That is about it, isn't it?"

The color deepened on Sara's cheeks.

"There was no one to take care of me, and no money," she said. "I belong to nobody."

"What did your father mean by losing his money?" said the gentleman, fretfully.

The red in Sara's cheeks grew deeper, and she fixed her odd eyes on the yellow face.

"He did not lose it himself," she said. "He had a friend he was fond of, and it was his friend who took his money. I don't know how. I don't understand. He trusted his friend too much."

She saw the invalid start—the strangest start—as if he had been suddenly frightened. Then he spoke nervously and excitedly.

"That's an old story," he said. "It happens every day; but

361

sometimes those who are blamed—those who do the wrong—don't intend it and are not so bad. It may happen through a mistake—a miscalculation; they may not be so bad."

"No," said Sara, "but the suffering is just as bad for the others. It killed my papa."

The Indian Gentleman pushed aside some of the gorgeous wraps that covered him.

"Come a little nearer and let me look at you," he said.

His voice sounded very strange; it had a more nervous and excited tone than before. Sara had an odd fancy that he was half afraid to look at her. She came and stood nearer, the monkey clinging to her and watching his master anxiously over his shoulder.

The Indian Gentleman's hollow, restless eyes fixed themselves on her.

"Yes," he said at last. "Yes; I can see it. Tell me your father's name."

"His name was Ralph Crewe," said Sara. "Captain Crewe. Perhaps,"—a sudden thought flashing upon her,—"perhaps you may have heard of him? He died in India."

The Indian Gentleman sank back upon his pillows. He looked very weak and seemed out of breath.

"Yes," he said, "I knew him. I was his friend. I meant no harm. If he had only lived he would have known. It turned out well after all. He was a fine young fellow. I was fond of him. I will make it right. Call—call the man."

Sara thought he was going to die. But there was no need to call the Lascar. He must have been waiting at the door. He was in the room and by his master's side in an instant. He seemed to know what to do. He lifted the drooping head and gave the invalid something in a small glass. The Indian Gentleman lay panting for a few minutes, and then he spoke in an exhausted but eager voice, addressing the Lascar in Hindustani,—

"Go for Carmichael," he said. "Tell him to come here at once. Tell him I have found the child!"

When Mr. Carmichael arrived (which occurred in a very few minutes, for it turned out that he was no other than the

father of the Large Family across the street), Sara went home and was allowed to take the monkey with her. She certainly did not sleep very much that night, though the monkey behaved beautifully and did not disturb her in the least. It was not the monkey that kept her awake—it was her thoughts, and her wonders as to what the Indian Gentleman had meant when he said, "Tell him I have found the child." "What child?" Sara kept asking herself. "I was the only child there; but how had he found me, and why did he want to find me? And what is he going to do, now I am found? Is it something about my papa? Do I belong to somebody? Is he one of my relations? Is something going to happen?"

But she found out the very next day, in the morning; and it seemed that she had been living in a story even more than she had imagined. First, Mr. Carmichael came and had an interview with Miss Minchin. And it appeared that Mr. Carmichael, besides occupying the important situation of father to the Large Family, was a lawyer and had charge of the affairs of Mr. Carrisford—which was the real name of the Indian Gentleman—and, as Mr. Carrisford's lawyer, Mr. Carmichael had come to explain something curious to Miss Minchin regarding Sara. But, being the father of the Large Family, he had a very kind and fatherly feeling for children; and so, after seeing Miss Minchin alone, what did he do but go and bring across the square his rosy, motherly, warm-hearted wife, so that she herself might talk to the little lonely girl and tell her everything in the best and most motherly way.

And then Sara learned that she was to be a poor little drudge and outcast no more, and that a great change had come in her fortunes; for all the lost fortune had come back to her, and a great deal had even been added to it. It was Mr. Carrisford who had been her father's friend, and who had made the investments which had caused him the apparent loss of his money; but it had so happened that after poor young Captain Crewe's death one of the investments which had seemed at the time the very worst had taken a sudden turn, and proved to be such a success that it had been a mine of wealth, and had more than doubled the Captain's lost fortune, as well as making a fortune for Mr. Carrisford himself. But Mr. Carrisford had been very unhappy. He had truly loved his poor, handsome, generous young friend, and the knowledge that he had caused his death had weighed upon him always and broken both his health and spirit. The worst of it had been that, when first he thought himself and Captain Crewe ruined, he had lost courage and gone away because he was not brave enough to face the consequences of what he had done, and so he had not even known where the young soldier's little girl had been placed. When he wanted to find her and make restitution, he could discover no trace of her; and the certainty that she was poor and friendless somewhere had made him more miserable than ever. When he had taken the house next to Miss Minchin's he had been so ill and wretched that he had for the time given up the search. His troubles and the Indian climate had brought him almost to death's door— indeed, he had not expected to live more than a few months. And then one day the Lascar had told him about Sara's speaking Hindustani, and gradually he had begun to take a sort of interest in the forlorn child, though he had only caught a glimpse of her once or twice, and he had not connected her with the child of his friend, perhaps because he was too languid to think much about anything. But the Lascar had found out something of Sara's unhappy little life, and about the garret. One evening he had actually crept out of his own garret-window and looked into hers, which was a very easy matter, because, as I have said, it was only a few feet away—and he had told his master what he had seen, and in a moment of compassion the Indian Gentleman had told him to take into the wretched little room such comforts as he could carry from the one window to the other. And the Lascar, who had developed an interest in, and an odd fondness for, the child who had spoken to him in his own tongue, had been pleased with the work; and, having the silent swiftness and agile movements of many of his race, he had made his evening journeys across the few feet of roof from garret-window to garret-window, without any trouble at all. He had watched Sara's movements until he knew exactly when

365

she was absent from her room and when she returned to it, and so he had been able to calculate the best times for his work. Generally he had made them in the dusk of the evening; but once or twice, when he had seen her go out on errands, he had dared to go over in the daytime, being quite sure that the garret was never entered by anyone but herself. His pleasure in the work and his reports of the results had added to the invalid's interest in it, and sometimes the master had found the planning gave him something to think of, which made him almost forget his weariness and pain. And at last, when Sara brought home the truant monkey, he had felt a wish to see her, and then her likeness to her father had done the rest.

"And now, my dear," said good Mrs. Carmichael, patting Sara's hand, "all your troubles are over, I am sure, and you are to come home with me and be taken care of as if you were one of my own little girls; and we are so pleased to think of having you with us until everything is settled, and Mr. Carrisford is better. The excitement of last night has made him very weak, but we really think he will get well, now that such a load is taken from his mind. And when he is stronger, I am sure he will be as kind to you as your own papa would have been. He has a very good heart, and he is fond of children—and he has no family at all. But we must make you happy and rosy, and you must learn to play and run about, as my little girls do——"

"As your little girls do?" said Sara. "I wonder if I could. I used to watch them and wonder what it was like. Shall I feel as if I belonged to somebody?"

"Ah, my love, yes!—yes!" said Mrs. Carmichael; "dear me, yes!" And her motherly blue eyes grew quite moist, and she suddenly took Sara in her arms and kissed her. That very night, before she went to sleep, Sara had made the acquaintance of the entire Large Family, and such excitement as she and the monkey had caused in that joyous circle could hardly be described. There was not a child in the nursery, from the Eton boy who was the eldest, to the baby who was the youngest, who had not laid some offering on her shrine. All the older ones knew something of her wonderful story. She had been

born in India; she had been poor and lonely and unhappy, and
had lived in a garret and been treated unkindly; and now she
was to be rich and happy, and be taken care of. They were so
sorry for her and so delighted and curious about her, all at
once. The girls wished to be with her constantly, and the little
boys wished to be told about India; the second baby, with the
short round legs, simply sat and stared at her and the monkey,
possibly wondering why she had not brought a hand organ
with her.

"I shall certainly wake up presently," Sara kept saying to
herself. "This one must be a dream. The other one turned out
to be real; but this *couldn't* be. But, oh! how happy it is!"

And even when she went to bed, in the bright, pretty room
not far from Mrs. Carmichael's own, and Mrs. Carmichael came
and kissed her and patted her and tucked her in cozily, she
was not sure that she would not wake up in the garret in the
morning.

"And oh, Charles, dear," Mrs. Carmichael said to her husband, when she went downstairs to him, "we must get that
lonely look out of her eyes! It isn't a child's look at all. I couldn't
bear to see it in one of my own children. What the poor little
love must have had to bear in that dreadful woman's house!
But, surely, she will forget it in time."

But though the lonely look passed away from Sara's face, she
never quite forgot the garret at Miss Minchin's; and, indeed,
she always liked to remember the wonderful night when the
tired princess crept upstairs, cold and wet, and opening the door
found fairyland waiting for her. And there was no one of the

many stories she was always being called upon to tell in the nursery of the Large Family which was more popular than that particular one; and there was no one of whom the Large Family were so fond as of Sara. Mr. Carrisford did not die, but recovered, and Sara went to live with him; and no real princess could have been better taken care of than she was. It seemed that the Indian Gentleman could not do enough to make her happy, and to repay her for the past; and the Lascar was her devoted slave. As her odd little face grew brighter, it grew so pretty and interesting that Mr. Carrisford used to sit and watch it many an evening, as they sat by the fire together.

They became great friends, and they used to spend hours reading and talking together; and, in a very short time, there was no pleasanter sight to the Indian Gentleman than Sara sitting in her big chair on the opposite side of the hearth, with a book on her knee and her soft, dark hair tumbling over her warm cheeks. She had a pretty habit of looking up at him suddenly, with a bright smile, and then he would often say to her:

"Are you happy, Sara?"

And then she would answer,—

"I feel like a real princess, Uncle Tom."

He had told her to call him Uncle Tom.

"There doesn't seem to be anything left to 'suppose,'" she added.

There was a little joke between them that he was a magician, and so could do anything he liked; and it was one of his pleasures to invent plans to surprise her with enjoyments she had not thought of. Scarcely a day passed in which he did not do something new for her. Sometimes she found new flowers in her room; sometimes a fanciful little gift tucked into some odd corner; sometimes a new book on her pillow;—once as they sat together in the evening they heard the scratch of a heavy paw on the door of the room, and when Sara went to find out what it was, there stood a great dog—a splendid Russian boar-hound with a grand silver and gold collar. Stooping to read the inscription upon the collar, Sara was delighted to read the words: "I am Boris; I serve the Princess Sara."

Then there was a sort of fairy nursery arranged for the entertainment of the juvenile members of the Large Family, who were always coming to see Sara and the Lascar and the monkey. Sara was as fond of the Large Family as they were of her. She soon felt as if she were a member of it, and the companionship of the healthy, happy children was very good for her. All the children rather looked up to her and regarded her as the cleverest and most brilliant of creatures—particularly after it was discovered that she not only knew stories of every kind, and could invent new ones at a moment's notice, but that she could help with lessons, and speak French and German, and discourse with the Lascar in Hindustani.

It was rather a painful experience for Miss Minchin to watch her ex-pupil's fortunes, as she had the daily opportunity to do, and to feel that she had made a serious mistake, from a business point of view. She had even tried to retrieve it by suggesting that Sara's education should be continued under her care and had gone to the length of making an appeal to the child herself.

"I have always been very fond of you," she said.

Then Sara fixed her eyes upon her and gave her one of her odd looks.

"Have you?" she answered.

"Yes," said Miss Minchin. "Amelia and I have always said you were the cleverest child we had with us, and I am sure we could make you happy—as a parlor-boarder."

Sara thought of the garret and the day her ears were boxed, —and of that other day, that dreadful, desolate day when she had been told that she belonged to nobody; that she had no home and no friends,—and she kept her eyes fixed on Miss Minchin's face.

"You know why I would not stay with you," she said.

And it seems probable that Miss Minchin did, for after that simple answer she had not the boldness to pursue the subject. She merely sent in a bill for the expense of Sara's education and support, and she made it quite large enough. And because Mr. Carrisford thought Sara would wish it paid, it was paid. When Mr. Carmichael paid it he had a brief interview with Miss Min-

369

chin in which he expressed his opinion with much clearness and force; and it is quite certain that Miss Minchin did not enjoy the conversation.

Sara had been about a month with Mr. Carrisford and had begun to realize that her happiness was not a dream, when one night the Indian Gentleman saw that she sat a long time with her cheek on her hand looking at the fire.

"What are you 'supposing,' Sara?" he asked. Sara looked up with a bright color on her cheeks.

"I *was* 'supposing,'" she said; "I was remembering that hungry day, and a child I saw."

"But there were a great many hungry days," said the Indian Gentleman, with a rather sad tone in his voice. "Which hungry day was it?"

"I forgot you didn't know," said Sara. "It was the day I found the things in my garret."

And then she told him the story of the bun-shop, and the fourpence, and the child who was hungrier than herself; and somehow as she told it, though she told it very simply indeed, the Indian Gentleman found it necessary to shade his eyes with his hand and look down at the floor.

"And I was 'supposing' a kind of plan," said Sara, when she had finished; "I was thinking I would like to do something."

"What is it?" said her guardian in a low tone. "You may do anything you like to do, Princess."

"I was wondering," said Sara,—"you know you say I have a great deal of money—and I was wondering if I could go and see the bun-woman and tell her that if, when hungry children— particularly on those dreadful days—come and sit on the steps or look in at the window, she would just call them in and give them something to eat, she might send the bills to me and I would pay them—could I do that?"

"You shall do it tomorrow morning," said the Indian Gentleman.

"Thank you," said Sara; "you see I know what it is to be hungry, and it is very hard when one can't even *pretend* it away."

"Yes, yes, my dear," said the Indian Gentleman. "Yes, it must be. Try to forget it. Come and sit on this footstool near my knee, and only remember you are a princess."

"Yes," said Sara, "and I can give buns and bread to the Populace." And she went and sat on the stool, and the Indian Gentleman (he used to like her to call him that, too, sometimes, —in fact, very often) drew her small, dark head down upon his knee and stroked her hair.

The next morning a carriage drew up before the door of the baker's shop, and a gentleman and a little girl got out,—oddly enough, just as the bun-woman was putting a tray of smoking hot buns into the window. When Sara entered the shop the woman turned and looked at her and, leaving the buns, came and stood behind the counter. For a moment she looked at Sara very hard indeed, and then her good-natured face lighted up.

"I'm that sure I remember you, miss," she said. "And yet——"

"Once," said Sara, "you gave me six buns for fourpence, and——"

"And you gave five of 'em to a beggar-child," said the woman. "I've always remembered it. I couldn't make it out at first. I beg pardon, sir, but there's not many young people that notices a hungry face in that way, and I've thought of it many a time. Excuse the liberty, miss, but you look rosier and better than you did that day."

"I am better, thank you," said Sara, "and—and I am happier, and I have come to ask you to do something for me."

"Me, miss!" exclaimed the woman, "why, bless you, yes, miss! What can I do?"

And then Sara made her little proposal, and the woman listened to it with an astonished face.

"Why, bless me!" she said, when she had heard it all. "Yes, miss, it'll be a pleasure to me to do it. I am a working woman, myself, and can't afford to do much on my own account, and there's sights of trouble on every side; but if you'll excuse me, I'm bound to say I've given many a bit of bread away since that wet afternoon, just along o' thinkin' of you. An' how wet an' cold you was, an' how you looked,—an' yet you give away your hot buns as if you was a princess."

371

The Indian Gentleman smiled involuntarily, and Sara smiled a little too. "She looked so hungry," she said. "She was hungrier than I was."

"She was starving," said the woman. "Many's the time she's told me of it since—how she sat there in the wet and felt as if a wolf was a-tearing at her poor young insides."

"Oh, have you seen her since then?" exclaimed Sara. "Do you know where she is?"

"I know!" said the woman. "Why, she's in that there back room now, miss, an' has been for a month, an' a decent, well-meaning girl she's going to turn out, an' such a help to me in the day shop, an' in the kitchen, as you'd scarce believe, knowing how she's lived."

She stepped to the door of the little back parlor and spoke; and the next minute a girl came out and followed her behind the counter. And actually it was the beggar-child, clean and neatly clothed, and looking as if she had not been hungry for a long time. She looked shy, but she had a nice face, now that she was no longer a savage; and the wild look had gone from her eyes. And she knew Sara in an instant, and stood and looked at her as if she could never look enough.

"You see," said the woman, "I told her to come here when she was hungry, and when she'd come I'd give her odd jobs to do, an' I found she was willing, an' somehow I got to like her; an' the end of it was I've given her a place an' a home, an' she helps me, an' behaves as well, an' is as thankful as a girl can be. Her name's Anne—she has no other."

The two children stood and looked at each other a few moments. In Sara's eyes a new thought was growing.

"I'm glad you have such a good home," she said. "Perhaps Mrs. Brown will let you give the buns and bread to the children—perhaps you would like to do it—because you know what it is to be hungry, too."

"Yes, miss," said the girl.

And somehow Sara felt as if she understood her, though the girl said nothing more, and only stood still and looked, and looked after her as she went out of the shop and got into the carriage and drove away.

Index